Sofia and Richard

A Regency Romance, Book1

PRISTINE
PRESS AND MEDIA

By T.F. Fig

TABLE OF CONTENTS

CHAPTER 1

Retirement and Moving to Somerset

"Today is your last day in the Navy dear. Your career, in reflection, seems to have flown by in an instant. One wonders where it all went," said Anne to James.

Anne laid out James's uniform on the bed for the last time. "He would put his uniform on, with the same routine, and then leave for the admiralty. Except today would be for the last time. After this morning, it will all change.", thought Anne.

"It's hard to believe I will be relieved of command and put to pasture. We can only serve so long. My advice to the younger officers was to make the best of their time, make great friendships, train hard, and enjoy each moment along the way. It goes by so quickly and then it's over. I think they heard me.", said James to Anne.

"Your carriage is here dear. Will this be a long day or will you come home early since all the celebrations are over?" asked Anne.

"I think early. I have the change of command ceremony this morning and after a final walk around the admiralty and the respectful good byes to my collogues I will come home. Don't you think dear?", said James.

Arriving at the Admiralty, with his son, James was greeted by all for the final time. "Well done, Admiral! Thank you for your service. You will be missed! Have a great rest and retirement Sir!" shouted many in good cheer.

After the change of command ceremony, the senior officers handed the Admiral, with some ceremony, a folded flag and some unique mementoes to remember the great appreciation of the Navy to the cheers of his coworkers. James was as well presented with a note from the King, in his handwriting, with words of a grateful monarch's reflection of his service to the Crown and an open invitation to visit the royal court anytime, "You are most welcome here.", it said.

"Son, let us visit the Naval Academy.", said James to Richard. "Yes, father.", replied Richard.

At the naval academy they received a full tour, met some of the instructors, received notes and instructions for a study plan for Richard's naval education prior to his application a few years from now.

Richard would be tested yearly. This assessment would determine the reduction in time at the academy to graduation upon acceptance and entry.

"Richard, be diligent with your studies we will assess you each year to understand your progress. Listen to your father he will guide you well, and at fifteen we will accept your application to the academy.", advised one of the instructors to Richard's concurrence.

At that James and Richard headed home. James to walk into a new and very different life from that of the past 25 years.

"Hi dear, it seems you only just left work and here you are back again. Did you say all your goodbye's?", asked Anne. "Yes, I did. I received the customary flag, a few bits and bobs, and a personal letter from the King! All wrapped in a nice decommissioning ceremony.", replied James.

"I take my uniform off the last time in active service. The next time I put it on it will be as a retired admiral. Such a strange and new circumstance for me. I suppose it is about time.", said James with a touch of melancholy. "Have no fear honey, I will keep you quite busy in your retirement!" said Anne smiling.

"What are those notes laid out there on the table?", asked James.

"Don't you remember dear? Our growing up in the village of Meare. I was from a titled family. My title, Lady Anne. You were from a well to do merchant family in the village but not aristocracy. You and I had no problems being the best of friend and spending every summer day together but our mothers and fathers had other ideas.

My mother and father made it clear you were not suitable to be married to me. And your mother and father talked to you about the class system.

One year you went away to the navy and I was left alone. None of the local, suitable, men wanted me and I resigned myself to living independent. Then several years and you returned a wealthy captain and a knight of the realm. My mother and father were astonished at the transformation, saying nothing to me they invited you to supper wanting to see if by chance the spark would ignite between us. You were very suitable.

Little did they know there was no spark but a full-blown barn fire all pent up. We married shortly after and the rest is our history.

It seems like yesterday dear. Today you retired from the navy and we will be off to Somerset.", responded Anne.

"I haven't thought of those days in a while. We were so young, so adventurous and so full of hope for the future.

We are here, about to close a big chapter in our lives and open a new one.

I have a note, just now, from our solicitor he sends word he found an estate in the area of Glastonbury, that we are wanting to settle. He thinks this place to be the one that meets all our requirements. It is called the Charlton Estate. It has a main house and two smaller estate homes, with a quite large land grant.

He says one can see Glastonbury Thor from a place on the property. There is much in the way of history to the place and stately homes all about it in a country setting. It is near the town of Wells. And of course, Wells is near the town Meare and all of our growing up.

Shall we venture from Portsmouth to this Charlton Estate and take a tour of it to see if this is where we are to settle? I think tomorrow should be convenient. What say you?" asked James.

"Yes, that would be acceptable.", responded Anne.

"Well dear, I have nothing better to do from now on and it is true we have settled on Somerset since we both have roots in the area. Let us visit this Charlton Estates!" announced James still with that navy keenness to explore some unknown corner.

The next day was sunny and warm but not to warm. "It seems like a perfect day to travel to the estate James" said Anne at breakfast. "The carriage we contracted will be here in a couple of hours. Richard, we will travel to our possible new home and if we all like it I shall purchase the place! What say you son?" asked James. "Let's be on our way to this house then!" replied Richard.

A few hours later, and still early morning, the carriage arrived to take them to the Charlton estate. Anne arranged lunch and snacks for the trip to and from the place, they would go in some comfort. They boarded the carriage and were on the way.

"It will be a couple of hours dear. Hopefully most of the way will be on smooth road and we will not be tossed around the carriage," said Anne.

"The driver mentioned he knows this area quite well and the back roads that will save time and are smooth for the ride," mentioned James as Richard did not care much and was ingulfed in the reading of some tale or other typical of an eight-year-old boy of his time.

"Dear, I did not realize the road to London was the main route into Glastonbury.", said Anne. "It seems so, if this house is what we want then an advantage is knowing we can go to town without too much adventure and easily when wanted," mentioned James.

James and Richard took a nap while Anne watched over everyone seeing the countryside race by, "Somerset is as pretty as ever, I do hope this Charlton estate is as stated and we find it a place to settle," thought Anne.

The carriage slowed as it approached a nearby village, "We will change the horses and give our travelers a short rest and the stretching of the legs before the second half of our trip. We are about an hour away from the Charlton estate," said the carriage driver.

"Thank you for bringing food and drink dear. I could not imagine such preparation and the need for this refreshment," said James eating some bread and cheese with Richard and stretching their legs to a very blue sky and green pastures all around them.

"We have been so used to the hustle and bustle of Portsmouth and town, we will have to get use to the small towns and villages, the quiet," mentioned James to Anne.

"Indeed....", whispered Anne.

With the carriage horses and driver refreshed, and everyone onboard and ready, they were off again to the Charlton estate. Sometime later the carriage slowed with the driver announcing they are on the main road to the Charlton estate. It was tree lined with a stone fence on each side, beyond the fence were green pastures some with sheep, some with cows grazing lazily in the sunshine. Every so often one could see the very top of the Charlton house chimneys.

"We have been on the Charlton estate since turning on this road. Just over this next rise you will see the great house fully, on the right," said the driver.

"It is very impressive on the outside, but what shall we see on the inside dear," said James to Anne engrossed in the view.

The carriage turned onto the main portal to the home. "It is grander than I thought. I hope we have a good feeling on the inside as we do on the outside," said Anne. "Anne, look Glastonbury is just there in our sites," mentioned James. Richard inspected grounds and house with his eyes not saying anything for the moment.

"Ah, our solicitor. Good morning, Sir," said James. "Good morning. I hope your travel here was uneventful and not to long. Shall we go in, take a short break and then tour the house and perhaps some of the grounds. I assumed you will stay the night before traveling back to Portsmouth?" inquired the Solicitor.

"Yes, we will stay the night. Let me guide you to the apartments then and after tea lets view the house and some particulars of the grounds," said Solicitor.

After a refreshment, the solicitor guided the Hawke's around the house with Anne saying I really like the place several times to James. " After a refreshment, the solicitor guided the Hawke's around the house with Anne saying I really like the place several times to James.," mentioned James. "It is very light and airy with all the requisite furnishings about. We have very little in repair or make over to do, but have a major cleanup and move in I suppose, said Anne.

"Shall we tour a few places on the grounds Sir now that you have seen the house?" asked the Solicitor to an affirmative. "I have an open carriage standing by so you can take in the views. There are two large houses on the property. They are guest homes. One is called the Hill house, the larger of the two with about 30 rooms and the other house just there is called the White House, it has about 14 rooms. Both houses are quite nice places indeed," informed their solicitor.

From the Hill house one could see the extent of the property's boundaries. "Just there in the distance is an area called the common. This area has a smallish wood, a rather large pasture and pretty stream running through it. It is part of the Charlton estate but left open so your neighbors on the Highbury estate may venture there. If you look carefully just now you can see young Miss Sofia Alton. She rides quite well and is seen at the commons often. Where there is sun and warm weather, she is likely on a horse and in the commons," informed the Solicitor.

"How old is Sofia?" asked Anne. "I believe her to be around eight or nine years of age. The Alton's are old society folk. There is Edward Alton, Baronet his wife Victoria, Baroness and Miss Alton the daughter. The name of the neighboring estate is the Highbury estate. Richard did not say much but did take note he might have a future friend on Sofia. They would have something in common that is the love of horses and riding.

At evenings end and just before bed Anne said, "I do like this place. What are your thoughts dear?" "I am of the same mind. Richard, could you live here?" asked James of Richard. "Yes father, this seems as fine as any place and not too far from Portsmouth and the Navy since this is my future someday.", said Richard. "So, it is agreed then. Tomorrow, I will engage to purchase the place," announced James.

At the Highbury Estate, "Mother, I saw some folks touring the Charlton estate today.", mentioned Sofia. "Perhaps we will have neighbors soon enough. Edward, do we know anything about this family?" asked Victoria. "Nothing as yet, all I know is someone may be interested in the place," replied Edward. "Whoever it may be, this will be a family of means since the Charlton Estate is quite Grand and with a price to match.", commented Victoria.

The next day James engaged his solicitor for the purchase of the Charlton Estate. "I will inform the owners of your request Sir and work with your bank in London to secure the purchase. Do I have your leave to transfer the funds and obtain the estate deeds?" asked the Solicitor.

"Yes, you do. Please assure all taxes and liens have been paid prior to turning over of funds and verify the deeds." requested James. "Yes, of course," noted the solicitor.

Back in Portsmouth, Anne began to plan the move from the Portsmouth house to the Charlton house. "Anne, I received a note from our solicitor saying the transfer is complete. We own the Charlton Estate." announced James. "I have begun to plan the move James, I have talked with servants and have begun several lists. This will be a complicated effort. We may have to send our items there in three separate shipments so it's not to much.

I will send some of our servant ahead to organize the move from there. They can manage the shipments from Portsmouth, organize the unpacking. We will need cleaners contracted, the servants manage the cleaning of the place, removing the dust since it has sat around for the last year," said Anne pouring over her lists to James's acknowledgement.

In my estimation the move may take six weeks to a full two months before we leave the Portsmouth residence for good. Does this sound acceptable?" asked Anne. "I believe so dear," replied James. "I will send two servants ahead in the next couple of days so they can organize the place for the shipments arriving. We will send cleaners to them to organize as well," mentioned Anne.

"Is there anything you want me to organize?" asked James. "Yes, your library books can be shelved, please organize your navy papers, maps and mementoes into boxes. If you have any clothing, you want donated to the church it would be a good time to begin separating these.

Would you organize the stables to have our horses and tac moved to the Charlton Estate this may mean additional servants sent with the animals for transport and care.", said Anne. "I will get to it directly dear." replied James.

At Highbury in Somerset, "Victoria the Charlton Estate has a new owner," said Edward.

"Do we know who the new proprietors are Edward?" asked Victoria. "I believe they are the Hawkes of Portsmouth. That is Admiral James Hawke, retired, Anne the wife and Son Richard, 8 or 9 years of age," mentioned Edward with Sofia listening carefully.

"I wish wealthy Navy folk would not try to buy their way into the aristocracy with the purchasing of Grand estate! Next thing you know they will hold a ball and expect us to come!" said Victoria to silence.

"Let us see how this plays out. In the meantime, when they do move in, we will have to announce ourselves as is customary and proper," said Edward annoyed.

A few days hence, "Dear the horse, tac and servants are on their way to the Charlton Estate to set them up. It will take a couple of days to transfer them properly. I have been organizing the library and separating clothing for donation. We will, once settled, have to organize a winter ball for some of our Navy friends, those in town and some at court. Since they want to know where we have settled. Many may stay the night so we will have to organize the main house and guest houses for this. Perhaps, we get settled first, what do you say!?" said James. To Anne adding to her list.

"And our local neighbors will have to be known and then invited. We know nothing of the local society other than it exists." said James to Anne. "A lot of planning there. It's on the list to be dealt with after the move." said Anne.

"The first, large, shipment of our possessions leaves in a couple of days. The two servants I sent ahead should be settled at Charlton and I will send another two with the shipment. The cleaners are leaving tomorrow for the estate and arrive the same day. By the time the first shipment arrives the place should be clean and ready for unpacking. The cleaners will stay on to help unpack", said Anne.

At Highbury, "Edward, I have noticed servants cleaning inside and out. Shipments arriving, horses about the stables and a general sprucing up of the place. Not long now before the family that will reside there will arrive to stay, "noted Victoria. Sofia wondered, "if the son Richard rode, that she might have a riding companion. As well, there is the idea are they suitable for her society or will they be savages not to be born."

Finally, the day came when the Hawkes would say goodbye to their Portsmouth home and make their way to the Charlton estate. It was sunny and late summer we know what to expect with the roads since we have been there before with this driver. So, with a packed lunch, some knitting and good books the Hawke's set out for Charlton as a merry band.

Arriving at Charlton one noticed the summer scape of thick trees and bushes, grasses and hedge lining the lane making the place very pretty. Richard thought of all the adventures he would have with his horse. Anne worried about the state of the place and did the servants organize and complete the long list of tasks so that they could just arrive to lunch and at evening supper and bedrooms already setup.

"Richard, let us see the state of the move and organize to help your mother with any tasks that urgently need to get done before we rest," mentioned James. Upon entering the home Anne and James found it organized, clean and with no crates to be seen. "James, much of our personal house items, pictures have been set out. Very nice indeed," said Anne to James

The servants offered lunch in the dining room, the housekeeper appraised Anne of the condition of things with a good report, "The bedrooms are ready for tonight and dinner will be served as normal ma'am," said the housekeeper. "Thank you, I was worried with the long list of tasks I asked staff to attend and am very pleased you were able to accomplish all of this," responded Anne.

"Ma'am would you like a tour to assure everything is to your liking?" asked the housekeeper.

"Yes, lets tour.", said Anne, as they walked.

James and Richard were intercepted by a servant guiding them to their bedrooms so they might refresh themselves. "The library is the only area not quite done with so many books and the organizing of maps and other Navy articles we are taking special care of all the one-of-a-kind items ma'am. We have a few more days of work.," mentioned the housekeeper.

After refreshing themselves, "Time for lunch son let us set out for the dining room when one of the servants came along knowing they might get lost offered to guide them to a very welcomed James and Richard.

Arriving at the dining room Anne found James and Richard waiting. "Hi dear, let's have some lunch and talk about the state of the house and what assistance we can lend.", mentioned James.

"The house is in very good order James. The only area not complete to the list we wrote is the library with so many books and being careful with the one-of-a-kind Navy items this will take a few more days. Overall, the house is in good shape," reported Anne.

"Expect some growing pains and missed items not on the list in the next days and weeks but this will be found out and manageable as we find them," mentioned Anne.

"It is strange to think a few hours ago we were in Portsmouth these last twenty & five years and just that suddenly our lives have changed and we are here in Somerset. Is this not a shock dear?", asked James of Anne, with a puzzled look agreed to the suddenness and having been so busy with the move she had not thought of the quickness of change till now.

"What are your plans this afternoon Richard?" asked Anne. I will have my horse saddled and be ready for a first exploration the property. Later to give you my full account of what I see here," replied Richard. "Have fun and be safe son. I will go to the library first, then walk around the place and discover its secrets." commented James.

Richard excused himself to go on his tour. While Anne mentioned she would continue her tour and learning this house. While James found the library and began to help organize his desk and book shelves.

A carriage pulled up letting two persons out at the front door of Charlton house. Edward and Victoria Alton stepped out of the carriage. Inside the house servants set themselves to search for Anne and James.

"I forgot how handsome Charlton can be when maintained. It seems our neighbors have a sense of propriety with respect to the image and being seen even though he is only an admiral in that respect. Well, shall we meet these neighbors," said Edward with Victoria at her side. "Shall we," responded Victoria as they stepped toward the main entry of the house.

"The grounds are interesting and will be fun to explore this summer and fall.", thought Richard as he rode his horse through the Charlton grounds. The grass is soft, and trees dotted the grounds in just the right places. There are many places to stop and just lean back on a tree and read or just take a nap if that is what one wants.

This commons place is just ahead. Let's see what is so special here, advanced Richard into the commons. There is the wood creating a nice'ish border to the place, the pasture is grand and the horse can eat as much as she pleases. The stream is really nice with a good flow of cool water for the horses to drink. I think I shall like it here at this Charlton Place, reflected Richard.

"You, you there! That is a beautiful horse. I don't think I have ever seen one of its kind in these parts. What breed is she? What is her name?", asked Sofia surprising Richard and his horse who became taught and turned to face the voice and assess the threat.

"Oh, you startled me and Fire. I did not see you just there in the brush," said Richard.

"Sorry, I did not realize you and your horse did not see me", replied Sofia as Richard assessed this girl with all her red hair, slat grey eyes and freckles. Richard noticed her horse just at the edge of the pasture happily grazing on the plentiful grasses.

"You must be Richard Hawke then, our new neighbor. Are you one with manners or a savage?", asked Sofia grinning. "I hope one with manners but not so society that I am a stiff board and can break a rule or two for the sake of fun," smiled Richard.

"Shall we introduce ourselves? I am Sofia Alton of the Alton's living here at Highbury and your neighbor," introduced Sofia bowing slightly. "Hello Miss Alton, it is a pleasure to meet you. I am Richard Hawke, son of Admiral Sir James Hawke, my mother is the Lady Anne, and we moved from Portsmouth at my father's retirements and now live here at Charlton.

"Do you mind it Sir if I continue to visit your Commons area between our property?", asked Sofia gently. No, not at all Miss Alton. Please feel free to come as often as it pleases you. "You may call me Sofia, Mr. Hawke.", said Sofia.

"You may call me Richard, Sofia., replied Richard.

"My horse is a pure-bred Arabian. Her name is Fire. She is powerful and quick but gentle and kind in temperament and always takes care of her rider," answered Richard.

"May I touch her Sir? She is so grand a horse I have ever seen," said Sofia. "You can do one better Sofia; would you like to ride Fire in the pasture just here?" asked Richard of Sofia.

"Oh, please, may I please? ", answered Sofia as Richard began to dismount. My father was given Fire as a gift from an Arab sheik while in his country on crown business," mentioned Richard now handing the reins to Sofia. Up close Sofia noticed, of Richard, as tall and handsome, with a quick mind, confident, dark brown hair and crystal blue eyes. I think we shall be good friends this Richard and I, at very least for the sake of this glorious horse!", thought Sofia, given a hand by Richard to mount Fire.

Sofia must be an accomplished riders she knew to look in Fires eyes while gently caressing her cheek asking permission to mount him before mounting him and then petting his neck to assure her, she is a friend and will be gentle with her noticed Richard as he stepped back.

Sofia, holding the reins squeezed her knees and gave a gentle "ooh" from her voice and Fire responded trotting off into the pasture curving his neck, ducking his chin, flipping tail straight up and jumping to a slow gate to give Sofia the full Arabian treatment.

Fire moved to Sofia's commands and he did all she asked, showing off noticeably. I think Fire will like Sofia as a rider and will want to see that often, thought Richard as he sat on a large stone by the stream and where he could see Sofia and Fire having a frolic in the pasture.

After a while, Sofia and Fire approached both smiling. "Do you know your eye go perfectly round and your pupils are so wide your eyes almost seems like two black dots. You must have really enjoyed riding Fire?" said Richard when Sofia was close enough to hear him.

"No, I did not realize this, Richard. I fear you must let me ride Fire since she and I are the best of friends now. Shall we be friends as well?" exclaimed Sofia with a smile as Fire snorted loudly as if in agreement flexing his curved neck. "I believe you may, and yes we shall be friends Miss Sofia," replied Richard to Sofia's broad smile as Sofia dismounted Fire releasing her to the inviting green pasture. Fire moseyed his way to Sofia's horse be become acquainted.
What is the name of your horse Sofia?", asked Richard.

"Her name is Willow. She is a quarter horse. She is nothing special but she is steady and true and I love her.", replied Sofia.

At ringing of the house bell, the housekeeper opened the door to the Charlton house. "Hello, how may I help you.", asked the housekeeper to the Alton's asking who they are and to state their business in the polite society way that is proper and expected.

"We are the Alton's, Edward and Victoria. We own Highbury the adjoining estate, just there, and wanted to greet our new neighbors," announced Edward. James and Anne approached and said, "The Alton's I assume," said James.

"Yes.", said Edward Alton.

"Please do come in. I am the Admiral Sir James Hawke and this is my wife the Lady Anne Hawke. I do have a son, Richard, somewhere about the property you will meet sometime in the future Sir. Wonderful to meet you both," announced James.

"I am Edward Alton, Baron and may I present to you my wife the Lady Victoria, Baroness," announced Edward as Victoria and Anne assessed each other discreetly of course. "Shall we go in to a cup of tea," offered Anne as Victoria agreed before Edward could react.

With Anne leading Victoria to the grand sitting room Lady Victoria commented.

"Lady Anne, when last I was in this house it had a layer of dust and a darkness to it. Now, it is full of light and welcoming," mentioned Victoria almost shyly.

"Thank you for the compliment, Lady Victoria," replied Anne.

"Dear, the weather is so glorious today would you like to pass through to the patio where we can sit in comfort. I believe at this time of day we have just the right shade. Edward, Victoria what do you say?", asked James. "Yes, let's do. We leave our patio bear not knowing what to do with it. I will be interested in your place.", mentioned Victoria interested.

"This is like your sitting room except outside. What a singular idea. A grand idea, and your gardens have been revived beautifully. You have already given life to this place," said Victoria out of character.

James, offered a seat to his guest as Anne sat next to Victoria and James within conversation distance to Edward. Their conversation began shyly but very quickly flowed since James and Anne held no agenda and just had a curiosity about the neighborhood and its people, places and things to do.

"You are both originally from the village of Meare. How wonderful, so you know the area.", said Victoria.

The Alton's stayed longer than expected just enjoying the time and asking all the questions one asks in meeting a new acquaintance. As it was time to leave, the Alton's excused themselves with not wanting to overstay the welcome.

In the carriage, "I believe this to be an unexpectedly pleasant visit, perhaps, I may have to change my opinion of the Hawke's. They have all the sense of society, yet they live quite outside the constraints. Did you notice this, Victoria?", mentioned Edward.

"In my conversation with Anne I noticed this as well. She is very subtle and considerate of those around her and not wanting to overshadow them. She has traveled the world with her Admiral. They are always invited to the Royal Court when in town and personally know the King. I expect we will have to reset our expectation of society since they will be in the neighborhood.

I should like to know this, Anne better. Even her name is so much in the way of plain but she is anything but... her mind is quick, she has many experiences, is quite grounded, very well spoken and understands what is happening around her," replied Victoria.

James is a knight of the realm and Anne is a titled Lady. I had no idea before our visit and yes it seems they are invited to the Royal Court regularly. They know of the King personally. We are rarely invited and therefore rarely go. I suppose the idea they are not of society is a false one to be sure," commented Edward as the carriage slowed and stopped at their estate. I suppose we will wait for an invitation to supper at the Hawke's, and only if we made a good impression on our new neighbors.

"May I show you around your commons?" asked Sofia. "Yes, please do," replied Richard still a bit formal with Sofia. As they walked along, Sofia leading, she pointed out the best reading spots, "this tree is the best leaning tree where one can sit in the shade, the stream is just here flowing, the view of the pasture exquisite and one can read, write or idle the day away quite happily. This spot is best to put one's feet in the cool water of the stream on the very hot days and over here just at the rise one can see the Glastonbury ruins. See, just there...., have you been yet to that place of King Arthur and the Knights?", asked Sofia.

"No, not as yet but I have read of the place and expect to go soon," replied Richard.

"Would you please invite me when you do go. I love the place and its history," mentioned Sofia.

"Yes, I will. I do know a Knight of the realm," commented Richard.

"Really, I don't have the privilege of that acquaintance," replied Sofia. "Perhaps, we can remedy this since my father is a Knight and you will meet him soon enough," mentioned Richard.

"I should like to know him then," replied Sofia.

"Sofia, I will have to return to the house. Would you like to ride with me the way since Highbury is just there? Perhaps, you can ride Fire I will ride Willow if you agree, and meet my mother Lady Anne and father the Admiral Sir James?" hinted Richard.

"Well, when you put it this way I cannot say no politely. Yes! please let's ride to the Charlton house then," agreed Sofia.

At Charlton house, "Mother, Father I would like to present to you Miss Sofia Alton," presented Richard.

"Very nice to make your acquaintance Miss. Alton. I wondered who was riding Fire," smiled Anne in reply.

"We just had tea with you mother Victoria and Father Edward. Wonderful to meet you as well." said James.

With the short visit over Richard walked Sofia to Willow where she said, "I go to the commons daily this time of year and would be happy to see you there where you have time and wish to meet. Of course, bring Fire with you since we are friends too you know," stated Sofia with Richard nodding in agreement.

"Sofia is quite striking a young lady. That flaming red hair and slat green eyes and freckles like stars all around the peaches and cream complexion that is quite tanned. I suppose she will be a problem for the male sex soon enough. Richard however, sees her. I wonder were that will lead," mused Anne as James said, "Enough about the match making dear let us let Richard have some childhood since life is coming fast as it is. And, we will see the character of Miss Alton over time. In the meantime, she does make a good impression and is skilled in the manners and acting in society as to be expected with a mother like Victoria,"

"I suppose we will send an invite to the Alton's for supper? Would sending an invitation out tomorrow for a date next week be to soon? As well, shall we invite the Lord and Lady Percy since they make a wonderful impression, we know them and they are in the area touring the Glastonbury?", asked James of Anne.

"Yes, that is a wonderful idea. I will get to the invitations. Let's not tell the Alton's of our guest since they are used to local society and perhaps not use to royal society.", mentioned Anne.

"Father, Mother can we arrange for me to tour this Glastonbury, perhaps invite Miss Alton sometime soon?", asked Richard.

"We can arrange this and invite Miss Alton. I will go as well since this is a society rule and I am interested in the Glastonbury as well. We must do our reading beforehand so we make the most of the ruins there and what it is about," replied Anne with a list of tasks in hand.

With invitations sent out to the Alton's and Percy's, and all agreeing to the dinner party Anne and the staff worked on the menu and details of the dinner party. As well Anne organized a tour of the Glastonbury ruins inviting Miss Alton, with her parent's permission of course.

The Lord and Lady Percy arrived a day before the Supper to visit with their Hawke friends and be at leisure for the next day's supper. "Welcome Lord and Lady Percy. Thank you for coming. Our servants will convey you to your apartment where you may refresh yourselves and when ready we will meet you on the patio with Lunch, relaxing and conversation," commented James with Lord Percy in concurrence.

"The weather is nice today, with it not being too hot nor cold and the breezes are glorious, would you like to lunch on the patio to beautiful views?" asked Anne of the Percy's. "We see no impediment. We do like the out of doors you know," replied Lord Percy with Lady Percy at his side.

Anne directed the housekeeper to have lunch served on the patio.

"It is wonderful to have you as our guest. As you can see, just there, is the Glastonbury Thor you are touring. Lord Percy, I remember you mentioning to me you had a great fondness for the histories. I took the liberty to secure a local and well know historian of the Glastonbury and the local area. He will arrive this afternoon and give you a recitation on the place and Somerset area," mentioned James at lunch. "This is a wonderful and thoughtful surprise Sir James, thank you," assessed Lord Percy.

"Sir, lodging in the local towns may not be up to what your used to and I offer my house for your use while you are in the area. Would you accept my and Anne's invitation to make this your port while in the Somerset. We would consider this an honor Sir," explained Sir James to his guest.

Lord Percy looked at his Lady and concurred that this would be very acceptable. "Tell us about your dinner guests for tomorrow's supper," asked Lord Percy. "There is a society here in the neighborhood, and its local. Not many for the Royal Court. However, they seem to be harmless and a bit of fun. I want to put on a good show but not be so grand as to scare them off," James said with a smile. "Do they know we will attend the supper?", asked Lord Percy. "No Sir, this has come about most unexpectedly," replied James.

"Perhaps you might inform them, we do show up often in the society papers and this may lead them to feel uncomfortable," said Lady Percy to Anne. "Yes, I see how that could be the case. I shall set about this task directly," replied Anne.

"Perhaps, they might invite one more family in the neighborhood so the conversation is varied and flows easy. What do you think James?" asked Lord Percy. "You and Lady Percy's advice on how to conduct oneself in the society is always impeccable, as you are, as well, a great protector of ours. We will ask the Alton's who we may invite." considered James.

Just then Richard and Sofia where, on each other's horses, and there walking by, "Richard, Miss Alton would you pause and say hi to our guests the Percy's. "Let us dismount and set the horses to grazing. Be there directly mother.", said Richard.

"Richard, who are the Percy's?" asked Sofia intrigued. They are particular friends of the Royal family, especially our King and Queen.

"Of course, you know Richard. "Lord, Lady Percy it is a wonderful surprise to see. Are you both in good health?" asked Richard. "Ah Yes, Richard wonderful to see you again young sir." Replied Lady Percy.

"May I introduce to you Miss Alton of the Alton's our neighbor," presented Anne as Sofia Bowed in that proper way.

"How do you do Miss Alton. It is wonderful to meet you. We will supper with your father and mother tomorrow evening," mentioned Lady Alton.

"It is an honor Lord and Lady Percy. You name sounded so familiar yet I have never met you and only now do I recall this familiarity. You are mentioned quite often in the society papers I believe. Is this so, lord and lady Percy," said Sofia to a surprised group with her frankness said in a very kind and curious way.

"Yes, I suppose we do get mentioned in the society papers perhaps too often at times," smiled Lady Percy.

"Richard, I understand it that you have an interest in touring the Glastonbury. If this is so, we will be there tomorrow and would be happy to take you along. As well, this afternoon we will have a local historian here to present some of the points of interest of the Glastonbury and surrounding area. Would you like to tour this place with us," asked Lord Percy.

"Lord, Lady Percy, I am very interested. It would be an honor to tour this place with you and lady Percy. Sir, would it be impertinent for me to ask that we invite Miss Alton since she is very interested in this place as well," asked Richard almost shyly.

"Yes, we can have Miss Alton, that would be a wonderful idea. Miss Alton, is this to your liking?", asked Lady Percy.

"Oh yes Lady Percy. May I as well listen to the historian's presentation this afternoon?", asked Sofia.

"Of course, you may sit with us.", replied Lady Percy.

"Then it is settled. Don't ride to far since in an hour or so the historian is to arrive. "Yes father," replied Richard bowing to take his leave with Sofia.

Anne, set about sending a note to Lady Alton mentioning the Percy's attendance and asking them to invite one additional neighbor they felt would enjoy the evening and that they should know.

"Richard, your family is not originally from aristocracy but it seems your father and mother know the best of society and regulars to the royal court. Not even my father a baronet is invited to the royal court. The Percy's are quite prominent in the whole of Society. I hope my father and mother are not overwhelmed with it all," said Sofia.

"I believe my mother will assure a good show and not one that is so overwhelming. Have no fear Sofia," replied Richard.

With the Glastonbury historian's arrival, all assembled to hear the historian's talk about the Glastonbury and surrounding Somerset area.

"It was a very interesting recitation. Even I, living in the neighborhood had no idea of many of the points of interest. I will be very happy to tour the Glastonbury tomorrow with you and the Percy's.

Thank you, Richard, for thinking of me and assuring I would be invited to make the tour, it is good of you," mentioned Sofia.

"Not at all. It was nothing. I am glad to tour the ruins together with you as planned and with much more knowledge of what we at touring. It is getting late, shall I walk you to your Willow and see you off to your place?", asked Richard. "Yes Please," replied Sofia smiling at a surprisingly enjoyable day.

At Highbury, "Edward and Victoria, we received a note from Anne about the supper tomorrow night. It seems we should invite another neighbor to the supper. Anne apologizes for the short notice and not knowing any families she is leaving it to us to decide who can be asked," said Victoria.

"Shall we invite the Spencer's they are our closest friends," recommended Edward.

"Edward, there is one more detail...., they have a guest already staying at Charlton house, they are the Lord and Lady Percy, of the Royal Court. They are the special friends of the Royal family, of the King and Queen, those Percy's.

"The Hawke's are a surprise with all their connection to the highest society and the royal court. Victoria, we will not show ourselves to be county bumpkins and to have some knowledge of the society. Let's be sure to dress in our best and perform all the society things that are right and proper under the circumstances," said Edward.

"Knowing a little of Anne and how careful she is we will get a good show but not be overwhelmed with the personages in the room tomorrow.

"Mother" shouted Sofia. "Yes, dear. We are in the sitting room and no shouting please. What is it child?", replied Victoria, at Sofia's arrival in the drawing room.

"I was invited to tour the Glastonbury with the Percy's and Richard tomorrow. This afternoon a local historian gave us the points of interest," mentioned Sofia.

"How did this come about?", asked Victoria with Edward listening intently.

"I was riding with Richard, as we passed the patio we were asked to stop by Lady Anne and I was introduced to the Lord and Lady Percy, and when the subject of their touring of the Glastonbury came up Richard was invited and asked if I could go as well since I am very interested in the place and all agreed," replied Sofia.

"Then you must be made ready considering the Percy' station in the society," replied Victoria motioning to a servant to prepare Sofia's clothing and more to assure she makes a good impression," instructed Victoria.

The day of the supper came quickly. The lord and lady Percy, Richard and Sofia were touring the Glastonbury. Anne worked with the housekeeper to assure all was ready for the supper tonight. A note arrived from the Alton's explaining the Spenser's invitation, and not yet met them, will be the additional family asked and have accepted the invitation to supper tonight. As well as a special thank you from Victoria to Anne for the invitation.

Anne asked the housekeeper to have a light lunch standing by for the Percy's, Richard and Sofia since they may not have had a meal. and may be famished upon their return from the tour.

Upon returning to Charlton House the Lord and Lady Percy, Richard and Sofia talked of their time at the Glastonbury. All seemed to have had a good time and applied the learning they gained through the historian to make the tour even more enjoyable.

"Lord Percy, you seemed to be especially keen at the sites. You have an interest in the Arthurian lore Sir?", asked Sofia.
"I do have an interest in history and especially in this place. You see the King asked me to assess the Glastonbury sites and the state of their protection since he has heard some reports of damage. I would like to see this place preserved since many not

yet born will have this place and our history. It is the least we can do for the generations to protect this place.

I will write a report for His Majesty so he might consider actions for the protection of the place you see," commented Lord Percy to a hushed crowd when he mentioned the King in the conversation. With lunch concluded the Percy's took to their apartments, while Richard and Sofia walked toward the stables and the horses.

"Shall I escort you back to Highbury Sofia?", asked Richard. "That would be lovely," responded Sofia realizing in the moment Richard may want to meet mother and father. With Richard on Willow and Sofia on Fire they set off for Highbury.
"Richard, would you like to meet my mother and father?", asked Sofia. "It would be an honor," responded Richard as they approach Highbury.

Dismounting the horses, a servant asked if he is to stable Willow with Sofia affirming this and asked that water be brought for Fire and let him graze here till Richard returns to her to ride her back to Charlton house.

Sofia led Richard into the house finding her parents in the sitting room discussing a topic and not wanting to interrupt waited at a distance until they signaled it was ok to approach.

At the signal, "Mother, Father I would like to introduce you to Richard Hawke of the Hawkes at Charlton house," announced Sofia. "It is wonderful to meet you Richard, your very welcome here. I am Victoria, Sofia's mother and this is my husband Edward Alton, Sofia's father," announced Victoria.
"It is my pleasure to meet you. My mother and father have only good words about you," returned Richard.

"Richard, do you know the Percy's? How did you come to know of them?", asked Victoria.

After a pause to think, "Well, as you know my father is a friend of the King going on one mission or another at the Kings request and accomplishing His wishes through his service to the Crown through the navy.

Going to the Royal court is a duty and so we know of many a lady and gentlemen, the nobility, many in government and of course the Royal family.

The Percy's are quite high up and friends of the Royal family. As well, they are quite good people, I do not know of a time of not knowing them as long as I can remember. The Percy's are family to me," replied Richard.

"Sir Edward, Lady Victoria and Miss Alton, I see you will be at supper this evening so I will take my leave so as not to take up your time unduly. Thank you for the inviting me into your beautiful home and the honor of meeting you.", said Richard bowing and withdrawing with Sofia asking to escort him out to Fire.

"A very will mannered and respectful young master," commented Edward to Victoria's concurrence.

"Richard, I will be busy tomorrow with mother so I will not be able to ride with you but perhaps the following day we can resume out exploring of the estates." mentioned Sofia. "It was a wonderful day today and fun spending it with you, till next we resume our rides Sofia" replied Richard smiling and waving.

CHAPTER 2

Supper with the Percy's

"Victoria we will leave soon," mentioned Edward with Sofia ready and waiting to see mother fully in her society dress, jewelry and bonnet.

Victoria walked down the staircase to a waiting Edward and Sofia in the sitting room. "Edward gasped in such a way as to make it almost imperceptible but Sofia noticed.

"Victoria, you look...., I forget how handsome you look when it calls for it. May I escort you to the carriage then?", asked Edward as if they were not married these many years, with Sofia taking it all in.

"Of course, you may!" replied Victoria looking at Sofia wanting her appraisal. "Mother you look magnificent," commented Sofia to her mother's smile and the assurance she will not let the Alton name down this evening!

Arriving at the Charlton house, the Spenser carriage was just arriving after the Alton's carriage had stopped. Disembarking both the Alton's and Spenser's arrived at the front door together and were met by James. "Sir James may I introduce you to the Lord and Lady Spenser of West Hill in the neighborhood," announced Edward. "It is a pleasure to meet you Lord and Lady Spenser. I am the Admiral Sir James Hawke, retired. My wife is Lady Anne, she is with our guests whom I will introduce you too. Please be welcomed here do come in, come this way please. Hello Edward, Victoria, welcome.", replied James.

James escorted his party to the sitting room with the Spenser's not yet familiar with the refurbished Charlton house and trying not to look here and look there and comment on the newness and lightness of the place since last they were in the house.

In a society way and with just the right flair, James introduced the Alton's and the Spenser's to the Percy's. Then he introduced his wife the Lady Anne to the Spenser's. "Wonderful to meet you Lady Spenser please be welcomed here. Victoria it is so nice to see you again. I do hope the note I sent was note to short notice," commented Anne as the women formed a group leaving, the men to talk about what men talk about.

"Lady Anne, I am sorry we have not met as yet. You are so new to the neighborhood I did not want to intrude with the whole business of moving in it can take up all of one's time, but I am so very glad to meet you now and to this invitation with your friends the Percy's to supper tonight.", said lady Spencer.

"Lady Percy it is truly an honor to be an acquaintance and to supper with you," commented the Lady Spenser.

"The honor is mine Lady Spenser. I am always keen on meeting new folks and I do so in my friend's house the Hawke's. As you will find out soon enough, the Hawke's are good company, always up for a laugh and loyal to our King and Queen.

Have you lived in this neighborhood for long Lady Spenser?", asked Lady Percy.

"I have lived here all my life Lady Percy. We have no children through a mishap of the first birth," commented Lady Spenser.

"So sorry to hear this, Lady Spenser. I did not mean to intrude.", replied Lady Spencer.

"No at all Lady Percy.", replied Lady Spencer.

"Lady Alton, I take it your roots are from here as well?", asked Lady Percy with Anne taking in the conversation.

"Yes, ma'am I am a Somerset girl born and raised. My father, deceased, was a knight of the realm and visited court regularly as was his duty.", mentioned Lady Alton.

"Lady Alton, I believe I knew of your father and that he visited my husband, at our home in town, a number of times on crown business. Was his title Brigadier Winston, British Army?", asked Lady Percy.

"Why yes, Lady Percy. Small world indeed.", responded Lady Alton feeling a bit less uncomfortable now.

"Dear," said Lady Percy. "We have established the Lady Alton's father was Brigadier Winston. Did he not visit our home and you on crown business many times in his day?", asked Lady Percy of her Lord Percy.

"It has been a long time since I heard that name spoken. Yes, I do remember Brigadier Winston. Good man that Brigadier. I am sorry to see him gone from us. I am happy to know of his daughter Lady Alton," replied Lord Percy.

At the announcement of supper ready, conversation ended in the sitting room as the merry group lead by Sir James headed in the direction of the dining room. The servants took special care this evening. The dinning looked magnificent, with candle light in just the right places, dishes, glasses, knives, folk and spoon laid out just so and sparkling. The food cooked to perfection and the servants danced around the table so the guests never had an empty class or plate. Desert was amazing for the guests and of Italian origins and not so common to the British table.

Conversation flowed easily this evening. With the neighborhood guests taking in all the goings on at the royal court since all they have to understand court activities is the society pages that are thin at best and more focused on the next scandal and not so much the many successes.

"Lord and Lady Percy, it is such a pleasure to meet you. Thank you for the conversation and insights into a part of society we have little access and helping us to understand the subtle nature of events.

We do hope you have a safe return to town and will be interested in the Percy's through our friends the Hawke's and the society papers I suppose.", said Edward Alton with Victoria in concurrence.

"You're very welcome, this was a pleasant evening, good conversation and the meeting of new acquaintances.

"Thank you for having us Sir James. It's been a pleasure meeting you and lady Anne. Lord and Lady Percy, an honor to meet the both of you. Thank you for your hospitality. This has been a wonderful evening. Good night, all," said Lord and Lady Spenser as they left just after the Alton's.

As the Charlton house settled down the residents and guests settled down to sleep in their apartments, the servant's completed cleanup of the dining room and kitchens in prep for the breakfast to come in the next few hours.

The next morning the Hawke's and the Percy's breakfasted together. "I have the kitchen packing lunch for your return to town. Since this is a few hours of travel Lady Percy. I did take into account some of your favorite items," mentioned Anne casually. "Thank you, Anne, for this consideration it is very kind of you. Now that we are advancing in age it is harder to find fresh healthy food about our stops and the switching of the horses," commented Lady Percy with Lord Percy's acknowledgement.

"This has been a wonderful stay. Thank you for offering to take us on Sir, you made our tour of the Glastonbury very pleasurable. And it was very nice to have your Richard with us since he was so helpful to us on the tour yesterday," said Lord Percy.

Richard having breakfast quietly looked up to an address from Lady Percy, "Thank you Richard and to Miss Alton. We thought we would be taking care of you on the tour when in fact you cared for us and watched over us during the tour assuring, we had the most comfort.", said Lady Percy.

"This is nothing Lord and Lady Percy. The two of you are like family to me and it was my privilege to assist you in any way and to assure your comfort. You're very welcome," replied Richard.

With the carriage loaded and the Percy's bags, and packed lunch on board, all that was left is the saying of goodbye. "We will see you at court soon?" asked Lord Percy.

"Yes, in a few weeks we will be in town and will see you and Lady Percy at court Sir. Safe travels," said James with Anne and Richard waving together.

I am glad the weather is perfect for travel, thought Anne.

"What are your plans today, Richard?", asked Anne. "I have naval readings recommended by father to study." replied Richard. "Shall we have lunch together," recommended Anne. "Yes, mother," replied Richard.

At Highbury, "Extraordinary supper last evening Victoria," said Edward.

"Very unique set of guests. I have to reassess my opinion of the Hawke's. There acquaintance with the King, with the royal family, and those high in society that we in fact have no access too forces a change in opinion.

In a few weeks they will be in town and at the Royal Court as a common circumstance. Let us be associated with them since we have a good relationship, although recent, with them," advised Victoria to the agreement of Edward.

"Dear I am off to the village to do some shopping with Sofia. We will be a few hours and then return," announced Victoria. "Please take one of the male servants for protection," mentioned Edward. "We are," replied Victoria.

"Hi mother, is it lunch shall we have some food then," said Richard casually. "Yes, sit by me. How was your naval study?", asked Anne. "Good, I covered a lot of material," replied Richard. "I wanted to ask you about your relationship with Miss Alton?", asked Anne.

"She is a friend. We are exploring both properties. She especially loves riding Fire. Is very talkative in private. Is this appropriate mother? Am I breaking a society rule I am unaware of?", asked Richard.

"No dear, I wanted to understand the nature of your being together and guide this if needed. But it seems harmless at this time. Let me know if anything changes is this understood.", said Anne.

"Of course, mother. What would change?", asked Richard. "You will know and you will tell me son, I am assured of this," replied Anne. "Yes mother," noted Richard.

At supper, "Anne, we will have to finalize the plans the winter ball. Which invitees from town will stay on the property, and the neighborhood to invite, you may want Victoria's assistance with who to invite. This event will come upon us very quickly. As well the invitations should give invitees, in receipt, time to plan their attending or not", mentioned James.

"This will be our first ball and must be a specular event. I have not mentioned it but planning has been going on since we moved to Charlton. However, I like your idea of asking Victoria and will send a note asking her over for tea and to chat about helping me put together a guest list of the neighbors to invite. My plan is to send out invitations to town tomorrow, the Navy Monday next week and later next week the neighborhood. This gives all invitees a full month or more notice.

As well I have been working with our housekeeper on food, music and events for the ball. If you have noticed, the grand ballroom and the adjoining rooms have been cleaned, furniture arranged and are generally being readied for the ball, so we have plenty of room, dancing and conversation and freedom to move about the house.", reported Anne smiling.

"You are so organized dear, what else could I have expected. If you need any assistance from me, just ask.", mentioned James to an acknowledging Anne.

At Highbury, "Edward, I received a note from Anne asking me over for tea and my help to put together an invitation list for their winter ball. I will be happy to suggest those in the neighborhood that should be invited. I expect there will be those from town and regulars from the Royal Court that may attend. Will it be a shock to the local society that Sir James commands great respect by many high personages.", asked Victoria of Edward.

"It did surprise us. I had my impressions of those not in the aristocracy buying there way into the class as you know, but in this case and probably many more there are those that earn their way into the class through true service to the Crown. Sir James is an example of that exception. We will be happy to be seen with them.", replied Edward.

"I will be at Charlton this afternoon and I will take Sofia since she is friendly Richard and the place.", commented Victoria.

Richard completed his daily naval readings and decided to go to the stables to brush down and care for Fire. "Mother, I completed my naval studies and will go to the stables to brush Fire.", said Richard. "Have fun," replied Anne at Richard left to the task.

"Ma'am, the Lady Victoria and Miss Alton are here to see you.", announced a servant. "Please send them through and would you have tea brought in, thank you.", mentioned Anne.

"Anne, nice to see you. Thank you for your note. I am happy to help you.", said Victoria.

"Hi Victoria, Sofia, thank you for coming today. Please be seated. I have tea coming. How have you been?", asked Anne.

"We have been good. I can't help but think of our supper. The conversation, the setting and the attendance made it a special affair. Thank you for inviting us. We very much enjoyed it.", said Victoria.

"I am glad to hear this. We were glad you attended. As you know we are quite new to the neighborhood and don't know all the neighbors and so with the winter ball coming in a little over a month I was hoping for your help with the neighborhood invitation list.", asked Anne of Victoria.

"I am happy you asked and am happy to assist you with the invitations for the neighborhood.", said Victoria, I have put together the list of acceptable neighbor invitees, the addresses, names, and a note about them. Here Anne," offered Victoria.

"Victoria, this is amazing. With this information I can quickly get invitation out and in the post in time for folks to consider acceptance and without a rush. Thank you, Victoria. With this list in hand, we can have a proper visit and chat about what we want. By the way, here is one invitation I will not need to post. I hope the Alton's will come.", commented Anne. "You can count on us Anne.", answered Victoria.

"Miss Alton, Richard is at the stable grooming Fire. I know of your fondness for Fire and if you want to visit her and Richard you may, if this is acceptable with your mother.", mentioned Anne.

"It is acceptable, Anne. Sofia, I will chat for an hour or so, so be back for a ride back to Highbury.", replied Victoria as Sofia excused herself.

"Anne, if I know a little about you. You would have invited some from town and the Navy. Who might be coming to the winter ball?" inquired Victoria curious. "As you know, James has a number of acquaintances in town that would travel to Portsmouth for our winter ball there and now, we are much closer to town they will surely come as well. Some are quite high in the society...Lords and Ladies all, gov't officials and several members of the Royal Family.

We will set aside apartments in the house and the two additional houses since the local towns will not support the kind of living, they are accustomed too, so Charlton will bridge that gap. Some will be driven back to town late in the evening or early morning.

We invited the Prime Minister and other ministers, the Prince and Princess, there will of course be officers and some from the admiralty, foreign diplomats, lord justices, a number of lords and ladies, a number of single ladies of the court to assure the officers have dance partners and of course our local society.

You may see some marine guards posted just before the ball if the royals accept. I expect one or more of them since this will be away from the town assemblies and they might be able to just let their hair down. Would this be too heady for the local society?", asked Anne of Victoria.

"Certainly yes! But we do need a good shake up and to witness real society folk.", replied Victoria smiling at the wonder of the coming ball.

"It may be a consideration to hint at the high personages that will attend the ball so they are not surprised. What do you think in this case?" asked Anne.

"This is a good consideration. I will as well make the hints to prepare our neighbors. As well, and I have to confess humbly dear Anne, I was not sure the Admiral was not just one trying to buy their way into the class. It was not till we met you that we realized you and Sir James are quite special and it is we that should be honored to know you. Indeed, we will have to prepare the local society to encounter broader society for the first time Lady Anne.", replied Victoria calling Anne by her title for the first time.

"I appreciate your frankness Victoria and am glad we are acquaintances. Have no worries or guilt in this matter. James and I have encountered this prejudice many times to folks who then realize we are very experienced in the society with powerful friends. But I never hold these acquaintances over anyone's heads since I would not like that treatment myself. We simply have many great and interesting friends that have a say in the empire that my husband helped expand in his day on mission for the King. And that appreciation is displayed when at court or in a ball we might put on.

Victoria, the neighborhood invite list you created will save me so much time. In a day or so we will post all the neighborhood invitations thanks to your kindness and forethought. I am very appreciative, thank you.", smiled Anne causally.

"It was nothing at all Anne, you're very welcome.", replied Victoria.

At the stables, "Hello Richard," said Sofia to a startled Richard. "Oh, hi Sofia, I did not realize you would come to the house today else I would have met you.", bowed Richard with a grooming brush in hand.

"Fire looks magnificent! Can we ride perhaps tomorrow if the weather is acceptable?", asked Sofia.

"Certainly, if I can ride Willow?", said Richard with a smile and a wink.

"I am done with Fire's grooming. Shall I walk you back to the house. Isn't your mother helping mine with the invitations for the winter ball?", asked Richard.

"Yes, she is. Richard, you spend time each day on naval studies. What is this all about?", asked Sofia shyly.

"Father set a course of study that I follow each day. It takes about one to three hours depending on that day's plan. When I am of age I will attend the Royal Naval academy, it is expected you know.", replied Richard.

"And how long will you be in the Navy?", asked Sofia slightly annoyed and not hiding it very well.

"It could be three years, maybe four at the academy and a few years of sea duty", replied Richard.

"Sofia, you seem put off by the Navy plan.", commented Richard. "I am not one for going away and the idea of leaving.", said Sofia.

"I am seven to eight years away from the academy. So, we have many years of riding and great adventures. Let us enjoy today and not worry about tomorrow's events until they come about. Shall we?", said Richard calmly.

Sofia, relaxed the tension and resumed easy conversation about tomorrow's planned riding adventure. At Charlton house they walked in together to both mother's chatting away over a cup of tea and smiling.

"Richard, I see you and Sofia found each other.", mentioned Anne. "Yes mother, we plan to go on a riding adventure tomorrow on the estates, weather permitting and after my naval studies.", replied Richard.

"I still don't like this idea of leaving for the naval academy for three to four years...and then the sea for several years.", whispered Sofia annoyed with the idea.

"Did you hear that, Anne?", whispered Victoria. "Yes, very interesting comment I thought. Are we forming an attachment already." mentioned Anne.

"Sofia, has never liked the idea of saying goodbye and of people leaving she cares about. This has always been a line for the most part for an easy-going young lady. I suppose Richard is someone close to her and she does like the idea of him leaving her. Yes, interesting, something to keep an eye on." replied Victoria discreetly.

"Shall we leave?" announced Victoria to Sofia. "Yes mother", interrupting her conversation with Richard. "Anne, thank you for having us and trusting me to assist you with the invitations. We will talk soon.

Anne, Edward and I wanted to invite you, James and Richard to supper, mind you we don't have some of the friends you possess. However, we would invite one or two from the neighborhood. Would you accept?", asked Victoria.

"Of course Victoria, we will accept. Send us an invitation with details so we can make ourselves free.", replied Anne smiling.

"Dear, what was the letter, you received today, about?", asked Anne of James. "It was from the Admiralty asking for assistance on a naval matter. I will have to travel to town for a few days to assist. I was thinking of taking Richard with me.

Richard you can be with me at the admiralty and we can visit the Naval Academy's new offices as well and be seen there. What say you?", asked James of Richard.

"Father that would be very acceptable, to see the admiralty and to visit the new academy offices for the first time. When are you planning to leave for town?", asked Richard hoping not tomorrow.

"Today is Monday, I was thinking we leave Wednesday and be back Friday. We don't want to leave your mother to long else there will be suitors banging at the door.", replied James with a big grin toward his Anne.

"You are so funny dear. First, I only have eyes for you and Richard. Second, they can bang away at the door but no one will be answering. I will miss the both of you and hope for the safe return of my two men.", commented Anne.

In that case we will be back as quickly as possible!", replied James.

"Dear we will need some clothing for Richard for the trip to town as I may take him to court with me since he is of age and should get use to this setting now rather than later. Then the admiralty and the academy offices. As well as travel cloth to and from....", said James interrupted by Anne.

"Have no worries, dear I know just the trick and will have the servants pack him properly." Answered Anne.

"Richard, gently tell Sofia, tomorrow on your riding adventure, you will be going to town with Father for a couple of days. You now know she is not one that the likes going away and the saying of goodbye.", mentioned Anne.

"Yes mother.", replied Richard.

The next day was all sun and warm, a light breeze and perfect for a riding adventure in Sofia's estimation. "Mother, I will be riding Willow to the Charlton Estate and go on a riding adventure with Richard.", said Sofia.

"Have fun, stay on the estates," replied Victoria.

"Oh! Sofia, would you deliver this supper invitation to Anne for me," asked Victoria.

"I would be happy to mother," replied Sofia. "If you're going to ride most of the day, perhaps you should pack a lunch for you and Richard?" asked Edward thinking ahead to Victoria's surprised look.

"That is a great idea father. I will go to the kitchen," replied Sofia.

At Charlton, Sofia found Fire saddled and ready to go. "Hi Richard, how are you?", asked Sofia. "Very well, and you?" responded Richard. "I brought us some lunch, and would you excuse me while I deliver this note into your mother's hand.", announced Sofia.

"Yes, of course...", said Richard holding the reins to both Fire and Willow.

At Sofia returning, "Ok, ready. May I ride your Fire?" smiled Sofia hand outstretch as Richard handed her Fires reins. "It seems Fire enjoys you riding her" said Richard as they rode off to Sofia smiling broadly.

At Charlton, "Dear, we have been invited to supper this Saturday evening at the Alton's. They caution us that they do not know such society folk as we may but they will invite a couple of the neighbors to make for an interesting evening. Shall we accept?" asked Anne.

"Of course, let us see what there is of our neighbors", smiled James.

"I will send an acceptance this morning. It seems Victoria and Edward are making an effort.", commented Anne.

"Let's encourage the connection." Replied James.

"Concerning the winter ball, all of the invitations are posted, including those to the local neighbors. I am receiving responses already, all acceptances thus far and mostly from town. I think folks are wanting a country dance this year and won't mind the travel to Charlton.", mentioned Anne.

"We had better be ready for a large crowd. Do you think Richard can attend this year for a few of the early hours or should we wait one more year?", inquired James for Anne's opinion.

"I think he may be of the maturity this year for a few hours of exposure to society.", replied Anne.

"When in town I will see how he acts at court at my side before we make the final decision.", recommended James.

"I will wait for your report then Dear.", remarked Anne giving an acceptance note to a servant and asking it be delivered to Highbury, into Lady Victoria's hand.

"I am off to the Hill house and the White house to provide my list to the servants there to ready them for our overnight guests to stay while at the winter ball. We have a total of eight apartments that can hold up to twenty-two persons comfortably, there is food, drink and parking for the carriages and horse care at each to considers....so quite a list dear. I will see you later this afternoon when this is organized.", chatted Anne on her way out with the housekeeper at her side and a carriage waiting to take her to Hill house.

"It does seem we are settling in at Charlton. It is becoming our home.", thought Anne scanning her list of to-dos for the ball yet to worked on.".

CHAPTER 3
Society and the Aristocracy

"Hi dear, the guest houses and the apartments here at Charlton house are organized in preparation for the winter ball. I have an orchestra I wish to engage but have not heard them play. They will be here tomorrow. I will ask Victoria if she would listen in with me since you and Richard are off to town and I may need an opinion for the music and dancing.", mentioned Anne handing a note to a servant to deliver to Highbury and wait for an answer.

"It seems to be coming together.", replied James excited.

A little later, "Let's get James and Richard settled for tomorrow's trip to town.", said Anne walking with one of the house maids.

"We have the clothing you asked to be packed for James and Richard, and have the bags ready for transport Ma'am. The cook asked if we are to prepare food for the trip?", asked the maid.

"Yes, to a packed lunch, that is a good idea. Something light but filling so they are not famished at arrival in town.", said Anne. "Yes, Ma'am" replied the maid.

At the commons, "Richard, shall we settle here and give the horses a chance to graze and refresh themselves. Let's have some food and drink to refresh ourselves, shall we?", asked Sofia.

"Yes, good idea.", said Richard dismounting and then hold releasing both horses to the commons pasture grasses and stream where the horses found cool inviting water to get a deep drink and lots of green grass for them to eat.

Sofia set out lunch. Richard returned after assuring the horses were taken care of, "Richard, would you tell me about the academy and what to expect.", asked Sofia.

"When I am fifteen years I will be accepted into the royal naval academy. My name has already been submitted and because my father is an admiral I should be accepted. The royal naval academy is located in Portsmouth. My stay there will be four years where at successfully completing of the course I will be made an officer of the rank of midshipman. I will be nineteen.

Typically, this is a four-year course, but because of my studies now and leading up to I will be tested and if sufficient I will be jumped ahead in class. During this time, I will have breaks to return home for weeks at a time. The longer breaks are Christmas/New Years and summer break.

It is a sacrifice to be sure. I did notice you do not like the idea of going away. Would you talk to me about this, if you feel comfortable.", asked Richard.

"I have never liked good-byes. It is distressing to see those I care about leave to some destination, uncertain of their return. I say, why do people need to go in the first place? So, it distressed me hearing you would be leaving. Until you reminded me the leaving is six to seven years hence. Still, I do not like it. Tomorrow, you go to town! I don't like that, but accept it.", replied Sofia eating one of her sandwiches lightly.

"Yes, we are off to town tomorrow, Father has been asked to assist the admiralty with his opinion on a number of naval matters, then we go to the royal court and finally I will visit with some of the academy instructors for advice on my studies and preparation for yearly testing.

Father says, they may take me at fifteen if I test well enough.

I realize this is distressing. You must know I am not an aristocrat and so must be employed and in the service of the Crown to maintain the level Father has established before me. Even though Father is quite wealthy money is not a ticket into the aristocracy but rather connections.

Serving the King, the royal family is a key to the royal court and connections in the realm. If I am to marry a lady one day, I would be unsuitable in societies eye unless my path through service to the Crown was clear to see, and of course being wealthy in my own right does not hurt the cause. So, I have work to do.", reflected Richard, as Sofia listened deeply.

"What is the royal court like Richard.", asked Sofia.

"It is a grand affair. The splendor of the palace can be overwhelming at times and necessary so that those in doubt of the power and majesty of the King would be brought to heal at the sight of it. The people invited are the most illustrious in the land. The best military men, knights, Lords and Ladies, scientists, business, government.... You name it and they can be found. I find these folk to be interesting, some kind, some not so kind like any society one is in.", said Richard.

"Have you met the King, or the Queen?" asked Sofia.

"Yes, mind you, I was a child in their eyes and their attention was upon father. They seem kind, very astute in manner and worldly in nature. I know to be still and attentive to them when they are near and only speak when spoken to.", replied Richard.

"I have never seen the King or Queen. And only know their looks through drawings found in the society papers to recommend me.", added Sofia.

We will leave tomorrow and will be back Saturday. I believe we have a supper invite to your house. We will be able to catch up and I will tell you all that transpired.", said Richard.

Back to the academy topic, after I graduate the academy and a few years of service to the King I will be back to Charlton since my mother and father will be elderly and need my help to run the place.

"Sofia, what about you? When are you off to finishing school?", asked Richard.

"Mother's plan is when I am fifteen years. This course will last two years, with breaks to return home during those times.", answered Sofia.

"Perhaps since we are both in our obligations we can correspond? Or maybe not since when you return you will be presented to society and there will be many eligible men for you of the aristocracy and I am nothing to that.", mentioned Richard.

"Yes, we will correspond and I am not a cow or horse to be sold to the highest bidder. I will make the marriage decision. When you perform your obligations, you will be as eligible as any and one to consider surely.", replied Sofia as Richard eyes met Sofia in that way of understanding something that is too soon to tell for sure but not too far away as to leave unsaid.

"We should begin to gather ourselves up, I will retrieve the horse so we can return since I need time to prepare for tomorrow.", said Richard as Sofia packed what was left of their lunch.

"Today was a glorious day and not many till the winter weather settles in for the season. I love a return to warm weather that we get in this part of England, before the winter takes over. I expect this to be the last of the warm till late spring next year. I was thinking during the time when it is too cold to ride you can visit me at Highbury and when my mother visits your Anne, I can visit with you. If this is acceptable?" asked Sofia.

"Yes, very acceptable. I am glad you think ahead in these matters. At some point I would have wondered what to do to chat with you. I suppose it's a man's nature not to think in this way until it is pointed out.", smiled Richard.

"Shall I ask my mother if it would be acceptable for you to specially visit me at Highbury during the winter months since riding is out of the question. And if you talk with your mother this will not be a surprise since they will talk about it between the other.", planned Sofia.

"This sounds like a good plan.", said Richard as he and Sofia arrived at Highbury.

Sofia's mother came out holding a note, "Richard, how are you today?", asked Lady Victoria. "I am very well, thank you for asking.", replied Richard as he dismounted Willow handing the reins to Sofia, as Sofia handed Fire's reins into Richards hands.

"Richard, would you hand your mother this note of acceptance to visit with her tomorrow?", asked Victoria. "Of course, Lady Victoria, I would be very happy to do this.", replied Richard.

"Did you have a fun time today. Not many warm days left to ride.", said Victoria.

"Lady Victoria, I wanted to ask your permission on a subject.", mentioned Richard with Sofia listening curious.
"Please ask," replied Victoria.

"Would it be acceptable if I came to visit with your Sofia here at Highbury, since riding will be too much in the cold.

"I think this would be acceptable. I will have to talk to your Lady Anne of course.", replied Victoria.

"Yes, I will talk with mother as well so this is not a surprise. And if this is acceptable for you Sofia.", mentioned Richard.

"Yes, this is acceptable.", replied Sofia standing next to her mother as Richard mounted Fire and rode off in the direction of Charlton.

"Mother, I have a note from Lady Victoria for you.", said Richard handing Anne Victoria's note.

"Thank you dear, did you have a good ride today?", asked Anne.

"Yes mother. Mother, I asked Lady Victoria if it would be acceptable to visit Sofia during the cold where we will not be able to ride. She thought she would chat with you first but saw no impediments. I did not want this subject to be a surprise when she brings it up when next you visit with her.", said Richard.

"This seems acceptable Richard, however I will chat with Victoria so all are in agreement. I will let you know what Victoria and I think.", replied Anne.

"Yes mother.", replied Richard.

The next morning, James and Richard were to leave for town. "Dear, it is time for Richard and I to leave for town. All the bags are on board. And we have food and drink for the trip, thank you for thinking ahead for us. We will see you Saturday then," said James with Richard at his side.

"Have a safe trip dear.", said Anne as Richard and James stepped into the carriage.

Anne waved as the carriage speed off down the lane headed to town. Later in the morning a group of musicians arrived at Charlton in preparation to demonstrate the level of skill and plan music for the winter ball.

Victoria's carriage came into sight before Anne went back into the house so Anne waited her arrival. "Hello Anne, I just passed James and Richards carriage on my way here. How are you today?", said Victoria.

"Very well, thank you for asking. And you?", asked Anne.

"Very well, I see some of the orchestras are arriving.", mentioned Victoria.

"Yes, they are assembling in the ballroom. We have some time to sit and have a cup of tea and a chat before they are ready. What do you say?", asked Anne.

"Yes, that sounds lovely.", replied Victoria.

"The housekeeper will let us know when the musicians are ready for us. Did Sofia ask you if Richard may visit her at Highbury during the cold months by any chance?", asked Anne.

"As a matter of fact, yes. Richard asked me. I said I did not see any impediments but would have to talk with you first. I suppose Richard talked to you as well.", responded Victoria.

"I am of the same mind. I do not see any impediments and we should keep an eye out for the two of them since you would agree there is an attachment forming. I know they are young at nine and ten but nonetheless. As well we will have to find reasons for you to visit Charlton, bringing of course Sofia and giving them a bit of time, and me to Highbury.", smiled Anne.

"Well, the cups of tea seem better tasting at Charlton and that is just as good an excuse to visit as any!" returned Victoria with both women laughing at it all.

"Ma'am, the musicians are ready for you.", said the housekeeper to Anne and Victoria walking toward the ballroom.

Seated before the musicians they played the music to a number of the popular dances. Victoria said, "I think they are strong, the music sounds wonderful, mind you I am not in the high circles as you at the Royal Court.", giggled Victoria.

"Yes, I agree. I think they will be just the thing for the Winter Ball. After making arrangements for the musicians Anne and Victoria discussed the ball plans overall.

"We have a number of very high in the society folks staying at Charlton to attend the ball. They are Prince Lionel and Princess Jenni, the Prime Minister and several cabinet ministers, Lord and Lady Percy and several others with that title, a number of ladies so the officers attending have dance partners and a host of other notables, and our neighbors. It would be best I think not to speak of what I just said since this may cause nervousness and a stir with the locals if they found out and waiting at the entrance road for the train of carriages to see what they could see.", mentioned Anne.

"I will not mention this to anyone. Well, may I mention this to my Edward asking him to be discreet?" asked Victoria.

"Yes, of course," responded Anne.

"Anne, this will be the event of the season. It will be exciting. Will you have Richard attend the ball this year?", asked Victoria. "Maybe..., what I mean is James will see how he behaves at the Royal Court while in town. We will make the decision at that.", answered Anne.

"Will you let me know your decision. Since if Richard will be at the ball a few hours Sofia will want to be there hoping for her first dance and conversation.", asked Victoria.

"I shall Victoria, I will know Saturday and be at supper at your place. We can chat about it then.", replied Anne.

In town, "Dad, we are arriving in town.", said Richard gently waking James from a light sleep.

"Ah, here we are in the hustle and bustle of it all. I did need a good nap. I was up to the early hours of the morning preparing my opinion for the admiralty today.

We will go to the apartments to refresh, then it's the Admiralty. There will be academy instructors happy to meet you, while I am in meetings. They want to start the yearly assessments.", related James as Richard listened intently.

At the house, James and Richard refreshed themselves and departed for the admiralty.

At the admiralty offices, "Good afternoon, Admirals Nester, Jones, Vincent. Would you gentleman give me a moment while I organize my son with the academy instructors Grimms and Cecil. Who should be here somewhere.", mentioned James.

"Of course, Hawke. Welcome to the Admiralty young master Hawke. We will be in the meeting rooms James.", responded Admiral Nester.

"A Hawke has retired with another Hawke on the way!", commented Admiral Vincent smiling.

"The young master will begin a yearly assessment of his knowledge of the navy then?", asked Jones.

"It seems so. They will assess his studies to this point and advise his father.", said Admiral Nester.

"Ah instructor Grimms, instructor Cecil it is very nice to see you two again. Thank you for meeting Richard here at the admiralty offices today. I have a meeting I must attend. Shall I leave my son in your capable hands then?", commented James.

"Yes, Admiral, we will take it from here.", responded Cecil as he approached Richard and shook his hand.

"Very nice to meet you, Richard. I am instructor Cecil, and this is instructor Grimms. Shall, we go into this room. We are from the Academy. Do you know why we are meeting with you today?", asked Cecil.

"I believe so sirs, my father said I was to meet academy instructors to begin a yearly assessment that will test my knowledge of the navy. But not much more Sirs.", replied Richard sitting up straight.

"We will be assessing your knowledge of the Navy, and reporting back to your father on your progress and make any recommendations for your education. Since you're intending to test for credits that may amount to a year or more this will require a yearly assessment by academy instructors. Your father is so well regarded that means you will be closely watching his son progress. Do you understand young master?", asked Grimms. "Yes, sir.", replied.

"Let's, begin then......", instructed Cecil.

With James at the admiralty meeting, "Admirals, I am very glad to be asked and to assist in these matters of the navy, as you see fit gentlemen.", said James.

After some hours of discussion and the giving of opinions the meeting ended, "I understand I will be back tomorrow for additional discussions?", asked James of the Admirals.

"Yes sir, if this is convenient.", replied Admiral Nester.

"Yes Sir, this is convenient. Until tomorrow then. Will you be at court tonight.", asked James.

"Yes, I will be. The admiralty has to show face and tonight I am that face. Pity those that look upon me! Knocked about as I am by the weather, beaten and tanned I am!", laughed Admiral Vincent.

"Well gentlemen, if you will excuse me, I will collect my son and have an early supper then prepare for court. See you, their Admiral Vincent!", said James leaving the meeting room.

"Sir James, shall we chat about your son?", asked instructor Cecil as instructor Grimms walked away with Richard so he could not see or hear the discussion.

"Yes, please.", replied James.

"Your son is ahead in his knowledge and understanding Sir. If he continues, we may be able to shave more than a year off his time to graduate the academy. We see you have had a hand in his readings, skills with navigation and the maps as well as history and command.

I would keep him on the same regime. As long as he is able to absorb the work.

Next year, let assess him around the same time but at the academy in Portsmouth. We will see what he has learned and report to you. I see great things here. Like father like son.

That is all Sir James.", reported instructor Cecil as he and James walked toward instructor Grimms and Richard.

"Thank you, for your time today to test me instructor Cecil and Instructor Grimms. I am grateful and appreciative.", said Richard to the academy instructors, to James surprise at the maturity.

"You are very welcome young master. Please continue your studies and only good things will come of it. See you next year at the academy in Portsmouth.

Sir James, if you will excuse us.", said Cecil as he and Grimms walked away.

"Father, I hope you I had a good report. I have kept up with and sincerely make the effort to follow your instruction in the naval studies.", said Richard.

"Son, I received a glowing report. I am very proud of you. We will continue your studies as is and at this pace if this is acceptable.", replied James.

"This is acceptable father", replied Richard.

"Let us get an early dinner then visit the Royal court this evening. What do you say?" asked James.

"This is very agreeable Sir.", replied Richard.

"Father I would like to buy a small present for Mother and for Miss Sofia perhaps tomorrow can you help me arrange this?", asked Richard.

"Yes, I can send one of the servants to this task. Mind you nothing too expensive. It's the idea that counts. Your mother is partial to English chocolates. What is Sofia partial too.", asked James of Richard.

"She is partial to Turkish delight. Would that be to extravagant father?", replied Richard.

"I think I can arrange this, Richard.", replied James as they arrived at their house to a nice supper waiting.

"Richard, your cloths for tonight, at the palace, should be laid out on the bed. One of the male servants will assist you and assure all is correctly adjusted. Then I will of course inspect you.", said James with a smile.

"Yes, father.", replied James.

"Son, it will important to follow all the protocols expected at court. You know, say nothing unless spoken to, smile and bow where appropriate, eat with me and in a very dignified way, stand at attention and put your hands away as you know. If you have any question wait until we are alone to ask so we don't cause a commotion. If one of the ladies asks you to dance, you may dance, remember showcase the lady, smile and be warm, bow after the dance thanking her and return to my side.", reminded James.

"Shall we both get dressed?", recommended James as he and Richard walked upstairs and to their rooms where servants awaited them to assist in the dressing.

Now dressed, "Richard, you look splendid. I am reminded you have your mother's looks and my statue to your credit.", said James.

"Thank you, father. I want to make you proud of me at court."

"Son, whether at court or not I am very proud of you. Don't steal all the ladies!", smiled James as they walked out and onto the carriage.

Arriving at the palace they disembarked from the carriage to a very busy scene of those arriving and empty carriages leaving. The palace entry was lit by lanterns, creating a golden hue to the stone steps and the grand entry into the palace.

Entering the main portal suddenly one encountered light cream-colored walls trimmed in gold, with candles everywhere so there was little to no shadows. The ceiling was very tall and slightly darker but on could see very intricate designs, the doors from one room to another where very tall, some mirrored while others painted gold, all of them opened so guests could move about freely.

There were servants everywhere assuring all the guest were taken care of, even servants in the background rushing to replace spent candles were found assuring the maximum light. While other servants assured food and drinks were plenty. Still, others assured the ladies special needs were attended.

This will be a grand affair with very experienced staff to assure the smooth running and that all the guests were taken care of for the evening. I have been to court before but this is the first time I am aware of everything going on around me, the people, the place, the environment thought Richard staying close to his father.

"Father for the first time I am aware of the Royal Court.", said Richard.

"It can be overwhelming but don't let it be so for you. We will meet many friends and acquaintances. The palace is a grand place to be sure and the show is for those needing a reminder of the Kings power. For those that serve His Majesty this is a Thank you for the many tasks we complete in His Majesty's service. You and I serve the King. Now let's enjoy ourselves.", said James.

"The Admiral Sir James Hawke and young Master Richard Hawke", announced the doorman as James and Richard entered the Royal Court. The scene was grand with many looking at James and young master Richard. "Ah, the Lord and Lady Percy. How are you this evening.", said James with Richard at his father's side smiling at the Lord and Lady Percy.

"Very well, Sir James. And how is the young master Richard,", asked Lord Percy. "Very well Lord Percy, thank you for asking.", replied Richard smiling and bowing slightly.

"Hi James, master Richard. I hope your evening is going well?", said Admiral Vincent approaching.

"Very well, Admiral and you?", asked James.

"Very well Sir. I had a chat earlier with the Lady Peal, she is very grateful to you and your Anne.", mentioned Admiral Vincent.

"Yes, I put in a word at the academy on behalf of her son.", replied James.

"I thought I saw a Peal sir name on the accepted list this year, and forgot to ask if he was a relation to Lady Peal. Well done, James!", mentioned Admiral Vincent.
Ladies Peal, Summons and the young Lady Bently arrived to chat. "Lady Peal, Lady Summons, Lady Bently let me present my son master Richard.", announced James as Richard smiles and bowed.

"Why lovely to meet you again young master Richard.", said Lady Peal. "Will you save a dance for me young master Richard.", asked young Lady Bently.

"Yes, of course, Lady Bently.", replied Richard.

"There is no time better than now. If you are free?", exclaimed the Lady Bently inviting Richard to take her arm to escort her to the dance floor several rooms away.

"Father, may I.", asked Richard.

"Yes, son.", replied James.

As the Lady Bently and Richard walked away, the Lady Bently mentioned, "I will find you Sir James after a dance or two depending on the skill here.", mentioned Lady Bently, smiling.

After a time and four dances later, the Lady Bently returned master Richard to his father.

"Those were two long dances Lady Bently.", said James.

"Well, Sir I have to say I did take advantage of your young master Richard with four dances since his dancing skill is quite good. And I had to fight off several Ladies who wanted him to dance with them saying they had to ask your permission since he is a young master. Expect a broken heart or two already.", joked the Lady Bently.

"Lady Bently, it was an honor and privilege to have danced with you.", said Richard.
"The pleasure was all mine master Richard.", replied Lady Bently.

As the Lady Persimmons and Lady Chatter approached, "Dear Sir James may we each have a dance with your young master Richard. We promise to return him unharmed.", asked the Ladies Persimmons and Chatter. "Well, Richard are you up for two more dances?" asked James of Richard with both ladies watching intently.

"It would be my honor dear ladies.", replied Richard to the two ladies commenting on how considerate the young master is while leading him to the dance floor.

Richard was returned by the very happy ladies exclaiming he must be returned to court soon if for nothing but a dance or two for the many ladies needing the dance floor.

"Let us find some food and drink and a quiet corner to sit, shall we son?" asked James as they went into a room filled with servants and many types of foods, drinks and desert. With plate and drink in hand James and Richard found a quiet place to sit.

"Father, there are circle here.", said Richard.

"What do mean son?", asked James.

"People revolve in their circle. Some circles are higher and some lower. The closer to the royal family the higher the circle. While other circles may revolver around an illustrious personage. Does this make sense father?", explained Richard.

"Yes, and you are quite right. I haven't thought of it in such terms but this is a truth. Your powers of observation are quite advanced and at such a young age.", replied James.

"Father, one more interesting observation, you move from one circle to another, from the highest to the lowest with ease while others restrict themselves to just be near their circles and only wanting to be seen in this way or that.", said Richard.

"So now you are learning of what confidence is, when one can travel between all the circles one displays a self confidence in oneself. One can as well, gain many friends and allies at all levels. This is an important skill to cultivate son.", said James.

"Father, I met the Lord Chief Justice and his wife Lady Rachael. They saw you in me and asked if my father is Sir James Hawke. I said yes and they asked I send you and mother their compliments.

"This evening you were no doubt watched by many in manner and treatment of the ladies you danced with by those in the admiralty and beyond. They assessed your willingness to be helpful to the ladies, your poise and ability to move about society fearlessly.

You did very well Son. I am proud of you. Your conduct has been exemplary", commented James.

"I don't know about you. But it seems this may be the best time to leave this place and retreat for the evening. What say you!", asked James of Richard as they walked slowly through crowded rooms.

"Sir James, Sir James," someone announced. Turning James laid eyes on Princess Jenni.
"Princess Jenni, wonderful to see you this evening. May I present my son young master Richard.", replied Sir James as he and Richard bowed as is customary.

"Please, Sir James would it be too much if my brother Lionel and I attended your winter ball and my we stay at your Charlton house?", asked Princess Jenni.
"It would not be too much and yes, it would be an honor to have you and Prince Lionel at Charlton.", replied James.

"May I inquire about your Lady Anne, and how is she?", asked Princess Jenni.

"She is quite well. Richard and I are in town for Admiralty and Academy business while Lady Anne is home at Charlton.", replied James.

"Please send her my warmest regards. I would ask a great favor of your young master Richard?", asked Princess Jenni.

"Of course," replied Sir James.

"Young master Richard would you be inclined to save a Lady friend of mine, just there, and ask her to dance. Her name is the Lady Penelope. She has not been asked this evening and would so like to take to the dance floor. Would you be a gentleman and save the Lady Penelope?" asked Princess Jenni.

"Father, may I do this favor for our princess and the Lady Penelope?", asked Richard.

"Yes son, you may and the Princes Jenni and I will be just here waiting for you.", replied James, as Richard carefully walked over to the Lady Penelope.

"Dear Lady Penelope, my name is young master Richard Hawke. My father is the Admiral Sir James Hawke, just there speaking with princess Jenni.

I wanted to ask you for the great honor of this next dance, if this is acceptable to you?", asked Richard of the Lady Penelope.

"Young master Richard, this would be very acceptable would you sit with me until this dance is completed then we can take to the floor.", mentioned Lady Penelope.

"Yes, I would be happy to dear Lady. Lady Penelope, would you tell me of yourself. You have the advantage of me knowing my father Sir James and I know little of you except that you are very grand indeed.", asked Richard kindly.

"How old are you master Richard?", asked Lady Penelope.

"I am nine years."

Quite true young master, I am aware of your father Sir James and his great service to the Crown. As for me, I am a lady in waiting to the Queen. I am alone because no one wants to approach the Queens lady. Does this make sense?", commented Lady Penelope.

"Yes, it does dear Lady and I sense a dance with you is a great honor indeed. I will try my best for you Lady Penelope.", replied Richard as the previous dance ended, as Richard led the Lady Penelope to the floor.

Richard danced flawlessly. Taking care of the Lady Penelope so that she was displayed and could just enjoy the dance.

After the dance, "Princess Jenni, Sir James, your young master Richard took great care of me on the dance floor. Thank you, master Richard, for the dance. I hope to see you at court again sometime soon. Please feel free to ask me for a dance you made my evening. Good evening to you.", said the Lady Penelope smiling.

"Young master Richard, you made the evening of a great servant to the Crown. Many here have taken note of your kindness to this dear friend of the Royal family. And I have taken note. I will attend your winter ball and hope you will save me a dance.", said Princess Jenni earnestly.

"Thank you for your compliment, your Highness, and yes I will be honored to save a dance for Highness.", replied Richard bowing and at his father's side.

"Good evening then Sir James, master Richard.", said Princes Jenni leaving James and Richard musing about the whole affair.

"Shall we leave for the evening else you will be dancing till dawn.", joked James as they waited for their carriage to pull up.

The next morning, "Son, I will go to the Admiralty for a few hours, during this time you may go with the house keeper to purchase a gift for mother and Miss Sofia. If you are agreeable and knowing you mother's love a chocolate, from you, and for a cup of tea in fine porcelain, from me, I think your mother would love Jones fine chocolates and a Worcester porcelain tea pot with matching cups and saucers?", said James.

"I think this a good idea father and she would use it and not let this gift collect the dust. Father, I thought twice about a gift for Sofia. Tell me your opinion. She is a reader of the modern novel. One novel that seems to be popular and that she does not have is called the 'Pride and Prejudice', as well I was thinking of the Turkish delight.", said Richard looking for father's opinion.

"I think this to be an agreeable gift. I will ask your mother to send a note to Victoria to assure she is in agreement with the novel and at her consent then you may give her the novel and Turkish delight. When I am done with my meetings, I will meet you here and we will leave for Charlton and be there for supper since I will be done before noon today.

That will leave us not in a rush Saturday for supper with the Alton's where you may give your gift to Miss Sofia.", said James leaving for the Admiralty while the housekeeper busied herself organizing Richard gift shopping trip.

With the gifts secured and meetings at the admiralty completed James and Richard departed to Charlton just at mid-day.

CHAPTER 4

Victoria and Anne

"Hi dears, I was not expecting you today and so soon but am glad of it. I do not like a separation. How was your return trip. Let me get some refreshment to the sitting room where you can be comfortable and tell me of all your exploits.", said Anne as servants rushed about to bring refreshments to the sitting room for the two travelers.

"The meetings at the admiralty were successful. I received glowing reviews of Richards progress from the academy instructors. The royal court is how we left it, much in the way of splendor and grandeur, the meeting of many friends and acquaintances.

Richard had many requests to dance with a Lady. On one occasion, Princess Jenni asked Richard if he would ask Lady Penelope for a dance as a personal favor. This made lady Penelope's evening since she had no offers, and this favor very much pleased our Princess, who by the way accepted our invitation to the winter ball for herself and Prince Lionel. It Is also expected they will be staying with us here at Charlton.", reported James.

"Mother, I wanted to bring you a gift. I hope you like it.", said Richard offering his mother an adorned box wrapped in a bow.

"Richard!", said Anne opening the first gift carefully, smiled, "I just love it! I have been wanting a Worcester porcelain tea set. This is really beautiful! Thank you very much. I will put this to use very quickly.", replied Anne smiling.

Opening the smaller second box, "You know I love a chocolate. And a Jones chocolate at that! Thank you dear.", said Anne smiling at Richard and her James.

"Richard, purchased a gift for Sofia. I thought perhaps we would ask Victoria's permission.", stated James.

"Richard, what gift is this?", asked Anne.

"As you know Sofia is an avid reader of the modern novel. I purchased the novel 'Pride and Prejudice'. She mentioned it was quite popular and wanted to read it soon. As well I purchased some Turkish delight, her favorties.", replied Richard.

"I don't see a problem however, adhering to form I will send a note to Victoria directly getting her opinion and will let you know son what to do in this case.", replied Anne as James and Richard retreated to their rooms for a change of clothes and to freshen up for supper and an early night.

"Would you take this note directly to Victoria Alton at Highbury. Wait for an answer and return directly to me.", instructed Anne to one of the servants who left for Highbury directly.

"I believe this would be acceptable Anne. I know of the 'Pride and Prejudice' novel. It seems to be quite popular and depicts that aspect of society we all know well. Thank you for always being considerate of Edward and I in the affairs of Sofia and in the asking of our opinion. We all look forward to supper with you tomorrow evening.", read Anne to James of Victoria's response note.

"That sounds very positive. You are forming a friendship with Lady Victoria I see.", said James.

"Yes, it seems so, she works at a friendship with the Hawke's". "Dear, I forgot one more item, while in town I did engage an opera singer since we will have the royals about and you know they like this type of entertainment. We will need a separate room for a concert away from the dance and a room for her to stay overnight since it will be too late to send her back to town.", said James.

"This will be a very nice addition to the events of the evening. Thank you for doing this. I will inform the house keeper and have a room set aside for her to stay. I think the south sitting room would be big enough, yet cozy with the fire place to hold a gathering for a concert?", inquired Anne of James.

"Yes, that is a good plan!", replied James.

The next evening, "It is time to leave for Highbury. Is everyone ready?" asked Anne of James and Richard. "Richard did you bring your gifts for Sofia?", asked Anne of Richard.

"Yes mother, thank you for asking Lady Victoria her opinion.", responded Richard as they all boarded their barouche.

Arriving at Highbury, "Hello Lady Victoria, Edward. Thank for the invitation to supper this evening.", said James. "Your very welcome, please do come in this way to our sitting room.", directed Edward as they walked along with Anne and Victoria already engaged in conversation.

Walking along, Sofia met eyes with Richard wanted to say hi but waiting patiently to sit with him. "Hi Sofia, how have you been?", asked Richard.

"I have been very well. Would you tell me of your exploits in town, at court and anything you think interesting. I will be interested in all you have to say", replied Sofia.

"First, I have a present for you and with your mother's permission.", said Richard handing her a ribboned box.

"Why Richard, thank you, you did not have to.... But I do love a present!", replied Sofia as she reached out for the box.

Carefully untying the bowed ribbon, she opened the box, pulling the paper fold apart carefully till she could see the contents. "Richard, Turkish delight lovely my favorites. I could never find this in the local village. Thank you. How did you know I love a piece of Turkish delight?", asked Sofia looking into Richards eyes.

"Sofia, you often talk about your fondness of the candy so I thought...", replied Richard as Sofia caught sight of the novel and quickly read the title.

Looking up, Sofia eyes round like two dots, she was so excited to finally have a copy of the 'Pride and Prejudice'.

"Richard, I have been wanting to read this novel for so long. I cannot believe it is here sitting on my lap. Thank you so much for these gifts. You know me well enough to know I am an avid reader of the modern novel. This novel is so well regarded as special. I could not find it in the shops since it is always sold. I will start reading it tonight. Thank you!" said Sofia.

"Sofia, I see you finally have your much wished for novel. I will take a try at reading it, after you of course and your good opinion.", said Victoria. "I am so excited to read this one mother. Thank you. Mother, thank you for granting me permission to read this novel. It is so well regarded a story. I will be quick about it so I can give it to you.", replied Sofia.

"I have come to understand this Pride and Prejudice novel to be popular among readers. Let me know how you like it?", asked Anne of Victoria.

"Dinner is served", announced one of the servants.

Sofia and Richard sat together with Victoria to the right of Sofia. "Richard, tell me about you trip to town.", asked Sofia.

"Of course, the first day we arrived in town in good time and before noon. We arrived at the house and refreshed ourselves to then go the admiralty. Father went to his meetings while I met with two academy instructors. I was tested in navy history, navigation, maps and command. Father seemed to have forgotten to tell me of the assessment testing. But by reports I did well.", said Richard.

"Well done, Richard. I am so proud of you.", reacted Sofia, with Anne and Victoria casually monitoring the conversation between the two.

"The same evening, we prepared for the Royal Court.", said Richard interrupted by Sofia.

"Please tell me every detail of what court is like Richard.", commented Sofia.

"We arrived at the palace to many carriages arriving and departing. The palace was grand, lit with candles, the splendor magnificent. There were many great personages one reads about in the society papers just there saying hi to father and me for being the son. He knows them all.

I was asked to dance by a number of ladies since there were not enough man to go around. In one instance the Princess Jenni asked me to dance with one of her mother's ladies in waiting which I did happily and was asked to save another dance when I return to court. The Princess Jenni thanked me for saving the lady.", said Richard interrupted by Sofia. "The Princess Jenni, really. She talked to you. Asked you a favor...", so impressive Richard.

"Later in the evening, father thought we should leave so I could be some rest for the next day and our travel back to Charlton.", said Richard.

"Would you describe the palace is it really grand as described in the society papers?", asked Sofia.

"Yes, and beyond. Father says it is done so those doubting the Kings Power and Majesty will then have no doubts at witnessing this place.

There rooms are with cream-colored walls, trimmed in gold, the door are tall. Some doors all mirrored while other doors ornate with designs. The pictures on the wall are exquisite, each room has servants just to maintain the large number of candles that light the place. The food is not describe-able, the taste incredible.

I met high government officials, admirals and generals, the Prime Minister himself, the Princess Jenni, saw the King and Queen and many others. And saved many a lady by dancing with them.", said Richard. "I suppose you will marry one of these ladies.", replied Sofia slightly annoyed she was not there at Richards side. Prompting Anne and Victoria to meet with their eyes at the comment.

"No, not my type. You're more my type. Your love a horse and the out of doors are superior qualities.", replied Richard quickly and to Sofia's delight giving her a bust of confidence.

Sofia turned to her mother, "Mother, will I be attending the first few hours of the winter ball?", asked Sofia of her mother.

"Anne will Richard be attending the winter ball?", asked Sofia. "Anne, have you made a decision about Richard in this case?", asked Victoria.

"Yes, Richard did very well at court so he may attend the first three hours.", replied Anne.

"Then, yes Sofia, you may attend the first few hours of the winter ball. If Richard will be your escort. What do you say master Richard?", asked Victoria.

"This would be an honor and privilege dear lady Victoria.

"Thank you master Richard. You may attend the ball Sofia.", said Victoria.

"Thank you, mother.", replied Sofia.

"May I have the first dance with you Sofia?", asked Richard in that gentlemanly way.

"Yes, of course, Richard.", responded Sofia with the adults looking at them and thinking they are growing up so fast now.

"Richard with all this dancing with the Ladies at court will you dance with a simple country girl?", asked Sofia of Richard.

"You are no simple country girl. Yes, of course. I will engage you all your time if you will have me. I do have to tell you the Princess Jenni has engaged me for one dance the evening. Do you mind this, Sofia?", asked Richard.

"No, it is the Princess after all and she must have her way.", replied Sofia.

"Victoria, the Prince Lionel and Princess Jenni will be attending the winter ball and staying the night at Charlton. His and Her Highness are quite disarming but one should never forget their place around them. As well James has engaged an opera singer to assure His and Her Highnesses are well taken care of from a country home.", said Anne.

"Will I see you soon Richard?", asked Sofia.

"I hope we can see each other before the ball. Your mother did say I might call on you. Perhaps later next week I can come to Highbury?", asked Richard.

"That would be lovely Richard.", said Sofia.

With supper done and all subjects exhausted it was time to depart Highbury. "Anne, if you need assistance with the winter ball all you need do is ask.", said Victoria.

"Thank you, Victoria, I will ask your assistance. Expect a note.", smiled Anne leaving for the carriage with Richard at her side.

The next day, at breakfast and in the society paper "it was reported that the Admiral Sir James Hawke attended court with his young master Richard. Who was found to be dancing with many ladies there since there were more ladies than men to dance with that night. It is especially noted that the young master danced with the Lady Penelope, Lady in waiting to the Queen herself as a favor to Princess Jenni. It was stated the young master Richard was the young image of his father and mother and a gentleman at that with the saving of many ladies with a dance that evening. Sir James was in town for meetings at the Admiralty and young master Richard met with instructor from the Naval Academy.

The Hawkes, in just a few weeks, will be putting on a winter ball at their country estate of Charlton in Somerset. It is expected many high in society will attend the country event.", read Edward to Victoria and Sofia listening intently.

"Indeed, the idea of this admiral buying into society does not have much merit since Sir James is well-regarded and a member of the highest society in the land.", thought Edward Alton, Baronet.

"Edward, I have to tell you and Sofia something important and in confidence concerning special attendees to the Winter Ball at the Hawke's. Prince Lionel and Princess Jenni will be attending and staying at Charlton. Lady Anne, asked me to keep this detail confidential since it may cause a stir. Anne mentioned they are quite personable but to never forget one's place in their presence.", said Victoria.

At Charlton, "Dear you and Richard were mentioned in the society papers. It seems our Richard was quite a hero at court.", smiled Anne.

"Father, I have naval studies this morning. No time like the present, I will be in the study.", mentioned Richard.

"Richard there is note from Highbury for you.", said Anne.

"Oh, thank you mother. It's a thank you note from Sofia for the gifts. She was very surprised and appreciated the thoughtfulness. Thank you, father for assisting me in purchasing the gifts.", said Richard.

"Your welcome son," responded James.

"Dear, shall we go through all the arrangements for the ball and assure we have not missed any details.", asked Anne. "Yes, capital idea.", responded James.

The following week, "Dear I will find a reason for Richard to visit Sofia. I think a note to Victoria should do the trick.", mentioned Anne to James.

"Richard, would you deliver this note to Victoria and wait for an answer.", asked Anne of Richard.

"Of course, mother. May I visit with Sofia while I am at Highbury?", replied Richard.

"I see no impediments, as long as Victoria is agreeable. "I will ride Fire since you may have need of the Barouche.", said Richard leaving with the note.

At Highbury, "Hello Lady Victoria, how are you today?", asked Richard.

"Hi Richard, very well, thank you for asking.", replied Lady Victoria.

"Mother asked me to deliver this note to your hands.", said Richard handing Lady Victoria the note.

"Lady Victoria, may I visit with Miss Sofia while I am here?", asked Richard.

"Of course, you may. She is in the sitting room just there.", said Victoria reading the note.

Richard walked in announcing himself to Sofia and a male visitor. "Hello Richard, I did not know you were visiting today. I would have....", said Sofia surprised and interrupted by Richard.

"Mother asked me to deliver a note to your mother and since I am here, I wanted to say hi and visit with you. I did not realize you had a guest. Let me not interrupt you and wait with your mother and for your mother's return note.", said Richard taking steps to leave the sitting room.

"Will you excuse me a moment.", said Sofia as she walked out of the sitting room after Richard. "Richard, Richard," said Sofia in that dignified way. Turning Richard locked eyes with Sofia.

After a moment, "Richard, would you wait for me please. I have to tell William in that way without saying it bluntly his time with me is up.", exclaimed Sofia with Victoria within hearing.

"I shall Sofia. I will wait with your mother so I am not in the way. Come and get me when you are ready.", replied Richard.

Some minutes later Sofia returned to find Richard chatting with mother about some topic when they both turned to Sofia approaching. "Mother, have you stollen my special guest?", asked Sofia.

"No, I have not, but Richard related events about the Royal Court and the goings on not mentioned in the society papers. Sofia, why had William come to visit you?" asked Victoria.

"He asked me if I were going to the Winter Ball at Charlton and wanted the first dance. I had to let him down and mentioned Richard holds my dance card the evening. I did do so in a very gentle way and according to all the society rules mother. What do you think?", asked Sofia with Richard observing the conversation while very much appreciating Sofia's favor toward him.

"It is always best to be truthful, frank and clear in such matters. It prevents confusion and hurt feelings that may never heal.", said Victoria carefully knowing this to be a teaching moment, with Richard saying nothing so not to interfere in any way.

"Richard, thank you for coming to see me. I so much wanted to talk to you about so many topics. I so miss our rides and spending the day together. I will have to pick and choose what to tell you since you cannot be here the whole evening. I....", said Sofia walking away with Richard toward the sitting room, and Victoria shaking her head at the sight of the two so engaged in conversation.

"There is something special there between those two. I wonder if it will lead to marriage one day.", thought Victoria.

"Richard, Richard....I will leave my response to your mother's note here on the table. Do pick it up and deliver it to your mother when you finish your visit.", catching Richard before he entered the sitting room, and Richard acknowledging Victoria.

"Richard did you ride Fire here?", asked Sofia.

"Yes, he is just outside grazing I suspect.", smiled Richard.

" Yes, he is just outside grazing I suspect.", asked Sofia now walking to the front door and putting on a coat, gloves and scarf.

"Fire, fire how are you girl. I have missed you.", said Sofia brushing her hands on Fires neck and shoulders with Fire snorting at the attention and seeing Sofia.

Back in the drawing room Sofia talked about all topics, "I am almost done with the Pride and Prejudice novel. It is so good. Shall I high light it for you?, asked Sofia. "Yes please.", replied Richard. You see there are sisters and officers and suitor, the aristocracy and much in the way of opinion and designs on one another. After a bit of trouble all the girls will get all they desire.", said Sofia.

I read in the society papers of your exploits at the royal court. I do hope you will dance many dances with me at the Winter Ball, but if not, I will be satisfied to just spend time with you." exclaimed Sofia.

"I will dance many dances with you. I do have to dance with the Princess Jenni if she remembers and engages me and there may be a lady or two. Mind you I have no marriage plans with any.., so get your dancing slippers ready.", smiled Richard.

"Richard it is late afternoon and I am sure your mother will be looking for you. Here is the note to bring to her.", said Victoria handing Richard her return note.

"Sofia, it was wonderful visiting with you. Lady Victoria, thank you for letting me visit with your Sofia it was a wonderful time.", said Richard bowing and taking the note for Anne.

With Sofia looking in her mother's eyes and in that womanly way that needs no word, "Richard, would you like to visit us next week, perhaps Wednesday, if this is convenient?", asked Lady Victoria.

"That is convenient Lady Victoria, Miss Sofia", bowing and exiting the room to go outside to mount Fire for Charlton.

"Thank you, mother. It makes a visit by Richard less awkward and we know when he will visit.", said Sofia.

"Sofia, you and Richard have a special bond be sure not to have interference from the local boys since they will be at the ball and will do what they can to interrupt you and Richard. We will have to chat about ways to manage this as the games develop. I did notice William eyeing Richard.", mentioned Victoria.

"William is an odd one. He has no love in him and wants father's title, wealth and lands, that is how he sees me mother. I am simply a means to his goals. It is not hidden in the least. I have no interest in him.

With Richard, he talks to me, listens when I speak, he is patient and always considers me. He has his father's strength and courage, and his mother's patience. I never feel nervous with him. And of course, he shares Fire with me!", said Sofia with a big smile and rounded eyes and Victoria taking it all in.

"If there was no Richard and only the local boys, I would have shared my dance card but it is hard not to be selfish in the case of Richard. I will have to share him with the Princess and perhaps a lady or two but it's an obligation and nothing more, the rest of his time while at the ball belongs to me with dancing and conversation. We only have three hours you know", said Sofia.

"When he is on the floor dancing through obligation come to my side so the local boys do not try to scheme some plan to distract you from Richard. If this is acceptable.", offered Victoria. "Yes, it is very acceptable mother. Thank you.", replied Sofia.

At Charlton, "Mother, I have a return note from Lady Victoria for you.", said Richard. "Mother, thank you for finding a reason for me to be at Alton's and to see Sofia since I worried, I would miss her this week.", whispered Richard.

"I will always take care of my boy! Do I need a reason for you next week?", asked Anne smiling.

"Actually, no mother. Lady Victoria asked me to visit Wednesday afternoon. Will that be acceptable?", asked Richard. "Yes, that will do the trick.", replied Anne.

"I understand you may be dancing with the Princess, says your father.", asked Anne. "It seems so mother, but it will come to nothing since she made me the offer to save a dance and being quite busy, I doubt she will remember. I do expect a lady or two might ask me to rescue them with a dance. I have prepared Sofia for such occasions if that occurs.", mentioned Richard.

"You forgot one dance with a Lady. Would you save me a dance?", said Anne. "MOTHER! that goes without saying! Of course, and I look forward to it.", replied Richard.

"I have a dance instructor coming Monday, next week to give a lesson or two. This is because the princess may ask you to dance and she is impeccable of course and I want you to shine as well.", said Anne to an acknowledging Richard.

Monday came all so quickly and to Richard's surprise Victoria came to visit and bringing Sofia with her. "Lady Victoria, Miss Sofia please do come in and be welcomed here.", said Anne directing them to the drawing room.

"Is Richard about?", asked Sofia. "He should just be completing his navel studies for today at any moment. He will be here shortly Sofia. In the meantime, would you give me your opinion of this novel you are reading. Do you like it? What is the plot? What stands out?", asked Anne smiling.

"Well, the plot revolves around two themes....", interrupted with Richard coming out of the study and not expecting visitors. "Oh, how do you do Lady Victoria and Miss Sofia. This is a lovely surprise.", said Richard.

"Sofia, will you partner to do some dancing lessons with Richard?", asked Victoria to a puzzled Sofia.

"Richard is sharpening his dancing since the Princess might remember a dance with Richard and we wanted to put on a good show. The dance instructor is here, in the ballroom." Mentioned Victoria.

"Yes, mother. Will you have me as a dance partner Richard?", asked Sofia.

"Yes, it would be an honor and privilege.", invited Richard for Sofia to come with him to the ballroom and to some dancing lessons as Sofia for the first time took a hold of Richard's arm they walked together.

"There is something special there I think.", said Anne.

"I thought the same thing the other day Anne.", replied Victoria smiling.

"I have been spending time with Sofia teaching her how to be observant especially of the male sex. Well, William of one of the local families visited unannounced to see Sofia. His purpose was to fill up her dance card.

When I asked Sofia his reason for the visit, she mention it was about dancing at the ball but she had told him Richard had her dance card for the evening and that he was only interested in father's land, title and wealth and she was just an means!", said Victoria to Anne's eyes wide with recognition of her observance of the boy's intent.

"The frankness of the young is astonishing at times. She did mention, Richard has his father strength and courage and his mother's patience with her. Can you imagine.... I did advise her to come to my side where Richard is on the dance floor so we can reduce the change of the local boy's and mischief.", said Victoria.

"Indeed, that is a capital idea and for any reason you are not seen she can find me as well.", replied Anne.

"I will mention this to her. Thank you, Anne. It seems those two have guardian angels!", replied Victoria.

"Hello, I am Richard and this is my friend Miss Alton. We are here for a dance lesson.", said Richard.

"Very nice to meet you two. Let's begin at the beginning. As the man you lead and display the women, assure she is comfortable and protect her on the floor from those that may bump into her and assure she is admired.

To display her put you hand out like such and lead her to an open place on the floor. Look into her eye so that no one else is important but her and then move close so she can place her hands here and here and yours as follows.

Always be attentive to her before, during and after the dance.

For the first time Sofia was very close to Richard and felt slightly nervous that her hands were on his person and his on her. Richard looked into her eyes. She steadied herself so not to show her nerves but Richard's person penetrated her whole being.

The dancing instructor sensing the nerves carefully coached them so they would be relaxed.

Richard sensed Sofia's nerves as well and softened his touch, smiled and squinted his eyes at her saying, "I will not let you down".

Sofia calmed a bit more, realizing dancing with Richard would always be special, when he took her into his arms and looked into her eyes in that way that all that existed was her, her heart would skip, and she would blush for being so close.

As they danced around the floor to instruction Sofia found she moved to Richards prompts and the slight pressure of his hand there and the other hand there. Her legs would just move that way.

"You two are of the same mind. You move as if one. It is quite beautiful to see. Well done. Shall, we do one more dance since we have the time. Ok, let's begin.", said the instructor as Anne and Victoria quietly viewed the dance from the door just out of sight.

"Sofia dances so well.", said Anne.

"They both move together. Richard is so attentive to her as if she is the only one in the room. It will be something to see at the ball.", replied Victoria.

"Have you noticed, Sofia is blushing noticeably.", smiled Anne to Victoria.

"Yes, I am her mother you know. I suppose they have never been so close touching and dancing together. Remember those early days with our husbands?", commented Victoria.

"I almost forgot. Yes, I do.", replied Anne as the lesson ended and they walked onto the dance floor.

"How was your lesson?", asked Anne of Richard..

"Very enjoyable and we learned quite a lot mother.", replied Richard.

"Very enjoyable, mother. Thank you, Lady Anne, for inviting me. I will be very comfortable dancing at the ball knowing Richard is my partner. He will take care of me on the floor.", said Sofia.

"You are very Welcome, Miss Alton.", replied Anne.

"We will be off then Anne. Richard don't forget to visit us Wednesday. We look forward to your visits don't we Sofia?", said Victoria.

"Yes, Richard we are looking forward to your visit. Thank you for dancing with me.", replied Sofia smiling.

As Anne and Victoria, Sofia and Richard walked to the carriage, "Sofia, I am sorry if I made you nervous in the dance lesson. I truly did not mean too.", said Richard discreetly.

"You were very gentle with me Richard. I realize it will be very special to dance with you and it is something I claim for my sex that when dancing with someone cared about one may blush and be nervous. Have no worries I look forward to dancing with you many dances at the ball. I know now you only see me.

See you Wednesday Richard!" said Sofia as she and Victoria boarded their carriage to leave.

At Charlton, a day before the ball and at mid-day there was a commotion at the door. A marine guard announced Prince Lionel and the Princess Jenni where in the carriage and requested leave to come into Charlton house. Almost stunned at the news and coming to her senses, "Yes, of course. Be welcomed here.", said Anne signaling the house keeper the Royals are here a day early. Prepare the house now, expect supper guests as well.

"Richard, quickly go to the Alton's and ask them to come to supper with us tonight, bring Sofia. Especially tell Victoria we have very special personages at the house tonight. Supper will be at 7pm, leave now Richard and come to me when you return.", instructed Anne.

"Yes, mother", replied Richard leaving quickly as James approached with Anne waiting at his side for the royals to approach the door.

Behind the scenes the servants assured the apartment was ready with lighting candles, starting a warm fire, setting out fresh flowers and all the things to make the rooms inviting for their special guests.

"Be welcomed, your highnesses.", said James as he and Anne bowed as it customary."

"Thank you for having us here at Charlton house Sir James, Lady Anne.", replied Prince Lionel with Princess Jenni in concurrence. We hope it not inconvenient that we are a day sooner than expected but it was convenient for us to leave town and visit with you in this way.", stated Prince Lionel.

"It is convenient and we are honored and privileged to have you as guests here at Charlton house your Highnesses. Please do come into the drawing room.", invited James as Princess Jenni moved to Anne's side to chat with her.

"Lady Anne, I love what you have done with the drawing room. The décor and the spacing of places to sit and be comfortable and chat while not interfering with other conversations. This will be a grand place to sit and be comfortable for the winter ball.

Where is young master Richard? I would remind him of a dance he will have with me.", smiled Princess Jenni. "He will be here shortly and will be very excited you remembered the dance. He had a dance lesson to assure he dances well for you.", replied Anne.

"Sir, how was your travel from town?", asked James of Prince Lionel.

"Our travel was uneventful and we arrived faster than I expected. Your Charlton is just outside the band of town activities yet close enough to easily travel into town when needed. Thank you, Sir for taking us in and earlier than expected. The next day and a half will be a much-needed rest for me and my sister. As you can imagine we have a busy schedule with each day representing our father to the people.

Your Charlton seems to be a quiet sort of place just out of the way and giving us a chance to catch our breath.", commented Prince Lionel.

"You're very welcome here Sir. I will endeavor to give you the freedom of the place and without interrupting your quiet.", replied Sir James as James and Prince Lionel walked to a quiet corner to chat.

"Mother, ... Your highness, welcome to Charlton.", said Richard bowing to Princess Jenni.

"Hello Richard, wonderful to see you again. My you have grown noticeably taller since last we talked.", said Princess Jenni with Richard acknowledging the comment.

"Mother, the Alton's will be to supper this evening. They will arrive 7pm.", mentioned Richard.

"Thank you, Richard.", replied Anne.

"The Alton's are our neighbors just up the road at the Highbury estate. They are Edward Alton, Baronet, Lady Victoria and their daughter Miss Alton.", said Anne to Princess Jenni.

"It will be nice to acquaint ourselves with new people in a quiet supper.", replied Princes Jenni.

The royals bring their own servants to assure all is in order in their apartments and the royal servants found the Charlton accommodations to be excellent. "Ma'am, the apartments are in order and ready for the Prince and Princess, as it please them.".

"Excellent, we shall take time to refresh ourselves in the apartments and come down to supper.", said Prince Lionel as he and Princess Jenni excused themselves following the house keeper and a royal servant guiding them to the apartment.

After a short while and with the house settling down from the commotion the Alton's arrived. "Hello Victoria, Edward, Sofia. Thank you for coming this evening and with such short notice.", welcomed Anne with James just now walking into the drawing room.

"Hello, welcome. Thank you for suppering with us tonight", said James.

"Not at all, thank you for the invitation.", replied Edward. "May I ask who your guest is and will they be suppering with us?", asked Victoria discreetly.

"Our guests are Prince Lionel and Princess Jenni. Yes, they will be supper with us this evening and look forward to meeting the Alton's.", said Anne casually.

"How should we act with His and Her Highness then?", asked Edward for the first time unable to determine what to do in this society.

"Be relaxed. They are very personable and want to rest before the ball. However, do not forget one's place in their presence. They do talk about all subjects and will do all they can to make you feel at ease around them. Address them as His or Her Highness unless directed otherwise.", instructed James.

"We trust you and regard you as friends and so we invited you to vary the conversation and add to the success of the evening. Do not be uneasy we will guide the evening to success.", said Anne.

Richard, entered the drawing room discreetly locking eyes with Sofia, then smiling. "Good evening, Richard.", said Victoria. "Good evening, Lady Victoria, Edward, Sofia wonderful to see all of you.", as Richard moved to Sofia side.

"Richard, would you let me look at your dress so I can assure you are ready for this evening's events. "Yes.", said Richard standing before his mother and turning slowly. "You look wonderful son.", said Anne.

Just then the Princess Jenni walked into the drawing room. As everyone stood and bowed, "I would like to introduce to you Her Royal Highness the Princess Jenni.", announced Sir James.

"Your Royal Highness may I introduce the Alton's of Highbury, Edward Alton Baronet, the Lady Victoria and their lovely daughter Miss Alton.", introduced James.

"Lovely to meet all of you. I did not mean to interrupt your chat, so I will sit in one of your sitting areas. Richard, would you sit with me, and Miss Alton?" asked the Princess. "Yes, of course Your Highness as the Princess found an area just out of hearing and within sight."

"Richard, would you introduce me to Miss Alton. I sense you are partial here. Is this the case?", asked Princess Jenni.

"It is true we are great friend. May I introduce to you Miss Alton. Miss Alton Her Royal Highness the Princess Jenni.", introduced Richard.

"You Highness it is wonderful to meet you. Please forgive my nervousness since I am not used to this high personage of society.", express Sofia.

"Be at ease Miss Alton. Shall we be friends? Would you tell me about the neighborhood here around Charlton?", asked the princess.

"Yes, of course. There is an aristocracy here in this part of Somerset but not so grand as that found at the royal court.

It's a quiet place with grand estates passed down from one generation to the next. We do go to town infrequently and prefer the countryside.", described Sofia. "It is very beautiful here and something not found in the London.", commented the Princess.

We supper between the families and hold a ball or two. Richard and I go riding as much as possible when the weather is agreeable. I read quite a lot in my free time.", said Sofia.

"What are you reading at the moment Sofia?", asked the Princess. "I just finished the Pride and Prejudice novel. It was quite good. In fact, better than good. It was brilliant.", replied Sofia smiling.

"I really want to read this novel. I hear so much about it from many acquaintances. Miss Alton, might I borrow this novel for a few hours. I am a quick reader. I would consider this a favor.", asked Princess Jenni. "Of course, Your Highness. It would be an honor to lend you this book. If you would excuse me I will have the novel brought here at once.", said Sofia bowing and leaving.

"Mother, can we send a servant to Highbury and have my Pride and Prejudice novel retrieved and brought here for Her Royal Highness?", asked Sofia of Victoria. "Anne, would this be possible?", asked Victoria of Anne discreetly. "Yes, of course and directly. Sofia come with me to describe where the novel can be found.", said Anne.

"Richard, what have you been doing of late?" asked the Princess with Sofia bowing and returning to sit with them. "I have my daily naval studies. I ride with Sofia when the weather permits. Help father where he wants me. Not long ago the Lord and Lady Percy visited and they took Sofia and I to the Glastonbury for a tour of the place. That was very interesting.", explained Richard.

"Wonderful!", replied Princess Jenni. "Richard, I have not forgotten I owe you a dance. Will you save me one for the ball?", asked Princess Jenni.

"Yes, it would be an honor Your Highness.", replied Richard.

"Ah, there is my brother. I will have to leave you two. Thank you for chatting and spending time with me.", said Princess Jenni standing and walking away as Richard and Sofia stood and bowed.

"Richard you are so familiar with the Princess. I had no idea.", mentioned Sofia.

"It is true I have had a conversation with Her Royal Highness and now so have you. Thank you for letting me guide you.", said Richard.

"I am grateful Richard.", replied Sofia.

As Prince Lionel walked into the drawing room all stood and bowed. Your Highness may I introduce to you the Alton's of Highbury. This is Edward Alton Baronet, the Lady Victoria and just there is their daughter Miss Alton.", introduced James.

The highnesses and the Hawkes and Alton's made pleasant conversation, when a servant announce supper is served.

Supper was lively with much in the way of conversation and the country life. "Richard, the weather tomorrow will be agreeable I understand you ride quite well. Shall we take a tour of the estate since my daily work does not give me much time to ride this would be a treat for me.", asked Prince Lionel.

"It would be an honor Your Highness yes. I will have everything ready for you. Sir, would it be acceptable if Sofia join us since she is an avid rider and we know all the interesting places you might find unique as well.", asked Richard.

"If Edward and Victoria are in agreement and of course Miss Alton, then yes she may accompany us.

As servant discreetly entered the dining room handing Victoria Sofia's recently read novel, Victoria handed the novel to Sofia.

Standing, "Princess Jenni, may I lend you the Pride and Prejudice novel?", asked Sofia shyly. The princess noticing, did what she could to make Sofia feel at ease,

"Yes, you are very thoughtful to have retrieved it for me. I can read it tonight. Will you save me some time tomorrow after your ride with brother so we can discuss the story?", asked the Princess as Sofia handed her the novel.

"Mother, may I?", asked Sofia.

"Yes, Sofia. Of course you may.", responded Victoria.

"Yes, of course Your Highness it will be an honor and I will be at your service.", said Sofia, as all were in agreement.

With supper done and tomorrows mornings activities decided. The Prince and Princess retreated to their apartments, while the Alton's returned to Highbury.

James and Anne reviewed all the plans for the winter ball to assure all was ready. "Guest will be arriving tomorrow all day so you and I will be quite busy dear. I will try to take as much of the burden so you can pay special attention to those who will be at the house.", said James.

"We should assure the royals are not caught in the rush of the day but that they have as much quiet and rest as they want before the ball.

Richard, would you get up especially early and have two horses ready for the prince. I believe he is an early riser.", asked James.

"Indeed, father. It will be as you have asked.", replied Richard.

"I did mention to Edward to have Sofia here with her horse for an early breakfast to wait on the prince for his ride. Let us all get some rest and be up early for a very long and wonderful day.", said James, as they all went to bed while the servants readied the house for visitors and and the ball.

"Good night, God bless everyone."

In the early morning, Sofia arrived at Charlton, with Willow, her horse, she was taken to the stables to be readied for the ride this morning. "Good morning, Richard", said Sofia entering the dining room smiling.

"Good morning, Sofia, please sit here and have some breakfast. How are you and Willow this morning?", asked Richard.

"We are both very good. I am hungry and this breakfast look delicious to me.", said Sofia as prince Lionel walked in as if a normal guest, all stood and bowed. "Good morning, Your Highness.", said Richard.

"Good morning, master Richard. Good morning, Miss Alton. The weather looks great with clear skies and not so cold this morning. The morning mist lends such an air of mystery to the place. Let us have some breakfast and go for a leisurely ride. I am so looking forward to this.", said the prince.

"Richard, I understand you have a pure bread Arabian that was gifted to your father on one of his missions to the Arab countries?", asked the prince.

"Yes, I do Sir. Although, I do not get to ride her much since Sofia and Fire have a special bond.", smiled Richard and the prince looking at Sofia who responded, forgetting herself.

"Well, it is true Fire and I are great friends. And Richard gives me leave to ride her. In return I give Richard leave to ride my Willow. She is as solid English quarter horse as there was one. Oh Your Highness please forgive me for speaking out of turn.", replied Sofia as all had a laugh.

With breakfast complete, Richard, with Sofia at his side, lead the prince to the stables to collect the horses and saddle up for the morning ride.

"Dear, the prince and the children are on their respective horses touring the estates. See just there in the distance. Princess Jenni found a corner of the library to her liking and is reading the pride and prejudice novel. She is more than halfway through and I suspect will be done in an hour or so. Let us protect their privacy since they have so little of it.", said Anne to James.

"Indeed," replied James.

"Ma'am, the Lady Victoria.", announced a servant.

"Show her in", replied Anne.

"Good morning, Victoria.", said Anne.

"Good morning, Anne, James. Anne, I came to lend a hand in whatever way I can help you for the ball. Please put me to work.", said Victoria.

"Wonderful, I am about to inspect the ballroom, and the apartments. I will chat with kitchen on food and drink preparations. And will chat with the housekeeper about the readiness of Hill house and the Whitehouse. Would you join me?", asked Anne of Victoria.

"Yes, it would be a pleasure to assist you.", responded Victoria.

"Sofia is on a ride with the Prince and Richard. The Princess is in the library finishing her read of the Pride and Prejudice novel. It seems I will have to have a read at some point!", commented Anne as she and Victoria entered the ballroom.

"Anne, this room is so well decorated and so grand. In the candle light is will be glorious room filled with music and dancing and many amiable conversations. I can see it now.", said Victoria.

"Anne, you may want to move those tables and chairs away from the that corner since the main entrance to the ball room is just there and your guest will need room to come and go unhindered.", commented Victoria prompting Anne to have the tables and chairs moved.

"Thank you, for the suggestion Victoria. That was a great observation. Shall we inspect the opera rooms.", replied Anne.

After going though a few more details Anne and Victoria went to the apartments to understand their readiness for the coming guests. Speaking to the house keeper Anne received a good report about the state of the Hill house and white house pronouncing them ready.

"Ma'am, a messenger is her with a note from the King for His Royal Highness Prince Lionel.", said the servant. "Tell him the prince is on a ride on the estate and will be back in a few hours. In the meantime, assure he is feed and refreshed. See to his horse. We will notify him when the Prince returns.", directed Anne.

"Sir, the Lord and Lady Percy have arrived from town.", said the doorman as Anne and Victoria walked into the drawing room. "Show them in.", commanded James.

"Lord and Lady Percy, please be welcomed here. How was your travel from town?", asked Anne.

"Our travel was pleasant, and we are glad to have arrived at Charlton.", smiled Lord Percy.

"If you will excuse me for a few moments, I will see your trunk is conveyed to your apartment.", said Anne with Victoria at her side.

"Thank you, Lady Anne, Lady Victoria.", replied Lady Percy.

"Sir, Admirals Nester, Vincent and Jones have arrived with a host of officers.", said the servant.

"I will speak with the admirals and have a servant guide them to the Hill house to be settled in their apartment.", said James as Anne and Victoria returned.

"If you will excuse me, I will be back presently.", said James, on his way to organize the admirals.

"I understand the Prince and Princess have arrived?", asked Lady Percy. "Yes, they have arrived. Prince Lionel is on a horse-riding tour about the estate and Princess Jenni is reading in the library.

Your apartment is ready lord and Lady Percy. Would you like time to refresh yourselves?" asked Anne.

"Yes, and Thank you Lady Anne, Lady Victoria for your hospitality in settling us.", said Lord Percy.
"You are most welcome, dear Sir, dear Lady", said Anne as a servant arrived to convey the Percy's to their apartment.

Prince Lionel, Sofia and Richard strolled into the drawing room to Anne and Victoria sitting there with list of tasks for the ball reviewing them. Both stood and bowed at the Prince's presence.

Prince Lionel, Sofia and Richard seemed thick as thieves talking about something or other having had a good ride.

"I cannot believe my daughter is just there talking to the future King and as if they have known each other for a long time.", thought Victoria.

With Anne and Victoria standing and bowing, "Be relaxed here.", said Prince Lionel.

"Sir, a royal courier arrived about an hour ago with a message from the King. I will guide him here to you.", said Anne.

"Let us find him together Lady Anne. Richard, Sofia thank you for a lovely ride about the place. It was just what I needed. I will see you two at the ball.", said the prince leaving with Anne to find the messenger.

It was lunch suddenly, so Victoria, Sofia and Richard went to the dining room in search of food. There was plenty to be found, with Princess Jenni just having a light meal. "Sofia! I completed the pride and prejudice novel. We must talk about Elizabeth Bennet and the Bennet sisters! Such propriety and such scandal.", said the princess with a smile.

"Your Highness and bowing, yes, exactly!", replied Sofia with everyone else looking on at the them taking about the details and this character and that in the stories main characters.

At the end of lunch, "Thank you for lending me this novel Sofia and the wonderful conversation about the story. For these few hours I was able to forget the many pressures and just enjoy the moment.

I had a great conversation with you, just the thing to feel refreshed again. Thank you, Miss Alton. Well, I am off to my apartment. See you at ball, please do share Richard with me since I owe him a dance.", said Princess Jenni smiling as all stood and bowed.

For a moment it was silent as Anne, Victoria and even Richard looked at Sofia in wonder as she crossed all the barriers of class to have a civil conversation with the Princess Jenni. "Well done, Sofia.", commented Victoria to concurrence from Anne and Richard.

"Anne, it's about time for Sofia and I to return to Highbury and prepare ourselves to return for the ball this evening. Sofia, shall we go.", mentioned Victoria, as the princesses servant returned her novel into her hands with a thank you note from the princess.

"Yes, Mother.", replied Sofia.

"Thank you, Sofia for entertaining the Prince and Princess. Well, done. Victoria, thank you for assisting in preparation for the ball.", said Anne as she and Richard walked them to their barouche.

"Shall we come a bit early to assist you should you need this, Anne?", asked Victoria.

"That is very thoughtful, do come early.", replied Anne at Victoria and Sofia drive off to Highbury.

In the distance one could now see the carriages on the road from town heading toward Charlton. In just a while we will have a full event.

"Richard it is time we readied ourselves for the ball.", said Anne.

CHAPTER 5

The Winter Ball

Guests were arriving at the estate regularly now. Some guests were escorted to apartments in the house, while other guests were routed to the Hill house or Whitehouse.

The house was a buzz with activity as the orchestra and opera singer were in place and preparing for the evening's events. Candles were being lite, as the sun faded, fireplaces glowed, food was laid out. The whitest cloths on tables, brilliant China, and sparkling glasses all ready for hungry guests. The ballroom looked magnificent. The house was ready.

With Anne and James dressed for the ball they were positioned so they could greet each arrival to the ball. With a little time before the ball was to start and guests arriving, "Dear, in a short while our ball will start. I will do a final walk around to assure all is in order. I will be back directly.", said Anne to an acknowledging James.

Richard, dressed and ready walked down the stair case to his mother's side. "How can I help mother?", asked Richard. "Walk with me. I am doing a final inspection. So far, I have not found a single problem to solve. It all looks quite splendid.", commented Anne walking back to the entry and James.

"Ah, I thought Victoria might arrive early. She has been attentive and being of help with the ball preparations.", said Anne to James.
"Hello Victoria, Sofia, Edward welcome.", said James.

"I know we are early, we wanted to assist Anne with any last-minute tasks.", said Victoria looking at Anne.

"The is very kind and thoughtful.", replied Anne as the two women took a walk around the place.

"Richard, would you walk me around the rooms and ballroom I should like to see everything?", asked Sofia of Richard.

"I would be happy to escort you around the place," said Richard as they walked along.

"The general splendor of the place is breathtaking. I don't remember a time it was ever shown in this way.", said Sofia.

"Mother, has done a great job.", replied Richard.

"Sofia, have you eaten. Perhaps now is the best time to get a bite since you can have your choice of all that is available. Would you like a plate?", asked Richard.

"I am a bit hungry actually and if I eat something now then later, I am not famished.", replied Sofia as they walked around and filled a plate with food.

"This is a nice corner. Sofia, there are small mince pies. I know you to be partial to these. Would you like one?", asked Richard.

"Yes, please. Will you have a plate and eat with me?", replied Sofia.

"Yes, I will, as well.", replied Richard leaving to get a plate and a small pie for Sofia.

Returning with a plate to Sofia's side, "Would you tell me your latest news and happening?", asked Richard.

"Well, as you know we spent time with the Prince and Princess. What a wonderful experience to be known by them certainly. I had an interesting discussion with Princess Jenni talking over the Pride and Prejudice novel. What a treat. I had more male visitors about dances at the ball and let them down easy since my dance card is quite full, smiling. Shall, we take a tour of the ballroom and dance floor before it is filled.", commented Sofia.

"Yes, let us take a tour. Have you eaten enough?", asked Richard. "Yes, I have.", replied Sofia as they walked toward the ballroom.

With all the candles lite the room had a soft glow. The orchestra was in place and preparing to play, they made all the sounds of tuning their instruments. And just that quick they started to play dances already. "Sofia, I know this to be a surprise but since the music is playing and no one else is on the dance floor and not to waste this moment, would you honor me with the first dance?", asked Richard reaching out his hand toward Sofia.

At no hesitation, "Yes, let's dance Richard.

Less nervous and more composed at the closeness and touching Richard, Sofia moved about the floor in Richard's embrace. Anne and Victoria, walking around paused to watch the two on the dance floor. They did not notice anyone being engrossed in the dance and conversation with each other.

Some of the neighbors arrived and were introduced to the Hawke's for the first time most thinking he is trying to buy his way into the society and not realizing as yet the very well-known and powerful friends he has attending the ball. The Prince and Princess, the Prime Minister, the Lord and Lady Percy as well as others will come a bit later.
Some of the young suitors that asked Sofia to dance caught sight of her on the dance floor with Richard, thinking how beautiful

she looks tonight and planning a scheme to pry her a part from Richard. "He is a no body.", thought one or two neighborhood boys.

"Thank you, Richard. You always dance beautifully and take care of me on the floor. Perhaps, it is my turn to ask you, if this is not considered bad form and we do know each other well enough now. Shall we dance again?", asked Sofia of Richard.

"I would love to dance with you.", replied Richard taking Sofia's hand and stepping to the dance. "Tell me more of your upbringing Sofia......", asked Richard as they glide around the dance floor just starting to entice one and two more couples to dance and not noticing because they were deep in conversation.

"Hello, Mr. Prime Minister, Lady Joycelyn welcome to Charlton and the Winter ball. Thank you for coming.", said James.

"I am fond of a country ball. As you know we have so little time with busy schedules. The apartments at the Hill house are excellent. A day away from town will give us a much-needed break. Thank you for inviting us. Has the prince arrived?", replied the Prime Minister.

"Yes sir, he is here.", responded James.

"Hello, Lady Penny, Lady Grace, and Lady Enis welcome to Charlton and the Winter ball. Please be welcomed here", said Lady Anne.

"Thank you for inviting us Lady Anne. Your Charlton is magnificent. I suspect the evening will be grand.", said Lady Penny.

"Since all f you are here it will be grand indeed.", replied Anne.

"Hello, Sir Graham, Sir Williams welcome to Charlton and the Winter ball wonderful to see the two of you.", said Lady Anne.

"Thank you, Lady Anne, for the invitation.", replied Sir Graham.

Many high personages from the society in town and at Royal Court arrived. "What a splendid place this Charlton...", said many guests. Each was announced to many already knowing each other.

"Victoria, who are the Hawke's. I took it that they were one's trying to buy their way into society. To find out, it is Sir James, a knight of the realm. The Hawke's circulate in the highest society circles and are well known to the King and Queen.", said Lady Stephany, Victoria's neighbor.

"The Hawke's do not need to buy a grand house and display wealth nor buy their way in to society. They are wanted and needed in the royal society. Sir James, a hero, is often at the Royal Court and sort after by our King and Queen. This evening there will be some special guests here prepare yourselves and know they do not put on airs and graces.", replied Victoria.

Sofia and Richard walked toward refreshments with three dances done already. "Here you go Sofia. Thank you for dancing with me. You are a wonderful dancer. Shall we take a break and get back to the floor?", said Richard.

 "Victoria, I would like to introduce you the Lady Penny, Lady Grace, Lady Enis.", introduced Anne to Lady Victoria.

"How do you do ladies, it is wonderful to meet you. I assure you I am nothing to the society you are used too but I will do my best.", replied Victoria as all the women laughed and enjoyed pleasant conversation.
"Victoria lives at the Highbury the estate just next to Charlton. Her husband is Sir Edward Alton, Baronet.", stated Anne. "Very

nice to meet you Lady Alton", said Lady Penny with Lady Grace and Lady Enis concurring.

"Lady Anne, I take it the Prince and the Princess are here this evening?", inquired Lady Enis discreetly. "You are quite right Lady Enis. They are here at Charlton and will show themselves when they are ready. Not often do they come out of the palace. You and your Sir James are such a friend to the family that they stay with you without a second thought. And I have to say Charlton is magnificent this evening", stated Lady Grace.

"Thank you, Lady Grace. Thank you for coming. With all of you here the evening will be a success surely", replied Anne.

"We will take a tour of the place and chat with you later. If I am not asked to dance by an officer or two, I may ask your young master Richard. I take it he is good dancer, loves a dance and is amiable in spirit!", smiled Lady Penny with Victoria making eye contact with Anne.

"Well Anne, there you have it, Richard is a ladies' man.", expressed Victoria.

"I do hope not and he is quite devoted to Sofia you know. See, just there they are thick as thieve and talking about everything and nothing. They enjoy being together.", said Anne to a smiling Victoria.

"Anne, there are broken hearts in the neighborhood. Well not broken heart rather ego's since the neighborhood boys don't care about Sofia. See Anne just there a group of the young men. Look at them watching Sofia and Richard. Let us keep our eye's out for our children and assure no schemes are successful.", mentioned Victoria.
"Yes, we shall.", replied Anne.

To music stopping and hushed tones the announcement of the arrival of "His Royal Highness, Prince Lionel, and the Her Royal Highness Princess Jenni, and the Lord and Lady Percy."

Where upon the music started and one could feel a more amiable atmosphere with the Royals and high personages about the ball.

"Anne, I would love a dance with you sometime this evening?" asked James.

"Of course, dear", replied Anne. "It seems the ball is a success thus far. Lots of dancing, eating and amiable conversation had by all.", said James.

"Yes, it seems so James. Many here are so wary of the many responsibilities and wanted a country ball that would give them a few moments way from the many stresses. I hope this is the place for them.", replied Anne discreetly.

"Richard, Sofia how are you this evening?", asked Princess Jenni to bowing.

"We are quite well Your Highness.", replied Richard.

"Miss Sofia, my I borrow your man and take a spin on the dance floor?", asked Princess Jenni of Sofia.

"Of Course, Your Highness.", replied Sofia with Victoria nearby to occupy her while Richard dances with the Princess.

"Would you guide me to the dance floor master Richard.", ask Princess Jenni. With Richard leading Princess Jenni to the floor the floor cleared for Her Highness and did not resume until the Princess and Richard started dancing then the floor filled up quickly with many just wanting to be on the dance floor with the Princess.

Prince Lionel, seeing this walked over to Lady Victoria and Sofia and asked, "Would you honor me with a dance Miss young Miss Alton, especially since I owe you a dance the excellent horse ride this morning.

"This would be an honor Your Highness.", replied Sofia slightly shy where upon the prince expertly made her comfortable and led her to the dance floor. The dancers moved aside for Prince Lionel and Miss Alton. Princess Jenni and Richard noticed, "How lovely Sofia is this evening..." thought Richard determined to dance with her more this evening and to find more topics to chat about.

With the dance over and all the courtesies performed Richard and Sofia found each other's company. "Sofia, you were so grand dancing with the prince.", said Richard.

"So, were you with the Princess.", noted Sofia.

"I want to dance with you're a few more dances if this is acceptable.", said Richard to Sofia noticing Richard standing just a bit closer and wanting to be near her, she did not mind it.

"Here let's dance now since we will have less than an hour before we will both retire.", said Sofia leading Richard to the dance floor smiling. After a couple dances Sofia and Richard found refreshment and a quiet sitting area to resume their conversations about whatever those of that age talk about.

"Sir James, thank you for the invitation. We are the Lord and lady Principal you neighbor in the area here.", said Lord Principal. "You're very welcome, I am glad you could come. Enjoy yourselves.", mentioned James.
"Sofia, Richard it is time to retire for the evening. We hope you had a good time.", said Anne with Victoria at her side.

"Yes, mother.", replied Sofia.

"Thank you for the dances and company this evening Sofia. It was an honor for me.", said Richard in the way gentlemen do for the women of society.

"You're very welcome Richard. I enjoyed my time with you. Good night, and God bless.", said Sofia to Richard.

"Richard, would you come visit with us this next Friday, if this is acceptable with you and of course your mother.", asked Victoria.

"Yes, I believe this to be acceptable Lady Victoria. Thank you for the invitation.", replied Richard as he watched Victoria being led to a waiting carriage and a ride back to Highbury.

"Good night mother. This ball is splendid.", said Sofia.

"Richard, did you have a good time tonight.", inquired Anne.

"Yes, mother. I enjoyed the dancing and company of Sofia. I do admit I do not envy you having to stay up to dawn while I make for my bed and some hours of sleep. Goodnight mother.", replied Richard walking up the stairs to his room.

"Good night son.", replied Anne.

"It seems our neighbors, not so acquainted with us, having found the society here quite heady. I am afraid they are us to in a quiet country group of society folk husband.", said Anne as James led her to the dance floor.

"Indeed, I have noticed. I suppose the thought of buying into the aristocracy through the purchase of a grand estate is washed from their minds now!", smiled James to Anne's acknowledgement.

After the dance, "Lovely dance dear.", said Anne.

Prince Lionel was engaged in a discussion with the prime minister and other high government officials while Princess Jenni approached to chat with Anne and James. "A lovely evening this is Anne. You must have worked hard to make this so. Thank you for having us as guests here at Charlton. My brother caught his breath and so have I.", related Princess Jenni.

"You very welcome Your Royal Highness. Where you and your brother would like a quiet weekend feel comfortable that Charlton house is open to you both.", replied Anne.

"Thank you, I will keep this place in mind. It is not so far out of town and not so close. There is a quiet and a calm here, also it is on a main road making the travel smooth and without incident.", mentioned the princess.

"Anne, it seems that Richard of yours will be a lady's man and dances very well!", smiled the princess. He is ten years now?", asked the Princess.

"Yes, he is of that age.", replied Anne. "So, you have a few more years of influence. Use them well!", commented the princess.

"He is for the naval academy?", asked Princess Jenni.

"Yes, at fifteen he will be there. James is guiding him carefully. At the moment he is being tested annually.", replied Anne.

"Wonderful, he is a special one. What about Miss Alton. She seems quite special and to him.", observed princess Jenni.

"Yes, there is something special there and both families are guiding this carefully.", said Anne.

"I noticed the prima donnas (opera singer) preparing for a concert. You must know I am very partial to these concerts and I do know her to be an excellent singer.", side Princess Jenni.

Just then an announcement was made that an opera concert would begin within the hour, there is limited seating with several seats set aside for the His and Her Highness, the Hawke's and certain personages. The concert would be in the gray's rooms away from the ballroom.

"Your Highness, shall we stroll over to the gray rooms.", asked Anne as she prompted Victoria to follow.

"Lady Victoria, I take it you like a concert?", asked Princess Jenni.

"Yes, I do. However, as you know the country life does not always provide the opportunity to have such events so I only attend concerts when in town.", replied Victoria.

"When you are in town with the Hawke's you should come to court. You will be welcomed there. We usually have the opera at some point. You would enjoy it.", commented Princess Jenni.

"Thank you, Your Highness, I will keep this in mind.", replied Lady Victoria.

The concert room was arranged in such a way that His and Her Highness chairs were set ahead of the first row with a small table in between to allow them to put a refreshment down. The rest of the room was even rows of chairs with a center aisle.

"Ma'am, there are considerably more that want to be at the concert then we have room. The dance floor and rooms have emptied to try and get a chance to hear the prima donnas. With your permission, if we open the adjoining rooms and arrange seating then all that want to listen may do so.", said the housekeeper.

"That is an excellent idea. I will delay the start of the concert and walk around to assure all that want to listen can do so comfortably.", replied Anne.

"Your Highness, do you mind a slight delay as we accommodate the extra folks for the concert?", asked Anne.

"Not at all.", replied Princess Jenni as Prince Lionel approached to sit with his sister.

After ten minutes, the connecting rooms were organized and those that wanted to listen to the concert were seated and ready Anne returned to sit with her James the concert began with some of the orchestra playing music for the concert.

For an hour or so time stood still as the opera singer embraced those listening with her voice, the candle light created a golden haze lending to the atmosphere , as everyone listened intently to the siren. For a short while all that attended were sweep away.

At the end of the concert, most seemed to sense an end to the evening. Many gave a positive assessment of the ball to then leave to their apartments or houses on the estate or the neighborhood, satisfied the ball had all the society, events, dancing and amiable conversations as any great ball should. When asked many would say yes, I was at the Charlton "Winter Ball", a fine a ball as any.

With only a few guests lingering and about to leave, "Dear, it seems the ball was a success. Every event went off without problem. Even the concert and having to open adjoining rooms to accommodate so many that wanted to listen. That was a special event. I think His and Her Highnesses enjoyed that moment as well.", said James.

"Indeed, the ball flowed along better than I could have hoped. I will talk with housekeeper about how pleased we are with her and staff, and there will be a lot of work tonight with the cleanup of the place and breakfast tomorrow for our house guests. Would you talk with the doorman to assure the carriage and horses are ready for tomorrow morning when our guests wish to leave, especially His and Her Highness. As well, the marine guard should have been feed and have their horses ready to go for early morning.", asked Anne of James.

"I will direct the butler directly dear.", replied James's walking away to the task, as Anne chatted with the housekeeper.

Lord Percy, His Highness and the Prime Minister were in the study having a sherry when Anne and James walked in, "Oh, let us not interrupt you Sir.", said James with Anne at his side.

"You are not interrupting Sir James, Lady Anne, as all stood with Lady Anne entering the room.

Lord Percy and I were just saying perhaps you would consider this Winter Ball yearly. It is refreshing to have a ball outside of town. This event was splendid, much more relaxed since it is in the country side. The accommodations at Charlton are a very high standard, and travel here and to town is not a bother really. We all feel refreshed from when we arrived only a day or so ago. Thank you for having us.", said His Highness with Lord Percy and the Prime Minister, for the first time smiling in agreement.

"Your very welcome Your Highness. We will plan for a Winter ball next year this time if we are all in agreement.", replied James. "Yes, and communicate this to our secretaries as soon as possible so we can accept and look forward to this event.", instructed the Prince with James and Anne bowing and leaving the study to the three gentlemen.

"I suppose that is a sign of the success of the winter ball. I expect we will have requests to attend and have to be sure where our space and limits are dear.", commented James.

"Indeed.", replied Anne to closing the house as the last guests left and dawn was just creeping up on the horizon to the west.

Checking on the dining room, Anne observed breakfast being laid out to a now cleared and cleaned room. "When breakfast is laid out completely, would you go to the study and announce there is breakfast in the dining room with coffee, tea, eggs, ham, kippers, toast and pastries.", asked Anne of one of the servants who acknowledged her request.

"Dear, it is too early to rest. So, I will go to our apartment and put on a fresh change of cloth and come down to breakfast. Until all the guest here in the house have left to town it will be proper to be available to them.", said James.

"Good idea, I will do the same. We can rest later. I will go first to refresh myself then you will go.", replied Anne.

Early, at breakfast Anne and James just enjoyed the quiet after a very active ball. Lord Percy, the Prime Minister and His Highness came strolling as if they had a full night's sleep but they never touched a bed. James and Anne stood. "Good morning, it seems none of us have taken to the bed save perhaps my sister who is the smarter of us gathered here.", smiled His Highness.

With all the guests satisfied with the ball and on their way to town, the house settled into cleaning and organizing. "After all is inspected, give the staff as much a break as possible and needed. As well thank everyone. In a couple of weeks, we begin planning next year's ball. In a few weeks after we will have to inform secretaries so they can schedule to be at next years winter ball.", instructed and informed Anne to the housekeeper.

A few weeks later, "Dear we are receiving many notes from the winter ball attendee's saying how they enjoyed the ball and are looking forward to next year's ball invitation. The house keeper and I have set the date for next year's ball, have begun to send invitations out to secretaries so they can schedule the event. I am waiting on an answer to the question of how early I may send an invitation out for a ball. It seems most need as much time as possible to assure their schedules are open and they may accept, they 'all' want to come to next year's ball.", said Anne.

"This Charlton is proving to be a special place for many in town. With you and I as host's and assuring the comfort of all, it is a special event. A highlight for the evening was the opera and the overflow showed everyone really took in all the events and just enjoyed the moments.", replied James.

"The idea of the prima donnas was so well received. Perhaps next year we will plan for more rooms and seating so everyone that may want to attend the concert can sit in comfort and hear the music. Ah, an invitation and a note from Victoria. It seems we caused a stir in the neighborhood with many asking the Alton's to hold a supper so they might have the opportunity to be introduced to us formally. We will have to accept.", said Anne to James approving.

"Dear, we have another very important invitation, from the Palace to attend a smaller gathering of only a hundred. And a note from Princess Jenni, inviting young master Richard and Miss Alton, if this is acceptable.", read Anne.

"What date is this?", asked James. "December 20, so a Christmas event, at the palace.", replied Anne.

"Of course, we must accept. This will mean we will ask Edward and Victoria since Sofia cannot attend without her mother and father. This will be a first time at court for the Alton's. We should prepare them.", said James.

"There will be acquaintances formed from the winter ball so this won't be so much of a shock. Yes, I will send a note to Victoria today using Richard.", said Anne.

"We can plan to travel to town together and they can stay at our house in town since we have more than enough room to make this convenient for them.", said James.

"Great idea!", replied Anne.

CHAPTER 6

The Royal Court, Christmas and New Year in town

"Richard," called Anne.

"Yes, mother.", replied Richard approaching.

"I have a note here I would like you to deliver to Highbury containing an invitation to the Royal Court as our guests. Also, a replied to their invitation. Would you assure Victoria, Edward and Sofia know of its contents. I wrote this in a note to Victoria and here is the invitation as well.", asked Anne.

"I will take these to Highbury directly mother.", replied Richard.

"Thank you, son.", said Anne to Richard leaving.

At Highbury, "Hi Sofia, how have you been?", asked Richard.

"Very well, thank you for asking and you?", returned Sofia.

"Very well, thank you. What do you think of this invitation?", asked Richard.

"I think it wonderful....", replied Sofia interrupted by Victoria,

"Richard, would you ride back with us to Charlton since I have to speak with your mother. I hope she will not mind me coming unannounced at your house.", said Lady Victoria.

"I am sure it will be nothing Lady Victoria. I would love to ride to Charlton with you and Sofia. I will tack my horse to the back of the carriage and ask the driver to be mindful and not go too fast if this is acceptable Lady Victoria.", replied Richard.

"Yes, very acceptable.", replied Lady Victoria.

With that settled Lady Victoria, Sofia and Richard arrived at Charlton. "Ma'am, the Lady Victoria and Miss Alton, with Richard are here to see you.", said one of the servants.

"Pass them straight through," instructed Anne.

"Welcome, Victoria. I take it this has to do with the note I sent you this morning.", asked Anne.

"Please forgive us for coming unannounced Lady Anne. Yes, this is an astonishing piece of information.", said Victoria.

"Princess Jenni, herself, asked that you and Miss Alton should be invited and come to town. I will prepare you and Sofia for court so it is not so much of a shock. And James can chat with Edward on the ways to behave and what not to do at the Royal court. We have a house in town with plenty of room and all of you may stay with us. As well, we can travel together to and from town to make the trip more pleasant and to and from court of course. You see it will be very little bother to the Alton's.", said Anne.

"It seems so.", replied Victoria still a little stunned at the invitation and what she may encounter at the Royal court.

"This will be your first time to the palace?", asked Anne.

"Yes," replied Victoria with Sofia confirming.

"It is a bit formal, with rules like never approach, speak to or touch the King or Queen. They may approach you and speak and only then do bow and you reply. You would encounter very personable people, while others may be too full of themselves to speak with. So being observant of the types will be important so as not to be embarrassed. In the next days we will talk about all the observances from arrival at the palace and what to expect, to leaving for the evening.", commented Anne.

"Sofia, shall we catch up while taking Fire to the stables?", asked Richard.

"Mother, while you catch up, may I walk to the stables with Richard and settle Fire?", asked Sofia of her mother.

"Yes, I will be with Anne for about an hour. So be back then so we can go back to Highbury.", replied Victoria, as Sofia acknowledged her mother's request.

"Richard, you have not visited me in a week. I look forward to chatting with you, you know.", noted Sofia.

"I apologize Sofia. Father took me to Portsmouth with him unexpectedly and I only returned last night. I will endeavor to send a note to you when these things happen and give that note to mother to send to Highbury and you.", said Richard.

"I did not realize Richard.", said Sofia.

"It was impossible for you to know Sofia and I had to leave with such haste I did not have time to think about a note. Next time I will be prepared and have a note ready for you. In the meantime, let us enjoy our time since we are together. Tell me everything you have done and thought about since last we talked.", asked Richard "Well, we were invited to supper at the Principal's. Their son has most of the neighborhood ladies falling over his title and inheritance. There is no love in him for another person. He thinks only of himself, the estate and money matters. And of course, the keeping up of appearances.", said Sofia as Richard acknowledged but said nothing.

"Speaking for my sex, a marriage to a person, without a sense of love in the heart, a deep friendship must be unpleasant since there is only obligation and nothing in the way of consideration and respect.", said Sofia.

"I think so as well, and not speaking for my sex, just me in particular.", replied Richard to a smiling Sofia noticing his sense of humor.

"What did you do while in Portsmouth Richard.", asked Sofia. "I attended the academy as a visitor to the place. I toured the place, even participated in a few activities. The purpose was to familiarize myself with the place. Father was at command headquarters in meetings. We had suppers out and sometime at the naval base.", replied Richard.

"I thought your father was retired? For someone retired he has many obligations to the Navy.", commented Sofia. "This is quite normal with retired experienced naval officer's advising and giving opinion to the next generation of commanders.", replied Richard.

"Richard, I am not use to the idea of you leaving for the Navy. I know it is expected. But I am quite use to you being here and at my side. It will be difficult not see you. I have not settled on the idea of it.", said Sofia earnestly.

"I realize the hardship. When I leave to the Academy, I can write to you and you may write to me. There will be breaks at Charlton. When I am a commissioned that is the bigger worry since when I am on a voyage that can last months, I will not be able to write to you until I am in port at Portsmouth.

On the advice of my Father, until I do two tasks. I should not be engaged to you. I must grow up as a man and I must accumulate wealth. It would be unfair to you and your family to be engaged to a nobody. I am not an aristocrat; I will have to earn my place. Are you sure I am your interest Sofia? You can have anyone.", said Richard.

It took a moment for Sofia to answer. She noticed it was the first time Richard ever talked about engagements and marriage so openly. "We will have to both think carefully and plan.", thought Sofia.

"We will have to plan carefully our next short years together and what it will be like when you are in the academy and later in active service separated for months at a time. It will take strength, courage and patience to overcome these obstacles. It is true my parents will want some qualifications to bless an engagement. Would you be constant, Richard?", asked Sofia as they approached Fire's stall.

"Yes, and we have time before all of this comes to that. Who knows you may change your mind about me and marry the principal boy.", replied Richard lightening up the mood, and smiling in a way to say "Not to worry, everything will work out in the way that destiny intends."

"Fire, here you are, home girl.", said Sofia engrossed and enjoying Fire, as a stable boy gathered fresh hay, grain and water.

At the house, "The winter ball was such a success Anne. I still, weeks later, have the neighborhood talking about this or that, of an experience at the winter ball, the general splendor of the place and the people that attended were very special. I do confirm it was special. What is unusual, for me, is in my experience most neighbors forget events from one moment to the next. But the winter ball lingers.", said Victoria.

"In less than a month you will be at the Royal court and know several high personages in the Percy's, the Prince and Princess, some of the ladies and of course Sir James, Richard and myself included. What do you think about it all?", asked Anne.

"I am still getting use to the idea that the princess thought to invite us. My mind is not use to such things. In a few days I will have an opinion I am certain. Sofia and I will need your guidance so we know what to wear and how to act at court. I look forward to your instruction. If you engage the dance instructor that sharpened Richard and Sofia, would you tell me and would it be too much trouble if Edward and I attend a lesson. One can always move more gracefully on the dance floor.", asked Victoria.

"That is a wonderful idea Victoria, I will engage the dance instructor and send you the details since it will be fun for Sofia and Richard and if you and Edward come it will be even more so. Who knows I might be able to get James on the floor leaving no one left to watch.", said Anne smiling.

Sofia and Richard walked into the drawing room. "Hi Lady Anne, mother.", said Sofia. "Anne, this has been a wonderful visit. Sofia and I shall return to Highbury. Would you let me know when you can instruct us on what to wear and how to act at court and when you may engage the dance instructor so I can fence in Edward.", said Victoria smiling.

"Richard, it seems we have another dance lesson in the next week or so.", said Sofia.

"Anytime I can have a dance with you, I am at your side.", replied Sofia.

The Alton's, in the carriage speedup the grand avenue then turned in the direction of Highbury and home.

Several weeks later, "Today, we will leave for town with the Alton's. It is agreed they will stay at our house in London, the Pearce House. "Victoria, Sofia if you have any more questions about court, please do ask I will do my best to answer. Also, know we are at your side throughout the evening. I expect all will go very smoothly.

Richard will dance with Sofia?" inquired Anne.

"Yes, mother. If Sofia will add me to her dance card.", replied Richard.

"Of course, you are on my dance card Richard.", smiled Sofia seeing right through Richard's humor.

"Sofia, would you tell me about the Pride and Prejudice novel. The story, the characters its end?", asked Richard as he and Sofia chatted about the novel.

Travel to town was uneventful and quicker than expected with calm weather and good roads. Arriving at the Hawke's house Victoria stated, "This is a grand town house."

"If you're in town and are planning a few days you may stay at our house even if we are not in town.", said James to Edward with Edward acknowledging the offer and thanking James.

With everyone settled in the house, supper was announced, and all were grateful for a good meal and amiable conversation. Plans were made for the next day with the Royal Court that evening it was decided to visit the Royal Museum and the gardens, return to the house to lunch and then prepare for the evening's events.

"Victoria, James and I have a quick appointment this morning. Do you mind if we leave you the barouche for your use? We will be back for the Museum and garden tour. Give us an hour.", informed Anne.

"That would be fine, thank you Anne for telling me. Are you sure we can have the carriage?", replied Victoria. "Yes, James and I are well experienced in traveling about town. I was hoping you would not mind taking Richard with you since he mentioned he would like to be with Sofia, if we are delayed. If this is acceptable with you.", said Anne. "We would be happy to have Richard with us.", replied Victoria.

James and Anne return just before the Alton's and they all lunched together to a full report of their trip to the museum and the gardens. "I am glad you had a wonderful time. Town can be overly busy with much in the way of going here and there for no particular reason but it does have its advantages for those that visit town in the seeing of sights not so common in the countryside.", said Anne to all acknowledging.

After lunch, both families began to get ready for the evening's events. The men, always done before the women, sat in the drawing room chatting about the event and what it will be like to be at the Royal Court. "Edward, you are a true aristocrat, this should be nothing to you and Victoria. As you know, I am common really, and the fell into a number of missions in the Navy important to our King and the Royal family and as destiny has it my circumstances pushed me into a very amiable circumstance. It took time to learn to act in a very civilized manner as expected at court but I learned. If at any time you feel uncomfortable Anne and I are at your side. As well, you are acquainted with many that attended the winter ball and they will look after you and your family.", said James.

"Sir, I had my beliefs about people trying to buy their way into the class but in your case perhaps the title was not at birth but surely you are more aristocracy than many with the title at birth. It is an honor and privilege to be an acquaintance of the Hawke's.", replied Edward earnestly, with the ladies entering the drawing room and the three men standing.

"Quite a sight.", said James to Anne while Edward tipped his head to Victoria and Sofia. The dresses were new, the head dresses fancy but not over the top. The hair curled just so and a ribbon was enough to set off the gowns.

When Richard was just close enough to Sofia and where no one could hear him, he said, "Sofia, you are so very beautiful.", making Sofia smile and blush in the comment.

Composing herself, "Thank you for the compliment, Richard.", replied Sofia standing close to Richard noticing he was a bit nervous and wanting to assure him it was the same Sofia with just a bit of polish this evening.

"I am looking forward to several dances sir.", said Sofia.

"You may have as many as you wish dear Sofia.", replied Richard as he extended his arm for Sofia to hold while they all walked out to the waiting carriage that will take them to the palace.

Arriving at the palace the scene and activity was as Anne described to Victoria. The palace was very imposing, the grandeur, the staff, the pictures and tapestries on the wall, candle light, food, the high society people one reads about never to meet where now just there to touch and see, some even smiled in greeting when they looked in the direction.

"Victoria, Sofia would you stay close to me and James at least for the beginning of the event. I am sure the sights are overwhelming. There are those you have acquaintance with from the winter ball who will want to meet you here at court and will, as well, assure your comfort since this is a first visit. Will this be acceptable?", asked Anne. "Yes, very acceptable and thank you Anne, James.

"The Admiral Sir James Hawke, his wife the Lady Anne and son the master Richard Hawke. Sir Edward Alton, Baronet his wife

Lady Victoria and their daughter Miss Alton.", announced the doorman.

Entering court, its main room was quite large with many personages walking about, chatting and visiting one person or another. The first persons they encountered were the Percy's. "Lord and Lady Percy, wonderful to see you.", said James.

"Sir James, Lady Anne, master Richard; and Sir Edward, Lady Victoria and Miss Alton. I take it this is your first time at court. If you're without the Hawke's and feeling uncomfortable come to our side and we will guide you. Have no worries.", said the Percy's earnestly.

"Thank you, Lord and Lady Percy this is very kind of you," replied Edward.

"Sofia, would it be too early to ask you for a dance since this will relieve any nervousness, we have for being here. What do you say?", asked Richard. "Mother, may I take a turn with Richard?", asked Sofia. "You may, come find us afterward.", replied Victoria with Anne agreeing as well.

Sofia and Richard found the dance floor and waited for the next dance to start to enter the floor. Richard noticed lady Penelope just there. "Sofia, after a dance or two with you may I ask the Lady Penelope, just there, for a dance she does not get many offers.", asked Richard of Sofia. "Yes, that would be acceptable and only if you introduce me.", replied Sofia smiling.

After two enjoyable dances, Richard approached the Lady Penelope and introduced Sofia. "How do you do Miss Alton, welcome to the Royal Court. I understand the Princess Jenni invited you. She does not invite many to court. You must be very special.", said the Lady Penelope.

"Dear Lady Penelope, may I have this next dance with you if this is convenient?", asked Richard.

"Yes, you may and this is very convenient.", replied lady Penelope. At end of the dance Richard walked the lady Penelope back to her seat to find the Queen approaching as all stood aside and bowed as did Sofia, Richard and the Lady Penelope.

"Lady Penelope, I worried that you would not get the opportunity to dance and was organizing some men for you to find you with this young master on the dance floor. What is this?", mentioned the Queen.

"Your Majesty, this is the young master Richard Hawke and his lady friend Miss Alton.", replied Lady Penelope. "Young master Hawke, are you by any chance a relation to the Admiral Sir James Hawke a dear friend of ours?", asked the Queen and seeing a little nervousness in the young master.

"Be at ease young master Hawke.", commented the Queen.

Richard gathering himself, "Yes, your Majesty the Admiral Sir James Hawke is my father and my mother the Lady Anne.", replied Richard.

"Miss Alton, I do not recognize you.", said the queen.

"Your Majesty, Jenni invited the Alton's to court having met Sofia at the Charlton winter ball in Somerset. Her father is Sir Edward Alton, baronet. He and his wife the Lady Victoria are society but not so much at court living in the countryside and are neighbors to the Hawke's", reported the lady, Penelope.

"Ah, I see, welcome to court Miss Alton. I see you have the most excellent escort in the young master Hawke. Richard, you have done me a service in dancing with our Lady Penelope. I will not forget your chivalry in this case.", said the Queen as the Princess Jenni walked over wondering who her mother was talking to.

"Hello, young master Hawke, Miss Alton. How are you this evening.", asked Princess Jenni.

"Very well Your Highness", replied Richard with Sofia close at his side.

"Mother, Richard and Sofia took our brother out for a horse ride one morning while we stayed at the Hawke's house. He so enjoyed it and was refreshed because of it. I invited the Alton's to court and since they are aristocracy anyway and do not come to court.", said Jenni to her mother.

"That was a wonderful idea. I will meet these Alton's then and pay my respects.", asked the Queen. "Yes, mother. They are there just with the Hawke's and Lord and Lady Percy.", said the Queen as she moved in that direction.

"Sofia, shall we dance one more?", asked Richard. "Yes, before the evening gets busy. If you will excuse us, Lady Penelope.", said Richard. "

Of course, enjoy yourselves.", replied Lady Penelope.

"That was a wonderful dance, Sofia. Thank you for dancing with me.", said Richard with Sofia holding his arm as they went in search of their parents.

"I can hardly believe we are at the royal court, I met and chatted with the Queen, Princess Jenni, met the Lady Penelope. You danced with her. I have so much to write about in my diary of today's events.", said Sofia as they spotted their parents chatting.

They were interrupted by Prince Lionel, "Hello young master Hawke and Miss Alton. I do hope the Royal Court is to your liking. Is there anything I can do for you?", asked Prince Lionel wanting Richard and Sofia comfortable.

Bowing, "Your Royal Highness, wonderful to see you again. We are enjoying ourselves. Thank you for having us.", replied Richard. "Capital, if you are in need of anything don't hesitate to ask.", said Prince Lionel walking away with a group of folks.

"I read the society papers of these events, to now be here and experiencing it myself.", said Sofia to Richard. "Did you two enjoy a dance?", asked Victoria.

"Yes, mother. We had a few dances. Richard danced with Lady Penelope as well, we were introduced and chatted with Her Majesty the Queen, chatted with Prince Lionel and Princess Jenni. Such an evening.", replied Sofia in disbelief.

"All we have left is to chat with the King himself. Just then, "Is that the Admiral Sir James Hawke! Old friend will you chat with me?", asked the King. As all turned and bowed to their King.

"Your Majesty, I will always chat with you. I am at your service", replied Sir James.

"Then how is your Lady Anne and the young master Richard who is gaining a reputation for his chivalry my wife the Queen tells me?", asked the King.

"They are all in good health and as you can see here and enjoying your great hospitality Your Majesty.", replied James.

"And who are these Lades and Gentlemen?", asked the King.

"Your Majesty may I introduce to too you Sir Edward Alton, Baronet, the Lady Victoria Alton and their daughter Miss Alton.

"Wonderful to meet all of you. I do hope you are enjoying court?", asked the King.

"Yes, your majesty we are very much enjoying court.", replied Edward unsure.

The King sensing this quickly said, "Be at ease we are relaxed here at court.", easing the shock of being introduced to and chatting with the King. "I am off, there are a number of people wanting a chat before the evening is done on some matter of importance to themselves.", said the King as all bowed at his leaving.

"Sofia, you will have to add conversations with Prince Lionel and being introduced and chatting with the King to your lines in the diary.", said Richard to Sofia smiling at his humor! "

Well, said Richard, well said!", replied Sofia.

The rest of the evening was a blur and just that quickly they were outside boarding their carriage to return to their house. "I declare this to be a successful evening.", said James to all agreeing!

At the Hawke's house, "Since Christmas is just a few days away does it makes sense to celebrate here in town and perhaps New Years as well?", asked James of the Alton's. "We never thought of this but it would be a pleasant change to the routine and the seeing how these holidays are celebrated in town and enjoy your company would be acceptable. Victoria, Sofia what is your opinion on the subject.", asked Edward.

"I would love to spend Christmas and New Years in town with the Hawke's. If you will have us?", replied Victoria with Sofia's concurrence.

"Anne, Sofia and I can organize Christmas decorations for the house. And in the following day we can go out to the shops for a present or two?", stated Victoria.

"That is a wonderful idea. Let us do this!", said Anne.

"Edward, Richard and I can find the greenery and presents as well for our women folk.", said James.

Christmas and new year passed so very quickly. "We had such a grand time with the Alton's.

With everyone back in Somerset, "Victoria, the society papers mentioned us being at court through an invite by Her Highness the Princess Jenni, escorted by the Hawke's. They even mention Richard and Sofia dancing and being introduced to the Queen.", said Edward to Victoria. "It was such a special time really and as well to spend Christmas and New Year in town.", replied Victoria. "We can expect our neighbors to ask questions.", said Edward.

CHAPTER 7
Spring

The last few years have flown by, and in the May of the season the warm spring winds came hinting of the end of winter.

At Highbury, "Richard will enter the Academy in the autumn with Sofia entering finishing school in late September as well, leaving the spring and summer months open for the two.", said Victoria to her Edward.

At Charlton, "Mother, I am riding Fire to Highbury to lunch with Sofia and family. I will spend time with her today since everyday now is close to when we part for a while.", said Richard.

"Give the Alton's our regards.", replied Anne.

At arriving at Highbury one of the grooms took Fire so that Richard was free to enter the house.

"Please come in master Richard. You may wait in the drawing room. Make yourself comfortable. Is there anything I might get you master Hawke?", asked the servant.

"Nothing, thank you. I will sit here and wait for Miss Sofia.", replied Richard.

After a few minutes, Percival, a neighborhood boy, arrived in the drawing room.

"Hello Percival.", said Richard remaining seated and not bothered.

"Hello Richard, what are you doing here?"

"I am having lunch with Sofia, and your purpose here Sir.", replied Richard.

"I am here to see Sofia and her father. You may not be familiar with the aristocracy and the rules of society so I will educate you. I am here to secure an engagement with Miss Alton.

I am the son of an Earl and a Countess and take precedence over ones like you. You must give way. You have no right to be in the house of a Baronet and Baroness, speaking to their daughter and socializing with her as if equals.

You are a no body, with no title, no connections, no expectations I say. Leaving you one course of action and that is to go and not return.", said Percival to Richard in such a way as to present himself superior in every respect.

Hearing this conversation, and just outside of the drawing room, were Sofia, and her mother and father, they were horrified and embarrassed at Percival's words to Richard and in their own drawing room. They devised a plan for Sofia to enter the drawing room and ask Richard to visit with mother and father in the library while she handled Percival herself.

"I am the son of aristocracy and so is Miss Alton, a union between the titled is expected.", said Percival.

"Do you not think there should be considerations for love, friendship and respect in these cases?", asked Richard.

"Of course not, that is where we differ Sir, the aristocracy marry for position, wealth and power. What else is there. Shortly, Miss

Alton and I will be in an engagement and I expect you never to speak to the girl again Sir.", said Percival.

Hearing the last comments and remaining poised, Sofia entered the drawing room. Looking directly into Richard's eyes with all the compassion she had in her and in the gentlest of tones saved only for him, "Richard, how are you today?", asked Sofia.

"I am very well and you?", replied Richard.

"I am very well. Mother and father are in the library and would like to see you. Would you..., I will come to you later.", asked Sofia.

"Yes, of course.", commented Richard as he bowed on his way out of the drawing room.

"Should that boy be allowed to roam this house so freely. Perhaps the servant's entrance for him. When I am master here, he will never be able to enter this place.", said Percival presumptuously.

Maintaining her composure and not showing her true feelings at the comments, "Percival, how are you. I was not expecting you. What is the purpose of your visit?", asked Sofia.

Richard, knocked on the library door and at leave entered the library. "Richard, thank you for visiting Highbury. I so look forward to you coming. We have such a high regard for you and your dear family.", said Victoria hurt by what Percival implied Richard could see.

"Richard, for a long time I thought like Percival, thinking of superiority over others and not realizing until I met the Hawke's the privilege of a title and its wealth should be used to uplift those around one and not for tearing down.
We are sorry for the comments Percival made this morning. Our opinion is far different than his. Victoria and I have such

a respect for you and your family. Please know this. Please disregard Percival and his manner.", said Edward earnestly.

"Sir Edward, Lady Victoria, thank you for your regard. I have known this for a long time in the way you treat me and granting me many favors and considerations. My father has prepared me well for these encounters both here, at court and even at the academy between other cadets and officers.

My regard for you and Sofia is the same. I have a great affection and regard for each of you.", replied Richard looking at Edward and then Victoria with sincerity.

In the drawing room, Percival announced, "I came here today to secure your agreement to an engagement with me. This is a very advantageous union with me coming from aristocracy and great family titles and the Alton's with family titles of Baronet and Baroness. Shall, I ask your father's blessing then?", asked Percival, sure of himself.

Remaining calm and almost enjoying the moment, "Isn't this premature Sir? There is love, friendship and respect to consider here for me and my mother and father.", replied Sofia in a very aristocratic tone suddenly and repeating Richards points purposefully.

"Aristocracy marry for position, wealth and power, and not the fickleness of love may I remind you.", stated Percival tiring of the discussion.

"Sir, I understand the seriousness of your proposal and will give you my answer now. I am grateful for the offer to an engagement with you but respectfully decline this offer.", replied Sofia in a very calm and clear tone.

Annoyed now, "Would you reconsider. Do you need time? Perhaps, I overwhelmed you with such an advantageous union without time to consider.", asked Percival.

"Sir, I do not need time to consider your offer further. I do decline a union between the two of us. If I had known this was on your mind I would have hinted this would not be possible.", replied Sofia.

After a stunned pause, "Is there anything else Percival?", asked Sofia.

"I do not believe so, I will see myself out. Good day Miss Alton.", said Percival bowing on the way out.

As Percival rode away, he thought, "So ungrateful not to take advantage of this advantageous union. What is this girl about? There are many ladies in the neighborhood who would be glad of my offer."

Sofia, entering the library, "Richard, I am so embarrassed at the comments Percival made to you. This is not the opinion of mother and father nor of myself, truly. You know I have the highest regard for you and have hopes for a future.

Perhaps today, we will not be engaged. The proper way is to make me an offer after your graduation from the Naval academy, then apply to my father for his blessing. I look forward to that day. In the meantime, I will be constant, as I know you will.

I am certain there will be more suitors and I will let them down.", said Sofia to Richard with her mother and father looking on amazed at the daughter they raised.

"I know this in my heart of hearts Sofia. I promise to work hard to earn my place so when I apply to you and your father, he and your mother will know you are in the best of hands, and they are not losing a daughter but gaining a son who cares about them as well.", replied Richard.

"We have this spring, summer and some weeks of the fall months before we part from each other for a period of time. So let us forget this Percival and enjoy the warm month together.", proposed Sofia with all agreeing.

A knock at the door, "Lunch is served", said a servant, as they all had lunch together to amiable conversation and talked of the summer events to come.

"Richard, shall we ride tomorrow. I don't want to lose even a day if at all possible.", said Sofia.

"Yes, if your mother and father are in agreement.", asked Richard being very respectfully.

"We agree.", replied Victoria.

"I will see you tomorrow bright and early with Fire warmed up and ready for you!", smiled Richard bowing to take his leave.

"Richard, would you deliver this note to your mother.", asked Victoria. "Of course, Lady Victoria, my pleasure.", replied Richard.

At Charlton, and Richard having delivered Victoria's note into Anne's hands, Anne read the note and advised James of the Percival event. "That in spite of the insults Richard conducted himself with great self-control. And the Alton's expressed their high regard for Richard, while Percival left empty handed.", wrote Victoria.

The next morning Richard rode to Highbury for a planned ride with Sofia, "Hello, Sofia. Fire is ready and looking for you.

Fire, is just there, grazing and seeing Sofia raised his head and nickered for her.

It's as if she knows.", smiled Richard.

"I was thinking we could settle at the commons. I have a packed lunch.", said Sofia. "Wonderful, let's go! Willow, lead the way!", said Richard.

Together, riding along a familiar path, "Richard, let's be together every day we can.", said Sofia.

"Of course, Sofia. That is my intention.", replied Richard.

At the commons pasture, and leaning against one of her favorite tree's, the horses grazed nearby to the sound of flowing water from the nearby stream, "This warm and sunny day seem like a dream. The wildflowers are in bloom, many of them in every corner radiating all the colors of the rainbow. My horses are near and my Richard just there. I wish this could last.", thought Sofia spreading out a cloth on the soft grass for lunch when ready.

"Richard, I will need your letters since I will miss you. It is hard for a woman, she is bound I'm afraid to be waiting for any word from the man she loves.", said Sofia.

"Indeed, while at the academy, I will write to you weekly. There will be regular breaks and I will come to Charlton. I have these dates written down, here in this list.", said Richard handing a list to Sofia surprised.

"Some dates are holidays and some are Navy days. When you're at school and these days match yours, come home when you're able and let me spend time with you.", asked Richard to an acknowledging Sofia reading the dates carefully.

"I have yet to get confirmation of my total time at the academy to graduation. Father mentioned, to me, because my testing scores were so high, I may be granted the maximum two years credit of the four-year academy course.", said Richard.

"When, however I am commissioned and, at sea letters will be few. I will write but have no place to send them. When back in port I will mail all of them. So, you will suddenly see a large number of notes come through in the post after a period of quiet.

My time at sea will be the most difficult of times. This period will last thirty and six months. This is when I must make rank, wealth and a name. It is not thirty-six months continuous but three to nine months at a time and when in port I will have some time off where I will travel here to you.", said Richard as gently as possible.

"We will do our best, I promise to be constant. When I can take leave, I will come home and if you're at Highbury spend as much time with you as I can.", said Richard.

"Thank you, Richard. I will depend on all of that.", said Sofia.

"I am about to say something prematurely, and ask your patience.", said Richard.

"Of course, ask Richard.", responded Sofia curious and taking his hand.

"May I marry you one day. You don't have to answer now. I just wanted to say it. I do care for you, for your mother and father. I, as well, realize I have work to do at the academy, and as a commissioned officer so when I return, I will be as eligible as any. Wait for me, I will be the best of husbands for you.", said Richard his heart pounding.

"There will be a suitor or two while I am away, I am sure of it. If by chance you decide to alter the plan just write me and I will understand and not be so hurt.", said Richard looking deeply into Sofia's slat green eyes.

"Richard, if I have not made this clear let me do so now. It is my intention to marry you. We will weather the separations and when you have made yourself completely eligible and father blesses your offer. I see our children, a boy and a girl, and such happiness. Focus on your work, write to me often, come here when you can and see me, and in the end, you will win your heart's desire.", replied Sofia holding Richard's hand tightly now and looking deeply into his eyes.

"Sofia, would you describe finishing school and what you will learn?", asked Richard listening intently.

"Well, the school will prepare me for my future role as wife and hostess, the finer arts of navigating in society. We will learn the arts of dinning, dress, holding balls and gatherings, addressing and conversing, dance, the arts and music and what a lady should and should not do, how to run a household and more.

I will not speak of my time in town and at the Royal Court unless it is wanted and respected since all of this etiquette and manner was on display there.", said Sofia.

"I have noticed your father's health is not the best. How is he really.", asked Richard sensitively.

"Father has had visits from the physicians and chemist they all agree to the illness but as yet to understand it and treat it properly. Mother and I are worried. He is not getting better.", said Sofia.

"God forbid the worst happening to your father, I understand the inheritor of the title and estate, your cousin, does not care much for you and your mother. Sofia, don't hide this from me so we can protect you and your mother if this relation puts you out of Highbury. I will do all in my power to help, you know that.", said Richard. "

Thank you, Richard. This is a great comfort ", said Sofia.

"Are you sure you would want me then.", said Sofia.

"Sofia! to say such a thing. I will not fail you or your mother. If the worst befalls your family while I am away, you must let me know. If your cousin puts you out of Highbury, we will not let you fall away. You and your mother will stay with us at Charlton. We are your friends never forget this, and I love you, Sofia. Not the status, not the title and not the power. Just you.", said Richard.

And be sure to stable Willow at our place as well so she cannot be taken away from you.", said Richard with Sofia looking intently into his eyes.

Riding back to Highbury house, "Such a gorgeous day today. Will I see you tomorrow, Richard?", asked Sofia.

"Yes, I was wondering if a walk through the gardens? And spend the afternoon with you.", inquired Richard.

"Yes, that would be a lovely change of pace. Bye Richard. See you tomorrow.", said Sofia.

At Charlton, "Mother, may I speak to you and father?", asked Richard. "Edward Alton's health is failing of late. If the worst should happen and the cousin comes to claim the estate and title and puts Victoria and Sofia out of Highbury, we must take them in. There is no simple way of saying it.", said Richard concerned.

"Your father and I have been aware of the concern for some time. If the worst happens and the cousin puts Victoria and Sofia out of Highbury, we will offer the White house for their use. Proud as they are I will convince Victoria our friendship and concern is more important than pride. It will be no bother to us and we will be glad they are in the neighborhood and safe.", said Anne.

"Thank you, this puts me at ease should events warrant. I also asked Sofia to stable Willow here at Charlton. I hope this to be acceptable?", asked Richard. "Yes, very acceptable. Then this is settled, do not be concerned. We will not let our friends fall.", said Anne.

The next day, Richard arrived at Highbury for his tour of the gardens with Sofia, however before Sofia was downstairs, "Lady Victoria, may I speak with you?", asked Richard. "Of course, you may, come sit with me.", replied Victoria.

"The topic I would discuss may not be my place and so I beg your leave since in this case I am worried.

Lady Victoria, I worry for your Edward's health. If the worst should happen and the cousin put you and Sofia out of Highbury my mother and Father have made provision for you and Sofia to stay at our place. We think the White house would not be a bother and is a very nice house. I realize I am speaking out of turn and of events that God willing will not come about. I beg your forgiveness for saying this.", said Richard concerned.

"And of course, we would want Willow taken to our stables so she is secured for Sofia.", said Richard.

"Richard, thank you for this caring for me and Sofia. I see you and your mother and father have spent much thought on our welfare. For making provisions if the worst were to happen. I and Sofia would be grateful to know we have dear friends that would not let us fall far if the worst were to happen.

I have been worried as a wife and mother. My hope is in Edward's recovery and that is my focus these days. To know the Hawke's are just there is a great comfort.", replied Victoria as Sofia strolled in the drawing room.

"I will be away at the navy soon but my mother and father will be close by.", said Richard standing bowing and leaving with Sofia for their tour. "Thank you.", said Victoria thinking, "What a young man already."

"What is this conversation with my mother.", asked Sofia. "I discussed a difficult topic of your Father and if the cousin put you and your mother out of Highbury. We have the White house ready and standing by for your use as long as you want to stay and that Willow be stabled in our place. I realize this is premature and our hopes are for Edward's full recovery but it must be discussed.", said Richard.

"It is the right time. You are not in the wrong. I am so grateful to know we are taken care of, so now we can concentrate on father and regaining his heath. Thank you very much for caring about me and mother Richard.", said Sofia.

"I may be away at the navy and will worry about you terribly should events warrant. You will write to me to tell me you are settled at Charlton. If it comes to that.", asked Richard. "I will Richard. I know I and mother are grateful and appreciative of this care from you and your family.

In the meantime, father is here and we are focused on his health and know the Charlton White house is there for us should we need this.", said Sofia.

"Let's tour the gardens now and speak of this glorious day!", said Sofia taking Richard's arm.

"I will miss this quiet and countryside with you Sofia. I will live for the day I may return and never leave you. For now, I live for each day and will enjoy the moments with you. Shall we have a late lunch?", asked Sofia. "Yes", replied Richard.

"I have a gift for your Sofia.", said Richard handing Sofia a small wrapped package. "Why Richard, what could it be?", replied Sofia carefully opening it. "It is an ivory portrait of you Richard. I will keep it with me always. Thank you, Richard. It's lovely.", said Sofia kissing Richard on the cheek.

"Richard, I have no etching for me. I will ask mother if we can have an image of me made for you to keep with you. It will be such a comfort to know you have me near and I have you near.", said Sofia.

"That sounds wonderful Sofia. I look forward to an etching of you.", replied Richard.

"Sofia, later this week we are to go to Portsmouth. I asked mother if she would talk with your mother, that you would be our guest. Even, perhaps if Victoria would like to come as well. We can tour the Naval Academy, the Navy yards and ships and just see all I will be involved with when I am attending the school.

I realize this is very short notice with only some days to decide but I hope you are willing and on agreement of your mother and father. Of course, you will be under our protection. What do you think?", asked Richard.

"Well, this is quite a surprise and very short notice. I would love to be your guest and put an image in my mind to all the places you will be so I know better what you do at the academy.

Since we are heading back to Highbury would you come in and chat with mother and father and introduce the idea?", mentioned Sofia.

"Yes, I will do this.", replied Richard.

At Highbury, in the late afternoon, Sofia and Richard entered the drawing room to find Anne and Victoria chatting away over a cup of tea. "Lady Anne, wonderful to see you.", said Sofia smiling.

"How are you, Sofia. How was your outing today?", asked Anne.

"It was wonderful. Richard surprised me with the possibility of mother and I being your guests on a Portsmouth trip later this week. That I may tour the Naval Academy, the yards and Naval Ships so I know what my Richard is doing in this place. It seems exciting. I hope for my mother's opinion on this topic.", said Sofia.

"Anne and I have talked this over and I think this a grand idea. We would travel with the Hawke's. Your father wants us to go and get a break from him and his illness. So, I see no impediments. Time is short and we have to plan and pack very soon.

Anne mentioned we will have the use of an Admirals home who is in town during our stay. So, you see it is all arranged and we just have to show up with bags in hand!", said Victoria.

"Richard, yes! I am so excited to see this academy and the Navy. It will be my first time to Portsmouth. In the cold winter months when all we have are letters, I will be able to imagine the place you study and write to me from instead of a blank image.", said Sofia to Richard.

"Lady Anne, thank you so much for thinking of me and my mother in this case. I am so grateful to have the opportunity to know this place. It is all so exciting.", said Sofia to Anne acknowledging her comments.

"You're very welcome Sofia", returned Anne.

At Charlton, "Dear, the Lady Victoria and Miss Sofia will accompany us to Portsmouth. We will leave time to tour the Academy and visit the yards and see a Naval ship or two. I have taken the lead in planning a night at the concerts, another night in the house and supper, and a day touring the naval museum. Is this too much?", asked Anne of her men.

"I like your plan dear. While I am in meetings you will not be bored and sitting around yet have some time to rest and sit as well.", replied James.

"I like your plan as well mother. We can visit the navy while visiting other sites with time to relax as well. Thank you, father, mother for inviting Victoria and Sofia. It is such a good idea that they see where I will be at school, the navy and Portsmouth. As Sofia says, this is all so very exciting.", mentioned Richard.

"We have two days to pack and prepare.", reminded Anne as they finished supper. And, the days flew by quickly to the morning they leave for Portsmouth.

At Charlton, "Dear, the carriage is packed with all our bags, the kitchen packed a lunch for the trip. Victoria and Sofia are just now arriving, the servants will load their bags, and when the ladies are ready, we are off to Portsmouth. Twenty minutes I should say.", said Anne.

"Thank you, dear. I will find Richard and assure we are both ready when the ladies are ready.", replied James.

"Richard, Victoria and Sofia are arriving, their bags will be stowed and when the ladies are ready, we are off to Portsmouth. We think twenty minutes or so.", said James.

"I am ready father. I will wait by the carriage and assure their bags are stowed, so no worrying about me.", replied Richard walking to the carriages.

On their way to Portsmouth, "Is it just my observation or are you and Sofia chatter boxes. What do the young people talk about with such animation these days.", asked Anne curious, arousing the curiosity of those in the carriage.

"We talk about the horses, the state of the estate grounds, our future, my dad and his health, all of you here, the places we have been. You know, all of the important topics one talks about.

Just now we talked about Portsmouth, the academy and what we will see there, ships and the yards. Nothing terribly important but to us I suppose.", replied Sofia musing at the adults in the carriage.

Having entered the port city of Portsmouth, one could see and feel the hustle and bustle as the carriage navigated the active streets to then stop at the Admirals house where the housekeeper came out with a number of servants, expecting visitors. "Hello, Admiral Hawke, Lady Anne and master Richard, and not so much young anymore I'm afraid.", said the housekeeper knowing the Hawke's quite well.

"Hello, Heather.", replied Anne.

"May I introduce the Lady Victoria and her daughter Miss Alton.", said Anne.

"How do you do Lady Victoria and Miss Alton, wonderful to meet you. Welcome to Stately house. Would all of you follow me so I can get you in the house and to refreshments. The servants will bring your bags in have no worries about this.", said Heather leading the way.

After refreshments and a light and late lunch everyone retreated to the drawing room.

"Portsmouth is so very busy. I could not imagine such a place.", said Sofia.

"Indeed, this is true compared to our little piece of country side. And it is more so busy during wartime and where the navy is engaged.", replied James, to Anne and Richard acknowledging since they had years and several wars they experienced while living in Portsmouth.

"Ma'am, this note was waiting your arrival.", said one of the servants to Anne.

"Tomorrow, will be an active day with a tour of the Academy, the Yards and a Naval vessel. It seems our Admiral James still knows one or two officers here in town.", smiled Anne.

"Then we are off to a concert in the evening. We would have had supper here first. If this is agreeable with everyone.", noted Anne.

"James, during the day your time will be taken up with meetings at the admiralty, however the evenings are ours to organize for you Sir.", said Anne.

"I look forward to you pointing the way dear.", replied James.

"Son, a cadet will be assigned to take all of you around the academy, the yards and one of the Frigates for a tour. You will remember him in your growing up here at Portsmouth. Do you remember Spencer Dobbs?", asked James.

"As a matter of fact, I do father. A good chap.", replied Richard.

"He will arrive at the house around nine in the morning if that is acceptable to all of you. He thinks when done you will be able to have a late lunch in the academy eating house.", said James.

"The eating house will be an experience in itself.", said Anne smiling.

"Thank you for taking a hand in the tour tomorrow, James. I know we all appreciate it.", said Victoria.

"You're very welcome, it's the least I can do since I am in meetings during the day.

The next morning, "Good morning cadet Dobbs. Thank you for taking us on a tour around the academy, the yards and a frigate.", said Richard.

"You're welcome Richard. It has been a while since I have seen you. I understand you will come into the academy as a third-year cadet. Your scores must have been very high to achieve that consideration. We will graduate in the same class. Congratulation.", said cadet Spencer.

"Thank you for the compliment, but I have no formal notification as yet about the two years. I will know before the trip is done. It does look promising. May I introduce our guests. You know my mother the Lady Anne, however this is the Lady Victoria Alton and her daughter Miss Alton.", said Richard.

"It is an honor to meet you ladies and a privilege to take you on today's tour. Shall, we board the carriage. This is an open carriage so I can point out a number sights along the way. We will start at the Naval academy this morning.", said cadet Spencer.

"Richard this Miss Alton is connected to you?", asked cadet Spencer.

"Yes, I hope to be her promised after graduation.", said Richard.

"I see why you studied so hard, to get high scores and save time at the academy.", replied cadet Spencer discreetly.

"If you direct your attention along this upcoming street this is named captain's row, since most of the current captain's live somewhere on this street. Note, the name of the street, "High Street", mentioned cadet Dobbs.

"The Naval hospital there takes up this entire block and has four floors of various medical departments. During a war footing unfortunately this place is quite busy saving sailors.

Along this avenue one can see just there a hint of the Naval Academy buildings above the tree tops, pointing. See the two domes?

These houses are filled with navy folk. Like the Hawke's these are navy families from one generation to the next. It is not an easy life but we make the best of it here in Portsmouth.

Just up the street and a left turn, we are at the Academy entrance.

Lady Victoria, Miss Alton have you been to the academy?", asked cadet Spencer. "No Sir we have not had the pleasure.", replied Lady Victoria.

"The Royal Naval Academy contains the Royal Naval College.... and museum. The various statues are of those admirals before this generation that distinguished themselves in a way to be remembered.

That building there is where the cadets live. The pitches behind those are for training. We cannot go there for obvious reasons. It would not be appropriate for the ladies but we can go into the college and view a class or two and see the place.

Richard your instructors are just there.

The museum entrance is here, we may enter to see what there is to see.", directed cadet Spencer showing the way and answering many questions.

"The museum was so informative, the history of the royal navy and the important figures to keep in mind. Thank you, cadet Dobbs.", said Victoria.

"Richard, I had no idea the organization and disciplines of the Navy. I am very impressed, and worry about you.", said Sofia to Richard.

"It will be a challenge. My advantage is I have been born into a navy family and have been well prepared for what is expected. As well, my hope is to receive the maximum credit so I am twenty-four months to graduation. My secret weapon, the things that drives my success is you.

So, you see I have no choice but to succeed.", said Richard.

"Have confidence in me. I will not let you down.", said Richard to Sofia.

"Let use take the carriage to the yards.", announced cadet Dobbs. Just then Academy instructors Grimm's and Cecil, walking along the corridor, recognized Richard.

"Hello cadet Dobbs, what is this?", asked Instructor Grimm's.

"Hello Sir, I am conducting a tour of the place at the request of the Academy Commandant on behalf of Admiral Hawke, for his wife, son and the Lady Victoria and her daughter Miss Alton, Sir.", replied cadet Spencer standing at attention.

Instructor Grimm's recognizing Richard, "Ah Richard Hawke. May we have a word with you. It will only take a moment and I will not delay your parties tour Sir.", asked Instructor Grimm's with Instructor Cecil at her side.

"It would be my pleasure Sir.", replied Richard his demeanor changed to that similar to cadet Dobbs.

"Hawke, it has been decided to give you the maximum credit of two years. Your grades were so high and your verbal tests whereas well excellent. You will enter the academy as a third-year cadet. You are from a navy family so you know the expectations. We will see you in a few weeks. You're dismissed.", said Instructor Grimm's as he and Instructor Cecil walked away.

"What was that son.", asked Anne with Victoria and Sofia listening intently as they walked to the waiting carriage.

"I will be allowed that I enter the academy as a third-year cadet.", said Richard.

"That is wonderful son, father will be so proud of you. And Sofia, if it is your intent to be promised at graduation from the academy that is just 24 months of time.", said Anne to Sofia's acknowledgement and grabbing onto Richard's arm tightly.

"Driver, there seems to be large crowd in that direction.", said Spencer.

"Yes, prince Lionel is in town to christen the new ship.", replied the driver. Let us take an alternate route to the yards.", instructed cadet Spencer.

At the Naval yards there was much in the way of activities, coming and going, cargo and crates, "The ships are so impressive, the officers, the crews, the organization to support all of this is a big effort.", said Victoria.

"Yes, Lady Victoria each department has a task, a mission to perform. Some stock food stuffs, others make repairs, there are crew that handle munitions while medical teams assure the health of crews and more.

Because of the professionalism of these teams, we have a navy that protects the sea lanes, assures trade is not interrupted by those that might harm this free navigation.", said cadet Dobbs.

"I cannot even count the number of cannons on that ship.", said Sofia wide eyed and confused something so heavy like can even float.

"A ship of this type is more to instill fear in those to never try this out, nor never even think of an exchange of fire. One volley from this ship will sink most vessels and we hope it never comes to that.", replied cadet Spencer.

Aboard a Frigate, "Even moored here I can feel the rocking, the swaying. It is very small cabins and almost no protection from the weather. You will come home to me Richard?", said Sofia looking at Richard.

"I will come home to you, you can be sure.", said Richard.

"The tour ended, it was an honor and privilege to have guided you here today. Richard, I will see you in a few weeks. Ladies, it's been my honor. Here comes your carriage now.", said cadet Dobbs as he turned to leave.

Thank you said the ladies as they boarded the carriage for a trip to their house and time to refresh themselves, have supper and attend a concert tonight.

"Sorry we were too late for the lunch at the eating house.", said Anne.

"We lost track of time and I am glad of it. Everything was so interesting and needed time to take in.", said lady Victoria.

At the house James was there in the drawing room since his meetings were completed. "Ladies, how was your tour?", asked James.

"It was wonderful and very interesting", said Anne.

"We will have to change plans tonight. We have an invitation that must be accepted. It is to spend the evening with Prince Lionel.", said James.

"What invitation is this dear?", asked Anne.

"Prince Lionel is in town and upon finding me at a meeting he attended he asked if it would be acceptable if we suppered with him this evening. It will be quiet evening, no balls or dancing and more in the way of conversation and relaxing with friends. One can only accept such an invitation.", said James.

"Yes, of course", replied Anne. I will inform the kitchen we will be dining out. Mind you we do not have out best dresses and accessories but we will do our best.", said Anne as the ladies went upstairs to get ready for the evening.

"Richard, I understand you will enter the academy as a third year. Congratulations. I am very proud of you. We should get ready for the evening.", said James.

"Thank you, Father and yes.", replied Richard.

Arriving at the royal residence, the housekeeper greeted the guests and led them to the drawing room offering them refreshments. After a short time, His Highness entered the room where everyone stood and bowed as is expected. "Thank you all for coming this evening and dinning with me.

It was a surprise to know you were in Portsmouth Sir James and with your family.", said Prince Lionel.

"We had a few missions while here. I had some meetings at command, and we thought it a good idea that Anne, Richard, Lady Victoria and Miss Alton go a tour of the Academy and the navy since Richard will be entering in a few weeks.", related James.

"Ah, a separation. There is nothing more difficult than a separation. What do you think of the academy Miss Alton?", asked the prince smiling.

"I think Your Royal Highness, my Richard will be very busy about navy business and I will be glad for a letter and to see him when he is home at Charlton on a break.", replied Sofia.

"These times will go very quickly in my experience. Richard, have you gotten credit in time from your naval studies before entry into the academy?", asked His Highness.

"Yes, Your Royal Highness. I received a full two years credit. I will enter as a third year cadet.", replied Richard.

"Well done! That is the maximum amount of credit. Your testing grades must have been the highest. Congratulations. Then it will be twenty-four months to commission. I will keep an eye on you Sir since my father always kept your father close since he can be trusted.", said prince Lionel.

"Lady Victoria, it is wonderful to see. I understand your husband has not been in the best of health lately. It is my hope that he recovers soon. Is there anything I can do to help?", asked the prince.

"Thank you, Your Royal Highness for your concern. It surprises me with how busy you are that you would know this small detail. We have the doctors looking at Edward and are hoping for a treatment soon.", replied Victoria.

"My thoughts are with you lady Victoria, Miss Alton.", said the prince as a servant announced supper to be ready.

After, a brilliant supper and very amiable conversation the Hawke's and Alton's left for their residence, and while in the carriage, "It was a surprise to receive such an invitation.", said the Lady Victoria.

"Yes, I thought maybe he wanted company but I think he more wanted a break from those that constantly ask and place a weight on him. Where we meet him as friends enjoying time together.", replied Anne.

"That is very true. You will be counted as a trusted friend where you can just be amiable and not making demands. This is a great secret to those that are close to the royal family. The weight of state affairs is constant. When they can get a few moments of break this refreshes them and those that give this short cover are considered special to the family. Lady Victoria, Miss Alton you are those that have been amiable to the great family. That he knows of your husband's health should tell you much about your standing. I expect more connections and visits to Charlton in the future.", said James.

Just that suddenly the Hawke's and the Alton's left Portsmouth and were back on their estates in Somerset having had a very successful trip. "Mother, who could have known we would be preferred by the prince. I know where Richard will be and only twenty-four months to a promise. We will see each other here during our school breaks and once in a while travel there with you mother to visit him were appropriate. Don't you think?", asked Sofia.
"Yes, daughter that sounds like a good plan.", replied Sofia.

"Will you see Richard today?", asked Victoria. "Yes, since it is raining, we will meet here at the house.", replied Sofia.

"Ma'am, said a servant, entering the drawing room, Robert House is her to see the Miss Alton.",

"This is unannounced mother. I have not talked with Robert in more than a year I think.", said Sofia.

"Let him pass through.", instructed Victoria to the servant.

"Sofia, I will stay here by your side to see what this business might be.", said Victoria. "Thank you mother.", replied Sofia.

"Ah, Robert, how are you? Nice of you to visit with us today.", said Victoria politely.

"Hi Robert, this is unannounced, what is the purpose of your visit?", asked Sofia politely.

"You are eligible now and it seemed only right that I would make you an offer and secure an engagement. You would make me the happiest of men if you would accept me?" said Robert blowing his nose in between statements, since he has always been sickly.

Stunned for a moment, then answering, "Sir, I understand the seriousness of your proposal and respectfully decline. I hope you will find acceptance with one of the other girls in the neighborhood, you are a very good man.", responded Sofia.

"Is there anything else I can help you with Sir?", asked Sofia.

"I do not believe so. Are you certain Miss Alton?", asked Robert stunned he was not accepted.
"I am very certain Sir.", said Sofia politely as Robert bowed to take his leave.

"Mother, am I on some list to be made an offer? It seems there is a train of men to pick from of late. Do they not consider love, friendship and respect. I think a marriage is much more amiable where love is a consideration.", said Sofia to her mother .

"In my time love was not a consideration. Marriage was about money and titles. Your father and I were lucky in two points. We knew each other in growing up and it was acceptable to make an offer since we were two aristocratic families.

This was rare in those days to consider love. After marriage we fell in love and here you are. It is true where love is a consideration the marriage is much more amiable indeed.", replied Victoria.

"You are quite adept at refusing offers I see. It's all done quite politely, to the rules of society and leaving no room to misinterpretion. I like at the end of the refusal you ask, "Is there anything else I can help you with Sir?", said Victoria smiling.

"Yes, it is true mother. I think it best to be quick about it. If they knew me in the least, they would know I only have eyes for Richard and spend all my time with him. They only ask out of obligation and not in the least care to even know me. It is only fair to refuse the offer, leaving no doubt.", replied Sofia.

"Hello, Lady Victoria, Sofia. Good morning.", said Richard smiling and holding a bunch of wrapped flowers, giving them to Victoria, leaving one of the stemmed flowers for Sofia. "Miss Alton.", said Richard handing her the single flower with ceremony.

"Thank you, Richard! This is very thoughtful of you. Lovely Flowers.", said Victoria.

"Thank you, Richard. I love it.", said Sofia.

"I saw Robert House leaving the estate as I approached. I said hello but it was not returned. Was there an offer made?", asked Richard looking at Sofia.

"Yes, and just that quickly declined.", replied Sofia.

"Lady Victoria, Sofia I have something I would like to chat about of a serious nature. I did talk to my mother and father about this consideration and have their opinion. May I chat with you about this topic.", asked Richard earnestly.

"Of course, Richard.", replied Victoria with Sofia sitting up and near her mother.

"We have all been concerned about Edward and his health. Our families are close. This may be putting the events before they occur, so please be patient and hear me out. What I am about to say is very sensitive to the two of you. I will try not to be clumsy.", said Richard.

"R", replied Victoria.

"In twenty-four months, I will graduate from the academy. It is the plan to make an offer to your Sofia and my hope is to be accepted. With Edwards illness these last months and him not getting better in twenty-four months he may be worse in health then today.", said Richard pausing and being sensitive to this statement.

"If this is the case one has to consider waiting to marry and not having your Edward for the wedding. Therefore, I beg your indulgence and would ask you to consider that when I graduate from the academy that I may make Sofia an offer, that she accepts me, we marry sooner so we have Edward and not to lose this chance.

I know what I have said is very forward and I have no standing here but it is my hope you might consider this idea.", offered Richard sitting silent now.

"I can leave and come back when you call for me. This is a big consideration and I have no right to even ask for such a consideration.", said Richard.

"Richard, what was the opinion of your mother and father?", asked Victoria. They like you were in shock at the frankness in speaking of your husband and father, and assuring he is in the wedding and not losing this opportunity. Their opinion was favorable if all three of you agreed to this idea they would be in support.

Sofia, I ask you special grace since we have not yet talked about this possibility.", replied Richard.

"I will approach Edward on the topic Richard. It may be a few days before we can say. Would this be acceptable to you?", asked Victoria. "Of course, Lady Victoria, this is very acceptable whatever the opinion. I will take my leave, and ask you both for your forgiveness again if in any way I offended you.", begged Richard as he took his leave.

"Richard, may I see you out?", asked Sofia. "I will be back directly mother.", said Sofia.

"Richard, it was a shock what you described. It took great courage to talk about this and I honor it. We need to face these things. I want to say this to you. If mother and father agree to moving up our vow's I will agree. To assure father is part of that special day is a very important consideration.

Thank you, for discussing this very difficult topic. I know it is rooted in the heart and takes into account mother, father and me and the special day. I think mother will bring this to father and we will see their opinion. If by chance I can only accept your offer and wait the three years for you to finish with the navy will this still be acceptable?", asked Sofia.

"Yes, dear Sofia", replied Richard.

"I will work on mother and father on our behalf. I hope to send you a note in a couple of days. Be patient for now.", said Sofia hugging Richard.

"Mother, are you ok?", asked Sofia to the drawing room. "I am daughter. It was just the frankness of the topic and the consideration of losing our Edward. I have done all I can to not think of this. Richard was so kind, so gentle, so considerate in his manner of bringing this up. We have to discuss this. It is time.

As for you, Sofia, what is your opinion on the topic?", asked Victoria.

"I just now told Richard, it took great courage to bring this subject up, to consider my father and not missing his daughter's wedding and I honored it. If you and father agree to this idea, I am willing to accept an earlier wedding date. So, you see mother this will be in yours and father's hands.", stated Sofia.

"I will go to Edward and chat about the idea. If this idea is acceptable, we will talk with you to confirm your acceptance then we will send an invitation to the Hawke's to supper and an evening and chat about this topic in earnest." Is this a good plan?", asked Victoria of Sofia.

"This is an excellent plan mother.", replied Sofia.

"Edward, may we speak with you?", asked Victoria.

"Of course. What is it?", replied Edward.

"The subject I talk about is quite serious and I only ask you to hear me out.

We worry about you leaving us too soon. It is deep concern. As you know Richard will be leaving to the Naval Academy and in twenty-four months he will be graduating. At that, the plan is that he makes an offer to Sofia and with your blessing she accepts him.

With the worry about your health and waiting three more years for Richard and Sofia to marry, and the thought of losing you before the wedding. Perhaps, if you agree, when Richard graduates the academy, he makes his offer and with all agreed we move the wedding date up with a better likelihood you are here for the wedding, for that special day. I realize what I am saying is very shocking.", said Victoria.

"I am so relieved you bring this up Victoria. I have thought of not being here for our Sofia. I have even considered asking Richard if he would be willing to marry our daughter earlier. I know this took courage to bring this up. I agree. If we can get both families to agree and most importantly Sofia and Richard then we should do this.", said Edward.

"I am so relieved this is not a shock and that you know we are not wanting you in the ground anytime soon.", said Victoria.

"I asked James to the house to chat with him and my solicitor this afternoon. I will bring this up to him and get his opinion.

James and I will discuss money and other resources I have set aside for you and Sofia for when I will go from you.", said Edward with tears now visible in Victoria's eyes.

"Hear me out. I need to know your taken care of, then I can enjoy what life has for me and rest in the end should that come unexpectedly . Would you both sit here close to me.?", asked Edward.

"Yes, Edward I will.", replied Victoria.

"Shall we call for Sofia and hear her opinion.", asked Edward.

"Sofia, your mother and I called you here to chat about the idea of marrying early so I can be sure to be part of your special day. I was hoping for your opinion and that will guide us.", asked Edward.

"I love Richard father. I so honor his courage in thinking of us and assuring, if accepted, that you would be a part of our wedding and not lose the opportunity. I told Richard if you and mother find this acceptable, I will accept his offer and marry earlier.", said Sofia calmly.

"I and your mother find this acceptable.

James, will be here at Highbury today to meet with me on some legal matters where I will invite the Hawke's to supper tomorrow night to discuss this proposal.", said Edward.

"Thank you, father, this is a very acceptable plan. Father what are these legal matters?", asked Sofia.

"I am setting aside money and other resources to assure mother and you are taken care of when I am gone from you.", said Edward to Sofia who paused at the gravity of the statement.

"Are you to leave us so soon father. Can you not stay as long as you can.", said Sofia with tears flowing down her cheeks.

"I will be with you more years to come dear child, but one must be prepared well ahead of time should it be needed. I admit to some illness now but I promise you not to leave one day sooner than I can help. Now cheer up and enjoy today and the moving up of your very special day! It seems in a little over twenty-four months you will be married. Richard Hawke is the best of men. I look forward to walking you down the aisle.", said Edward.

"Father, may I be present for your discussion with James on the matter of our welfare?", asked Sofia.

"Yes, you may. Now let me sit quietly since James and our solicitor will be here in an hour.", replied Edward as the girls kissed and hugged him before leaving for the drawing room.

James arrived with Anne at Highbury, walking into the drawing room to a surprised Victoria and Sofia. "Anne, how are you. I was not expecting you but am glad you have come. Please be welcome, come sit.", said Victoria.

"Father is in the study Sir James. Let me walk with you there, Sir.", said Sofia.

"Thank you, Sofia", replied James.

"Sir James, thank you for your care for mother and I, especially if the worst happens and father leaves us too soon. We are so very grateful to you and lady Anne.", said Sofia sincerely.

"Sofia, your eye's are quite red. What has distressed you so? Can I be of help?", asked James.

"We have discussed the worst, preparations, you and lady Anne's kindness to the family. All heady topics.", replied Sofia.

"It is my honor and privilege Sofia. If the worst should befall your family....., you will be under my protection, and we will not let you fall.", replied James as they entered the library.

"Sir James, thank you for coming. Have you met my solicitor, Mr. Martin.", said Edward. "How do you do Sir.", said James.

"Father, Anne is here so mother and I will spend time with her while you, Sir James and Mr. Martin work on your important details. If you will excuse me.", said Sofia.

"Anne, Richard is already such a man as there was. He came to chat about moving up the date of the wedding to assure Edward would be here for the event. He was so kind, so gentle so considerate of me and Sofia and wanting not to hurt us and assuring consideration of Edward to be at Sofia's special day.", said Victoria as Sofia came in with a servant bringing tea for them.

"I was so surprised when Richard approached us on the topic. We did not prompt him. Asking his motivation, he said he was thinking of you and Sofia and wanting Edward to walk Sofia down the aisle and not lose the opportunity. He worried not to offend you and Sofia since this is such a sensitive subject. Even now he is nervous. He shows it when he sits for hours very still.", said Anne.

"Oh Richard, mother can I write Richard a note?", asked Sofia. "Yes," replied Victoria.

"Lady Anne, would you deliver this in his hands when you return to Charlton?", asked Sofia. "Of course. I will Sofia.", replied Anne as Sofia set to write the note.

"My Dear Richard;

I love you. Have no worries about your suggestion to move our wedding up. All here are in agreement, especially me! How kind and gently you opened the subject. How considerate you were about our feelings of the matter.

I can't wait for that special day! I will see you tomorrow at supper here at Highbury where we can chat about this as one family.

Yours Sofia Alton,"

wrote Sofia folding the note and sealing it with red wax dripping and handing the note into Anne hands personally.

"Have no worries, Sofia, Richard will see this note in his hands.", said Anne. "Thank you, Lady Anne.

"I was telling Richard we are so grateful to you and Sir James for caring about our welfare. Thank you, Lady Anne.", said Sofia sincerely with tear about to burst from here eyes.

"You very welcome, we are almost family now and family relations are worth preserving!", smiled Anne.

"So, there you have it, James. This is the list of money and resources I have put aside for Victoria and Sofia should the worst befalls this family.", said Edward.

"Have no worries, Edward, we will not let anything happen to Victoria and Sofia. We have a place for them on the estate and will work with Mr. Martin to assure they have a living. If

Victoria and Sofia want to live in the big house, we have plenty of room or in one of our two guest houses. So be assured they will be in the neighborhood and safe.", said James.

"Edward, would you explain the character of this cousin. Can he be worked on? What is the history here. Would you enlighten me Sir?", asked Edward.

"He is from an impudent relationship. Illegitimate by society standards, but provable in relations that he is the son and heir. The mother is long passed away. The son was never recognized and over time the resentment has grown to the point he wants the title and the inheritance as soon as he can get his hands on it, and to make what is left of the family pay. He has no character and therefore there is no means to work on him with a reasonable discussion. All one can do is to get out of his way. He will fall to his level.", said Edward embarrassed about the whole topic.

"You see, I was without thinking in my youngest years. I could not comprehend the consequence any actions in the moment would effect ones in the future years.", mentioned Edward.

"I see Edward, we will know how to act at the appropriate hour. Have no worries.", replied James.

"Edward, I would speak with your Victoria as well, Anne and I was thinking of a wedding present for Sofia and Richard and we have the idea to build a home in the commons area. Since we have so much land and this a favorite spot for the two.

The advantages are they are close to us, a favorite spot, a home of their own and one day they will inherit Charlton just here. What is your opinion Sir.", mentioned James.

"This is a wonderful Idea. Would you let Victoria and I have hand in the place as well. Perhaps we can provide the furnishings, paintings. Even more, we can offer a piece of land next to the commons so the commons remain as untouched as possible. Can we continue to talk about this and be part of the planning?", asked Edward.

"Yes, Edward. This would be a wonderful present for the two. Let's next discuss the land parcels to dedicate to this project and then the position of the house, build while they are at school, etc....", offered James.

"Shall we meet here next week. We are not telling Sofia and Richard. We want to keep it between you and Victoria and Anne and I.", said James.

"Yes, good suggestion.", replied Edward.

"Anne, I was going to send you an invitation to supper tomorrow night but since you're here. We would like to invite you and family to supper and an evening with us here at Highbury. We can discuss, as a family, the wedding and these plans.", offered Victoria.

"This would be very acceptable. We accept.", said Anne.

At Charlton, Anne handed Sofia's note to Richard. "Thank you, mother.", said Richard.

"Now what does it say?", asked mother teasing Richard with James standing right there.

"Mother! it is private. She asks me not to worry, all are in agreement and see me for supper tomorrow evening, she sends her love.", replied Richard holding the note tightly.

The next evening at Highbury, "Hi Richard, I am glad you are here for supper and the evening. We have so much to talk about.", said Sofia before supper.

 "I will graduate in the January twenty-four months from the end of September.", said Richard.

"I know your mother and father and mine will talk about the possible wedding dates, the church, a ball, guests. It is all very exciting and to know my father will be at my side is the best of gifts.", said Sofia.

"Attention, everyone shall we talk about the Sofia and Richards wedding. I wonder though, if Richard should make an offer first and at Sofia's acceptance and your blessing Edward perhaps, we should talk about the wedding.", said James to a suddenly very quiet group at the thought.

Richard and Sofia looked at each other and with the same thought, "Sofia, this is completely unplanned and not at all in private. We talked about this moment so many times. Rehearsing what I would say to your father.", said Richard to Sofia.

"Courage Richard. My heart and hopes are with you.", said Sofia.

"Sir, may I speak with you? I suppose in company.", asked Richard of Edward.

"Yes, son. What would you speak to me about?", asked Edward having some fun as Anne, Victoria and James sat as if watching a play unfold. Sofia feeling for Richard in these strange circumstances wanted to be at his side but patiently sat there.

"Sir, as you know I have grown up with your daughter these last years. She loves horses, reading, the out of doors, dancing. She has a keen sense of humor, a wonderful smile. We have a strong friendship, a great respect for each other and there is love.

Sir, I would like your permission and blessing to make an offer to your daughter. Our engagement will be twenty-four months to a wedding since I will be at the Naval Academy and she at boarding school for young ladies.

Some may say I have no right to ask. But I ask Sir for your opinion?", asked Richard.

"It is true Richard; you have grown up with my dear Sofia. I can see a deep friendship, a respect and love. On one point I do not agree. You have every right to make an offer. Of all the so-called worthy in the neighborhood your family are the truest.

I have no doubt how you will treat our Sofia. You as well care about my Victoria and myself. You have every qualification and I give you my blessing wholeheartedly. You may ask my daughter and if she accepts you we can talk about the wedding.", said Edward as all eyes turned to Sofia.

As Richard approached Sofia, Sofia wanted to put Richard out of his misery as quickly as possible since the whole family were watching him and thoroughly enjoying themselves.

"Sofia, would you give me one more moment?", asked Richard to Sofia's confused nod.

Turing to Lady Victoria, "Lady Victoria, may I speak with you?", asked Richard to a very surprised Victoria.

"Yes, you may.", said Victoria confused.

"I just now received your husbands blessing to make an offer to your Sofia and I would like your blessing as well.", asked Richard to a very startled and touched Victoria.

"I love your Sofia. I will be the best of men for her. Would you give me your blessing dear lady?", asked Richard.

Startled and snapping back, "Yes, Richard you do have my blessing and with all my heart. I have no concerns", replied Victoria then looking at Anne in that surprised and pleased way. "

What a son you have Anne. This took my breath away and at my age that takes a lot of doing", said Victoria to Anne discreetly, both smiling.

Turning to Sofia now, "Sofia, I have just now received your father and mother's blessing and my mother and father's blessing, to make you the offer of marriage.

This will be a long engagement since we can marry when your done with finishing school and I graduate the Naval Academy. We have so much in common. The love of horses and the out of doors, dancing, a deep friendship and love. Would you make me the happiest of men and accept my offer dear Sofia?", asked Richard.

"Yes, Richard, yes!", said Sofia to the parents clapping and congratulations all around, as Richard and Sofia hugged.

"Well done, Richard! fine show of courage!", said James with Edward smiling and Victoria still in awe of the moment Richard asked her blessing!

"Father, can we put this in the paper, that an offer was made and accepted to at least stop the parade of men at the door.", asked Sofia to everyone laughing.

"Yes, and tomorrow directly!", laughed Edward.

The rest of the evening and supper left all satisfied with amiable conversations, the planning for the wedding and the asking of blessings and the plan to work together to build a house for the future couple.

CHAPTER 8

The Academy

At Charlton, "In two weeks, Richard is off to Portsmouth and the Academy. And, I will miss him.", said Anne.

"It will not be forever and there will be winter and summer breaks where he will be here. And a time or two we can go down to Portsmouth to visit him. We can bring his promised as well. For now, let us enjoy him each day. He will need our support and strength.", replied James.

"I have been thinking about a couple of events we should organize. We should have a special supper with Richard, and we should have a supper with the Alton's since both families are on the same road it seems. Should we have the Aton's here at Charlton or are we to go to Highbury?", asked James.

"I will chat with Victoria today and make it a point to organize the get together between families. No worries there.", said Anne.

"I will set time aside to chat with Richard in the next day or so and have a father son talk. Soon enough he will be a man in the outside world and I will lose my chance.

As well, I am meeting Edward and our Architect to talk about building a home for the kids near the commons. We have parcels of land to dedicate to the new home project and the Alton's will provide land and furnishings as well.

Victoria suggested we have some items from both houses and of course new furnishing too so the home will seem familiar for them. Edward wants to do the land transfer, furnishings and more up front, so if the worst were to happen the cousin cannot interfere in the plan and it will be on us to just complete the work.

Edward has wrote letters to Victoria and Sofia and Richard and us, and entrusted them to me to give to them, before the wedding, if he should leave unexpectedly.

I think both families will be busy the next twenty-four months with this project.", mentioned James.

"Once we start work, if they go to the commons and that is very likely when the weather is warm, they will see the work. What shall we say?", asked Anne.

"I think perhaps we are building another guest house or the truth? Perhaps, we should get agreement from the Alton's on this.", replied James.

"I will ask Victoria's opinion.", said Anne.

"Good morning, Richard. Will you have time for me tomorrow. I was planning on a trip into Wells to pick up a few things. We can have lunch there and talk. It may be our time before it gets busy. What do you say?", asked James.

"Yes, father that would be acceptable. I almost asked you for some time, since we have just two weeks.", replied Richard.

"We are setting time aside for a family supper and I will be talking with Victoria on setting time aside new week for a supper between the families. What do you think?", asked Anne. "I love the idea. Do we know when?", asked Richard.
"The family supper would be Friday of this week. That is in a few days. The get together with the Alton's will be next week

and I will meet with Victoria this morning to work that out. So, tonight, I will have details.", replied Anne.

"Father, may Sofia and I borrow a carriage this morning. We were wanting to do a walking tour of the Somerset coast. We would leave early, well when Sofia arrives and is ready, take a packed lunch from the kitchen and will spend the day walking about the place with a small group also interested in a walk of the place with a tour leader talking about the history and legend of the places we tour.", asked Richard.

"Yes, you may, do you mind taking the barouche so your mother and I can take the other carriage to go to Highbury.", replied James.

"Yes, of course, thank you father.", commented Richard with Sofia just arriving.

"Hello everyone! Wonderful to see you.", said Sofia.

"So, it's a walking tour of the Somerset coast I see.", commented Anne smiling. "Yes, since we both like the out of door and are not bothered by drafts. We like to know of the history of a place and of course just being together.", replied Sofia.

"Richard, I will freshen up and we can go.", said Sofia.

Arriving at the coast meet up location, just outside of Wells, the group gathered in preparation for the walk. Richard arranged for the carriage to meet them in several hours at the end of the tour location. "We picked the perfect day Richard. The weather will be nice and warm throughout our walk and no rain.", said Sofia excited to see new sights.

"Indeed, the weather will be glorious today. Sofia, my parents are planning a supper with our families next week. Mother will be talking to yours to work out the details. I have a chat with dad tomorrow and a private supper with my parents later this week.", said Richard.

"It seems our parents will be missing us and want some time together. I have very similar events.", said Sofia as the leader of the walking tour began to organize the group and what direction to walk in and what they will be seeing and talking about.

As they began to walk, one could see the coast line and cliffs. The guide explained, to the group, the history and legend in the fabric of Glastonbury lore.

"Sofia, thank you, for agreeing to marrying me. I don't see myself with anyone else. You're such a friend, someone I am so acquainted with in our growing up, and there is love. Sometime, I do not want to leave you, and so there is attachment.

But I leave you as a boy and will return as a man. Your man.", said Richard discreetly as Sofia moved close to take his arm.

"It won't be easy. As you go to your navy, I go to my boarding school to learn how to be a proper lady. Just twenty-four-month Richard and we will be married. Then 36 months of sea duty and we will not be parted. Surely, we can endure this for the sake of our future years.

James and Anne at the Highbury estate, "James our parcels of land will make Richard and Sofia's home an estate in its own right. Let's do all the legal documents directly so there are no worries later. I asked the land surveyor and solicitor to be present so the papers can be drawn up and signed. I see you're adding the commons to the estate parcel. We will have to give this place a name.", said Edward.

"Ladies shall we all decide on the name for the new estate. I took the liberty of putting a list of names. If these are not one's were interested in then we can recommend alternate names. Here is the list of names "Edenwood Park, Common's Estate, Ashdown Abbey, Somerset House, Alton Hawke Manor, or Wells Place.", said James.

"I vote for 'Alton Hawke Manor' since the name contains both family sir names.", said Victoria with Anne musing and then concurring with her reasoning.

"I would be happy with the 'Alton Hawke Manor' as the estate name.", said James. Then it's to be the "Alton Hawke Manor.", said Edward.

"Shall we talk about the parcels of land to dedicate to the project. The surveyor was ready with both property maps with the marked-out land parcels discussed, with a third map that combined the parcels into one property showing Highbury, Charlton and the Alton Hawke Manor as discussed.

The solicitor had finalized the legal documents, there were several, mentioning all they needed were the family's signatures to finalize the transactions. He would then go to the magistrate's office to register the land transfer and creation of the Alton Hawke Manor estate.

Each looked over the proposed property lines. "James should we not add a few more acres of land knowing the two love a horse ride. If this is acceptable.", said Anne.

"I think we can extend the manor's property line here by adding this parcel. What do you think?", asked James.

"That parcel really opens the property to riding. They will enjoy this place since we are thinking of them and their likes.", commented Victoria.
"A year from now this house will be visible to them when they are on break and riding to the commons, they will see it and

ask. I think it's ok to tell them the truth. This is the families wedding present for them, Alton Hawke Manor. What are your opinions?", asked Victoria.

"I think this is the only way.", replied Anne as all agreed.

"Now to the house design.", said James asking the architect to display the design. "This will be a square two-story structure with ornate exterior adornments. The first floor will contain the drawing room, study, library, dining room, a small ball room, kitchen, grand stairway, servant's stairway. The second floor contains the family quarters and guest quarters, and the attic containing storage and servant's quarters.", described the architect.

"Lots of windows and fire places. It will be a very cozy place for the young ones and they are in the neighborhood and near us after the separation.

"Victoria, James and I thought it would be a great idea for both families to supper next week?", said Anne. "Yes, this is a good idea. It will be a while before we are whole again. Which house shall we have supper?", asked Victoria.

"We would be happy to hold this at Charlton if this is agreeable with you.", suggested Anne.

"This is agreeable. Do you think Wednesday evening would be the best day?", asked Victoria. "Wednesday at Charlton it is.", replied Anne.

"Richard, there is Barrington Court home of the Strode's, they own quite a bit of the land one see's in Somerset.", said Sofia. "Indeed", replied Richard.

"The history here is more in the way of legend I think.", said Richard.

"This is true. I wonder about the King Arthur legend and can more be found one day. Some say he is buried around these places and not so much at Glastonbury Tor. I suppose one is left to wonder until we know more.", said Sofia.

"It's lunch time and I am famished!", related Sofia smiling.

"Sofia, can we pick and choose what we will eat for lunch and what is left over can we offer it to those in the group that do not have a packed a lunch. I realize it's not much but it is something.", asked Richard.

"I think this is acceptable Richard.", replied Sofia.

"Thank you for sharing your lunch with us we are very grateful and appreciative of your kindness", commented a number of the follow walkers enjoying the lunch offered.

"I am glad we followed your suggestion, Richard. It all went quite positively.", said Sofia.

"Hello, everyone, we will finish lunch and resume our walking tour. Thank you to those that shared lunch with those that did not have a packed a lunch. I am certain this was much appreciated.

We have two more stops before the end of the walking tour. These stops are very close and near here so shall we continue.... And then leave the rest of the afternoon for you to enjoy the out of doors and explore freely", announced the tour leader.

At Highbury, "We have made so much progress on the house plans, made many decisions together and agreed to one approach over another. It is all so exciting. When will the work begin?", asked Victoria.

"As early as three weeks with ground work and foundations being set as a first part of the work. Now that we know the land parcels, we can approve the road work so that can be laid out and workers can get to the site of the house, bring all the needed supplied and equipment needed to build the place.", replied James.

"Making decisions, approving this detail or that is one thing but to talk of roads laid out to the future house site and house foundations being laid makes this all so real. Indeed, this is very exciting.", said Edward.

"In the next weeks and months, we will see much in the way of progress along this house project. Both families can select items from our houses we would like to add to the new furnishings. We have a secure storage building for this purpose picked out and ready. So, we don't have to wait to purchase new furnishings, as well we may donate sentimental items from each house we want in their home.", commented James.

Retuning to Highbury after the walking tour, "Hello," said Sofia and Richard entering the drawing room, as Edward, Victoria, James and Anne changed the subject.

"Hello, how was your walking tour?", asked Victoria.

"Wonderful mother, there is so much to see and learn in the way of history and legend. The weather was glorious, we shared our packed lunch with those that did have a packed lunch and Richard and I talked of many subjects. I pointed out the Barrington Court home of the Strode's along the way.

It all sounds like a success!", said Anne smiling.
"Yes, a special and wonderful day today. I am sorry to see it come to an end.", replied Sofia pensive.

"I am certain it will be hard as we approach the separation period. I will be melancholy.", said Victoria.

"Yes, that is it, what I feel. I wish my Richard would not leave, on one hand. And on the other hand, I know this is necessary for his own person. As for me, I am off to boarding. I will be glad when Richard will never be away from me and we will never be away from this place since all of you are here. Our roots are here.", replied Sofia to a silent room and Richard standing ever so close to Sofia and trying to give her his strength.

"This time will pass quickly have no worries, Sofia. The following two years will go by with many visits and weeks Richard and you will be here. These next twenty-four months will be the challenge. Live for the breaks at Christmas and the summer. And at its end there will be a grand wedding.

Some days later and at Charlton, "The days slipped by so quickly father. Tonight, we host the Alton's and, in a few days, we are off to our respective schools locked away with only letters to talk to each other.", said Richard.

"How I will miss my Sofia, this place, my mother and father.", thought Richard.

"The Alton's are arriving.", said the housekeeper.

"Welcome Edward, Victoria, Sofia.", said James. "Please do come right in to the drawing room.", invited Anne.

"Anne, it's come around so quickly.", said Victoria, as Sofia searched for her Richard finding him just coming to her side.

"Sofia," said Richard as he approached the group, with Sofia moving to his side almost unconsciously they walked together entering the drawing room and sitting together. Everyone could tell every moment together mattered to them now and did little to interrupt their time.

 "James and I took the liberty of buying a present for Richard and Sofia.", said Anne as James and Anne handed a wrapped present for each of them. Surprised, Sofia and Richard sat with the presents on their laps, not knowing what to do next.

"It is really Ok to open them, the presents will not bite.", said Anne smiling as Sofia and Richard began to carefully remove the wrapping.

"It's a writing box and supplies of writing paper, envelopes and even ink and quill. This is a lovely gesture lady Anne, thank you so much.", said Sofia.

"Thank you, mother. I am grateful for the gift and knowing I am more organized to write to Sofia and each of you is a great relief.", said Richard.

"Such a thoughtful gift. It's a wonder I did not think of this a well.", said Victoria with Edward's concurrence.

"Father, I see there is some work being done near the commons area. Do you know about this?", asked Richard. "Yes, both families are working on a wedding present for the two of you. So don't ask about details since we want to keep this as much a surprise as possible.", smiled James.

"Dinner is served.", said one of the servants.

"Have you had any offer's lately?", asked Richard discreetly with a big smile. "No since father posted my acceptance of a certain offer.", replied Sofia, needling Richard's arm and smiling at his humor.

"I would like to propose a toast to our dear children. You are truly stepping out into the world. We hope and pray for your many successes. Know we are here waiting for your return, ready to support you in any way we can.

In twenty-four months, you will be married and what an occasion this will be for all of us. God's speed on your journey's. We wish you happy.", proposed Edward to glasses clinging together

"Congratulations and safe adventures.", said Edward.

The evening ended all too quickly with both families settling in their homes.

"Son, what are your plans these next few days?", asked James. "Tomorrow, I finish packing and spend time here with you and mother. Friday, I spend some time with Sofia and her mother and father. Of course, Saturday late morning I leave for Portsmouth and the Academy.", replied Richard, thinking a week later Sofia leaves to her boarding school, and we will live on the written word and letters.

The next afternoon, Sofia arrived unannounced. "Hello Sofia, please excuse me Lady Anne for coming unannounced. I just wanted to see you're Richard, nothing more.", said Sofia.

"Sofia, you do not need an invitation to come here. Just come!", said Anne with Richard entering the drawing room.

"Hello Richard.", said Sofia.

"Hello Sofia, is everything alright?", asked Richard surprised.

"Yes, I .... I just missed you and wanted to see you. So, I asked mother's permission and here I am.

"Well, wonderful we can spend some time together.", said Richard.

"I was expecting you to tease me but you didn't.", replied Sofia.

"This separation is nothing to tease about. It would be too hurtful. I honor your love and commitment to me. And, I miss you too. Let's just be together.", said Richard earnestly.

"I was overwhelmed thinking Saturday evening you will be at the academy, a week later I will be at boarding school and will not be able to see you until our break at Christmas. It does not seem real. Yet, it is true.", said Sofia.

"Courage, strength and patience dear. Focus on your work and the time will go fast. Write to me often and I will as well. I will imagine you sitting next to my writing box, looking at the sketch you gave to me, and just telling you about all my comings and goings since last I wrote.

We live for the Christmas break, then the summer break and so on till the twenty-four months are done. When you miss me write to me. Tell everything in your heart. Let me encourage you, give you strength. I will let you know I have not moved from your side.

And, there will be times I will need your encouragement.", said Richard with Sofia sitting so close and squeezing his arm so firmly.

"I will Richard. I have to go. I look forward to seeing you at Highbury tomorrow. Come soon to me. I will wait for you.", said Sofia stepping on to the carriage with Richard's help as he stood there till the carriage turned and crested the hill to Highbury and was out of sight.

"Don't worry Sofia, I will be there early and spend all my time with you.", thought Richard.

The following morning after breakfast, "Mother, father I am off to Highbury to visit Sofia and the Alton's. I will give your compliments. I will be back for supper.", said Richard.

"Richard, would you give this small package to Sofia.", asked Anne.

"Of course, mother. What is this present?", queried Richard.

"A few items my mother passed to me. Some ribbons, special writing paper and handkerchiefs not so easily found in today's village shops.", said Anne.

"Bye mother, I will deliver this package to Sofia, see you a later.", said Richard.

At Highbury, "Hello, Lady Victoria. May I speak with you?", asked Richard. "I wrote a note to Sofia. I thought if it could be placed in her writing box. When she is at school and opening the writing box she would find my first letter, and at a time she is missing home, you and me. What do you think of this idea?", asked Richard.

"I like your idea. I think I can do this if I am careful. I will write her a note with Edward as well. Would that be acceptable?", asked Victoria.

"Yes, very acceptable. Sofia will be away from home for the first time and need all of our good wishes. I am very thankful Lady Victoria.", replied Richard as Sofia approached.

"Hi Sofia, I hope I did not keep you waiting long? I rode Fire since I thought you might want to say goodbye for now.", said Richard. That was very thoughtful of you Richard let's go see Fire.

And, No, you did not keep me waiting. Thank you for your words yesterday. They gave me strength.", said Sofia.

"Fire, fire.....how are you girl? I will miss you. Save me lots of rides for when I am back.", said Sofia rubbing Fire's forehead and neck.", said Sofia, Fire some how knew and stood perfectly still giving Sofia all her attention.

"Sofia, mother asked me to give this to you.", said Richard handing Sofia a package.

"Richard, what is this?", asked Sofia.

"I suppose you have to open it and see.", replied Richard.

"I will open it later. Do tell your Anne thank you.", said Sofia.

Finding a place to sit in the library, "Have you packed Richard?", asked Sofia.

"Yes, I have everything ready. Including my writing box! I double checked my writing supplies so composing a note will be no trouble at all.", replied Richard.

"It does not seem real we will be separated until Christmas. I remember six years ago, like it was yesterday, when I first found out about your naval studies and you leaving one day for the academy, and now we have arrived in the moment.", said Sofia with a crack in her voice.

"Like you, I will depend on your notes to me. Tell everything and anything you want. I will tell you of my days, and live for the Christmas break. I imagine breaks to be like an islands, like sailing from one break island to the next. We have four islands to our wedding. Two Christmas islands and two summer islands.", said Richard.

"I like the idea of four breaks to our wedding. It makes it seem much shorter away from each other.", replied Sofia.

"Then let's live from one island to the other and to our reunions.", said Richard.

"I have the feeling that these winter months will go by quickly. We will see each other at Christmas and New Year then, spring and summer and we are halfway there. What do you think Richard?", asked Sofia.

"Indeed.", said Sofia.

After lunch with the family, "I will leave you now and spend the evening with mother and father. Tomorrow, I leave at 10 in the morning for Portsmouth.", said Richard with what seemed to Sofia watery eyes, although he would never admit it if asked.

"Richard, I will see you off tomorrow morning. I know we are parting now but I can't be here knowing you are leaving for the Navy and not be there to say...", said Sofia, choking.

"Please do come and don't worry I will be happy to see you.", replied Richard.

"Well, I am off and a quiet evening with mother and father and then to the Navy tomorrow morning. I will see all of you at Christmas and send notes between now and then.

Thank you for all your considerations I am grateful and appreciative.", said Richard earnestly.

"Thank you, Richard, we will all miss you. Richard, would you wait a moment I have a note for your mother in the library. Sofia, would you come with me and help me find it.", replied Victoria.

"Yes, mother.", replied Sofia.

"Sofia, I would like you to write a note to Richard. A first Letter, quickly. I will ask Anne if she would discreetly place this note in his writing box. So, at his first letter to you he can find your first note just there waiting for him.", said Victoria.

"Mother! What a wonderful idea!", sitting at the desk writing a note,

> My Dearest Richard,
>
> You are by now at the academy. I wish you all the success possible. I am thinking of you and sending you all my love and encouragement. I know you to be strong and courageous.
>
> Your path is laid out in front of you. God's speed my darling.
>
> I can hardly wait for your letters, telling me of all your adventures.
>
> As you read this, I send you all my love, my hopes and wishes. Know this! Please be safe, do great things!
>
> I await your notes,
>
> Love and hope to you.
>
> Your Sofia, xoxo

"Mother, here is my note to Richard.", said Sofia handing her mother the note and Victoria placing the note in another note and in an envelope to give to Richard to place in Anne's hands.

"Richard, would you place this note into your mother's hands for me.", asked Victoria. "My pleasure Lady Victoria. Good bye then till Christmas.", replied Richard.

"I will see you off Richard.", said Sofia walking with Richard and waving as he rode off on Fire.

"Mother, that was such a wonderful idea to have a note placed in Richard's writing box for him to find the first time he writes me a letter.", said Sofia chaffed and having no idea it was Richard's idea and a note in her writing box that inspired this return idea.

"I am glad you like the idea. Richard will be surprised and happy to read your note. Will you see Richard off tomorrow at Charlton?", asked Victoria.

"Yes, mother.", replied Sofia.

"May I come with you? If anything, to give you strength and also to give Anne strength. You see she is hiding it but she is missing Richard terribly. Like you she does not like a separation. And he is almost like a son to me, I will miss him as well.", said Victoria.

"I should come as well. Since, we can represent the whole family in this case and encourage Richard.", said Edward as Victoria and Sofia realized Richard is like a son to the family now, and one day a husband to Sofia.

"Richard leaves at ten in the morning, I was planning to be there are nine in the morning. Is that time acceptable?", asked Sofia.

"I believe so.", said Victoria.

At Charlton, "Mother, Victoria asked me to place this note in your hands.", said Richard hand her the note.

"James, would you keep Richard engaged until I am back.", asked Anne discreetly.

"Of course,", replied James.

"Richard,....", said James as Anne slipped out of the room and up the stairs to Richard's room to assure Sofia's note is placed in his writing box and then repacked.

Returning to the sitting room directly, "With a discreet thank you node.", communicated Anne in that way only a husband and wife would notice, mission accomplished.

"Mother, Sofia will be here at nine in the morning, to see me off.", said Richard.

"Wonderful, it will be nice to see her.", replied Anne.

The next morning came all too quickly. Breakfast was a blur and bags were brought downstairs ready to be stowed in the carriage. There was an excitement and an unease with Richard leaving soon for the academy not to be seen until the Christmas break.

"Mother Sofia is just arriving.", said Richard, waiting for her carriage to stop.

At the door, to his surprise were Edward, Victoria and Sofia. "Hello, what a wonderful surprise. Please do come in.", said Richard.

"Wonderful to see all of you. Mother and Father are in the sitting room. This way. Mother, Father the Alton's have come for a visit.", announced Richard.

"Edward, Victoria, Sofia, please be welcome here, come in.", said James standing and bowing as is customary.

Sofia moved to Richards side, and as if one they knew to find a quiet corner of the room, in sight, but private enough to have a final chat before Richard was to leave.

"James, we wanted to see Richard off. We realized he is like a son to us. Like you we will worry and be glad to hear from him.", said Edward.

"Anne how are you doing really?", asked Victoria discreetly.

"Like Sofia, I do not like this coming and going of loved ones. So, it's been hard. I put on a brave face but will be glad when he is home again.", said Anne.

"Was it this way with James? When he was at sea?", asked Victoria.

"Oh yes, but like now this has to be hidden so as not to affect the men on their mission.", replied Anne.

"I suppose it's a woman's lot to sit and wait in the quiet for their men to return home from some far-off place or other. And in that time our thoughts and fears prey on our nerves. We bare it.", said Victoria to a full acknowledgement from Anne.

"Indeed.", replied Victoria.

"We can keep busy.", said Victoria smiling.

"We will have a wedding to plan..., a house to keep progress on and of course look for posts from both our children.", mentioned Victoria. "Yes, we can dive right into that!" replied Anne feeling better.

"Richard, you should get ready now.", said Anne as servants carried Richards final cases down the stairs for loading onto the carriage.

After Richard refreshed himself and returned to the drawing room. "Well, all that is left is for me to board the carriage to Portsmouth. Shall we go outside?", said Richard.

"Richard, Richard...", said Sofia, for the first time Richard embracing her, as she leaned her head on his shoulders.

"I will not let you down, I will be constant, I will write regularly, we will see each other at Christmas break. That is three months.", said Richard, giving Sofia strength.

"Father, thank you for everything up to now in my life. Mother, I know it is hard for you, like Sofia you have never liked the coming and going. I will write often and tell you all.

Edward, Victoria what can I say except Thank you for everything. You are like another mother and father to me. You will hear from me regularly.

Sofia, I wish I could be here to see you off but I will do this in spirit. Write to me, tell me everything you are doing. I will be interested in anything you share with me.", said Richard hugging Sofia, and at boarding the carriage he was off as everyone waved until the carriage was out of sight.

Victoria noticed the tears in Sofia's eyes. Staying close to her knowing this will be hard on her. Anne, realizing this as well moved close to Sofia as well, as the men acted like this leaving was quite normal. Victoria discreetly handed her daughter a handkerchief.

In the drawing room and after some tea, "When are you leaving for school Sofia?", asked Anne.

"Next Thursday, around the same time. And be back during the Christmas break.", replied Sofia.

"We will miss the two of you so very much. You are a light in our lives. Write to us when you can. Tell how you are and all your adventures.", replied Sofia.

"Sofia, would it be too much if James and I come to your Highbury to see you off?", asked Anne.

"Not at all. I would welcome it.", replied Sofia.

"You may come here, and to Fire as much as you want between now and when you leave for boarding school. You don't have to ask.

"Thank you, I should like that.", said Sofia feeling better.

The next day, at the academy, and not having started training yet, Richard unpacked his writing box. "This will be the best time to get my weekly posts out to Sofia, her mom and dad and of course mine.", thought Richard.

"Here, what's this, a note. It's from Sofia.", thought Richard reading Sofia's note and composing a note for Sofia to post when done.

"Dearest Sofia;

Thank you for your note. It was so very thoughtful of you, to know how I am missing you in this moment. I know better what you mean about not liking the idea of coming and going of people you care about. I pray for your strength and for mine, these next few months.

I arrived at the academy safely. With training and classes starting Monday. I am ready to move through these months and back to your arms. I will live for that moment.

My room is empty still with third year cadets arriving tomorrow. It will be a surprise to some when they find a new member to the class. I am prepared for that and will slip right in since I know what is expected.

My room is on the third level, very plain with wood floor, a wood stove, a bed, desk, lamp, and large trunk for uniforms, a common showers and personal items locker. This room fits three cadets.

Tomorrow, I pick up my uniforms and training cloths and class materials. It will all begin very quickly.

Just two years darling to being married to you. I will count down each day, each hour and each minute.

I will end this letter here. Thinking of you. I will write next week. Thank you again for your note, I am so grateful for your sweet words. I will carry your image and your note with me in the spirit of keeping you close.

I will be thinking of you especially Thursday and at ten in the morning when you leave and later when you arrive at school. All the best dear Sofia. I am near you in spirit always.

God bless,

Lots of Love, oxox

Your Richard", posted Richard.

Richard completed letters to Edward and Victoria, and his mom and dad, and posted them.

Thursday the following week, at Highbury, "Sofia, come down for breakfast so later you're not so rushed.", said Victoria heading to the dining room.

"On my way mother.", replied Sofia.

Mother, father thank you for escorting me to school. I am grateful for your send off. It will be the first time away from home.", said Sofia.

"Remember, all the lessons and talks we had this last year about being careful outside the home, with strangers, and to look and listen to think before you act to assure you are not in the least careless.

Because someone claims the aristocracy does not mean they are of a clear heart, and a clear mind. Sometimes they are the worst offenders of the privilege. Recognize this and do not fall in with them.

"I remember mother, and will employ all you have taught me. If a situation comes about that may lead to an unfortunate circumstance I will side step this before it can multiple in size. ", said Sofia sure of herself.

"The Hawke's will be here this morning to see us off.", said Victoria.

"I will look forward to seeing Anne and James. And, if I want to see them, I had better go up to my room and finish any final tasks.", said Sofia.

"I had better be sure to have Richard's sketch.", thought Sofia as she entered her room with two large trunks in the center of the floor.

"Miss Sofia, may we remove the trunks to the front door?", asked one of the servants as another stood by waiting for her answer.

"Yes, you may, thank you. I am all done with the trunks and have a small bag I will carry to the carriage myself.", said Sofia.

"Mother, I am all packed. The trunks are being removed to the front door, awaiting the carriage to arrive. I will carry this bag with me. It is not so heavy but has important items Richard gave me that I would like with me at the school.", said Sofia.

"What special items?", ask Victoria.

"Well, for one I have Richard's sketched image. I don't want to forget this or lose it since this is all I have for a while to see Richard's face.", replied Sofia.

"Yes, take great care of that sketch.......", said Victoria.

"Ma'am, the Hawke's have arrived and will be here in a moment.", said the housekeeper.

"Edward, Victoria, thank you for having us over to see you off. It is hard to believe little Sofia is off to boarding school and so suddenly.", said Anne.

"Time did fly. I do hope the next two years will fly by as well.", said Sofia smiling.

"We will be leaving in thirty minutes.", said Edward.

"Victoria, I know you told me but how far is the school?", asked Anne.

"The Mayfair Manor Finishing School for Girls is just in town, with smooth roads. It will take us about one hour and thirty minutes to the place.", replied Victoria a bit stressed knowing for the first time in many years she will be without her Sofia.

"I suppose it runs in the family.", said Anne smiling.

"What is that, Anne?", asked Sofia curious.

"Of not liking the idea of coming and going of loved ones. I noticed your mother is not one for you leaving her. I think all mother's want is their children nearby. I know I would do a lot to have my Richard here. I think this is a women's nature.", said Anne.

"Sofia, when are you to return for the Christmas and New Year's. I know I am asking the same questions but to James and me you are like a daughter and we want so much to hear from you. To know of you. If you will allow us to know and hear from you.", said Anne to Victoria's surprise at the frankness.

"Anne, if I in anyway led you to think I do not care for you and James. Please forgive me. I want you to know where I am and what I am doing. I am very happy for your questions. I plan to write to you regularly so you know my business. I will return home for the Christmas break at two weeks before the day and leave to school to arrive a week after the New Year.", said Sofia sincerely.

"James and I look forward to your notes.", replied Anne with James's acknowledgement.

"Ma'am, Sir, your carriage is ready to leave when you are.", said one of the servants.

"Thank you, we will be along shortly.", said Edward.

"Sofia, shall we freshen up for the trip?", asked Victoria.

"Yes, mother", replied Sofia.

"Take care of yourself Sofia. Write when you can and want too. James and I will look forward to hearing from you. Safe trip there and back Victoria, Edward.", said Anne.

"Safe travels, God's speed.", said James as he and Anne waved goodbye, the carriage sped away out of sight.

"It is so quiet suddenly. I will miss Sofia and our Richard. It seems our dear children are on loan. They come and bring us great joy, sometimes great challenges, then they go out into the world. All one has is the hope they are prepared and they will return and live near.", said Anne pensively.

"Indeed, and my hope is they come back in a hurry."

Arriving at the Mayfair Manor the Alton's registered their daughter. "It is so hard to say goodbye. I told myself to be strong for you since you will miss us, but I will think of you every day, wonder what you may be doing hoping for a note of your latest adventures to come in the post.

We are so very proud of you. Do well! I will be glad of Christmas so I can see you gain even for a while.", said Victoria.

"Mother, my hope is for time to fly by so we can all be together again. I will write you a note often telling you of all the nothings I do here. Have no worries about this. Richard, told me recently this time will require courage, strength and patience. So, I gift this to you as well.

Father, please keep well. Wait for me. Be at my wedding. I will be thinking of you especially.

I will work extra hard with the goal I can speed the time to graduate. I want to lessen the two-year course and be home to you both. I love you. Let me live in your hearts for the moment.", said Sofia trying to be brave but not liking the coming and going of loved ones.

Waving as her mum and dad's carriage rode away and out of sight.

The next morning, Sofia unpacked her bags and thought since school starts next week this is the perfect time to write notes to Richard her mum and dad and Anne and James.

"My Dear Richard,

I hope your travel to the academy was uneventful. How I wish the twenty-four months were complete. You know I have never liked the coming and going of loved ones, and in these days, I acutely feel it.

I found your note in my writing box. What a wonderful surprise. I sat by one of the window sills where one can sit and read your darling note. How I loved your words of encouragement and hope.

Thank you darling, thank you for caring about me.

I also remember you saying, these days will require strength, courage and patience. So, I live by that motto. I did pass that motto on to my mum and dad since they were feeling it.

I will be here for months at a time for the next two years. I will concentrate and work extra hard and see if I can cut my time down like you, did with the academy. That will mean when others are on break, I will be in a class and my school day will be an hour longer.

When you're able to write tell me of the Academy, what your days are like and anything you want to say. I will be interested in all you tell me.............

Your
Sofia xoxo", posted Sofia.

With letters to Richard, mum and dad and the Hawke's posted Sofia focused on school and pushing hard so she could gain credit to reduce her time there.

At Highbury, "Edward, how are you. Today was a lot of activity with getting up early, taking Sofia to school and the travel back. Do you need to take a rest?", asked Victoria.

"I am tired and will take a break. Overall, I feel fine. Thank you for asking.", replied Edward leaving the drawing room.

"Anne left us a sweet note, she says if we need anything they are just a short distance up the lane.", said Victoria.

"We are like one family and I am grateful they are our neighbor.", replied Edward.

At the Academy, "Cadet Hawke, lay a course from point a to point b in this part of the world, in this part of the sea. You have exactly nine minutes to respond.", requested one of the academy instructors as Richard set to the task of the laying course and direction, and calculated approximate time of arrival.

"Well done, Hawke that is correct! Cadets let walk through the course Hawke just laid and why.

Did any of you pick up the trap we laid in the navigation question. To get from point a to point b one has to lay a course from point a in the direction of 40 degree 30 minutes and 15 seconds longitude then lay a course for point b.

This is the case because the shoals are quite dangerous in this location. There is only one known safe path through this area. Hawke took time to understand this part of the world and this part of the seas and knew to proceed with caution through this area in the only safe direction recommended at his location, adhering to longitude 40 degrees and 30 minutes then changed course to location b only after 30 min and 15 seconds.

The lesson here is "study your maps well", "understand what may limit your navigational choices at your sea location", "lay a course to your destination taking into account the navigational limitations", and "always proceed with caution". Is that understood.", drilled the academy instructor as class concluded.

"That Hawke boy is very well versed in the complexities of navigational sciences.", said the academy navigation instructor to another instructor discreetly.

"I encountered the same level of expertise in mathematics, physics and hydrodynamics studies. I believe his father is the Admiral Sir James Hawke.", said one of the instructors.

"Yes, his father is Admiral Hawke retired. He has taught him well indeed.", said another
instructor.

"Perhaps, we should have a meeting of instructors to encourage him to push the standards expected and see where he lands. We always need a cadet that can be admired and followed by those in the ranks to aspire. What say you?", said an instructor.

"I think he would make a great role model. Let us wait thirty days to see if he continues his personal commitment to excellence. Then let us meet, plan and apply ways to give him opportunities to advance the flag.", said an instructor.

"Capital idea.", responded the group of instructors.

With almost two months gone by, one Saturday morning early before the days training, Richard wrote his weekly note to Sofia.

"My darling Sofia,

In two weeks, you and I will be in Somerset again. I can hardly contain myself in wanting to see you. I can't wait to hear your voice, look into your eyes and just be near you. Time has flown and I will be glad to sit with you, walk with you and know all you have to say.

You mum and dad and mine will be glad of us as well!

I think Willow and Fire will be glad to see us too! What do you think?

See you in a couple of weeks,

Love,
Richard, oxox,", posted Richard.

At Charlton, "Dear, I received a note signed by a number of instructors at the academy.", said James.

"Really, is it about our Richard. I do hope he is doing well.", replied Anne interested in a response.

"He is doing better than well; Richard is doing excellent. He is doing so well in his academics, physical training and seamanship he has impressed all the other cadets and instructors at the place.

The cadets see him as a leader to emulate. His peers have gained a great trust in him and the instructors see him as someone special and to be watched. We only have reasons be proud of our son.", said James.

"He will be home tomorrow. I know he will be very interested in us, but he will want to know of Sofia. I will send a note to Victoria to assure we get the together, and in the next day find a reason to go to Highbury. What do you think dear?", asked Anne.

"That is a great plan.", replied James.

At Highbury, "Ma'am, I have a note just come from Charlton.", announced a servant handing the note to Victoria.

"Edward, Anne suggested we invite them over Saturday so that will give Sofia and Richard their first meeting since the separation. I agree.",

"At the Mayfair Manor, "I will see all of you after the Christmas New Year's break. Go safely. Genni, I look forward to your visit to Highbury in a few weeks.", said Sofia as she left for her carriage ride back to Highbury.

At the academy, "Cadet Hawke, your carriage is here. See you after the break. Well done this term Hawke. God's speed on your way home.", said the senior cadet as Richard returned the compliment, saluted and left for Charlton.

At Highbury, "Edward, Sofia is just arriving. Shall we...", said Victoria as they greeted her with hugs for the first time and to Sofia's surprise.

"Hello mother, father wonderful to be back Highbury and be with you. Shall we go in. I will freshen up then see you in the drawing room.", said Sofia more mature since she left.

"Sofia, you seem so much taller and your manner of speaking is more refined since last we talked in person.", said Victoria

"I am your same Sofia mother. Father, how are you? How is your health? I worried everyday while at school.", said Sofia.

"I have been as good as expected. Thank you, for asking daughter. We missed you very much and just wanted you near, to hear your voice and know of all of your experiences there at school.", replied Edward.

"I have been working hard. I am in class later in the day then most, as well when most are on break, I am in class. I do this because already I have reduced my length of school by almost three months. By continuing to do this I may be home in sixteen to seventeen months. That is between six to seven months earlier than planned. This is not certain, but if I continue it is a good possibility.", said Sofia.

"I would be glad of any shaving of your time at finishing school and having you here sooner. Have you made acquaintances?" asked Victoria.

"Yes mother. A particular friend is Genni. In a couple of weeks, she will visit Highbury if this presents no impediments mother, father.

"I do not see any Sofia. It will be nice to make an acquaintance of one of your school friends.", said Sofia.

"Mother, father I miss Richard so much I cried a couple of times on the carriage ride home. Is he back from the academy?", asked Sofia her emotions almost on the surface.

"My understanding, from Anne, is he is arriving at any time now. The Hawke's will be here tomorrow morning to spend the day with us. I suppose, with breaking all the society rules, you could take the carriage to Charlton, if you can't bear it. Go now, you may be able to greet him at his arrival. If you can be home for supper since we have missed you as well.", offered Victoria.

"Mother, father would this be acceptable. I missed you both as well and don't want to leave you worried.",

"Yes, it is best you see Richard, then when you're back, for supper, we can have you all to ourselves for the evening. So go, go quickly!", said Edward.

Sofia, arrived at the Charlton. "Ma'am Miss Alton is here to see you.", announce a servant.

"Send here straight through.", replied Victoria getting up and working out to find her and not waiting.

"Sofia, Sofia so very nice to see you! Welcome, come in. We are expecting Richard any time now.", said Anne.

"I was hoping you did not mind me coming unannounced.", said Sofia.

"Sofia, you are never not wanted here. We are grateful you feel comfortable to come and we welcome you.", replied Anne to James just entering the drawing room.

"Welcome Sofia. When did you arrive?", asked James.

"I arrived a couple of hours ago. Visited with my parents and found Richard would arrive at any time I wanted to be with you to greet him. Stay a short while, then spend the evening with my mum and dad. Would be acceptable.", asked Sofia.

"Very acceptable. And we will spend the day together tomorrow.", replied Anne.

"Ma'am, Master Richard's carriage is just arriving.

"Let's all go outside to greet him.", said James as they all stood up to go outside.

As the carriage stop the footman put down the step and opened the carriage door to Richard stepping out and in his white dress Naval cadet uniform.

"Welcome home son, welcome home.", said Anne, said James. Just next to them stood Sofia as Richard turned to her she stood there with tears in her eyes speechless and shaking. Anne noticed first and took her arm to give her support, then Richard realized and held her hand and looking deeply into her eyes as James came close to Anne's side realizing as well.

"Sofia, I am sorry. Is my dress too much. It is the first time you have seen me in these months and in all this uniform. Please be at ease. I assure you I am the same Richard, truly.", said Richard as they all escorted Sofia into the drawing room to console her from the shock of this new and powerful man of hers.

"Please forgive me, I was not expecting to react this way. I miss Richard so much and seeing him in his uniform and so handsome I was quite overwhelmed with it all.", said Sofia so tenderly with Anne handing her a cup of tea and sitting next to her.

"Sofia, I was the same way with James. We were not so different from you and Richard. He came to visit me and my mum and dad. When I saw James in his dress uniform for the first time, I stood frozen and crying was all I could do. Only later after much consoling did I calm down enough and be as we were relaxed and talking and being together. I understand the feelings you are having. I could see myself a young girl in love with my James.", explained Anne.

"Sofia, I can run upstairs and change if this would make you feel more relaxed?", asked Richard.

"No, please don't. I was just momentarily overcome. You are so much taller, so handsome. And I missed you so much. I am just catching my breath.", said Sofia regaining her poise.

"And you, Sofia, are so much more beautiful than I remember and speaking so refined. I look forward to many conversations and being together again as much as we can.", said Richard in his endearing way.

"Yes, I have been waiting many days for those words Richard.", said Sofia squeezing Richard's hand.

"Richard, I will return to Highbury since I promised my mum and dad to be with them this evening.", said Sofia.

"Of course, mother, father may I escort Sofia, say Hi to the Alton's and return to be yours all this evening?", asked Richard.

"Yes, son. Take our carriage.", said James and Anne waiving them goodbye.

"I am so sorry for overwhelming you, Sofia. Please be at ease. I promise you I am the same Richard as always and nothing has changed. I love you dearly.", said Richard holding Sofia gently to comfort her.

"You are so handsome in your uniform Richard. I missed you and I love you so much Richard.", said Sofia.

"And you are so very beautiful and refined Sofia. Believe me, when I tell you, you take my breath way, leaving me only one course and that is to marry you since I can't live without you.

If I can get half the impression at seeing me from your father, he is sure to have an even better impression of me.", said Richard to a smiling Sofia.

"That's my girl.", said Richard his arm around Sofia as the carriage slowed at arriving at Highbury.

"Ma'am, Sofia has arrived with Master Richard.

As Sofia and Richard entered the drawing room to silence. It was not until Sofia spoke that the silence ended, "Mother, father our Richard has returned to us shall we not greet him.", said Sofia.

Snapping out of it, "Richard, I have to say you took my breath away. I was overwhelmed with you in your uniform, how tall you stand, and you were handsome before but I believe even more so now.", said Victoria, to Richard bowing.

"Thank you for the compliment's dear lady Victoria. I assure you even with all this I am the same Richard. I love your daughter and care about the two of you. How is your health Sir?", asked Richard of Edward.

"Richard, if I had any doubt, you were not for my daughter that idea has completely vanished. My daughter is in the best of hands. Welcome back son, how have you been Richard?", asked Edward.

I am doing well, thank you for asking.", said Richard.

"That is wonderful to hear. For the rest of the break, I will put this uniform up and not overwhelm you. I came to say hi, to check in on you and to escort my Sofia, she herself was overwhelmed and I could not have her travel here alone. I will see all of you tomorrow. Thank you for inviting us to Highbury and spending the day together. I shall leave for now.", said Richard.

"Bye, bye.", said Victoria.

"Till tomorrow.", said Edward.

"Have a lovely evening, Richard. Looking forward to seeing you tomorrow.", said Sofia walking Richard to his carriage.

"Sofia, Richard mentioned you were overwhelmed at seeing him?", asked Victoria.

"Yes, quite unexpectedly. All of the poise training went out the window. All of my emotions of missing him, and then suddenly seeing him in his uniform, so handsome, so tall...even now I am shaking thinking of it. He was so very gentle with me mother, he held me and talked so gently and was patient with me. He reminded me he is the same, his feelings for me are the same, and he has been constant.

I was surprised he had the same effect on you and father and neither one of you are easily surprised. What did you feel?", asked Sofia.

"It is true he is taller and more handsome and, in that uniform, he has an overwhelming power to him.", said Victoria.

"Indeed.", said Edward in concurrence with the comments.

"Let leave the subject of Richard for now and talk of you and school this whole evening.", said Victoria.

At Charlton, "Hi Mother, father I am back from Highbury. The Alton's are looking forward to seeing us tomorrow.", said Richard.

"I hope you did not overwhelm them with the dress uniform.", said James.

"I fear I did father. I will put this uniform away till the day I leave. And be a bit more country society so Sofia and family are not overcome. Speaking of changing may I put this uniform up and come back down with country cloths, if you will excuse me.", said Richard.

The next day, at the Hawke's, "We leave in a few minutes to the Alton's dear, are you ready?", asked the Anne.

"Yes, dear. Is Richard ready?", asked James.

"He has been for a while now. Dear even without his uniform our Richard is taller and handsomer, and his manner of speaking is more to the point but with politeness to it. He is you, but young.", smiled Anne to James's concurrence.

"Shall we be off to the Alton's." said Anne as they all boarded the carriage for the very short trip.

At Highbury, "Hello, Anne, James, Richard." said Victoria.

"Hello, Victoria, Edward, thank you for having us today.", said Anne with James's concurrence.

Sofia slipped to Richard side and not so overwhelmed since Richard was in country cloth. "You still looked more handsome and standing taller Richard but I would talk to you and know everything.", said Sofia as Richard gave her all his attention.

Finding a quiet corner of the drawing room they began a talk that would take each other through all the happenings during their separation. Not realizing and hours later they were interrupted with a late lunch announcemet and after lunch only to go back into conversation as if they were making up for months of separation. Both parents could see the connection between the two and were glad in spite of the separation the two just resumed the relationship.

"Sofia, I was constant for you. At the periodic navel balls and the many ladies invited I never danced and made it clear I was engaged and it was not appropriate. As well the purpose of the balls is to teach young cadets the ways of society and I know these ways.", said Richard.

"Thank you, for your surprise note I found in my writing box. It was so sweet and at a time I was missing you and home. I still carry your note and image with me since I miss you, except on the athletic pitch, that would damage them.", said Richard sincerely.

"I had that same experience with your surprise note to me since the first few days were very hard and all I wanted was to go home to be with you. I still miss home and want to be with you. So, I am trying to do more work and longer days to shorten my stay at the school. If I continue on pace, I will cut short my stay from six to seven months and be here quicker and visiting you at the academy when allowed.

We have periodic balls with men from a nearby college attending and I have done the same and mention I am engaged. I will not dance with other men.", said Sofia earnestly.

"I suppose in many ways we are an old married couple and just need the ceremony to make it official.", said Richard with a smile.

"Shall we join our mothers and father so we are not so profligate in sitting together and talking all evening?", mentioned Sofia to a smiling Richard.

"Yes, let us join them. And tomorrow may I see you. Shall we go on a first ride? If the weather is permitting. Or, stay in together here at Highbury.", said Richard.

"Yes, a thousand time, yes!", replied Sofia so happy to be with her Richard and that all is well in their plans and love wins the day.

"Hello.", said Sofia and Richard sitting with their mums and dads.

"Have you exhausted all topics big and small?", asked James with a mischievous twinkle in his eyes.

"No, but we did not want to seem to profligate in sitting together and talking all evening when we both missed our families as well. Tomorrow, we will pick up the conversation where we left off and learn more of our months of separation.", said Sofia as Richard enjoyed the new and confident Sofia who expressed herself in such a refined way displaying grace and intelligence.

"You are so much more in the way of grace; in the way you carry yourself and the manner of speaking. I reminded myself I will be married to you. Can I marry you now?", asked Richard discreetly to a laughing Sofia squeezing his hand.

"As soon as possible, Sir!", replied Sofia.

"Edward, since we are all together, and having been away these months, how is your health? How are you Sir?", asked Richard honestly.

"I am glad for each day. Victoria keeps a close eye on me. I am following the physician's directions, eating well, exercising with walks and resting regularly. Overall, this has slowed the worst. My goal is to walk my accomplished young daughter down the aisle.

I worried for the longest time. Now, I am free to live each day. This is because I have you, your father and mother and I know if the worst happens my girls are in very careful hands. I cannot thank all of you enough.", replied Edward with Victoria and Sofia discreetly taking his arm and being close to him.

"You're very welcome. It is an honor and privilege for us to be of any help Edward. You must know this.", replied James.

"Victoria, we have some guest from town staying at the house later next week. Would you like an invitation? If anything, it will be an interesting evening.", said Anne.

"What evening? We accept of course. And we need to get Edward out of this house even for a few hours.", replied Victoria.

"Thursday evening.", replied Anne.

"We will be at Charlton the normal time then.", responded Victoria.

After supper and good conversation and amiable company the Hawke's departed to Charlton. "I will see you tomorrow, Richard.", said Sofia.

"Yes, you will. If the weather is nice let's ride and if the not let's stay in and find a quiet corner, we can talk to our hearts content.

The Next day was cloudy and cold so Sofia and Richard decided to stay in at Highbury.

"Hello Sofia.", said Richard.

"Hi Richard, thank you for coming. Let's go to the library. That is always a cozy and private place to sit in peace, as well the servants have a nice fire going where we can sit.", said Sofia as Richard followed.

"Mother, Richard and I will be in the library.

In the library, "Sofia, describe your school day. Its people and your classes?", asked Richard.

"Boarding school is an established place with some history to it. The dorms hold up to four girls per room all depending on the money arrangements. Those in the single rooms show off the wealth but they lose with no knowing close friendships and the knowing of others.

I share a room with another girl. Her name is Genni. She will be visiting for a couple of days next week. She will arrive next Tuesday.

The dorms are all in dark wood, from floor to ceiling. Each room has private baths, a window, coal fire places, desks and chairs for each girl, a chest of draws and a large cloth press. We have uniforms but nothing like your naval uniform. We bring something of home to it, like a throw rugs, porcelains here and there, a picture or two, our own pillows and bedding.

The class rooms vary. Some class rooms have desks for sitting, listening, reading and writing assignments. Other classes lend themselves to sewing, knitting. While other classes are designed for practicing walking, talking in assemblies and presenting one's self. One class is just for dancing the same space used for school dances.

I have been taking two extra classes a term during morning break and at the end of day.", said Sofia.

"Pace yourself dear.", commented Richard as Sofia noticed he called her dear for the first time and it made her feel close to him.

"Most of the girls are very nice and personable. And, like in the general society there are those full of themselves and no one can measure up. I feel sorry for them, they have few friends since most of the girls don't want to measure up and just avoid all the frustration they create.

This last term we trained on how to present oneself, how to carry ourselves into a room and the manner of speaking and responding. I think you noticed the difference when we first reunited.", said Sofia.

"Yes, I do. You are very elegant at the times you choose to be. You are so much more", responded Richard looking into Sofia's eyes deeply.

"During the weekends I wash cloths, write letters and read in my room. Sometime, take walks with Genni on the school grounds, when the weather is mild. I do what I can to stay out of mischief since I can see the groups of girls that just look to go amuck outside the school grounds.

I want to complete the course can come home to mother and father and to you Richard.", said Sofia leaving Richard sitting close to her wanting to let her know he is here for her and grateful for her attentions.

"Will I meet your friend Genni?", asked Richard. "I am planning on it since she knows how very important you are to me. One time I dropped one of your letters and not realizing it. She picked it up and put it away. At the evening when I returned from my last class, she returned it. Having glimpsed at its contents, she asked me about you.

I talked about you. Our growing up. Our fondness and our promise. She, was confused having not encountered an instance in her life where in a marriage it could contain respect, friendship and love together. She has always been told the acceptable marriage is about title, position and wealth.

When I mentioned your mother and father, she remembered reading of Sir James and his wife the Lady Anne in the society papers. So over time she has wanted to know of you, if anything to know what to look for in a man since in her estimation love, respect and friendship are very amiable traits to have in a marriage.", replied Sofia.
"I shall be happy to meet your friend, and stand by your side ever so close so she knows I belong to you. I will make you proud.", said Richard.

"You always make me proud Richard.", replied Sofia.

"Shall we find some lunch and say hello to mother and father?", said Sofia.

"Yes, let's do." replied Richard.

Lunch was amiable with lots of conversation and talking to Edward and Victoria. At its conclusion, Sofia and Richard found their quiet corner to continue talking.

"Sofia, may I be quite forward with you in a request?", asked Richard.

"Of course, Richard, what is it you ask?", responded Sofia.

"It has been a whole separation since we kissed. I think about this often, of kissing you. May I have a kiss? Yes, you may and when we are married you may have as many as you want, when you want Richard.", said Sofia moving toward Richard to invite a kiss.

"That was three kisses!", said Sofia feeling Richard's love surround her heart in a warmth.

"Sorry, I could not help myself. Did this offend you darling.", asked Richard.

"No, not at all. I know your warm love. At times I can feel you surround my person, like now. It makes me think even though you are at the academy and I at Mayfair I imagine you sending me your heart of hearts, and I feel it and return it to you.

I am grateful we found each other and Richard. Do you feel my love?", asked Sofia.

"Yes, I do. Your love drives me to keep going. To work hard. Do the best I can. When I write to you, I especially feel it and I forget where I am, feeling right next to you, like we are now.

Other times I imagine what marriage will be like with you. I even imagine our children. I know I have gotten away from myself.", explained Richard.

"No not at all Richard. A woman always imagines these things. We hope for happy circumstances, children, protection and more. I suppose it is part of a woman's nature.

To know you think of me is such a great comfort. It makes me want to marry you more and sooner since my instincts is to never be away from you.

Please be constant Richard since I am quite attached to you, I depend on you.", said Sofia.

"I have been and I will continue to be constant. Have no doubt, Sofia.", said Richard confidently.

"Thank you, Richard, I am grateful for your forthrightness. Some of the girls at school are in a one-sided partnership. Where the male is all that matters and they mean little. How sad to be in such circumstances.

The girl sits and waits and then is there to be the servant. There is no love, no respect and no friendship. I am grateful to you Richard. We will be a real partnership. To know we can talk about anything, we trust each other and even when we don't always agree we have a respect for each other that protects our love.

When the girls are sharing and I describe our relationship, since those of our sex are always interested, they are shocked and have never thought such men existed. They all want to steal you from me. They say this cannot be. I must be exaggerating.

So, you see Richard, I am quite spoiled.", explained Sofia.

"No one is stealing me from you! Let us continue to work on ourselves so we both can forever enjoy each other.", replied Sofia.

"Supper in an hour dear", said Victoria.

"Would you like to stay for supper Richard?", asked Sofia.

"I have nothing particular planned with mother and father. I think supper would be acceptable, if you will have me?", smiled Richard.

"Of course, we will have you!", said Sofia giving Richard a look to tell him she understood his meaning.

Entering the drawing room Sofia excused herself for a moment, "Lady Victoria, may I sit with you.", said Richard.

"Hello Richard. I think you may be less formal with me and call me Victoria since we are so familiar. I see you and Sofia are catching up on every detail.", replied Victoria.

"Yes, this is true. Victoria, how are you these days. It has to be hard and you bear it well.", asked Richard to a surprised Victoria not use to being asked how she is doing.", asked Richard.

"I am surprised at your question, since I hardly get asked about my feelings. I see why Sofia loves you and why you and her will have a great marriage. I am doing well as one can in the circumstance.

I worry about Edward. He needs more rest these days. Like you I have an attachment to Edward. We found love after our pairing and at that time it was a rare. I am so grateful Sofia will have love with you Richard. Marriage is so much more acceptable with love. Please be faithful to her and never let her be too far from you.", said Victoria.

"I will be faithful to be sure.

If there is anything I can do to assist you with Edward, in any way dear lady, all you need do is ask and I will do my best.", said Richard.

"I have known this for a long time now Richard.", replied Victoria

"You have known what mother...", asked Sofia entering the drawing room.

"Richard mentioned, if I need anything, all I need do is ask him, and I replied I have always known this. You have a very special man here and a very special pairing.", replied Victoria.

"Indeed, I do know this and appreciate him.", replied Sofia.

"Richard, will be staying for supper since its almost on the table!", said Victoria.

"Thank you for having me.", replied Richard.

"A mother's curiosity, what do you talk about so intently. If you feel comfortable saying this to me?", asked Victoria.

"We talked about what our schools are like, the acquaintances there, plans for our future, about you and father, and yes about our marriage, love and friendship.", replied Sofia smiling.

The next day at the Charlton, "Father, can we talk?", asked Richard. "Yes, walk with me to the library. What is on you mind son?", asked James.

"Edward is slipping away. That is clear. Has all been done to assure Victoria and Sofia. I mean if the worst happens to Edward?", asked Richard.

"I recently reviewed the money and resources set aside for them. They can stay at the house or one of the guest houses. When your married then there will be Alton Hawke Manor for you two and all the land, house and furnishings are secured and without risk to be taken by the cousin. All in all, I think we have secured them when needed.

If the cousin were to hire a solicitor to try and attached assets from Victoria and Sofia and or the new Manor, I am not worried since I am owed a few favors yet and he will quickly realize the Hawke's are under the protection of the Crown. Have no worries son.

I am watching events carefully. If we see Edward slipping, we will take further actions to secure Victoria and Sofia.", replied James.

"Thank you, father.", said Richard.

At the Alton's, "Mother Genni is arriving this morning. Remember? She is the Mayfair Manor school friend. She will stay the night and leave tomorrow evening for town and her grandparents.", mentioned Sofia at breakfast.

"Yes, I remember dear. Did you check with the housekeeper to assure her room is ready. As well we must welcome her and assure, she is comfortable for the stay.", said Victoria.

"I checked with the housekeeper and her room is ready. I have a plan for the two days.", replied Sofia.

"Will she meet Richard?", asked Victoria.

"Yes, of course, he will be the highlight of her trip since she has never encountered such a man. A man that cares about his lady and parents. Assuring their comfort. She could not imagine a marriage where friendship, respect and love are considerations.", replied Sofia with Victoria listening intently.

"She will be here in less than hour.", said Sofia.

"At Charlton, "Father I will visit Sofia this afternoon, one of her school friends is arriving this morning and she will need time to settle into Highbury. This afternoon, a visit will give this friend time to study me, for some reason or other.

At Highbury, Genni carriage arrived at the front door. "Hello Genni, hello. Welcome to Highbury.", said Sofia.

"Hello Sofia. Thank you for having me. I did not realize Highbury was so grand. I did see a glimpse of the Charlton estate just their on the road before we turned to the Highbury road.", said Genni as Sofia lead her into the house to meet mother and father.

"Genni, let me introduce you to my father Edward Alton, Baronet and my mother Lady Victoria.

"Wonderful to meet you. Thank you for having me.", replied Genni.

"Genni, let me lead you to your apartment so you may refresh yourself.", said Sofia, leading the way.

Later in the afternoon , "Miss Alton, Richard is just now arriving.", said the housekeeper.

"Thank you, send Richard straight through to the drawing room.", replied Sofia.

"Hello Richard, wonderful to see you. How are you?", asked Sofia.

"I am very well dear. And who is this may I ask?", replied Richard.

"I would like to present to you Miss Alistair a school friend, who has come for a visit.", introduced Sofia.

"How do you do Miss Alistair. I am Richard Hawke, naval academy cadet. I am the son of the Admiral Sir James Hawke, and Sofia's promised", said James.

"Wonderful to meet you. I have heard much about you. Please call me Genni Sir.", replied Genni.

"Sofia promised me a tour of the estate and a place called the commons. Will you accompany us and lend us your protection?", asked Genni, smiling in Sofia's direction.

"It would be my pleasure to be your escort.", replied Richard as they walked out to waiting carriage.

"I have noticed the two of you are of one mind. I am in a dilemma and left wondering since all I knew previous was marriage to be an arrangement for money, for position, for title. In your case I see one can consider friendship and love. This leaves me with the question of how does one find a compatible and eligible partner for the lifetime endeavor. What is your opinion on the matter?", asked Genni of Richard.

"What you said is true Genni. Marriage, I think is much more amiable when love, friendship and respect is a consideration. In the general society and speaking for the male sex, we are raised to live by societies rule where one is raised to be a gentleman. This leaves little in the way of consideration for combining love and marriage. One is focused on maintaining one's level or bettering their level.

Your question, I think is, of where to find eligible men that meet societies requirements and have a sense of love in the heart. In these cases, you will have to use all you're, senses to see the truth in one.

Does the man you interested in know, a woman is not an object. Would he appreciate a woman's value. Is the man looking for a life partner.

One still has to be very careful to assure the considerations one wants in a marriage would be present but when you know what to look for you can quickly separate those men that are dead inside and those that are not.

If those that are not, is there a spark between you and them. If so, and the path is clear then pursue your heart's desire. I think. Of course the man will have to want to pursue you as well.

I am certainly no expert but this is what I think.", replied Richard.

"It is a very good opinion Sir. It gives me something to think about in earnest.", said Genni.

"Genni, Richard and I usually go riding on the estates. I mention this because the weather is glorious. You're a lover of riding a horse as well. What do you say we ride then have a late lunch?", suggested Sofia.

"I would, but I did not bring riding cloths.", replied Genni.

"We are about the same figure. You may borrow some of my riding clothing.", replied Sofia.

"In that case, let us see what you have to wear.", replied Genni.

"Richard you will have nothing better to do but wait on us. Will this be acceptable?", asked Sofia.

"Perfectly, Sofia. I shall go to the stables to have the horses tacked and ready. I look forward to a ride with the two of you.", replied Richard smiling, standing and bowing as the women left the room.

"Sofia, did you know Richard watches you. Perhaps not so much watches you but looks over you. It is as if, when you move, he moves along with you. And you do the same, discreetly but it is noticeable.", said Genni.

"I know he look over me but did not realize it was noticeable.", said Sofia.

"I like your Richard, instead of waiting and doing nothing while we dress for riding, he knows to go to the stable and have the horses ready for riding.", said Genni.

"The girls at school will be jealous that I have meet your Richard. He really is so handsome, so well-mannered and considerate of those around him. He has a power around his person. I mean, the navy and being a warrior. Yet he is a kind soul. You are so very fortunate Sofia.", said Genni selecting riding clothing.

"We are ready. Shall we gather up some horses.", said Sofia.

"Yes, let's do. Fire is grazing just here. Let me take his lead and hold him for you Sofia.", replied Richard.

"Wait! What is this magnificent animal. I have never seen anything like this before.", said Genni.

Richard smiling, "Her name is Fire. She is a purebred Arabian. The Admiral Sir James Hawke was gifted this animal on a mission for the King in the Arabia's.", said Richard.

"The first time I saw him I had the same reaction. Fire and I have a very special friendship and he likes it when I ride him. So, Richard is left to ride Willow and I to Fire. Today you will ride Chesnutt a beautiful bay.", said Sofia.

"These estates are so pretty said Genni. I especially enjoy the commons.

What is the house being built there?", asked Genni.

"That will be our home when we are married. It is called the Alton Hawke Manor. Both families dedicated land and building, furnishings and more. When Richard graduates the academy, we will be married and this will be our estate. One day, the Charlton estate will fall to Richard and we will live there.", said Sofia.

"Richard, will you supper with us tonight. I would love to but should inform mother and father.
Since we are so close to Charlton shall we stop in, introduce ourselves.", replied Richard.

At Charlton, "Mother, father I would like to introduce you to Miss Genni Alistair of Hampshire. She is a school acquaintance of Sofia's", announced Richard.

"Hello Ms. Allister it is very nice to meet you. I am Anne, and this is my husband, James. It is a wonderful day to ride. The weather is just right I say. James and I are about to have a late lunch. Would you like to join us?", asked Anne.

"Yes please, I for one am famished.", smiled Sofia to Genni and Richard's concurrence.

"Mother, would it be acceptable to supper at the Alton's this evening.", said Richard.

"If you wish son. I see no impediment.", replied Anne.

"Sofia, will you supper with us sometime this week, since we have hardly seen you and caught up.", said Anne.

"Yes, I will. Tell me when it is convenient to come to Charlton.", replied Sofia.

"I see a lot of progress has been made to the new estate.", mentioned Richard with James acknowledging the comment.

"Sir James, may I be frank in my comments?", asked Genni.
"I do not see why not Miss Alistair.", relied James.

"Are you and Lady Anne the same Hawke's I read about in the society papers?", asked Genni to Sofia, Richard and Anne smiling broadly.

"We are the very one, I'm afraid.", returned James.

"And Richard, you danced with Lady Penelope, Her Highness Princess Jenni and conducted yourself with great a plum at court not to long ago.", commented Genni.

"I see you study the society papers. I would not take too much stock in them, you see how we really are, very relaxed and easy here young Miss Alistair.", smiled James.

"I have never encountered people like you. You have titles, wealth, great connections yet your so...., well so relaxed. Those that I meet spend all their time accumulating this only to die alone since they don't have real connections. I think.", said Genni.

"You have a very keen mind, Miss Alistair. Not many can understand what you have just said. When the time is right and with your mother and father's approval find a man that shares this view and you will live a very happy life indeed.", said James.

"Since you are so keen about the royal court and in the summer months I am commanded to go, when next I go to court, with Anne, Richard, Sofia and Victoria perhaps, since your father and mother are titled count/countess, if you're in town you might come with us and you can see the palace for yourself.", offered James waiting to see her reaction.

"Sir, I will make myself be in town. Sofia, I look forward to a note from you and would'be happy to see this place I only read about. Going to the royal court would not be so much to be seen but rather to see. I am curious.

I was taught one is an aristocrat or not. We are born to it. Yet you have earned your place Sir, in service to the Crown. The King and Queen know you and trust you. You know the highest personages in the land. You're a knight, Anne is a lady. I even read about the winter ball you hold and those that attended.

The society I meet have titles and use them to dimmish those around them or to gain entry or privilege where other may not. Yet you rarely use your much earned titles and gain entry anywhere.

I think Sir birth perhaps should not always be the standard for one's level in life. You're a perfect example of one that has earned all the rights. You are the highest society surely.", replied Genni.

"Thank you, for your frankness and your compliments. Miss Alistair. I assure you we are not perfect. So, no pedestals for us. It is true we have over the years served His Majesty and earned many honors, we have great friends at court and are trusted for advice in the services and government. We protect and work to be a voice without influence to those in public with high responsibility.

Does this make sense?", asked James.

"It does Sir. I am grateful to be a friend to Sofia and now her Richard, and to know of you and the Lady Anne, and Victoria and Edward as well.", replied Genni.

"Sir", announced a servant to approach. "Yes", replied James. "Sir, a royal messenger with dispatch from the palace.", said the servant.

"Send him through directly.", said James.

"Sir, a note from His Majesty", handing the sealed note to James opening it to read its contents.

"If you will excuse me. Dear I will not have to travel to town. I can answer this with a return dispatch.", said James to Anne.

"Please be sure to feed the palace messenger, and refresh him and his horse while I write a return dispatch.", said James to a grateful messenger.

CHAPTER 9

Death and Friendship

The precious few weeks ended with Richard now back at the academy and Sofia at Mayfair Manor.

At Mayfair Manor school, "What was this Richard like that we heard tell from Sofia.", asked one of the girls in the dorm block with many other girls listening.

"Sofia did not tell the whole story here. Richard is far more handsome and dashing then she admitted. He is very well versed in the manners of society. He attends the royal court is mentioned in society papers when there. Has an acquaintance with the prince and princess and is known to the King and Queen, and many at court.

I found him to be powerful, yet kind. He has a deep affection to Sofia and her mother and father. They are engaged as she said. When he graduates the naval academy, they will marry. Both parents are building an estate for them as a wedding present.

Sofia's mother and father are titled, earned. Her father is the Admiral Sir James Hawke's, knight of the realm, and her mother is the Lady Anne. They are the Hawke's mentioned in the Society papers and are personal trusted friends to the royal family.

One afternoon, having lunch with the Hawke's a royal messenger arrived with a note from the King himself. Yet, when you are with the Hawke's they have no need to make one smaller, rather they lift everyone around them.
The Hawke's and the Alton's are those one would want to be seen with anywhere. They invited me to come with them to

the royal court in town this summer break when Sir James is commanded to court by His Majesty.", said Genni.

"What an honor", said one girl. "I suppose Sofia did not exaggerate.", said another girl. "I wish I could find a man like this Richard.", said yet another girl.

At the academy, Richard settled into the routine working as hard as he could to maintain a high standard but as well helped any and all that asked him gaining many loyal friends and admirers.

Richard was faithful with letters written to Sofia. Telling her of his days at the academy. While Sofia was as well faithful with her writing. Each living to the next note and wanting the winter months over so spring would herald the last months of separation and a nice summer break to come and be together.

Sofia would write letters to the Hawke's and Richard would send a note regularly to the Alton's. "Such a nice young master said Victoria to Edward", said Victoria after reading a note from Richard.

Edward's health was slipping away and sometime Victoria would call for the physician to come. She never wrote to Sofia of these times for fear of interfering with her school. She remained close to Anne thus the Hawke's knowing if the worst were to happen, they would be left without Highbury, but James and Anne planned to be there for Victoria and Sofia.

James monitored the situation at the Alton's quite closely. One week Victoria came to Charlton with the ownership papers for Willow and Chesnutt and these horses were moved to the Charlton stables. The ownership was transferred to Sofia so no one can take them from her. She was not told of the transfer so this did not raise any question about father's health.
Edward wrote long letters to Victoria and Sofia and had a servant deliver the letters into James's hand to give to his girls when he

is gone from this world and close to the wedding. He wanted them to know how much they mean to him, it was such an honor to be in their lives, he will look over them soon enough. James locked the letters away until that fateful day.

"Anne, I fear Edward will not be with us for Sofia and Richard's wedding.", commented James.

"We cannot determine destiny dear. What we can do is be there for Victoria and Sofia. I have already set an apartment aside in the house so they do not have to suffer the cousins wrath and the taking away of their Highbury home.

Yesterday, I received a note from Victoria. She will come here later this morning. I fear our conversation will be about her worries for Edward. I will be the very best I can for her.", said Anne.

Later that morning, "Hello Anne, thank you for having me.", said Victoria in a tired and sad tone.

"Come Victoria, sit here. Let me pour you some tea.

I want to tell you I and James are here for you. Be at ease and say anything you wish to say. I will keep your confidence.", said Anne sincerely.

 "Anne, it's happening Edward is slipping away from me and Sofia and there is nothing I can do. Each morning he takes just that much longer to breakfast, during the day he takes longer naps. There are times often now he is there and with me but not, if this makes sense. It seems he is moving between the worlds.

We started our marriage out of duty but as time went on a fondness grew and Sofia is the result. He has never treated me inferior but as an equal. I never considered our time would come to an end. It just never occurred to me this would be possible.

Soon enough, he will leave us and life will change. Like Sofia, I don't like the coming and going of loved ones. In this case I do not have a say.", said Victoria.

"I am so sorry Victoria. I was hoping Edward would be in good health for the coming wedding. What does the surgeon say?", asked Anne.

"He is interested more in Edward's comfort than in a cure now. He showed me what to look for and to call him when I observe it.", replied Victoria.

"What will we do with the children. I mean in telling them?", asked Anne.

"I thought it would be hard to tell Sofia about Edward since she is in school and this would distract her. But, when it's close, that is when we tell Sofia and Richard and ask them to come home. I will, as well, keep the state of Edwards health between our families so I can delay my cousin and that unpleasantness.", said Victoria.

"On that count, we have a place for you and Sofia here at the house. Have no worries about this Victoria. We will not fail you.", said Anne.

"Anne, my cousin is known for using unscrupulous solicitors to intimidate and take what they want using the law. So, I worry about you and James.", said Victoria

"We have many very powerful friends that are solicitors, prosecutors and Lord Justices at many levels that will quickly surround us. As well, we have the King who on his orders can change circumstances as he pleases since he is the law. So, you see, do not worry. We will be your protection.", replied Anne.

"Anne, I can never thank you and James enough for all you are doing for Edward, Sofia and I. It is such a comfort to be able to focus on Edward and Sofia. Our cousin stopped by last week saying 'at his last breath move out', and the land dedicated to the new estate will be returned to the Highbury and he has the solicitors able to do just this."

Anne, may I have the contents of Sofia's rooms moved to Charlton as well has her many novels. Would you grant me such a favor?", asked Victoria.

"This is not a favor, of course Victoria. How quickly can we plan this so this is no longer a worry for you. Can we move some of yours and Edwards possessions to your apartments here so this is no worry for you.", replied Anne.

"Shall we see these apartments?", asked Anne.

"Yes", replied Victoria.

"Anne, these apartments are so grand. Are you sure you will dedicate these apartments to me and Sofia?", asked Victoria.

"You are like a sister to me. It is the least a sister can do for another sister. James and I are glad we are able to offer these to you. Let's plan moving Sofia's apartment contents here and any contents of yours here as well.", replied Anne.

"Thank you, Anne, you and James are so good", said Victoria.

"I have to leave now. I don't like being away from Edward too long these days.", said Victoria taking her leave.

"Anne, I have to visit Portsmouth and will visit the academy and our Richard.", said James.

"When will this be James?", asked Anne.

"Next Monday dear.", replied James.

"I would offer to come with you but with Edwards condition I think it best to be here and ready to assist Victoria. And I would like to move Sofia and Victoria's possessions to their apartments here at Charlton. Do you not think this a good plan dear?", asked Anne.

"This is a very good plan.", replied James.

In Portsmouth, "Admiral would you like to have supper with us this evening?", asked Admiral Cook.

"I would like to accept but I will spend the few hours tonight with my son Richard, at the academy.", replied James.

"Well then Sir, I will see you at court when the weather is warm again.", said Admiral Cook taking is his leave.

"Hello Son.", said James to Richard.

"Father wonderful to see you. What brings you to Portsmouth?", asked Richard.

"Naval college meetings. While there I did hear about the Hawke boy at the academy and his extraordinary abilities to retain information and the helping of those around him to reach for excellence. I supposed that be you?", asked James.

"Yes father, that be me. And you taught me to work hard, be excellent and raise all those around me.", said Richard.
"I am glad to see this son. You are appointing yourself very well and are gaining many friends who later in your career will be great allies of yours. Well done indeed.", said James.

"Thank you, father. Father how is Edward Alton these days?", asked Richard.

"What I am about to say must be kept in confidence, even from your Sofia. Do you agree son?", asked James.

"Yes, of course father.", replied Richard.

"Edward is fading. We now realize he will not be long for this world. We are supporting Victoria, since she is managing these events as best, she can. She does not want to burden Sofia and you with breathless report on Edwards health.

She is also feeling the weight of a hostile cousin wanting the house, the title and wealth as soon as Edwards last breath. Anne has been a great support to Victoria. Your mother has moved Sofia's apartments to Charlton and most of Victoria apartment so they can avoid the cousin's unpleasantness. As well, Willow and Chesnutt have been moved to our stables with all their papers. Sofia, at this time knows nothing of this, let her mother be the bearer of the news son.

It will be best not to mention this to Sofia since her mother wants to inform her when the time is near. We will ask you to come home when it is time.", said James earnestly.

"Indeed, father. It shall be as you have asked. Thank you for telling me, and thank you for supporting Victoria and Sofia. I am grateful for it. This eases my mind and heart and lets me focus on the work I have here at the academy father. Thank you.", said Richard.

"Your welcome son. I will have to go in a few minutes since I promised the instructors not to overstay since you are in training and this is a privilege granted only because of my service and rank. Do you have anything you wish me to convey to your mother?", asked James.

"Yes, father I have a letter written but not yet posted to the both of you. Would you deliver this in mother's hands since she is keen to hear from me and my reports from the academy. And a letter for Edward and Victoria who as well are interested in my life here.", asked Richard.

"Yes, son this will be my pleasure. Take good care now. Continue this working toward excellence and uplifting all those around you it is very noticeable to many even in the admiralty. You will go far indeed with such an approach. I will be here to pick you up for summer break or before this if the worst should befall the Alton's.", said James.

"Father if the worst happens would you consider collecting Sofia, since she will not have someone for her and I am here and unable?", asked Richard.

"Have no worry son, I will.", replied James.

Thank you, father for the visit, for your confidence in me and trusting me with Edwards state of affairs. Send my love to mother and Victoria.", said Richard taking his leave.

The next afternoon and back at Charlton, "Dear, I have a letter from Richard for you. Not yet posted, and another one for the Alton's I will ask a servant to place in Victoria's hands.", said James to Anne taking Richard's sealed letter.

"Dear, did you inform Richard of the Alton circumstance?", asked Anne.
"Yes, I did and in confidence not even to mention it to Sofia since her mother will tell her when the time is near and to come home. The same will be for our Richard and he will keep the confidence.", replied James and an acknowledging Anne.

"Dear, we have completed moving all of Sofia's rooms and most of Victoria's. I believe this to be one less burden for Victoria. She is very grateful to us. We must make them feel very welcomed here.", said Anne.

"Indeed, we will.", responded James.

In the May of the season, just at summer break for Sofia and Richard, "Dear, I will pick up Sofia first from Mayfair Manor, then we will ride to the Academy to collect Richard, rest the night in Portsmouth and then ride to Charlton the next morning. Expect us for supper tomorrow afternoon.", said James.

"I sent a note to Victoria, saying you would be leaving for Mayfair this morning to collect Sofia, then you're off to the academy. Please go safely and all of you return to me.", replied Anne.

"Of course, dear.", commented James.

At Mayfair Manor, "Your bags are loaded to the carriage, Sofia. Shall we leave for the academy.", said James.

"Yes, thank you James for coming to collect me.", said Sofia.

"My pleasure Sofia.", replied James.

"Sofia, don't forget I will come to visit this summer. You promised to send me a note or two and invite me to visit again. Until then.", said Genni.

"Bye Genni, see you soon.", replied Sofia.

On their way to the academy, "Sir James, how is my father really.", asked Sofia.

After a pause, "Your mother wants to be the bearer of this news..., but I will tell you some. Edward is fading for some time now. I can't help but think he is waiting for you to return home. I am hesitant to say more since your mother would want to tell you all. Prepare yourself, it won't be long now. And know Richard, Anne and I are at your mother's and your side", replied James.

"Willow and Chesnutt are stabled at Charlton, safe and healthy.", said James to lighten the mood.

"Thank you, Sir James for your kindness to mother and I.", said Sofia earnestly.

Arriving at the academy, "Sofia, we will collect Richard, then spend the evening at Admiral Cooks house and leave for Charlton tomorrow mid-morning.", said James.

"Richard, Richard, I missed you so much. Come your father is here. We will spend the evening at Admiral Cook's house and leave for Charlton tomorrow mid-morning.", said Sofia.

"Sofia, it is so nice to see you. I have missed you to. We have the summer months and I want to spend all my time with you.", said Richard.

"You will Richard.", said Sofia.

"Sofia, how is your father?", asked Richard.

"Perhaps if we ask Sir James this evening.", replied Sofia.

After supper and at Admiral Cooks house, "Father, how is Edward Alton?", asked Richard as he sat with Sofia and James in the drawing room.

"I am hesitant to tell all since Victoria will do this, but Edward has been slipping away. I believe he is hanging on for your arrival. It is not long now. Sofia's apartment has been moved to Charlton and almost all of Victoria's apartment as well. We are stabling Willow and Chesnutt at Charlton.

I am sorry to say, it will not be long now. Focus on your father, we will watch over you and your mother. We will not fail you.", said James earnestly.

The next morning was clear and crisp, perfect for the trip to Charlton. When everyone was ready, they boarded the carriage and set off for Somerset.

The carriage paused to switch the horses, an hour later they were back on the road, "We do have a packed lunch if anyone is hungry. We can refresh ourselves.

"I do miss home and will be glad for the summer break. Spending time with you Sofia, is my plan and spend time with mother and father. My first mission is to be there for you and your mother in the case of your father.", said Richard to Sofia as she squeezed Richard's hand.

"Sofia, we will stop at Highbury first and see your mother and the state of your father if this is acceptable to you.", asked James.

"This is very acceptable Sir James. Thank you", said Sofia.

Stopping at Charlton to unload bags and refresh before taking the ride to Highbury.

At Highbury, "Mother, mother I am home.", said Sofia entering the drawing room to find her cousin and some of his acquaintances there waiting. "Like vultures.", thought Sofia.

"Oh, excuse me. And who are you?", asked Sofia with Richard and James at her side.

"I am your cousin.", was the reply in a slimy tone.", said the cousin.

"Ah yes, I see. May I introduce the Admiral Sir James Hawke and his son cadet Richard Hawke of His Majesties Navy. They are our neighbors at Charlton. Where is my mother?", asked Sofia with great poise.

"She is with your father.", was the reply.

"If you will excuse me sir.", said Sofia, as she, Richard and James left the room to go to Victoria and Edward.

"Mother, father.....,", said Sofia softly as she fell upon her mother at Edwards bedside holding his hand, with James and Richard standing back so not to interfere in the moment.

"Daughter, come to my side. I waited as long as I could for you to come. What can one say in a fateful moment.

I adored you from the moment your mother said she was with child. You're such a young lady now. I am so very proud of you. You have always been full of sunshine.

I fear I will not be able to be at your wedding in the flesh but I promise you if there is a way I will be there in spirit. I will look over your life. Send you every blessing I can. Hope and wish you all the happiness I can.

Your future husband is already a great man. I see him just there standing ready to be your strength. He is the image of his father a knight of the realm. I see why the King has a great trust in him.

Don't stand so far back. We are all family here are we not.

Sir James, thank you for protecting my Victoria and Sofia. I will never forget your great kindness. Someday, I promise to stand before you and shake your hand.", said Edward.

"Have no worries, Edward. I will not fail your girls. They will be protected. You have my word Sir.", replied James.

"Richard, I trust you with my Sofia. I will be at your wedding. Treat Sofia well. She is a good girl. Have as many children as you please and share them with Victoria, Anne and James they will be the best grandparents. Tell them of me.

My darling wife. I am so sorry for adhering to the society rules and not showing you affection, not being endearing. I was made aware of this failing in meeting the Hawke's and how James would address Anne. Such a simple word like dear, but with much meaning.

In this moment society is so unimportant only you and Sofia matter. I have been so happy since you came into my life and even more so with our Sofia. Forgive me for the many mistakes. I always tried my best to assure my girls well-being.

If it is possible, I will be by your side in spirit, hoping, praying and sending all my love.", said Edward.

"It seemed only a moment and Edward was gone from this world. He passed peacefully. I think knowing he received a great grace in saying good bye to his family." , thought Victoria.

"Cousin, Edward Alton, Baronet has passed.", said Victoria with James at her side.

At the shortest pause, "When will you vacate the house then so I may move in.", replied the cousin.

"In a forte night replied Victoria, exhausted now, as the cousin and his folk left to return, in a forte night, to take the estate.

"Not even the courtesy to offer a condolence. Even though they warned me of his low character it is even worse than expected.", thought James.

"Victoria, I will ask you to grant me a great favor and this is to let me make the arrangements for your Edward. For now, you are exhausted and I would like to take you and your daughter to Charlton to rest now. Would you grant me this great favor dear lady?", asked James earnestly.

"Yes, thank you James. It has been a long winter and I need time to rest.", replied Victoria in a sad tone. Sofia, at Victoria's side seemed smaller and pale. Edward took to their side doing all he could to support them.

At Charlton and learning of Edwards passing, Anne and the house staff moved heaven and earth to accommodate Victoria and Sofia. Once in their apartment and settled. The servants brought them tea and sandwiches and made themselves available to them. The servants assured the fire place was lite and the place was warm, turning down the beds and staying near to assist in any way.

"Dear, I am making arrangements for Edward. I sent a servant to the village to have the body removed and prepared for burial. I have to tell you. This cousin is worse than described. There is no hope in him at all. He could not even find it in himself to offer a condolence. He just asked when they could move out of Highbury so he and his folk can move in, then left. It was horrific to witness.", said James.

"I am so sorry to hear of this James. Victoria and Sofia are with us now and we will protect them. Dear can you ask the servants there to collect and move the remainder of Victoria's belongings and anything sentimental to the family removed, to Charlton?", asked Anne.

"Yes, dear. I am going back to Highbury now and will stay there until Edward's remains are removed for the last time. I will engage the servants to collect the remainder of Victoria's possessions and Edwards personal possession and send them here to Charlton.", replied James.

"Dear, you have not eaten or refreshed yourself.", said Anne.

"Mother, I will go in father stead.", said Richard.

"Father, let me do this. I heard everything you have said and will execute all of this without bother. I am young this will give you a much-needed rest from all the travel, and events of the last days. As soon as all is in order I will return and report to you.", said Richard.

"Are you sure Richard?", asked James.

"Yes, father. It would be an honor to assist in this way. I will leave now to the task. Mother if Sofia should ask for me....", replied Richard.

"Not to worry, I will manage this for you.", replied Anne as Richard went to the task.

The next morning, Victoria and Sofia put on a brave face but there was a sadness that could not be hidden. Anne, James and Richard went out of their way to be a support for them, even the staff did all they could under the circumstances.

Later in the day, James and Anne gave her an update. "Victoria, Richard managed Edwards remains to collected by the undertakers for preparations for burial. Yours and Edwards personal items are being collected by the staff and will be sent here in the next day or so. Have we missed anything that you want done at the house or taken from the house and brought here?", asked James with Anne at his side.

"Nothing I can think of. Thank goodness we made plans well in advance with Edward to assure we are out of the way of the unpleasantness. Thank you, James, thank you, Anne. Please Thank Richard on my behalf.", said Victoria.

"Actually, you may do this yourself. Since you live here now and Richard is just coming to us.", said Anne.

"Richard, thank you for your assistance with managing Edward to the undertakers and our personal thing to be removed and sent here.", said Victoria.

"You're very welcome dear lady. I have a few more details I would ask you if you're up to this?", asked Richard.

"Please ask Richard.", replied Victoria.

"Please forgive me if I in anyway say this in a clumsy way. Where would you like your dear Edward to be laid to rest?", asked Richard.

"I think in the family plot on the estate.", said Victoria sadly.

"What day would you prefer the service to be performed?", asked Richard.

"Today is Wednesday, would Saturday be appropriate?", asked Victoria.

"Of course, Lady Victoria. I would ask a final question. I am

assuming All Saints church just up the lane for the service?",
asked Richard.

"Yes, thank you Richard for your assistance with this task.",
replied Victoria.

"You're very welcome. It is an honor. Is there anything I have
missed that you want done?", asked Richard.

"Perhaps some flowers Richard. Edward for all the stuffiness
loved the spring show and green of the out of doors", replied
Victoria grateful.

The following Saturday, the Hawke's surrounded the Alton's
at the service. Having invited the neighborhood, the church
was packed with many long-time friends. Save for the cousin
everyone else was there and gave their condolences.

Many of those in attendance, distant from the Hawke's not
knowing what to make of them drew near and, thanked the
Hawke's sincerely for taking the Alton ladies into their home.
Expressing, that they wanted to help but did not even know what
to do. They expressed that if any assistance was needed, please
do ask and they will offer what they can.

 Edward was laid to rest, this day. Victoria and Sofia left him
white roses, many colorful spring flowers Richard selected,
and many a tear. Some tears of sadness but many grateful tears,
grateful to have had him in their lives.

The following week, "Sofia, do you feel up for a walk or perhaps
a short ride?", asked Richard carefully.
"Actually, I do need to get out of doors or I will go crazy. Would
you walk with me Richard?", replied Sofia.

"Yes, of course. I will.", replied Richard.

"Shall we walk to the stables and check on the horses.", mentioned Richard.

"Yes, that is a wonderful idea. Richard, I am sorry to have not spent time with you these last days. I have been paying attention to mother she is only now starting to come out into the sun again. Anne, has been so caring and gentle with her, with us. I don't know what we would have done without all of you.", said Sofia.

"This is nothing, Sofia. We have surrounded you and will protect you. However long it will take for you and mother to grieve we will be here for you.", said Richard.

Hello Fire!", said Sofia, approaching fire, who neighed and ran to Sofia's side as if he could sense the sadness and wanting to comfort her he wrapped around here tucking his head on her shoulder.

"Hello Willow, Chesnutt!", said Richard.

More than month gone by with Victoria and Sofia feeling at home at Charlton. The summer weather settled in with bright sunshine and warm breezes, made it easier with walks and rides and the being out of doors.

At Charlton house, "Sir, there is a solicitor at the door asking to see you.", said one of the servants. "I will go to the door with you.", replied James.

"Hello, how can I help you.?", asked James.

Handing James some papers and a court date, "Sir I am serving you papers suing for the land dedicated to the new estate being built to be returned. Here you go Sir.", said the solicitor..

"Thank you. You may go.", said Sir James.

"Dear, what was that about. It was legal papers stating the cousin's intent to sue for the Highbury land dedicated to the new estate.", said James.

"You warned me of this happening and the nature of this cousin's solicitors. I will prepare a note and travel to town to meet with the Lord Chief Justice. I am prepared on a number of fronts for just these possible events.

I did not mention this but the Lord Chief Justice has in his hands a command signed by the King himself. The first level is to warn this cousin to withdraw the suit and go away. If they don't the solicitors will lose their licenses to practice, if they continue the King's command will be executed, this is to strip any titles, seize all their wealth, and the estate and turn these over to the lady Victoria Alton.

All of this will start when I turn over the legal papers to the Lord Chief Justice. This has to be done in person.

Let us not tell Victoria about the papers since this will be taken care of.

Dear, a thought just came to me. Tell me if this is appropriate, to invite Victoria, Sofia to town with you Richard and I. This would be a change of scene. Perhaps a show, a concert or museum. What do you think?", asked James.

"It may not be too soon and a change of scene may be good. I will ask Victoria and Sofia directly. Would you organize the servants for the trip to town.", said Anne.
"Victoria, Sofia we are to go to town unexpectedly would you come with us if anything to take a break from Charlton. Please say yes, please come with us.", asked Anne.

"Yes, if this is no trouble for you.", replied Victoria with Sofia's concurrence.

"Wonderful, this is no trouble at all. We leave tomorrow morning just after breakfast.", said Anne.

"Darling, we will all set off to town with you!", said Anne.

"I will be a couple of hours with the Lord Chief Justice the day we arrive. I have a note on its way and tomorrow when we arrive, I will have a note from the Lord Justice office and know what time to be at his offices to meet with him.", said James.

"Dear you will have your hands full, so I will work to arrange for events while in town. Shall we stay three nights then?", asked Anne.

"Yes, and you may want to let the Alton's know the length.", said James, smiling.

 The next morning, arriving in town and at the Hawke's house James found a note from the Lord Chief Justice office waiting for him:

Dear Sir James;

It was wonderful to hear from you and to know your family is well, and sad it is under these circumstances.

Can you come and see me today at two PM in the hour at my Lord Justice chambers at King's Bench Division of the Royal Courts of Justice in Westminster.

I would like to know the details of this suit and dispatch this non-sense quickly on behalf of the King and myself.

I am sorry this has happened to you Sir.

Sir William Moors,
Lord Chief Justice

"Anne, I will be at the Lord Chief Justice chamber at two PM today. I will see you later this evening. If I leave now, I should make the two PM hour. Richard, would you stay here lend these women your protection.", said James as he took his leave.

"Yes, and with pleasure father.", replied Richard.

James, took a carriage to the Lord Chief Justices offie.

"Anne, I am sorry but I fell upon this note. I typically avoid reading anything and never want to intrude but this letter drew my attention as I went to replace it on the table. May I ask why James has a visit with the Lord Chief Justice and that the Lord Chief Justice is sorry for the circumstances?", inquired Victoria with Sofia at Anne's side.

"I will tell you but don't worry. We received papers from your cousin's solicitors saying they want the Highbury land dedicated to the new estate returned. Knowing before Edwards passing this could be the case, James prepared for this eventuality.

He received a note from the Lord Chief Justice, that an order from the King was prepared and that if executed was to seize all his lands, title and wealth if your cousin does not withdraw the case.

Prior to this he will be warned to stop, the solicitors will be told they will lose license to practice law, the local magistrate and sheriff will be notified of the Kings command directly.

James has to personally turn over the suit papers today. He is doing so now. When he returns, he will give his understanding of this matter from the Lord Chief Justice himself. Please be patient a little longer.", implored Anne.

"Anne you and James have only been most kind to us. You take on so much in our protection. We will always be grateful. I am so sorry for the troubles you take on for our sake. Please forgive us.", replied Victoria.

Victoria, Sofia, you are family to us. Victoria you are the sister I never had and wanted so much. Sofia, you're already a daughter to me and James. You are family and we protect our own. You are no trouble. There is no forgiveness needed in this case.

What I will say is your cousin will find out shortly he stepped into the wrong place. James, has done so much for the Crown, the Crown will immediately protect him. The Lord Chief Justice was commanded by the King himself to handle this situation.

So, you see have no worries nothing will go wrong.

Victoria and Sofia, you are important to us and we will not let you down.", said Anne with Richard at her side.

At the Lord Chief Justices offices, "Hello, Admiral Sir James it is nice to see you again. Would you come with me to the Lord Chief Justice's chambers.", said the Justice's secretary.

"Yes, of course. Wonderful to see you.", replied James.

A soft knock at the door, "Enter", said the Lord Chief Justice.

"Sir James, wonderful to see. How are you and your beautiful family?", asked the Lord Chief Justice.

"I am well and my family is doing very good. We have settled in Somerset. Just there near the town of Wells and Glastonbury.", replied Sir James.

"I understand your son, Richard, is attending the Naval Academy at Portsmouth and doing outstanding.", said the Lord Chief Justice.

"Indeed, Lord Chief Justice.", replied James.

"I received a note from the King himself concerning your circumstance and that of the Lady Alton and Miss Alton.

First, I should say congratulations on the engagement of your son to the Miss Alton. Tell them, I wish them happy. They grow up so very quickly do they not?", commented the Lord Chief Justice.

"I shall, and yes they do!", replied James.

In the note from the King there was enough information to set several of my clerks the task of collecting the details of the case here. I ended up finding more than I wanted. The cousin of Edward Alton Baronet is not a very honorable man.

Would you turn over their warrant. My team has already notified the magistrate and sheriff in Somerset about the Kings command and my orders as the Lord Chief Justice. I understand you will spend a few days in town. When you return to your Charlton this concern would have disappeared completely. Have no worries and enjoy a show, a concert or come to court and socialize with all of us since we miss your company!", said the Lord Chief Justice.

Sir James, for years I have admired you and all you have done for the Crown. I my station I never thought I would ever have the opportunity to be of any assistance to you, a servant, a trusted knight of the King. It is my honor and privilege to be of service in this small way Sir James. I consider this service a personal highlight in my career.

Sir, I have a court session in thirty minutes and should prepare. Don't worry about this matter Sir James it is being handled as we speak.

At Highbury, "I wish to see the Baronet of this house. Take me to the drawing room.", said the Sheriff with a number of armed marines, the magistrate and the lord Justice for this region of England.

The Lord Justice sat while the marine guards surrounded him with the magistrate to the right. The baronet entered the room about to voice his distain when two armed marine guards with hands on their weapons and without a word where instantly at his side and stopping him from saying a word and taking a further step.

"Sir, only speak when spoken to and only provide the truth in your response else the consequence could be dire indeed. You are to address the Lord Justice as Lord Justice is that understood.", said the Magistrate.

"Sir, summon your solicitors here now.", commanded the Lord Justice.

The baronet asked one servant cowering in the corner to summon his solicitors to this place directly.

Since the solicitors happened to be at the estate, they were present within minutes. Armed marine guards escorted the solicitors into the drawing room, they realized something was wrong.

"Who here initiated this warrant against the Hawke's?", asked the Lord Justice.

"The lead solicitor spoke up, "I did Lord Justice."

"You will withdraw this warrant directly.", ordered the Lord Justice.

The Magistrate suggested they, "do this immediately or suffer the consequences."

The lead solicitor looked at the Baronet, who signaled to comply.

"Did you not know the Admiral Sir James, his family and those under his protection are all under the protection the Crown. If you ever even speak to the Hawke's, the Lady Victoria Alton or Miss Alton you will feel the full weight of the Crown and be crushed into dust. Is that understood!", commanded the Lord Justice.

"Yes, Lord Justice. Yes, Lord Justice.", replied the Baronet.

"Sheriff, see to it if any issues arise where they are approaching the Hawke's the baronet and any of his solicitors involved are to be arrested. The Crown will then strip the baronet of the title, seize the wealth and estate, they will be arrested, we will throw the key away in this case. Is that clear.", said the Lord Justice.

"Perfectly clear Lord Justice.", replied the Sheriff and the Magistrate.

"I think we are done here then.", said the Lord Justice leaving the premise with his party.

At the Hawke's house in town, James returned after his meeting with the Lord Chief Justice. Entering the Drawing Room he came upon Anne, Victoria, Sofia and Richard saying nothing but wanting to know the outcome of his discussions with the Lord Chief Justice.

"Dear Sir James, I came upon the note asking you to visit the Lord Chief Justice and wanted to Thank you for protecting us and as well wanted to know the outcome of your discussions with the Lord Chief Justice in this case Sir.", asked Lady Victoria shyly.

"It has all been resolved. Your cousin knows he is dealing with a family under the protection of the Crown. He will withdraw his suit and we will hear nothing of him again. Have no worries.

Victoria, Sofia, I kept this from you because you're still grieving and this warrant was ill advised and ill-timed with no knowledge that the Crown will not tolerate these tricks.

So, please forget this matter. Let us have a wonderful time in town these next couple of days. The Lord Chief Justice sends his compliments to you, Sofia and Richard and wishes them happy.

Dear, what do we have for activities this evening?", asked James of Anne smiling.

The two days flew by and had the effect of recharging everyone's spirits to the point of being refreshed and renewed in life again. Sofia and Richard were smiling and having long conversations again. Even though Victoria was still grieving she resumed coming to meals, chatting with Anne.

Returning to Charlton brought an aire of lightness and living.

"Sofia, shall we go for a ride this morning?", asked Richard.

"Yes, I thought you would never ask. I will collect a packed lunch. Then, let us go for the horses.", replied Sofia, smiling and full of life.

With the horses saddled, Sofia riding Fire and Richard on Willow and ponying Chesnutt they headed in the direction of the commons.

"Sofia, it is so wonderful to see your smile, your eyes round with the excitement of life.", said Richard.

"Thanks to you and your family, I am able to catch my breath. To enjoy the simple pleasures. I miss my father and always will. He is with me in heart and thought but I can live again.

I want to focus on you, our marriage next year. We have two more islands of break.

Look at the new estate. The house there is getting done, our house. You and I are constant. During this very trying time you sustain me. I will never forget your loyalty to me and my mother.", said Sofia.

"It is my honor to support you and your mother, Sofia."

Releasing the horses in the commons to graze. Sofia and Richard laid out the pack lunch, eating and chatting about all manner of topics.

"I enjoyed the shows and concerts while we were in town.", said Sofia.

"So, did I. I find I enjoy towns diversion but prefer the countryside. What is your opinion, Sofia?", asked Richard.

"I am of the same opinion. I like the social aspects, the assemblies, shows and concerts, even court but in moderation, the countryside is home and our lives here in Somerset is my focus.", said Sofia.

"Can we chat about marriage?", asked Sofia.

"Of course, we can.", replied Richard.

"It is a woman's nature to think about marriage, the household and children. Do you see children in our future?", asked Sofia.

"Yes, I do. Some boys and a girl. Is this being presumptuous?", replied Richard smiling.

"No, not at all. You said boys and a girl. Am I to assume two boy and a girl?", inquired Sofia.

"Whatever children we have will be a blessing and our own. That we have them, they are healthy and you are healthy is all that matters. If we have boys and girls or girls or just boys, this is all acceptable. I will be supportive of you and our children.", said Richard.

"It seems so natural to talk about these topics with you. I was educated that men do not talk about these topics so the women have to manage all of this herself. But you do talk about this and partner with me. How strange and wonderful. Can we marry now?", commented Sofia to Richards smile and steady gaze.", said Sofia.

"I would love to be married to you now. However, lets us stay the course and at graduation we marry and make the event wonderful for all that attend.
At Charlton, "Anne, the house build is progressing very well. We are under costs and ahead of the schedule. If we continue, next year when Sofia and Richard are married the estate will be ready for them to take residence.

Time is flying by with one a week now before Richard is back at the Academy and Sofia at Mayfair Manor.", said James.

"This is wonderful news. I will share this with Victoria.", replied Anne as Victoria walked into the drawing room.

"What would you share with me?", asked Victoria

"The progress of the new estate is ahead of schedule and looks to be ready for Sofia and Richard when they are married next spring. What do you think?", asked Anne.

"I think this is wonderful news. Several times when I walked by the place, I could see from the outside how wonderful this looks and how much has been done. This is good news indeed.", replied Victoria.

"Sir, many of the neighborhood families have arrived at the door. It is quite a crowd.", said a servant.

"Excuse me, would you repeat this.", asked James with Anne and Victoria listening intently.

"Sir, many of the neighborhood families have arrived at our door. What would you like me to do in this case.", send them through.", said James.

"Dear we cannot accommodate them in this room, we can pass them to the patio and see them there.", said Anne with James concurring.

"Hello, please pass through the drawing room unto the patio since the drawing room is too small for the number of visitors.

With everyone there now on the patio and James, Anne and Victoria before group, and Sofia and Richard just now arriving from a walk and curious walked up the patio.

"Sir James, Lady Anne, Lady Victoria I will speak for the neighborhood. Many in the neighborhood here have kept our distance from you Sir James, Lady Anne not knowing what to make of you. We witnessed how you protected the Lady Victoria and Miss Alton in the recent situation and from the cousin's wrath. From the moment of Edwards passing we realized we should have helped but did not even know how to act, not even what to do. But you knew how to act, what to do and when to do it.

Your actions made us all compelled to come. To say thank you. For educating all of us at what action is and a helping hand really is.

We had to come, to apologies to, Lady Victoria, a longtime friend for abandoning her in her hour of need.

One cannot know how they will act until the vital moment. We are thankful the Hawke's were in the neighborhood saving the Alton women from a very uncertain fate.

Please forgive us for coming unannounced we just could not let this stand unaddressed any longer. We would like to know you better if you will permit this.", asked Lord Principal.

"Thank you all for coming. These statements are quite a shock since it was only natural to be at the Alton's service. Yes, we would like to know you better as well. Please stay refreshments are on the way and the weather is glorious not being too cold or warm today. Let us introduce each other and make acquaintance. Be welcome here are Charlton.

While at the front of the house Prince Lionel and the Lord Chief Justice arrived unannounced having been in Somerset on Crown business and did not want to just pass the place.

A servant discreetly walked over to James and waited for him to grant his leave to speak. "Sir James the Prince Lionel and the Lord Chief Justice request entry.", said the servant.

"Of course, yes. Dear, very important personages prepare.", said James, walking to greet his honored guests.

Walking on to the patio, some there knew immediately who these personages were and bowed, "I would like to present His Royal Highness the Prince Lionel, as all acknowledged and bowed and I would like to present the Lord Chief Justice as all acknowledged and bowed.

The Prince Lionel and the Lord Chief Justice were instrumental in dispatching the warrants the Lady Victoria's cousin presented some time ago.

The group of ladies and gentlemen almost collectively thanked the Prince and the Lord Chief Justice. "Thank you, Your Highness, Thank you, Lord Chief Justice." was repeated often.

Seeing Prince Lionel off and the Lord Chief Justice to their carriage the entire group participated wanting to show respect but also a collective and sincere Thank you.

"Miss Alton, Cadet Hawke nice to see you again. We hope to see you at the Christmas ball at Court in town this year. I understand you are to be married after graduation from the academy. Many congratulations and wishes for happiness.", said the Prince Lionel. "Thank you, Your Highness. I will apply to my father that we all go to the Christmas ball at the palace this year.", replied Richard.

"Let me apply for you cadet. Sir James will you not come to the Christmas ball this year at court?", asked the Prince, to a startled gathering.

"We will plan to be there Your Royal Highness.", said Sir James smiling and bowing.

Those in attendance learning of and now witnessing the connections the Hawke's have to the Royal Family to be so friendly.

"I am glad we stopped to visit the Hawke's it is always special when I encounter them. All of these people in the neighborhood convinced me the King, you and I did a very good thing here in saving the Alton's. And I am glad of it.", said the Lord Chief Justice.

"Indeed, this is so Lord Chief.", replied the prince.

"We do not accept any invitations to supper or balls at the Highbury estate. They are quite alone there. We have a term we never use however in this case these are a perfect example of savages.", said Lord Principal.

Sir James, we all want to be acquaintances with you and your family. We are missing our dear Victoria who has supported us for so long and we abandoned with inaction.

Even now the connections you have, the people you are acquainted with for sure tell the story of your true nature. You see Sir you are the true society.

"Let us all be aquaintances here", replied Sir James.

CHAPTER 10
Graduation and Marriage

"The neighborhood surprised me with their show of support. And all at once.", said Richard.

"What really surprised me, was the visit of Prince Lionel and the Lord Chief Justice. I think this surprised everyone as well. They must realize now how prominent your family is.", said Sofia.

"Yes, if that does not get the attention then nothing will. Dear, less than a week now we set sail till our next island break at Christmas. I cannot wait.", said Richard.

"We have had such an eventful break, starting with father's passing, cousin's antics ending with the Lord Justice and the marines making the situation quite clear, and the neighborhood inviting themselves over for a visit at Charlton and the Prince and Lord Chief visit and an invitation to attend the Christmas ball at court..

"All of these events ended our lazy summer days and made for what seems a very quick break. We did have a few days of being together and just enjoying a moment. Don't you think?", asked Sofia.

"Yes, on those days we talked of marriage, children and the wedding. Time is flying by. When we get past the Christmas break our life will begin in earnest since our wedding will only be months away. Sofia, I have a request.", said Richard.
"What is your request, my Richard.", replied Sofia.

"I know we will have a whole lifetime and it may not be appropriate. Please say no if this makes you uncomfortable. May I embrace you, and kiss you? If this is acceptable.", asked Richard.

"Yes, you may.", said Sofia standing and waiting for her Richard's embrace and kiss.

"I will take this to the academy with me.", said Richard almost breathless.

"So will I Richard. This makes our connection more real. When we are married you never have to ask.", returned Sofia.

Riding back to Charlton house, "Tonight is our special sendoff supper. Our mothers and father have always thought to make our leaving special.", said Sofia.

"And our returning as well.", replied Richard smiling.

The day will come when we will care for them. Let us do the best we can in this case.", commented Sofia.

"We will endeavor.", replied Richard as he and Sofia handed the horses to the grooms at the stable.

"There is some convenience to living in the same house.", replied Sofia.

"I thought so too recently. With having supper together, just now riding, chatting in the day, walks, never needing an invitation... we are very fortunate.

The day to depart arrived, "Richard, Sofia your carriage is here to take you to Mayfair and the academy. I believe James is ready as soon as each of you are.", said Victoria with Anne at her side.

"Sofia, this is for you when you are settled at Mayfair.", said Richard handing Sofia a letter.

"A note, for me? Thank you, Richard, this is very thoughtful", said Sofia putting the note away in her book to be read later.

With Sofia settled at Mayfair, the carriage, carrying Richard and James, headed down the lane toward Portsmouth and the naval academy.

"Son, Christmas break will be here in no time. Then your graduation and wedding.", said James.

"You said, more than a year ago, time will fly and it has father. I will walk you to the carriage father.", replied Richard.

At Charlton, "Hello Anne, what is this book and all these papers?", asked Victoria entering the drawing room.

"These are the beginnings of our plans for our children's wedding. If one thinks a couple of weeks will be enough for the planning, it is not. We have to organize the church, guests, the reception and ball, her dress, rings, flowers, psalms, vows, invitations, bridal tour, his cloths, a carriage, food, drink, gifts and more.

Will he wear his uniform? This is just the big items to consider. Shall we begin Victoria? This will take about eight months to organize.", said Anne.

"Yes, please let's do organize these many tasks. Where shall we start. With the Church and guest list?", asked Victoria eager to do something that would distract her from missing Sofia and her late husband.

At the academy, "All the best this term son. Do well, take breaks, write to your mother and I when you're able and of course Sofia and Victoria. We look forward to your latest news.", said James.

"Thank you, father. I will write with news and see you all at Christmas break. Go safely, tell mother and Victoria I send my love.", replied Richard.

At Mayfair, "Hello Genni, when did you arrive at school?", asked Sofia.

"I arrived about an hour ago. When I arrived, the room was empty and only now just found you.

Thank you for letting me visit you, during the summer break. And the invite to the Royal Court is something I will never forget.", replied Genni.

"You were at the Royal Court?", asked one of the dorm girls.

"Yes, invited by the Hawke's and Sofia.", replied Genni.

"The Hawke's..., do you mean the Admiral Sir James Hawke? I have read about him in the society papers.", asked a dorm girl.

"Yes, the very one. I stayed at his house for a few days and he invited me to court with the family if I were in town. I was in town.", replied Genni.

"I have to go. I have some letters to write and post before the busy term starts. I will chat you up later Genni. I am very glad to see you and you're very welcome.", said Sofia as she walked toward her dorm.

At Charlton, "Victoria, shall we split the wedding tasks to we can get a good start on this. I would hope when Sofia is back there will be a number of bridal tasks to keep her busy and her nerves in check. What do you say Victoria?", asked Anne.

"I think this to be a good idea. I have the church, the ball and reception and, the supper before the wedding day.

"We will organize the new estate house together. James said the house will be ready for furnishing at the end of January or first half of February.

"I think we should help with the expenses of the bridal tour. But where to send them?", said Anne.

At the academy and in the month of December, "I can hardly believe we are in the second week of December. In another week we will be on Christmas break and all will be headed their destination home.", said Richard to his roommates.

"Hey Hawke! you keep showing up at the top of the class in many categories. You will have your pick of assignments you keep this up!", said the senior cadet.

"I have been very fortunate with so many talented classmates.", replied Richard.

"No need to be modest Hawke. You work hard that is clear and this is a great example to the younger cadets that hard work and dedication has its rewards. Well done.", said the senior cadet congratulating Hawke saluting and walking away.

At Charlton, "Anne, you have posts from Richard and Sofia. Shall I bring these to the drawing room?", asked Victoria.

"Yes, please.", replied Anne.
"I am always glad our children think of us and show this with the posts when they are away. It is only a week now and both

will be within wall of this house. Then they leave again but Sofia will be back at the end of February and Richard will be back at the mid-May.

Then a wedding. I am so pleased we have organized and completed most of the tasks for the big event. Soon, we will have the new estate house to furnish and have cleaned and readied for them."

"I hope you have a post from one or both Victoria.", said Anne.

"I do have a post from Sofia. Richard, when he writes usually comes a day or so later. So, you see not to worry.", replied Victoria as she and Anne sat quietly reading their posts.

"When they leave again for school and the academy, we will be busy with organizing their house and more wedding task by the time we miss them Sofia will be back from school and done and two and a half months later Richard will be preparing to graduate from the academy.

So, let's enjoy this Christmas and new year since the next month will be so very busy.

"Dear, have you heard. Highbury is up for let or sale. Your cousin has moved away.", said James strolling into the drawing room.

Anne and Victoria looked at each other surprised, "No I did not know this dear.", replied Anne.

"I suppose the neighborhood ignoring them and not accepting invitations or socializing made them realize their actions toward Victoria and Sofia was considered abhorrent here and there is no way back from that. I am sorry to see your home out for let or sale Victoria. I do hope Charlton is home for you now. We certainly want you here.", said James.

"Thank you, James, Anne. This is home to me. I look forward to my time with the both of you. I am in the neighborhood and quite welcomed here. It seems we have always been family somehow and I am glad of it.", replied Victoria.

At Mayfair Manor, "Sofia is Sir James coming to collect you tomorrow?", asked Genni.

"Yes, then we are off to the academy to collect Richard.", replied Sofia.

"I know you cannot wait to see your Richard?", said Genni.

"And how do you know that...", smiled Sofia teasing Genni.

"You, in all the time here and all the dances never once showed any interest in dancing with another man, disappointing many a starry-eyed gentleman. But at court last summer you and Richard lived on the dance floor, so I know you love a dance.", said Genni.

"I love Richard. We are to be married. I want to be his wife. I want to have his children. I want to be a great mother. I want to be a great wife. I will dance with Richard all my life.

It is simple really. It seems from the first time I met him and fire I have known he would be the special man for me. So, yes you are correct Genni.", replied Sofia.

"Good night God bless, Genni.", said Sofia snug in her bed and turning down the lamp.

"Good night, Sofia. Try to get some rest.", replied Genni.

"The next morning, after breakfast, Sofia your carriage will be here in less than an hour. If we get lost in the hustle and bustle of all the girls being picked up and bags and trunks being flung here and there one carriage or another. Have a wonderful Christmas and New Year. See you next term.", said Genni.

"Have a wonderful Christmas and New Year. I will see you next term. Go safely Genni.", replied Sofia.

"Sofia, your carriage is just arriving. See there.", said Genni pointing to Sir James distinctive box.

"Bye Genni, see you next term. Go safely.", said Sofia and to her surprise in the Naval Cadets best dress stepping out of the carriage was her Richard, looking so handsome, and impressive. All the girls at the same time gasped collectively, all looking at him and not wanting to be seen doing it but it was obvious. "Who is the lucky girl he will escort.", thought many a girl. But Richard had his wits about him and focused his attention on Sofia giving her every confidence that he is for her.

As soon as he spotted Sofia he walked in the military manner directly to her, took her bags, took her arm. He greeted her, kissed her hand, talked a moment and then turned to escort her to her carriage. The girls there that knew the story of Sofia's Richard realized this was him in the flesh, Even more handsome and dashing than described by Sofia and Genni.

Richard chatted with Sofia, laughing and smiling with her while waiting for the bags to be loaded.

"Hello dear, how are you? Would you like a ride to Somerset?", asked Cadet Hawke.

"Yes, and directly since I have missed you and only want to spend every moment with you. I have to catch my breath since when I see you in uniform or otherwise, I want to run to you. Everyone here wants your attention but you give that only to me.

I am so grateful to you Richard.", said Sofia.

"You have all my attention, and gladly!", replied Richard as he helped Sofia unto the carriage. With the carriage door closed and all secure the carriage drove in the direction of the road to Somerset and home.

Richard typically does not show affection in the open but on the ride, but he held Sofia's hand, all be it, discreetly. James did not notice since he was engrossed in Navy papers and reports he was asked to provide opinion.

"Richard, what is this?", asked Sofia softly looking at his hand caressing hers.

"I missed you. Is it too much?", asked Richard.

"No, I feel closer to you when you hold my hand. You usually hold my hand in private, You, are sitting close, holding my hand in the open and I wanted know the change.", replied Sofia.

"Tell me everything you have been doing and seeing, learning and thinking. I am all ears for you.", said Richard looking deeply into Sofia's eyes as she began to talk about all her topics.

Time flew by for the two and before they knew it, they were on the lane to Charlton in Somerset.

"Compared to the academy you must think my school simple.", commented Sofia.

"It is true we have very different topic but never think your school to be simple. We are a team. I do task you're not able and you do tasks I am not able. Together we make a formidable team. I will always be interested in you and respectful of what you do.", said Richard.

"I can't wait to be done with school and for Richard to graduate so we can be married.", thought Sofia as the carriage came to a stop at Charlton.

"Richard, Sofia, welcome home!", said Anne and Victoria outside and waving.

"Let's go in, we have an early supper laid out for us.", said Anne as they all walked in.

"Mother, I know we are not to ask but I could not help but see the new house. It looks magnificent. It is so exciting, I know when I say this I can speak for Richard as well, we are so excited and thankful to all of you for making this possible for us.", said Sofia with Richard's concurrence.

"Indeed, there has been a lot of progress to your future home. As you are excited, we are as well excited for you! During the break, we will talk with you about your wedding plans. Anne and I have made great progress with more to do and your input needed so we can proceed.

For now, enjoy supper. Let us have a quiet evening in, since traveling is tiring. You can be off to bed early and get some much-needed rest.", replied Victoria.

The next day started bight and early, "Mothers!", smiled Sofia.

"I will be done with school mid-February. The date I confirmed was the fifteenth of the month. All the extra work has paid off with an early finish. I will however go back for the graduation ceremony, with all of you!", said Sofia.

"Richard knows?", asked Victoria.

"Yes mother, and he will be at the academy until he graduates in May. I am grateful to be able to attend Richard's graduation, however sad Richard will not be able to attend my certificate presentation.", replied Sofia.

"We will endeavor to make this a very special event for you darling. I am sure Richard feels it, he is missing your moment.", said Victoria.

"He is, it is just not possible to get leave before academy graduation, as you can imagine.

"I am excited about the wedding plans and look forward to talking about it and answering any questions.", commented Sofia.

"Time is racing by and before we all know it the wedding will be weeks away. And here we are five months way.

"We do have some events planned during the break. We will have special suppers for Christmas eve and New Year's Eve, stay up after midnight New Year's Eve to see in the new year, we will have a few of the neighborhood to supper in between.

And spend time together, we miss you!", said Anne to Sofia, with Richard just now arriving having been up early and doing chores around the place with James.

"Richard, would you like some breakfast?", asked Anne.

"Yes, thank you mother. I am famished!", replied Richard dishing some eggs, and bacon, toast and biscuits then sitting next to Sofia who looked at his plate in wonder how he could eat so much.

"Richard, I received a note from the commandant of the academy will be arriving late tomorrow and staying overnight on his way to town. Would you assist me to assure he has all he wants?", said James.

"Yes, of course Father. It would be my pleasure. I had no idea he would be visiting.", replied Richard.

"He is an old friend. We went to the academy together and graduated in the same class.", replied James.

"Anne, we have to inform the kitchen since he will arrive here after supper most likely and will have a hot meal for him. And we will provide an apartment for the evening.", said James.

"Anne, James, if you will permit me, I will inform the kitchen and inform the house keeper an apartment will be needed for the visitor. James are there any special meal requirements I can assure?", asked Victoria.

"Thank you, Victoria. I will do this with you. Every day you are less and less a guest and more and more a sister in this household!", replied Anne smiling with Victoria and Sofia, leaving the men behind in comprehension.

The next evening, James and Richard stepped outside just before the carriage conveying academy commandant arrived so he could be greeted properly.

"Commandant, welcome to Charlton. You're very welcome here.", said James.

"Admiral, thank you for having me. I realize it was short notice so any accommodation is welcome.", said the commandant.

"I have supper standing by for you.", said James.
"Welcome commandant.", said Richard.

"Thank you, cadet Hawke.", replied the commandant.

"Father, I will have commandant's bags transferred to his apartment and assure his drivers and horses are put up for the evening and refreshed and ready for the travel to town tomorrow when the commandant is ready to take his leave.", said Richard very efficiently.

"Thank you, Son, this is much appreciated.

"Your son is doing very well at the academy as I am sure you know. Time flies and he will graduate in a matter of months. He has set the example to the underclassmen and they look up to him.

Remember in our day. You became that example. You upheld the Navy well in your day too.", commented the commandant.

"We upheld the Navy Sir! We upheld this, Navy.", replied Admiral James in a reminiscing tone.

"Too soon we will be gone and forgotten. The Navy is truly for the young and adventurous. It will be their tune and it will be gone that quickly from them as well.", said the commandant.

James sat with the academy commandant talking through naval affairs while he ate supper. Anne, Victoria and Sofia visited for a short while to pay respects but not to interfere. Richard returned after taking care of the carriage drivers and horses standing at the side ready to assist when needed.

"Thank you for this very lovely supper admiral. I will turn in since I am not so young and must pace myself. Perhaps, your cadet Hawke might guide me to my apartment?", asked the commandant. James turned to Richard and signaled to approach, "Richard would you guide the Commandant to his apartment and assure he has all he needs.", requested James.

"Yes, father it would be my pleasure.", replied Richard.

"Sir, if you would follow me.", said Richard.

"Goodnight Admiral.", said the commandant.

The next morning early, Richard having had breakfast was waiting outside the commandant's apartment so he could guide him to the dining room for breakfast. Richard had already assured the carriage drivers and horses were readied with their meals and tacking up the horses to the carriage so when the commandant wanted to leave there would be nothing to delay him.

Richard also was sure to have a packed lunch for the commandant and the drivers so to make the trip more pleasant.

"Good morning, Commandant. May I guide you to the dining room and breakfast?", asked Richard.

"That would be wonderful cadet, thank you.", replied the Commandant as Richard lead him to the dining room.

"Sir, may I have your luggage conveyed to the carriage so when you're ready to resume your trip there will be no delay. As well, we provided a breakfast to your drivers and assured the horses were well taken care of and refreshed for the ride to town.

I had a lunch packed for you and your drivers. The roads from here to town are smooth, the weather looks to be clear and calm. This way to the dining room Sir.", pointed Richard.

"Good morning, Commandant. Please be seated and have some breakfast with us.", said James.

"Good morning, Admiral, Lady Anne, Lady Victoria and Miss Alton. Wonderful to see you again.", said the Commandant.

"Did you sleep well Commandant?", asked James.

"Yes, I did, very well. Not my usually fits and starts only to get out of bed tried to begin the day's work. There is something to be said about a country home and the calm that comes with it.

After breakfast and time to refresh himself, the commandant was ready to leave, "Commandant, it was a pleasure to have you at Charlton. Please do stop by again. Perhaps for a longer period of time to enjoy the place and our countryside.", said James as the Commandant climbed aboard his carriage with Richard, Anne, Victoria and Sofia waving goodbye and saying safe trip.

"Sofia, the weather is cool today and if we layer and wear scarfs and gloves, we can take a walk. What say you?", asked Richard.

"Yes, let's do since I miss the out of doors. Can we visit our horses?", replied Sofia.

"Of course.", replied Richard.

Some days later and with Christmas only a few days away, it was snowing lightly these days and with more than six inches on the ground already no one could be found in the lanes.

"Today is a perfect day to go through all the wedding plans and answer any questions.", said Sofia to Anne and Victoria with Richard at her side.

"Indeed, I will get wedding notes and papers.", replied Victoria. That evening, after supper, "Victoria and Anne had made so much progress with the wedding plans. But for a few things yet to do, we are left with just showing up.", said Richard.

"When we went through ideas for the church, then the reception and ball, it's all so exciting. It was wonderful to see mother smile again and be full of life again.", replied Sofia.

"Yes, it is wonderful to see your mother's spirit return.", commented Richard.

"I will be done with school mid-February, as you know, and will help with the final wedding tasks, then take a trip back to Mayfair for certificate day, you know graduation. A week later we are all off to the to the academy and your graduation. These two years are coming to a close.", said Sofia.

"I wish I could attend your ceremony.", said Richard.

"It is not possible Richard. I will tell you all when we attend your graduation.", replied Sofia.

"I believe I made this observation previously, but I am glad for the advantage of living at Charlton. I can see you throughout the day, we don't have to send notes between estates, we can go to the out of doors with little delay, suppers together and conversation. Do you not see this too?", observed Richard.

"I do! I am grateful for being near you. When we are married I will not like being away from you. I have a three-year obligation to the navy and times when I will be at sea or at Portsmouth and after that I will devote myself to you, our children, our mothers and father.", said Richard happily.

With the New Year over, Sofia and Richard were off to school for the last time. Experienced now they knew exactly how to act with working hard, writing letters and demonstrating patience.

At the Alton Hawke Manor, "Anne, I am so very glad we selected the sentimental items of our family and removed them to be placed in this house. If we had not these would have been lost to some unknown new owner at Highbury not knowing any of the history.", said Victoria to Anne's acknowledgement.

"Victoria, I was thinking these set of pictures make sense hung in the upstairs passage. What do you think?", asked Anne.

"Actually, yes that makes perfect sense.", replied Victoria as Anne directed servants to do just that.

"These four chairs are part of the dining room set", commented Anne to a servant asking them to move the chairs to the dining room. "I am not sure what to make of this piece. Victoria is this a Highbury piece?", asked Anne.

"Yes, this piece would go well in a corner of the library or study. What do you think Anne?", asked Victoria.

"I think the library since the study will be too small for this piece.", replied Anne.

Victoria agreed asking one of the servants to have this piece removed to the library.

"We have made such good progress in the house. With a few more visits we can have the cleaners come to tidy this place from top to bottom in preparation for the newlyweds.

Dear Richard,

I this will be my last letter authored from Mayfair Manor since next week I will be done here and be collected by your father. When you write to me you will want to send your post to Charlton since that is where I will be. Waiting for you, hint, hint, hint, smiles.

Time is now flying. I cannot wait for the day when I will see you graduate. Please do not feel guilty in any way for not attending my certificate ceremony. A certificate for managing a house, socializing in society, dressing and walking pales in comparison to the Royal Navy graduation. All of my new skills will be employed well and to the benefit of our home but your endeavor is our focus dear.

I will join our mothers and help with the wedding planning and answer any questions on your behalf as best I can so when you graduate there is little left of the wedding tasks to be done.

I am so very proud of you Richard. For years now you have worked hard to make a name for yourself, to appoint yourself. You are about to succeed. I am ready to be your wife and live in our new home together.

Your loving promise,
Sofia",
xoxo

p.s.

I look forward to your notes to me. I live from one letter to the next. Write when you can.",

posted Sofia.

At Charlton, "James, next week you go out to collect Sofia for the last time from Mayfair Manor. Two and a half months later we go back to Mayfair for Sofia's certificate ceremony then leave for the Academy and Richard. We will need a place to stay since we arrive a few days ahead of schedule.", said Anne with Victoria listening intently.

"I can hardly wait. Sofia brings such color to the life around us. Don't you think?", asked James.

"Yes, she does. She is full of life. We were all this way in our prime.", replied Victoria to agreement.

The following week James collected Sofia from the Mayfair Manor school. Genni promised to write and they both promised to remain the best of friends and plan visits.

"Do you mind if I call you father since you will be in a matter of months, you treat me like a daughter now and I think it well past my father's passing?", asked Sofia of James.

"Indeed, it is true, I think of you as a daughter. I would take it as an honor you call me father. I do not replace your Edward but I will be as much of a father as it pleases you.", replied James earnestly.

"This is a bitter sweet moment for me with leaving Mayfair. I met wonderful girls I believe will be friends a life time and when I came all I wanted to do was to finish so I can be with my Richard. I am grateful to be done with the term and I know I have only a few months to a most wished for wedding. Life seems such a strange affair at times father.", said Sofia.
"From someone who has been on this road of life a little longer than you. Enjoy each moment, Love, bring grace, and uplift all those around you. When you awaken each day run into your moments. When the curtain closes you will be glad having enjoyed many moments.", said James.

"I look forward to Richards notes to me. I hope my posts to him comes in time to remind him I will be home and not Mayfair.", commented Sofia.

"I am certain it will Sofia. Richard and you have a special connection he knows where you are and you know his whereabouts as well.", said James, knowing Richard already posted at least three notes and a package to his Sofia, and they are all delivered and waiting for her to arrive at Charlton. Let this be the surprise Richard wants it to be for his beloved.

Arriving at Charlton, "Mothers, I missed you both and am glad to be back home. Thank you, father, for collecting me.", said Sofia, to Anne and Victoria's surprised and pleased she called James, father. It was a pleasant surprise.

After a late lunch they all settled in the drawing room to the latest news from Sofia of the last term at Mayfair.

"Sofia, you have some posts from Portsmouth.", said Victoria, carrying at least three notes and a package from Richard.

"He did not forget me. He remembered me.", whispered Sofia with tears in his eyes.

"Mother, Richard did not forget me.", said Sofia.

"No, he never forgets you dear.", replied Victoria, with Sofia engrossed in the contents of the notes.

"What did Richard post in the box?", asked Victoria.

"He put a scented Handkerchief, a beautiful locket and a note to me.", replied Sofia.

"How is our Richard?", asked Anne.

"He is well and sends his love! I will bring these notes and presents to my room.

I will skip supper tonight. It was a long day of good byes and the travel has me fatigued. Good night to all of you.", replied Sofia.

"We have to do all we can to assure their special day a special day.", said Anne, to James and Victoria agreeing.

The next day's saw Sofia writing a number of notes to her Richard, chatting with Anne and Victoria about the wedding plans. Anne and Victoria even took Sofia for a tour of the new Estate house.

"Mother, the house is magnificent. I can hardly wait to live here with Richard, raise our children, be near to you and visit as I hope you will visit us. Suppers and more. What do you think?", asked Sofia very excitedly.

"Yes, to all you have said!", replied Anne and Victoria together.

With just one month to the academy graduation, "I am thinking this is the perfect time to visit Portsmouth and a certain cadet. Would any one like to accompany me?", asked James to all the girls saying when can we go. We will be ready!

With this settled, the next day everyone was packed and ready and waiting for the carriage to Portsmouth.

Arriving in Portsmouth, James arranged a very nice house with a late lunch ready and waiting.

"We will visit the academy this afternoon. I sent a note to the commandant yesterday and believe our visit to be welcomed. Let us have lunch first and refresh ourselves.

At the academy, the senior cadet attended Admiral James. Admiral James was announced and Richard was excused to visit with family for the evening.

"Father, mothers, Sofia, it is a wonderful surprise to see all of you. I did not expect you since I am less than a month from graduation. I am very glad and pleased to see you all. How was your trip here? How are each of you. Sofia, you look beautiful!", said Richard.

"We had the weather on our side, smooth roads all the way through and no carriage problems to worry us, so we had a merry time here." replied James.

"Ladies, I see you have many questions and comments. Please feel free to make yourselves comfortable.

"How are you, Richard?", asked Anne.

"I am quite well. I am in the senior class so I get some privilege but also some responsibility with following all the rules and being an example to the underclassmen. If one were to make a mistake here the consequences would be severe. I try not to think in a month I will graduate. It is a day at a time in this place.", replied Richard.

"Son, I get very good comments from the commandant. Many are impressed with your work effort and willingness to help any and do. Those you help in your class and those underclassmen will all graduate someday and remember you and when you need support or allies, they will naturally go to your side.", said James.

"Richard, this may be unimportant in the moment but I have been helping with the wedding plans. I have toured our future house at the Alton Hawke Manor and it is wonderful. Willow, Fire and Chesnutt are all doing very well.", said Sofia.

"Nothing you say is unimportant Sofia. I am surrounded with navy affairs day and night. To hear about your day. What you have done. What you're thinking about, is refreshing to me. I remember there is more to life than ships and seas and navigation. So, please do not think your notes to me are ever unimportant.", said Richard sincerely.

"What are your school activities like these last days?", asked James.

"It is study, study, study since we are preparing for final examinations both written, verbal and practical. All of you coming here to visit me is such a welcomed break. Thank you for coming.

As well, I asked the cadet leader if I may supper with you and it was approved for six to eight. I will have two hours of leave and then must return at eight. May I supper with you?", asked Richard.

"Indeed, what a surprise. Yes! Let us organize to collect you. We can leave now. Have supper prepared. I can come and collect you and when we arrive supper will be on the table and we can enjoy as much of your time as possible.", replied James organizing the party.

"We will leave you for now. Come collect you here at six and take you to our house.", said Anne with Victoria and Sofia in agreement.

A couple of hours later, James was with the carriage at the academy at the appointed place and time to collect Richard to find him waiting, "Hi Richard, come! Supper is ready and the girls are anxious to see you.", said James as the carriage began to drive away from the academy and toward their let house.

"Hello Richard, supper is on the table and as soon as we all assemble, we can go in and eat and we want to hear all your latest news and stories.", said Victoria.

Supper was pleasant with much in the way of amiable conversation much missed due to time at the academy. Everyone conversed as if we were never parted to begin with.

"In three weeks and a few days, we return for your graduation. Our wedding is six weeks aways. We are no longer years away, or months away rather we are weeks away.", said Sofia to Richards concurrence.

"I cannot wait to see you at Charlton and marry you.", said Richard discreetly.

The evening ended ever so quickly, have a safe ride home tomorrow. I look forward to seeing you at graduation. "Come a day or so earlier and get some rest, the academy ceremonies will last the day.

On the day, you can come for me and attend various smaller ceremonies and traditions. The graduation ceremonies will be on the pitch and you will be seated to witness this moment.", said Richard upon leaving for the academy.

Back at Charlton, and only a week before the academy graduation, "We will leave today for Mayfair Manor since Sofia's certificate ceremony is Tuesday, then the academy graduation is Friday and we will endeavor to be at Portsmouth Wednesday, we will have a few days to rest and organize ourselves for Richard's ceremony. Hard to imagine we have two children graduating this week. Next week we take on the idea of marriage only weeks away.", said James.

"We have waited years for this moment. Let us have fun with this. Enjoy, each child and each moment.", replied Anne.

"Our carriage is here, we should make a start to be ready to board our ride.", said Victoria as everyone organized themselves for the trip.

"This is a fateful few days. I have dreamed of this moment for what seems many years and now we have arrived in the moment. When next we return to Charlton, we will bring our Richard home and we attend to the biggest of all ceremonies and a life together.", said Sofia to James, Anne and Victoria listening intently, understanding the full meaning but not saying anything to break the moment.

"We are so very proud of you and Richard. You both have worked hard, made your way to this moment and are determined as ever to make a life together. We all here wish you happy.

For the moment let us focus on you and your ceremony. Since this is your time. When we are in Portsmouth, we can enjoy our Richard and his time.", said Victoria.

The morning of the certificate ceremony at Mayfair. It was raining quite hard and the outdoor plans were moved to the indoors plans. Many families were there to witness their daughter's completion of the schooling at Mayfair and would enter society proper.

Sofia, arrived at Mayfair to Genni waiting for her. "I really missed you friend. How have you been Sofia?", asked Genni. I have been good, busy with wedding plans, helping with preparing for Richard and our new home, of course wedding plans. We visited Richard at the academy and now we are here for the ceremony and tomorrow we are off to Portsmouth for Richards academy graduation in a few days.

We are back to Charlton and fully focused on our wedding. It has been busy and fast these last weeks.", said Sofia.

"Well, let us make this ceremony fun and easy. Come with me and I will get us organized. Have no worries.", said Genni to many saying hello Sofia, and wishing her many congratulations.

"We will stay in touch and may I come visit you as often as I like?", asked Genni.

"Of course, Genni you may and I will be glad of it.", said Sofia.

The certificate ceremony went flawless with many speeches on the value of manner and the rules of society being upheld and the running of the household. Whereupon each graduate's name was called to receive a certificate of completion of the program. Afterward there was a reception where instructors and graduates mingled and each thanked each other and said their goodbye's.

"We are so proud of you Sofia. Many congratulations and wishing you happy. Your father is smiling so broadly and wishing you happy as well.", said Victoria.

"We are having a wonderful supper in your honor tonight. Sofia, I have a note here from Richard to you.", said Anne with James at her side handing her Richards note.

"My dear Sofia;

Although I am not there physically, I am with you in spirit. No matter what I am doing at the academy In this moment I am thinking and hoping for you, sending you happy and many congratulations!

I hope ceremony was grand and your day is beautiful. We all surround you with love.

Many Congratulations!

Love to you my dearest,

Richard,
xoxo, wrote Richard to Sofia.

Sofia had tears in her eyes, a bit choked up, and using her handkerchief, "These are tears of happiness I assure you.", said Sofia.

"I should have known Richard would be thinking of me and even prepared a note. What a man I have. I am so very grateful for his attentions.", said Sofia.

A day later, James, Victoria and Sofia were off to Portsmouth. "I can hardly breathe wanting to see my Richard. I have waiting so long.", said Sofia as Victoria and Anne each on either side took her hands to try and calm her knowing she would burst otherwise.

"Take a deep breath child, not long now. See we arrive at our house here in Portsmouth and tomorrow we will see Richard. Let us have supper, a quiet evening because the next days are quite busy.", said Anne calming Sofia's nerves.

The next morning, Portsmouth was buzzing with excitement for the Naval Academy graduation. Richard would be waiting for us at nine this morning to follow him from one ceremony to the next and at two this afternoon for the graduation ceremony.

Traveling to the academy the town was abuzz with excitement for the new graduates and wishing all of them congratulations. The weather was sunny and warm. Prince Lionel and Princess Jenni were in town representing the Crown and all manner of admiral showing off their rank and surrounding the graduates.

"Sir, sir, are you the Admiral Sir James Hawke sir?", asked a Royal Currier.

"Yes, I am. State your business.", replied Sir James.

"Have a message for you and was asked to return your response.", said the currier.

"We have an invitation for the Majesties the Prince and Princess to supper tonight at the royal residence.", said Richard to Anne, Victoria and Sofia.

Please relay our compliments to His and Her Royal Highnesses and our grateful acceptance of their invitation and look forward to seeing them, our party is the size of five.", said James to the currier as he confirmed the message he will deliver.

Richard approached dressed in his graduate uniform, all white, with rank and naval insignia in gold, white gloves covering his hands. "Hello everyone, thank you for coming. I hope your trip was uneventful. Would you all walk with me.", said Richard, as he greeted each of his party warmly.

"Sofia, how was your ceremony? Tell me about it.", asked Richard as Sofia described her day and special supper.
"That is wonderful to hear Sofia.", replied Richard.

"Richard, thank you for your note. I was surprised and touched by your words of encouragement.", said Sofia squeezing Richard's hand.

Richard led his family through a number of traditions and small naval ceremonies until the noon hour where they had lunch together.

"I will have to leave you now and prepare for the graduation ceremony. I can walk you to your seats where you may view the graduation and will come to you after the events and we are dismissed.", said Richard shaking James's hand, hugging Victoria and Anne, waiting to last to hug and kiss Sofia's hand.

"See all of you soon.", said Richard walking away.

"He seems so much taller, walks so much straighter and talks so much more directly.", said Sofia in awe of her man.

The graduation was completed in what seemed a moment and Richard was at their side, now an officer in her majesty's navy. With many congratulations, and much commotion the crowds parted to His and Her majesty's approaching.

All bowing to His and Her majesty's as they passed, "Congratulations Midshipman Hawke, you look very dashing in your naval uniform. I can hardly believe the time that has passed to now see you as a naval officer. You are an image of your father. Many congratulations Sir.", said Prince Lionel with Princess Jenni's concurrence at his side.

"Thank you, Your Majesties.", replied Richard.

"We will see you tonight for a special reception and supper party at the residence?", asked Prince Lionel.
"Yes Your Majesties, and with pleasure. Thank you for the invitation.", replied Sir James.

The next morning, "The evening with the majesties was a wonderful cap to the day. I cannot believe we are off to Charlton and after years of anticipation can focus on my wedding.", said Sofia to her mother.

"Just when it seemed always in the distance, we are weeks away from the ceremony. I am so excited for you and Richard. I am glad the wedding tasks are completed. We will review all of it this week and complete anything we missed or may need more consideration. Have no worries for your special day.", replied Victoria.

CHAPTER 11

With Child and Orders to go to Sea

With the wedding less than a week away James asked Anne and Victoria to organize a special supper for Sofia and Richard.

"That is a wonderful idea, James. Shall we do this tonight?", asked Anne.

"Yes, it is time we as a family send them off in style.", replied James to Anne and Victoria's agreement.

Sofia and Richard were out riding together. Catching up on all the latest since they were away from each other.

As supper approached James went into the study to find an important box with some very special contents. He carried the box to the dining table and placed it to the right of where he was sitting.

As Anne and Victoria and Sofia and Richard entered and sat James made an announcement before the meal.

"This is a special meal tonight. We wanted to honor Sofia and Richard only days now to being married and beginning their life together as husband and wife.

Sofia, you have been a daughter to us for a long time and we are glad of it. Richard, you are the best of sons. The best of men.

We hope and pray for your happiness and look forward to being in your life as much as you will let us. We believe in you and we know you will bring us many wonderful surprises. Maybe some grand children soon enough.", said James, smiling.

"Let's eat!", said James to laughter and Sofia and Richard looking at each other in that way to understand a meaning and yet never speaking a word.

"As each person finished their meal James stood up, "Thank you all for tonight, but it is not over. I have a commission I must discharge to you all. Edward made a request of me touching each of you here.", said James to Victoria and Sofia now intently listening to each word, wondering what would be next.

"Edward asked me to deliver a number of items to each of you just before the wedding and to hold these in trust through these last years he has been gone from us. I will be fateful to his request and complete this task now.", said James opening the wooden box to his right.

First a quick prayer, Heavenly Father, as your humble servants, we ask you grant us a great favor. This favor is that Edward can know I deliver his gifts now with his love to each sitting here. As well we send our love and best to him. Amen.

I have letters from Edward for each of you. Edward mentioned to me these words. I will read from my note of that time since I did not want to forget his true meaning. There will also be a private sealed letter just for your eyes.

He said, 'You have become my family. I thought it was just Victoria and Sofia, but quickly realized I had to expand, I had to grow. I have to be more than I thought I was. I will be thinking of all of you. Sofia, Richard I will be there on your special day. Smiling, hoping, sending all my love.
Your private notes, from Edwards hands.

Dearest Victoria, I can never thank you enough for teaching me to love, to be a man, to be a father, to just be aware of all the blessings. I love you and will be thinking of you always. Please accept this letter from me to you. In the beginning it was you and I, and in the end, you are in my heart of hearts. Always and forever light, love and hope to me.

My Darling Sofia, I loved you before you were born, and when you were born, I knew I would never get over you. You take my breath away when I even think of you. I can see your mother and I in you, your grandmother and grandfather in such natural ways. I wished so much to be in person at your wedding but my body will fail me. I will be there in spirit, at your side, watching every moment, wishing you happy and believing in every good thing for you. I love you darling Sofia know this! Live life, love and laugh as much as you can and have a bushel of children, this will be a blessing and keep you busy!

Richard, by the time you would read my letter to you, you would have graduated the academy and must now be tall, and straight, powerful and true, an image of your father. What a young man you must be. I can only see it in my mind but I know it to be true. Both families knew early of your special connection to Sofia and Sofia to you.. Something very rare and special. Please don't be too hard on yourself. Protect our dear Sofia, protect the children to come, guide them as the leader to light, love and hope all their lives. Give them strength and courage, patience and kindness. I give you all my blessings to marry my dear Sofia. I hope and pray for you. If you ever need advice, find a quiet corner and talk with me I will always be listening, I will always be there. Thank you for respecting me and granting me great recognition even when I may not have deserved it. I hope for your success in the navy. Be safe, follow your father's lead, stand on his shoulders. He is the best of examples. If it is in you, please protect Victoria as well since I am away from her now. God's speed son.

Dear Lady Anne, I quickly knew I was out of my depth with you. Your ideas, your words, your manner is so endearing I felt immediately we could have been brother and sister. You taught me it is not a title that makes one but rather it is one's person that makes one special. You taught me to uplift those around me. To grant grace and live without fear of losing or winning. You became a sister to my Victoria and did the same for me. How can I ever thank you dear lady. Sending you every blessing and hoping for your happiness.

Admiral Sir James Hawke, I thought you to be a savage that we would have to endure in the neighborhood. I was so wrong. It was I that was the savage. We, had the titles, of being a member of society, aristocracy but we played at society and you were the real society. Instead of pointing out this fact you invited us in, you encouraged us, you helped to be better people by your example. Thank you, Sir. I will always remember the experiences at the royal court and you and Anne guiding us in such rarified air. Sir, thank you for discharging this difficult task. Thank you for protecting my Victoria and Sofia. If I face God, I will remember you and your dear family to Him.

James, would you hand each there my personal note as a final task, thank you Sir James. With this I will be in each of your hearts.", read James handing out each sealed note from Edward for them personally with a deep reverence.

Sofia and Victoria were silent and with tears pouring down their cheeks. Anne's eyes were a pools as well. Richard, like his father clung to some strength and maintained their composure but inside they knew this moment to be very special and to be remembered a lifetime.

For some time no one moved from the dinner table. Each read the personal note from Edward and wanting just one more page of words to read but grateful for what Edward wrote to them. One could hear Sofia whisper, "Yes father, I will."

Richard declared, after reading his note, "Sofia, I will love you and protect you all the days of my life. Victoria, I will protect you all of your days. Have not worries.", said Richard sincerely.

Finally, and not too soon everyone stood and went to the drawing room but even there talking and conversation was hard to find. It seems all felt Edward's closeness and sent him as much love as they could thanking him for what he left them.

James, stood and asked if he might say a pray to end the evening. Everyone agreed needing this grace. "Heavenly Father, thank you for the time we had with Edward. He granted each of us such a grace this evening we can hardly speak of it. Heavenly Father, if Edward does not know it, please Father send him all our love and admiration for the gift he left us. Tell him how much we are grateful for this grace given. Amen.", prayed James.

The next day seemed lighter. Victoria, Anne and Sofia continued to work on the wedding details, her dress, the flowers, travel to the church and back, music, food and so much more. The business and the feeling of Edward watching over them made tasks so much more special.

Richard and James worked on the wedding as well with vendors and staff to deal with, and what to wear. "Richard, will you wear your dress uniform or a more civilian clothing?", asked James.

"Father, you wore your uniform at your wedding, so I will wear mine. The maid is pressing them so I look sharp for all. If this is acceptable.", said Richard.

"This is very acceptable.", replied James

On the day of the wedding, it was sunny and warm, Victoria asked the groomer if he would move Fire, Willow and Chesnutt to the front lawn of the house to graze, so when Sofia leaves for the Church and returns with Richard, they may see their three favorite horses.

Genni arrived the night before the wedding and stayed at Charlton, several of the girls from the neighborhood came early to help Sofia on this special of days too.

"Sofia, you are so beautiful he will die to marry you.

Remember you promised to introduce me to some of the nice boys in the neighborhood.", said Genni.

"Thank you Genni and I will. I will point out several at the ball. And Richard has four academy graduates coming to the wedding and mentioned they are good men. All of them from titled families.", replied Sofia as Victoria and Anne arrived to say it was time to leave for the church with two carriages standing by for them.

As if on cue, Fire, Willow and Chesnutt grazed close to the carriage so to be seen, "How wonderful my three girls are seeing us off.", said Sofia smiling.

At boarding the carriages, the bridal party was off to the church. Arriving Sofia's bridal attendants came out to assure when the bride exited the carriage there were no mishaps. It all went smoothly. At the entrance James was waiting for Sofia. Edwards request was, James was to walk Sofia down the aisle in his stead. When the Victoria and the attendants were seated the church doors opened for Sofia and James to enter. The organ was playing a hymn and everyone stood admiring the bride, discreetly wishing her happy with many whispers of happiness. The ceremony seemed to fly by with the vows and exchanging of rings, the blessings and then the walk to the registry and their signatures to witnesses. The church empty now save, for the vicar, Richard and Sofia, and Victoria, Anne and James.

A carriage waited to transport them to the ball at Charlton.

"The wedding, the weather, all of those that attended the ceremony, the church and even Fire, Willow and Chesnutt seemed so special today. The most special of all was seeing you waiting for me at the altar in all that white uniform, handsome and tall Richard. I could hardly wait to say I do and put your ring on, and sign the register.", said Sofia to Richards embrace and help into the carriage.

"I will quickly get use to you sitting close to me, holding my hand and more. We are one now and belong to each other.", said Sofia as Richard move in and kissed her gently.

The carriage arrived at Charlton, where the couple was led to their rooms to refresh themselves. Sofia and Richard stood to a knock at the door where the butler lead them to the reception where they were announced to all the guests and many congratulations and wishes of happy.

Richard and Sofia assured Genni and her school friends had plenty of dance offers and opportunities to know the eligible men in the place. "Perhaps one might catch their eye.", thought Sofia.

After much dancing, socializing food food, and amiable conversations, in the early morning, just after dawn a carriage pulled up, loading some bags, and waiting for the happy couple to board, many at the reception congregated to see the Sofia and Richard off for a week-long bridal tour of northern England and some of Scotland.

James, Anne and Victoria came out to the carriage and then Sofia and Richard walked to the carriage saying goodbye to all and boarded the carriage for their tour.

"See all of you in seven days. Thank you for everything, bye bye!", said Richard and Sofia as the carriage surged forward and was gone in a moment.

"What a wonderful wedding and reception. Edward would have been proud. Thank you, James, thank you, Anne.", said Victoria satisfied all that could have been done was done to make this day a very special moment.

"You're very welcome Victoria.", replied Anne.

"I felt Edward was with us in spirit.", thought Victoria walking along with Anne and James.

With more than a week gone by the wedding carriage returned carrying a very refreshed Sofia and Richard. Sofia had very rosy cheeked and Richard sporting a smile. James, Anne and Victoria came out of the house to greet them.

"Hello, everyone. Wonderful to see you. Glad to be back.", said Sofia embracing her mother then Anne, as Richard did the same and shook his father's hand.

"Welcome back son.", said James.

"We should all board the carriage and take the short ride to your new estate.", said Victoria, as they all did just that.

"Sofia, you have the advantage of me, having been in our new home. It will all be new to me.", said Richard.

"I am so excited for you to see the place, Richard. It is wonderful. I worked with our mothers to assure we have a familiar and comfortable place for you.", replied Sofia as the carriage slowed at the front portal of the Manor.

As they all entered, "Welcome to your home.", said Victoria at Anne's prompting.

"I am speechless. It is so beautiful. I see so many hints of Charlton and Highbury at every turn. This place feels quite comfortable truly. Thank you, Anne, Victoria, James and let me never forget Edward.", said Richard.

"We have toured the study, library, the drawing room, dining room, kitchens and the washrooms on this first floor, shall we visit the upper floor?", asked Sofia.

"Yes, please.", replied Richard.

"This is our bedchamber.", said Sofia.

"The pictures on the wall, the furniture and the carpets are from our two favorites houses.", said Richard touring more rooms.

"We will leave you dears and go back to Charlton house. Would you like to supper with us tomorrow night?", asked Anne.

"Yes, that would be lovely. Thank you for escorting us here. It is all so lovely really.", said Sofia.

"Good night and God bless lovelies. See you tomorrow!", said Victoria as they left in the carriage with Sofia and Richard waving.

"I am exhausted, shall we go to bed to recover for tomorrow's activities.", asked Sofia.

"Let's do.", replied Richard.

The next morning, "Richard are you awake?", whispered Sofia.

"Yes, I am. I was just laying here enjoying the quiet and knowing how much I appreciate being near you. I will always appreciate you.", said Richard.

"I can look out the window, to the commons. We do not have to ride to the commons, we live right here. Can you see? Our mothers and fathers have been so thoughtful.", said Sofia.

"Yes, now that you mention it. Let's have some breakfast and walk around the property so I can see all the out of doors points of the estate.", said Richard.

"That is a wonderful idea. I will walk with you.", replied Sofia.

"You will let me know if you get tired? I have noticed with the bridal tour, returning, the new house, and staying up all night seems to have caught up with you. There are times when you are just exhausted. So, on our walk we do not have to see everything and spend hours doing it. Rather let's make this a leisurely walk in the out of doors and fresh air.", said Richard walking slowly to accommodate Sofia.

"We were gifted such a beautiful estate by both families. At supper tonight let us please say thank you again and how much we appreciate this gift.", said Sofia.

"Indeed, I agree. We are very fortunate to have such loving families.", said Richard holding Sofia's curved arm.

"We should turn around for the house, I sense a slower step and perhaps some tiredness in you. Will you take a mid-morning siesta? And, let us not stay up all night and get some sleep this evening.", commented Richard.
Late afternoon and after Sofia's early afternoon siesta, "Hi dear, are you rested, feeling better?", asked Richard.

"Much better.", replied Sofia.

"I received a letter from the admiralty today. They are orders to report to the HMS Ajax and Captain Pierce for duty. This duration will be six months we are to sail to a duty station at the India colony. Because, of the unusual length of this commission we will have three-months shore leave at our return. I am to report in two weeks.", said Richard in a navy tone he rarely demonstrated.

"Such a short time then. We will make the best of each day.", said Sofia.

At supper, at Charlton, Richard mentioned the orders received and the details.

"I knew Pierce before he was a captain. He is a fine officer and will teach you much. If he remembers me to you, please give him my compliments.", said James.

"Sofia, while Richard is at sea would you mind it much if you stayed here at Charlton so you are not alone in the house and I am not up all night worrying about you. Please consider this request?", asked Victoria in such a touching way.

"I think this to be a brilliant idea, Sofia. I would not be worried about you as well if you were here at Charlton surrounded by family.", said Richard discreetly.

"I will stay at Charlton when Richard leaves for Portsmouth and the sea, until his return. Thank you for the offer and considerations. I am grateful and appreciative.", said Sofia.

"We wanted to say again how fortunate we are to have such a family to give us the Alton Hawke Manor. It is magnificent. Today, we took a small tour and everything seems so grand, so well thought out. We have more to see, not yet explored. But so far, we are left breathless at your careful planning for our sake. Thank you.", said Richard.

"You're very welcome dears. We planned many surprises in the out of doors, since we know of your love for the open skies and green grasses. I am surprised you have not looked through the whole of the out of doors of the estate as yet?" mentioned Victoria.

"It is my fault mother since I am exceptionally tired since returning from the bridal tour. I fear it is late nights, excitement and not resting properly. I have started to take mid-morning siestas to help me catch up and not staying up all night.", said Sofia with Anne and Victoria eyeing each other, as women can do, in that way as to say something important but without a word.

With supper finished and Sofia and Richard gone to their house, Anne and Victoria talked about Sofia's tiredness.

"Victoria did you get the meaning of my look when Sofia talked about her unusual tiredness and the taking of Siestas.", said Anne.

"Do you think the cause of her tiredness is she is with child?", asked Victoria.

"In a short while, after Richard has gone to sea, we will know.", said Anne.

"Indeed, we will. Perhaps, while she is at the manor, we should find excuses to visit her. We can assure she is watched with someone about for ready help if needed. What do you think?", asked Victoria.
"I think this a good idea. Who should go first?", responded Anne.

"I will tomorrow.", said Victoria.

Over the next days it became clear to Victoria and Anne there was something to Sofia's tiredness. Sofia seemed healthy, she had a good appetite save in the early morning where she felt queasy, she had regular restful siestas at mid-morning. Anne and Victoria assured she did not over work herself.

"Darling, supper is organized for tonight with our Charlton family.", said Sofia.

"Thank you dear. I am so reassured that with you residing at Charlton while I am at sea all will be well here in Somerset. There will be little connection to me until I return to Portsmouth. The three-year obligation in the navy starts in earnest. We will be strong and bear it. I will appoint myself with distinction and in my heart be focused on you. I will write to you but will have little means to post them, I will deliver them when I return.", said Richard.

"Thank you darling, I will be praying for you every day, hoping for your safe return. Please be careful in these foreign lands.", responded Sofia.

"I will be careful. Shall we get ready for our mothers and father.", said Richard to Sofia's concurrence.

At supper everyone wished Richard a safe voyage and quick return, knowing this will be a six month wait for all of them. It would be spring before he is returned.

"What time do you leave for Portsmouth?", asked Anne wanting to hear it again.

"At nine in the morning mother.", replied Richard.

"Son, the three-year obligation will be inconvenient but once completed you may retire and not have to leave Somerset unless it pleases you. In the meantime, while you are gone to sea I will care for the family, rest assured.", said James with a half father and half admiral tone.

"Thank you, father", replied Richard.

The next morning, the whole family waved Richard goodbye as his carriage to Portsmouth lurched forward in the direction of the port city. Upon arrival, Richard reported to captain Pierce and the HMS Ajax.

"Midshipman Hawke, your father has meant a great deal to me in my career in the navy.", said captain Pierce.

"The admiral sends his compliments captain.", replied Richard in a formal tone.

"It seems I need a second in command. I make you my number two. Let's us go through your responsibilities. Like your father did for me, I will guide you if you are willing.", said captain Pierce.

"I am very willing sir. It would be an honor Sir.", replied Richard.

Some week later, second in command became routine for Richard. He executed the captain's orders. While treating the men with respect and the crew returned the respect by following orders quickly and efficiently.

At Charlton, "Sofia the physician will be here this afternoon to look you over. This tiredness seems to be persistent. You do have very rosy cheeks so we hope for nothing serious here. Your health is paramount to your family.", said Victoria with Anne at her side.

"Of course, mother's", said Sofia smiling as both mothers knew her meaning.

"That is a stack of letters Sofia?", inquired Anne.

"Richard wrote me a letter, in advance, for every two weeks he is gone knowing he would not be able to post them to me, so here I am found out with my secret box with a pile of letters I pretend to receive every two weeks. I made a promise to him concerning you and our James. This is to give you a letter once a month that he has written in advance. To keep my promise to my Richard I will be in possession of the letters until the appointed time of the month and then personally deliver one to each of you.

This month Anne receives the letter next month Mum, then you, the following month James and again until the six months are exhausted.", said Sofia sighing and handing Anne the first of six letters.

"Richard is so thoughtful I cannot imagine I raised him at times.", replied Anne.

"Indeed, you did raise him and such a wonderful son and husband.", said Sofia.

At the arrival of the physician and several hours later, the physician and Sofia, entered the drawing room. The physician confirmed what Victoria and Anne suspected. "Sofia is with child. I can confirm twins in this case. Sofia is quite healthy but moderation is the key here.", said the physician.

"Sofia will need much in the way of a calm life. Good healthy food, sunshine and fresh air.", prescribed the physician. Riding horses is out of the question and would jeopardize the health and safety of the mother and the child.

"Congratulations Sofia. We are so excited for you. Have no worries.", related James, Victoria and Anne.

"If only Richard could know this glorious news but it will wait until he is back home.

It was a month into the voyage to India that the admiralty was informed of the sudden and untimely passing of Captain Pierce. Richard assumed command of the HMS Ajax until decisions were made and communicated to him from the admiralty.

It was two months, where the HMS Ajax was on station at Bombay port India, since the initial communication to the admiralty of captain Pierce's passing when promotion letters and orders from the Admiralty arrived.

October 22, 1809

Acting Captain Hawke,

HMS Ajax,

I am pleased to inform you that, following careful consideration of your service and merit, and with the approval of Vice Admiral Winston, you are hereby promoted to the substantive rank of Captain in His Majesty's Royal Navy, effective of the date of receipt of this letter or October 22, in the year of His Majesty 1809.

Your dedication, leadership and exemplary service as Acting Captain of HMS Ajax have not gone unnoticed. The successful navigation of a passing captain and maintaining the ship and crew to continue the ordered mission had demonstrated your skill, professionalism and commitment to the service of the Crown.

In accordance with the regulations of the Royal Navy, you are to assume the full duties and responsibilities commensurate with the rank of Captain, including the command of the HMS

Ajax.

This promotion is a testament to your accomplishments and the trust placed in your abilities. May you continue to serve with honor, and may this promotion mark the beginning of a distinguished chapter in your naval career.

You should by now have read the mission orders the HMS Ajax is under for this voyage. Execute the mission as ordered and return to port at the appointed date captain. Upon return prepare for the routine debrief of the mission.

Wishing you fair winds and following seas.

Yours faithfully,

Vice Admiral Winston, Fleet Operations

A copy of this letter was sent to Admiral Hawke as a courtesy.

"Dear, it seems our son has been promoted from acting captain to full captain of the HMS Ajax.", said James proudly.

"You have always said he is charmed. I guess this proves it. We must inform Sofia and Victoria.", said Anne.

"Inform us of what Anne.", inquired Sofia with Victoria at her side.

"Richard has been promoted to the rank of Captain and given command of the HMS Ajax. You see captain Pierce unexpectedly passed during the voyage to Bombay Port India, he was laid to rest at sea.Richard became acting captain. October twenty second Richard received a promotion and orders that raised him from acting captain to permanent captain.

Vice Admiral Winston sent me a note stating he has been brilliant and earned the rank. He has arrived at Bombay Port India and is executing the mission with excellence.", said James in that navy way of speaking.

"I hardly know what to say. I am so proud of my Richard. He said he would work hard for me, for this family, for you father (James). He is a man of his word.", said Sofia, and missing him.

"We are here for you Sofia. You are not alone. In four months, Richard returns. After that since he has taken the longest and most difficult of assignments, he will have one to three month voyages the remainder of his obligation. For now, we are focused on you and the babies.", said Anne.

It was a month later a worn and slightly torn dispatch arrived for Sofia. "I have a post from Richard!", everyone gathered around.

Reading the letter,

"My darling Sofia;

As you may know by the time you receive this letter, I have been promoted to Captain of the HMS Ajax. Captain Pierce, passed away suddenly. He was beloved. He remembered me from my father and assigned me second in command so he could teach me well. He remembered father helped him when he was a young midshipman. I am sorry to say his lessons only lasted a month before his passing.

Thanks to father's careful navy education I felt comfortable taking command of the Ajax while the admiralty made decisions. I was surprised to receive promotion letters and orders. I am one of the youngest captains. I know understand what father meant when he said 'always protect your ship and crew.'.

I am safely at Bombay port India performing the mission specified in the orders that bring us to this foreign land.

I have some uncomfortable news for you. I will be a month later to England than expected. Instead of, Portsmouth at the end of March, I will port at the beginning of May. I have received order to sail to China a month before I was to leave for Portsmouth. I will assist the Crown with an issue around the British East India Company.

My darling, would you read this one line to father, he will know my meaning:

'Helmsman, steer for open water! Trim the sails to catch the wind!' Make full sail! Let her feel the wind! Give way together!

Steady as she goes!'

You taught me well father, thank you.

The good news is when we do port England. I we will have a full three months leave. I look forward to April, May and June in your arms dear love. Let us go out of doors for the whole summer and ride horses, talk till the sun goes down, picnic, have suppers with the whole family, drink in every moment I pray.

Dear, if you are still finding the tiredness when I left please see the physicians for a cure. Eat well, get plenty of sunshine and air.

I have to go. Remember to read my letters every two weeks. I promise to think of you each day and I send you, my love.

Yours warmly,

Richard Hawke, Captain in His Majesty's Navy, commander of the HMS Ajax
oxox

"I ...", said Sofia unable to speak further with tears running down her cheeks and holding Richard's letter close to her breast, Victoria and Anne wrapped around her consoling her.

Aboard the Ajax, in the first week of February now, "Captain, we are prepared to set sail for China as ordered.", said his number two, midshipmen.

Richard barked out the orders to set sail, "All hands make ready to sail. Call to quarters! Hands to weigh anchor! Man, the capstan and the windlass! Heave away, hands! Heave away! Hands aloft! Set the topsails! Man, the yards!

Helmsman, steer for open water! Trim the sails to catch the wind! Make full sail! Let her feel the wind! Give way together! Steady as she goes! Set a course for China."

At Charlton, "Not long now dear.", said Victoria to Sofia.

"You and the babies are doing so well. Richard is three months from port, spring is on the way. All I see are blue sky's now.", said Anne.

"You are having twins. Look at the size of your belly.", said Victoria smiling with all of them laughing at the lot of a woman to bare the children.

"I have to wonder, as I think you may as well, what sex they will be. It is not possible to know in this case.", said Anne.

"Well, we know it could be all boys, all girls or a boy and a girl. God knows. Sometimes, I think they are girls when they are quiet. When they are kicking up a storm, I think they must be boys. So, I have no idea to guide me.", said Sofia.

On the Ajax, "Captain, we will make port at Canton by tomorrow if the winds remain steady.", said his midshipmen.

"We do not know the state of affairs there. The marines will protect the ship and crew while in port with twenty-four-hour guards and no shore leave. We will anchor in the harbor with room to withdraw quickly if needed. We will be on alert and ready to defend the ship and crew. Your primary orders are to protect this ship and her crew while I am on shore.. Is that understood. If I am on shore and an incident occurs, I will protect myself. Wait till you find it safe to come into the port. Assure the crew have their firearms at their side. While in the port, no foreign ships are to sail near the Ajax. Any ship approaching are to be warned to turn away or be destroyed. If a ship does not turn away sink it.

I will leave for the East India Company offices with marines guarding me there and back. I then will better understand what is needed. Ask the marine commander to come see me", ordered Captain Hawke.

"Understood captain.", said the midshipmen.

"Captain Hawke. I am lieutenant Smith, marine commander. You asked to see me captain."

"Yes, when we port at Canton, I will need a detachment of marines to escort me to the East India Company offices in town and back to the Ajax when meetings have concluded. I do not know the state of affairs except that there could be some instabilities.

You and the rest of your marine detachment are to protect this ship and crew. While I am on shore be vigilant. The ship will anchor in the harbor and not at dock. There should be no ships sailing near the Ajax including small ships. Assure the crew is active at assisting the marines to protect this vessel. There will be twenty-four-hour guard at every siting of the ship. If you determine the harbor is not safe order the Ajax to with draw until it is safe. If I am on shore your marines and I will protect ourselves awaiting the Ajax return to the harbor. Protect the ship and the crew.", said the captain Hawke to the acknowledging marine commander.

"We will have twenty-four-hour guards and looking for small ships and large that come near the Ajax. We will fire warnings first then protect the vessel where a threat is not deterred.", replied the marine commander.

The next day, at port in the harbor, the Ajax laid anchored in a watchful position. Captain Hawke and a marine detachment were already at the East India Company offices discussing the need for the Ajax's assistance.

"Captain Hawke, thank you for coming to our assistance in this matter. There are important shipments arriving via road from various parts of China in the next days. There will be shipments to be stowed away to several ships that will need an escort through the South China Seas to the open pacific where you will return and ready for the next group of vessels. There will be three groups of ships with these special shipments. The shipments are so important they are directly tied to the King himself, who will be watching the progress of these ships.", said the East India Company representative.

"Sir is it possible to prepare all three groups of ships as one and we will escort these ships directly to port at England? I see they are to land at Portsmouth. Would that make your worries less?"

"I think this a very good idea. Since we have the ships here at the harbor. Two of the shipments can be stowed and by then in just one day we should receive the last shipment via land road to then stow to the final ships. Would we be able to anchor the two initial groups of ships in the outer harbor near the Ajax for protection and when the final group of ships have their cargo you can all set sail for England?", asked the East India Company representative.

"I believe this to be a very good idea. Do you need marines on the dock while the ships are stowing cargo and before they leave dock?", asked Captain Hawke.

"We have good security at the dock so I do not foresee issues. Would it be acceptable to have two marine guards per ship once you make sail for England?", asked the East India Company representative.

"I believe this to be acceptable. Would you make provisions for food and lodging on each ship for the marine guards? Sir, I will return to the Ajax, so I will not see much in the way of dock activity and will depend on you to assure the ships are properly secured and readied for the voyage. I would like as well to have two marines on the dock to monitor and report to me and my security detail that all is well and the ships are secure while at dock and stowing cargo bound for the Crown.", said Captain Hawke.

I am expecting two groups of ships to be readied and sent to the outer harbor near the Ajax for protection. I expect tomorrow early afternoon the last group of ships to be sailing to the Ajax at after noon time.

"This is very acceptable. May I say, thank you captain Hawke for your timely considerations in this case. I will report to my superiors and that of the Admiralty of your attentiveness and extra care to this mission.", said the East India Company representative.

"I will leave you Sir. God save the King.", said Captain Hawke.

On board the Ajax, Richard relayed the mission details to his security commander and ship officers. Later that day two groups of ships approached the Ajax communicating they are part of the special group. Two marine guards were dispatched to each ship to billet there for the voyage and assure all was in order.

A day later, the final group of ships approached and when ready they set sail per orders of the Ajax in close formation and under the protection of His Majesty's Navy, and a full week earlier than expected.

At Charlton, Sofia now seven months with child. She is showing and although a brave face she is quite uncomfortable. The physician says all is well and she is quite healthy.

"Good morning, Sofia, how are you today?", asked Victoria

"As well as to be expected considering my condition and being so for seven months now. I understand what you endured to carry me!", replied Sofia smiling.
"James, there is a marine currier at the door for you.", announced one of the servants.

Reading the note,

> Dear Father;
>
> The HMS Ajax is at Port in Portsmouth a week early having completed my missions. I was wondering if you might come and collect me. If possible, would you do so discreetly so I may be a surprise to our woman folk upon returning to Charlton.
>
> I am at the admiralty debriefing on the missions to India and Canton China.
>
> I look forward to seeing you.
>
> Yours truly,
>
> Richard Hawke, Captain in His Majesty's Navy, commander HMS Ajax

"Dear, I have received a note from Portsmouth and will travel there for a day, maybe two. This is very short notice but necessary. I asked the marine to stay here on property for the day to two I am gone and to be available to assist the women while I am away. He is provisioned and organized.", said James to Anne with Victoria and Sofia listening.

"When do you leave?", asked Anne.

"Within the hour. It's ten in the morning, I should be in Portsmouth by one and the half hour in the afternoon. If all goes well, I could be back this early evening however it may be tomorrow mid-morning. I sent a note to the physician he will stay at the house while I am away. You will all be safe while I am gone.", said James.

"Dear, be safe and I want you back quickly please. I should like to meet this marine so I know him and where to find him should I need him.", mentioned Anne.

"Sir your carriage is here and ready to convey you to Portsmouth.", said one of the servants.

"I have a packed lunch since we will not stop along the way.", said James about to board the carriage.

"Safe travels.", said Sofia with Victoria at her side.

"Come back to us dear.", said Anne as the carriage sped away.

"I wonder what was so important the navy sent a currier and a note that asked that James leave for Portsmouth directly.", thought Anne worried for just a moment.

With the physician in residence, he performed a thorough check of Sofia and the baby's health.

"You and the babies are in perfect health, Sofia. Continue to moderate. At this stage it will be uncomfortable. The size of your belly says it all. I am here if you need me. Have no worries.", reported the physician to Sofia, Victoria and Anne.

In Portsmouth, James headed right for the Admiralty offices.

"Admiral Hawke, wonderful to see you. I just saw another Hawke, just there in that office.", said the Vice Admiral Winston smiling broadly.

"Son, son....", said James.

"Captain Hawke, your debrief is complete. Congratulations on successfully completing your first voyage sir. You will receive order to report and take command of HMS Ajax three months from now. In the meantime, the Ajax is being refitted and repaired. You are dismissed Sir.", said the attending officer.

"Father, thank you for coming to collect me. Can we stop by the Ajax so I can get my bags and some items from India and China.", said Richard shaking his father's hands.

"Of course, son. Would you like to stay the night or leave today?", asked James.

"I would prefer we leave today since the girls are missing you and we can chat along the way to make the time go quickly. If this is acceptable.", mentioned Richard.

"Yes, very acceptable. Let us go to the Ajax.", said James.

"It has been a few years since I was on a warship. The Ajax and crew are very impressive. Your marines are very intimidating. This ship is ready to fight.", commented James to Richard.

"If it comes to that. You taught me well father. You would say, 'Don't look for a fight but if it comes, always come with overwhelming force.' The Ajax is an instrument of overwhelming force. The idea is do not try it you will lose. As you know admiral.", said Richard in that captain's manner.

While on board everyone addressed him as captain and or stood aside when he walked along the deck. One could easily see a great respect in his person and as captain. With the bags secured on the carriage they headed in the direction of Somerset.

Son, I was saddened to hear of Pierce's sudden passing. He was a good man, a good officer and someone I had the privilege to assist once upon a time.", said James.

"He remembered you to me. He needed a second and assigned me that duty with the idea of teaching me. I found him to be brilliant. Of the type of men, you described to me. At his passing I assumed interim captain never expecting considerations beyond. When I received promotion letters and order at port Bombay it was a surprise and great weight.

Because of the excellent education you imparted to me, I felt comfortable taking command. I completed two challenging missions successfully to start. Your three lessons have served me well, Protect the ship, Protect the crew and Protect the Navy.", said Richard.

"Sofia, Victoria and your mother are doing quite well. They will be very surprised! Remember, secrets go both ways son. Thank you for your letters. Your mother and I, and Victoria lived on them once a month. We are grateful for your thoughtfulness."

"I am so very proud of you.

You seem a bit fatigued Son. Rest I will watch over you. Have no worries.", said James as Richard took the deepest of breaths and fell fast asleep.

CHAPTER 12

Captain Hawke and Son's

"Son, son awake.....we are home.", said James as Richard stirred.

With the carriage coming to a stop first James stepped out and then Richard. James could see the tiredness of the long voyage and the weight of the captain rank.

"Come son let us find our woman folk and give them a surprise and get to know them again.", said James.

"I have waited seven long months for this moment. It is hard to believe I am here. Let me straighten my uniform. I do not want to appear disheveled but somewhat in order for my wife.", said Richard entering the house and walking to the dining room where the girls were having supper.

"Hello, everyone. I am back from Portsmouth.", said James to Anne greeting him.

"Who is this...you bring?", asked Anne almost and only for a moment not recognizing her Richard.

Sofia, recognizing her husband sat frozen with tears in her eyes unable to move and wanting to throw herself at her husband.

"Darling! Are you with child! How long! How are you? I did not mean to startle you? Are you Ok?", said Richard.

"I am so surprised I can hardly move, hoping I am not in a dream.", said Sofia with Richard now by her side.

"Yes, seven months, healthy, it's ok and yes.", responded Sofia.

Richard, confused looked at Sofia, "Yes, I am with child, your children, it's been seven months, I and the babies are healthy, you startled me but I am ok.", stated Sofia.

"Babies?", said Richard.

"Yes dear, we are having twins.", said Sofia to a startled Richard.

"Darling, you seem shattered from the long voyage and trip her from Portsmouth. Let me get you settled in a bed and tomorrow we can all catch up. What do you say?", asked Sofia.

"This is a good plan. I am cream crackered.", said Richard.

"Goodnight, everyone...", said Richard in a tired voice as Sofia led him to their apartment.

"Glad you are back Richard.", said Victoria.

Later that evening, "Richard looks so different and so much the same. Do you know what I mean?", said Anne.

"Indeed, he had to mature quickly. He advanced to the rank of captain, assumed command of the HMS Ajax a powerful warship, completed two complicated missions successfully and brought his ship and crew home safely. Took on the great responsibilities in protecting his ship and crew. These are heavy burdens.

The mission to China was to escort three groups of ships out of the south China seas and away from pirates, instead the Ajax escorted them back to England safely. Little does he know the cargo is a rare medicine that will save thousands of lives in the north of England, southern Scotland and eastern Ireland where an infection is spreading rapidly and is killing many men, women and children. It can now be stopped.

The medicine is on its way to those regions as we speak. He is not aware but His Highness's name was on this shipment since he gave his word of a safe arrival and date. Our captain delivered the medicine safely and beat the date by a week. This has solidified the Admiralties decision to raise him to the rank of captain and quieted those that might have questioned the decision thinking it was done because of his father, the retired admiral.

Now that he is visible to the King, they dare not say a word. As well, his escort of the groups to Portsmouth demonstrated his dedication to the Crowns business. Those with question respect that example.", said James.

I will spend time with him during his time off daily to go through the captaincy protocols and procedures, responsibilities, ship preparedness, crew preparedness, mission preparedness and conflict preparedness. An hour a day, early, should give him knowledge and ability and not interfere in his rest period. The goal would be he goes back, in three months, ready for command at that level.

The next morning, "Would you consider staying here at Charlton?", asked Victoria of Sofia and Richard, at breakfast with James, and Anne listening for the answer.

"I think this a good idea, since Sofia is getting close and I am not sure what to do when the time comes. If this is acceptable to you Sofia?", asked Richard.

"This is very acceptable since I am use to being here and being spoiled with two mothers and a father looking over to me to assure my health.", said Sofia.

"Good, then that is settled.", replied Victoria.

"Father, I reviewed your plan for naval studies with you while I am here. I cannot thank you enough for this special education and special time with you. I now understand the gravity of what you teach me and am eager to learn from experience. When I became interim captain of the Ajax I used everything you taught me. At the time I did not know what was to come and without your time and patience with me I could not have survived the weight.

When do we start.", asked Richard.

"Tomorrow morning if you're willing.", said James.

"Yes, I am very willing father. One hour at the early morning is a good time since this leaves the rest of the day for Sofia and being with all of you.", replied Richard.

After breakfast, "Richard let us sit together. I have so much to talk about as I am sure you.", said Sofia.

"Let's", followed Richard.

"Sofia, I had no idea you were with child. I was so surprised and so pleased. I am pleased! I count my blessings that you and the babies are healthy and you have all of us by your side.", said Richard.

"There was no way to contact you while you were at sea, as you know. Our mothers wrapped around me. Father became a protector and assured we were all safe here at Charlton. Even when he went to Portsmouth just now to collect you, he arranged for the physician to be near and the marine currier became our guard while he was gone.

So, you see, even though I could not communicate the news to you, I and your babies were well cared for and safe.

In less than two months we will be parents of two very healthy children.", said Sofia.

"I left a midshipman, returned a captain and am about to have children! What a fate.", replied Richard.

"How are our four-legged friends?", asked Richard.

"They are very well. I have not been able to ride as you can imagine. But When I could go to the stables I did see them healthy and happy, groomed them and gave them a treat or two. They are on a regular exercise routine and are let out to the pasture regularly.

However, it is true they miss the both of us and our adventures on the estate. I think late summer we may resume when I am not with child and quite healed from the birth.", mentioned Sofia.

Talking through many topics the hours flew by, to suddenly being late afternoon. At entering the drawing room, they found James, Anne and Victoria chatting away.

"We were wondering when the two of you would come up for air. We did not want to intrude since you both have much to talk about and there is the missing each other as well.", said Victoria smiling.

"Yes, it is true. We talked and listened and talked and listened some more. I am so grateful you are home Richard. How I missed you I cannot tell you. As well I am grateful to have two mothers wrapped around me and a father who protects us well.", replied Sofia.

"I am grateful for all of you as a family and as well protecting my Sofia.", said Richard sincerely.

"Sir, we have some unexpected guest at the door.", said one of the servants.

"Who might they be?", asked James.

"Very high personages Sir.", replied the servant.

"Send them straight through.", said James as the women and men organized themselves.

"Admiral Hawke, Captain Hawke, Ladies, please excuse us for coming unannounced. We are here at the request of His Highness.

"Richard Hawke, would you stand please, Sir,

> Captain Hawke, Commander HMS Ajax, of His Majesty's Royal Navy,
>
> at the King's request and with the concurrence of the Admiralty, of His Majesty's Royal Navy,
>
> you have been awarded the peerage title of Richard Hawke Baronet, and that of your wife the Lady Sofia Hawke, be titled Baroness.
>
> Under normal circumstances you would be awarded this title by the King himself, at the palace in town but considering your wife's condition we did not think travel to town be prudent.
> The Queen sends her complements to Baroness Lady Sofia and the coming birth of the twins. "I look forward to your visit to court lady Sofia and a story or two about the twins.", the Queen.
>
> Awarded title details, are as follows,

You were ordered to extend a long tour even longer, the mission was to sail to Canton, China and assist the Crowns servants at the East India Company.

His Majesty has taken special note of the Canton mission, where the protection of the Crown was extended through the instrument of the HMS Ajax, through her captain Hawke, servant of the Crown.

This mission was to protect and escort three groups of ships and their cargo from port to the open pacific. You went beyond that and escorted these important ships and cargo safely to Portsmouth and ahead of schedule.

The cargo was especially important in that it is a rare medicine only found in China.

In the northern regions of this United Kingdom, parts of Ireland and Scotland an infection is raging. Many, men, women and children, have already succumbed to the infection and it is spreading unabated. This medicine will halt the spread and cure those ill.

The medicine is on the way to the affected regions of the UK, Scotland and Ireland.

His Majesty, sends his personal thanks and congratulations.

"When your children are born and you captain and the Baroness lady Sofia are able, please be welcomed to court at any time. Many here want to know you as they know your father the Admiral and great servant of the Crown. You are both very wanted here. We look forward to meeting you. the King. P.S. bring your father and his beautiful wife and the lady Victoria."

Read the Royal Currier and the Kings representative handing Richard signed peerage papers making these peerage titles official.

"Like I have said many times, 'charmed'.", said Anne discreetly to James. James arranged for the royal currier and royal representative to a meal, while the stable grooms attended the horses. When all were refreshed the royal party left for town satisfied they served the King well.

Life finally settled down into a routine of early morning naval lessons with father, everyone caring for Sofia as she is getting noticeably closer to birthing. Everyone could see Sofia, no matter the level of discomfort, made time for Richard, was patient with him and encouraged him in all he was doing.

On an early spring like day Sofia's water broke. Victoria and Anne were instantly by her side. James made sure the physician was living on the estate so they would have easy access to him and he was summoned to the house.

James and Richard remained close to the drawing room knowing this could be hours of long vigil. All Richard wanted was a healthy mother and two healthy children. All the signs leading to today were this would be a difficult but normal birthing.

"What do I do father?", asked Richard.

"Indeed, what. Well, I brought some naval lessons to make the time pass and keep you calm since I remember your birth and all the worries, I had endured waiting for the call to see my wife and child.", said James.

Good Idea father let us talk about the navy since there is not much I can do in the upper stairs.

Some hours later, Anne walked into the drawing room to say, "You have two healthy sons and a healthy but very tired mother. You may see her and your children but for a short time since she and the children must rest.", directed Anne leading Richard and James up the stairs and to her rooms.

"Oh Sofia, how are you? This is so amazing. I can hardly believe we have two healthy sons.", said Richard.

"May I present your son's Richard jr. and Alexander.", said Sofia.

"I can see your dad in Alexander. Richard jr. is much like me.", replied Richard.

"I see you are exhausted. I will leave you to rest dear. Well done, rest now.", said Richard.

"Stay with me till I fall asleep Richard.", asked Sofia, taking Richard's hand in hers.

Later in the evening, the house was quiet and everyone asleep save for Richard. He was sitting in the study near the fire place to a soft fire. Every so often he would go upstairs to his apartment and watch his Sofia and now Richard Jr. and Alexander.
"Hi son, I thought someone was up. Since, I am up may I sit with you?", asked James.

"Of course, father."

"A captain gets use too little to no sleep at times.", said James.

"This is very true, even when one may have the opportunity to sleep it may escape him.", replied Richard.

"Is there something on your mind?", asked James.

"I have children. I am a father. I am captain of one of the most powerful warships in the royal navy. The King and Queen of England know my name and now I am a Baronet.

"Yes, very heady events.", replied James.

I go up regularly to Sofia and the children. I remember the moment I met Sofia at the commons as if it was yesterday. And today, we are married and have two children. All I can do is try to be the best of men for them.", said Richard.

"It is natural to not feel so confident especially where children are concerned. You will be a good and steady father. Initially you have your navy obligation but that will be over in two years and some months now, then you can be here full time.

Children need a mother and father that are present and interested. You and Sofia are.", replied James.

"Sofia and the boys are asleep. The image of the three of them is such, it will be forever burned in my minds eye. It will only last a moment.", said Richard.

"Enjoy each moment. Live for them. In the end they are all that matter.", responded James.

"It is dawn already. We should see about breakfast especially for the girls, they had a very long and trying day yesterday. Today will not be much different with two boys wanting attention every moment.

I will bring Sofia breakfast to start her day.", said Richard.

Congratulations son, you are a husband and father, and a good one at that.", replied James to Richard's surprise.

With breakfast on a tray and he in his apartment, "Good morning, dear.", whispered Richard.

"Darling...", replied Sofia.

"I brought you breakfast.", said Richard.

"Thank you, I am sure I am very disheveled.", responded Sofia.

"You look absolutely beautiful dear.

I am hoping a good breakfast, before your time is taken up with the twins, this will replenish your energies.", said Richard.

"You're very thoughtful dear. While I eat and the twins are asleep let's chat. I feel I went into a long tunnel and only now are emerging to a very different life that will include our children.

Tell me, how are you? Where did you sleep? I reached for you to find you were not in bed. Did you sleep?", asked Sofia.

"I am well. No, I did not sleep much. I was up with father. We talked about fatherhood and our women folk.", replied Richard.

"You must take care of yourself. I am sorry to say I am focused on our children. For the foreseeable future they will take up my time, as you can imagine. Even now, in this early hour they are just stirring and will need feeding and changing.", said Sofia suddenly a new mother.

"I will take care. I know there is not much for me to do, but to stay out of the way. Nevertheless, I am here when you need me and will do what you need of me.", mentioned Richard.

James, Anne and Victoria were just finishing breakfast. "Where is Richard?", asked Anne.

"He brought breakfast to Sofia this morning. They are probably chatting while they can and before the twins need feeding and changing.", said James.

"A good man that Richard.", remarked Victoria.

At mid-morning a naval messenger arrived, "Sir, I have a message from the Admiralty for Captain Hawke."

"Richard there is a naval messenger arrived with admiralty dispatches for you. He is waiting in the drawing room.", said Victoria interrupting a longer than normal naval lesson.

"Captain Hawke?", asked the naval messenger.

"Yes, sir.", replied Richard.

"Sir, I was asked to convey this package to you. You are to report to the Admiralty in two days for mission briefings. Expect at least two days in Portsmouth before you may return here Sir.", communicated the messenger.

"With your leave Sir, I will return to Portsmouth.", said the naval messenger as he withdrew when given leave, on to his horse and in a flash was on his way.

"Son, are you able to share your message?", asked James.

"It is a special mission. I will report to the admiralty in two days for two days of mission briefings. Pirates disrupting trade and business in the west indies. The Ajax will be dispatched to assess the threat, assure open trade routes and put an end to it.

With most of the fleet engaged in the east indies I will be the only war ship in the west indies to manage the pirate problem.", related Richard."

"I will tell Sofia in a while since she is busy with the twins and we will need quiet to talk about this leaving for Portsmouth for a couple of days. I have yet to understand the sail date and the length of the voyage. Of course, mission planning will take up time.

Shall we discuss the mission once I have all the mission details?", asked Richard.

"Indeed yes, I would give any advice and put to use my experience and what to expect. There will be much in the way of planning to do.

I will relay your orders to mother and Victoria, while you focus on Sofia.", said James.

"This sounds like a plan.", said Richard.

"Sofia, how are you and the babies?", asked Richard.

"Good, they are active and healthy, growing like weeds. I am regaining my strength steadily.", smiled Sofia.
"Dear, I will travel to Portsmouth in two days for mission briefings that will last two to three days. I will not be leaving before planned but this mission will require planning since the Ajax will be dispatched to the West Indies. It seems there is a problem with Pirates and the jeopardy of open trade routes.", said Richard.

"Does this mean fighting and dying?", asked Sofia bluntly.

"Yes, however, if I plan this correctly the dying will be that of the pirates. I will piece a good plan together with father and assure we are ready. This will be as much as possible a routine sea operation.

"Richard, I don't mean to interrupt you and Sofia, however you have a package, just arrived, from the admiralty that you must provide your signature of receipt.", said Victoria.

"I will be back directly.", said Richard

"Father, I just received the mission briefing documents. They contain the mission objectives, operational details, intelligence, rules of engagement, communications protocols and more.

I will finish my chat with Sofia. Then, shall we lunch and delve into this material?", asked Richard.

"Indeed yes. Leave these materials to me. I will lay them out in the study for our inspection and planning. After lunch we will begin.", replied James.

"Dear, pardon my delay. I secured fathers to review and assist me with mission planning. So, you see I will have the best plan to assure a successful mission, and the safe return of the Ajax and her crew.", said Richard reassuringly.

"It is a women's lot to worry about their men. You will be far from home and waring. I will be hoping and praying for your safe return each day.", said Sofia being strong.

"Dearest, in those moments when I am far away and you ask yourself, 'What should I do?', just Love, Love is all there is, Love is everything that is. With that, there will be no distance between your heart and mine. I will know you are thinking of me and send you all my love and strength in return. Sounds singular, I know, but in the heat one realizes quickly what is important.

We talked about these times, they will require strength, courage and great patience.

I lunch with father and then go through the mission briefing materials and begin to sketch a plan. Shall we spend time together later?", asked Richard.

"Yes, darling", replied Sofia as the twins began to rustle wanting food and changing.

At lunch, "Son, I took a preliminary look at the briefing materials and find several points of planning. With the documents arriving today, I anticipate the admiralty is wanting your ideas in a plan presented to them detailing how the pirates will be dispatched when you arrive at the admiralty.

If we are done with lunch let's get to work.

"The operational details are minimal at best, and the first point for planning. There is no mention for resupply, since you will essentially be at sea for three months. You cannot port without significant threat to the vessel and crew. So, let us talk about resupply plan.

Since intelligence estimates a significant pirate fleet of twenty or more ships I expect, sea battles, some damage to the Ajax which means a plan for on station-at sea repairs. This has never been attempted, medical aid, admiralty dispatches to and from, perhaps the use of the resupply vessels being fitted for some types of at sea repairs.

There will be medical needs of the crew and the supply vessel could provide for this as well.

And you may consider using the resupply ships to deliver messages to the admiralty and to have them deliver messages from the admiralty.

My understanding is the Ajax has been refitted and repaired.

There must be provision for at least two marine units. I would recommend the light infantry units since they are very highly trained in shot and close fighting. You and the crew would be focused on disabling pirate ships and crew, while the marines would fight the hand-to-hand battles that may arise. Pirate's like to board ships and fight hand to hand; they would take over cannon duties as well since they know very well how to disable ships.

An advantage of the Ajax is the guns are more powerful, longer range and can be aimed. As well, the Ajax is very fast, very maneuverable given a highly trained navigator and crew.

Pirates, have a unique pattern to fighting..... Ah, let's start with planning the resupply. Locations change and are pre-determined with irregular locations and dates so it will be impossible for enemy to anticipate.", said James to Richard astonished at his brilliance in naval affairs.

Crew Training with Navigation, Gun crews and aiming and shooting, marine sharp shooting, owning the winds, the sea currents, keeping your distance and more.
This will take patience, and remembering to protect your ship and crew. Learn from the pirates you encounter. How do they fight? When do they fight? Pirate tactics and strategies. How well are enemy crews trained and act in concert. Do you see what I am saying.

A good approach may be to disable their ships at distance keeping the Ajax and crews save. Then give them the choice to surrender or be destroyed.

After two days and long hours in the study planning, both men emerged with an initial draft of the mission plan with some details yet to discuss and document.

"I am ready for the admiralty father. Although there is more to hammer the base plan is here. Tomorrow, I will leave for Portsmouth ready for the mission briefings thanks in no small part to your assistance. I will secure ship upgrades as suggested. Start crew training and exercises, secure two marine units from your suggested marine division talking with marine commanders and discuss refitting supply vessels for medical as well as light vessel repairs", said Richard.

"It seems you have much of the plan in hand son. All the best in Portsmouth and at your briefings. I look forward to great reports.", replied James.

"Sofia, James, Anne and Victoria saw Richard off watching the carriage leave for Portsmouth.

"It will be two to three days we will be without our Richard.", thought Sofia.

At Portsmouth, at the Admiralty offices, "The plan seems brilliant Captain Hawke. We have never provisioned supply vessels to handle medical treatment or at sea vessel repairs. And to use the resupply ship to deliver messages to and from the admiralty, that will give us a link we have never had before, just brilliant.

This seems so common since the way you designed it I wonder why we have not thought of this before. I suppose you will request several vessels be refitted for this purpose. The admiralty will be in support of this plan and assure this be done directly and to your specifications. Have you engaged marine division commanders yet for the two units you would like to have assigned the Ajax and this mission?", ask Vice Admiral Winston.

"Not as yet Sir. After this briefing I will attend a scheduled meeting at marine division headquarters and make this request. With your permission Sir.", replied Captain Hawke.

"You will be escorted by two Vice Admirals to Division since we must assure your success in having the marine units assigned this mission Captain.

Before we conclude this meeting, we have a special guest who asked to lend his weight to the proceeding.

I believe you know His Royal Majesty Prince Lionel.", said the Vice Admiral as all stood.

Captain Hawke, how is your father, your mother, your wife and the twins!", smiled the prince.

"A pleasure to see you, Your Highness. Everyone is doing very well.", replied Richard.

"Would you please give all of them my compliments. And that we miss all of you at court. Perhaps you might come soon.

In regards, to my visit here. This pirate concern in the west indies has caught the attention of the Crown. You and the Ajax are being dispatched at the request of my father himself.", said the prince.

"Understood Your Majesty", replied Captain Hawke.

"Your Highness, we reviewed the plans for the mission. They are excellent and we believe them to be sufficient to dispatch the savages.", said one the admiralty.

"Well then, God's speed, Captain Hawke. After the mission we will want to see you at court.", replied the prince as one of his advisers reminded him of his schedule and he left the meeting room to his next appointment.

At the third day at Portsmouth and everything on his planning list checked off, and with the permission of the Admiralty, Richard returned to the Charlton. With less than three weeks before he sails to the west indies Richard refined the mission plans with his father, would take trips to Portsmouth to assure the Ajax, crew training and provisioning for the marine units, supply and progress briefing show steady gain to the plan goals.

With only one day to leaving for Portsmouth and sailing for the West Indies, Richard spent all his time with Sofia and the family. At supper everyone wished Richard every success, to be careful, protect the ship and her crew and to come home safe.

"Have confidence, the plan is strong. Father and I have been through it many times to find and fix any weaknesses. I have implemented all the elements needed. All that is left is to sail to the Indies and dispatch the pirates and that is about to happen.

Of course, we will miss each other and worry. This cannot be helped. In three months, the Ajax will be back in Portsmouth with a successful mission completed. I will not over extend the Ajax and crew to unnecessary danger when a bit of patience is what is needed. Father, thank you for all your advice and experience in helping me formulate a plan. This has been invaluable. The plan is strong and will assure mission success.

After supper, "Sofia, I will miss you. Here are some letters I wrote in advance while I am at sea. I hope this will be enough for you. I expect you will have your hands full with the twins. They will have grown quite a lot while I am gone. You will take care of yourself and our children. I will look forward to many stories of good things while I was gone away.", said Richard.

"Thank you for the letters, dear. And yes, I look forward to your return. The twins will keep me busy but I will be thinking of you day and night.", said Sofia.

"I leave at dawn, so don't get up. I will awaken you just before and quietly say good bye. Shall we go to bed.", said Richard as he and Sofia put down their heads to rest.

In what seemed a moment, Richard said his fair well to Sofia, the twins and was off to Portsmouth.

In Portsmouth, Richard worked his crew through the final preparations to ready the Ajax to sail.

"Will you be ready to sail Friday morning?", Captain Hawke asked each officer. All was on schedule or ahead and nothing seems to be a hindrance to meeting the planned sail date.

Walk with me, I want to tour the ship and see the crew.

On the way, the marines were given leave to train on deck. The crew knowing the importance of their training did all they could to work around these men. The Ajax gun crews practiced loading, aiming and firing, while the navigation teams practice maneuvering quickly and efficiently to orders. They began to show adeptness in understanding where the sea current were, the winds and how to use all of this to maneuver the ship to advantage.

It was expected within a few days of reaching station just outside of Puerto Rican waters, they will meet the first supply ship and resupply all their stocks in preparation for the pirate fleet they will encounter. And as planned the supply ship met the Ajax at the designated coordinates and was given new coordinates and date for the next resupply.

The Ajax entered Puerto Rican waters and made itself visible and not menacing so as to lure the pirates into a false sense of confidence.

"Captain, we have spotted ten ships heading out to sea from port San Juan. They are confirmed to be pirate vessels, at coordinate latitude 18.46655 degrees north and Longitude 66.1057 degrees West. Shall we take a heading to intercept and engage?", asked the Exec.

"Yes, notify the crew to battle stations, set course to intercept, and prepare to engage the ten-ship pirate fleet. Gain favorable position. Gun crews to the ready. Marines protect the Ajax from any boarding attempts. As soon as possible and maintaining our distance advantage let us disable each ship in turn move as quickly as possible through their fleet.

I will walk around and inspect gun crews and marine units.

"Be ready, trust your training and do your duty. All will go our way. Disable these ships. I will protect the Ajax and crew.", said Captain Hawke to his crew giving them confidence.

Captain Hawke back at the command deck, "Navigation, move into position catch the winds to the north. Exec, the pirate ships seem to be positioned as a long string and by twos. Gun crews at the port and starboard ready for continuous fire, on my orders.

Fire, Fire! Marines fire on their crews at will. Navigation all possible speed through this course.", ordered Captain Hawke.

Each pair of ships reached were disable and heavily damaged. At pirate ships seven and eight under heavy attack and being disabled the two final pirate ships broke off to escape.

The Ajax did not pursue.

"Marines to board and clear those ships of pirates put them on row boat and set them in the direction of San Juan. When all ships are emptied of pirates seize all treasure found. Send two midshipmen to report the weapons found, stocks of ammunition and general condition of the ships then sink them.

Keep one ship to hold the treasure and sail that ship to a safe part of the seas since we cannot weight the Ajax down and slow ourselves.

After most of the day all but one ship was sunk and one ship was kept to hold all treasure found.

"Exec, what is the damage to the Ajax.", asked Captain Hawke.

"Sir, minor damage. We did have a failure with one of our cannons on the starboard side. The maintenance team is now determining the problem and during the battle the gun crew spread out and assisted the other crews. We have several crew injuries. They are being given medical treatment.", reported the Exec.

Exec, move us out of these waters and to a safe distance. We can expect now a surprise attack with multiple ships, they will want to bloody our noises. Let us not give them the chance. Marine, commander let us have twenty-four guard looking for small ship and ship at sea. Let us stay out of fog so we can see.

Maintain our small ship observation for the larger pirate fleet. Exec prepare for the next battle giving rotating groups of crew's rest before they are put back to the task. Keep the Ajax moving in a southerly direction", ordered Captain Hawke.

The next day, "Sir, six confirmed pirate ship are making way to our position. They are several hours from sighting.", reported the Exec.

"The surprise attack is upon us. This will be their best ships and fighters. We will inform crew let us go to battle station. However, let us seem to be surprised. Do we know the six-ship formation?", asked Captain Hawke.

"The are spread out but this may not be a final formation Sir.", responded the Exec.

"Do we have all cannon?", asked Captain Hawke.

"Yes Sir, and test fired for assurance.", responded the Exec.

"Marines are we ready for this next battle?", asked Captain Hawke.

"Yes, Sir.", replied the Marine commander.

"I will do a quick walk about to see the crew and marines. Exec assure we have the wind and position when we come upon the pirates. Men, these pirates are the hardened members. They will not run from a fight. Today is the day to use all your training. Trust each other and trust command. This is the group of ships we must destroy.

Gun crews, every shot counts, disable then destroy these ships.

Marines, identify and kill every one giving orders on board those ships.", commanded Captain Hawke.

"Your, walk about before a fight to the crew and marines give them great confidence Sir.", said the Exec.

"Sir, the pirate ships are just in sight. See, just there.", said the navigator.

"Steady as she goes. Give not reaction at this time to being spotted. Marines be prepared to protect this ship and crew.

They will try to get close in to the Ajax with the intent to board and fight hand to hand.

They will not board and we will destroy these ships using our distance advantage and knowledge of the seas and winds.

Navigation, keep us at distance give us position. We have bigger, more powerful and longer-range guns. Let us fire on them until all that is left is kindling wood floating on the sea.", said Captain Hawke.

In range of cannon, the Ajax turned into the wind and at speed fired what seemed continuously disabling each ship they fell upon. The marines bared down and aimed their rifles at all those that barked orders on the pirate ships taking them down, seriously limiting the ability of those crews to know what to do.

As the Ajax kept its distance and used the warship's ability to navigate quickly this gave the gun crews another run at the six vessels disabling all of the six and forcing the crews to abandon ship, as the pirate ships one by one sink in the seas.

The Ajax kept its distance for the sinking ships. "Captain, shall we strafe the seas with fire and kill as many pirates as possible?", asked the Exec.

"That will not be necessary, many will perish on the way to shore and those that make it will leave a tale of fear and not to oppose the Royal Navy else die in the attempt.

"Exec, it looks like we sustained some damages to the Ajax, as well have several injured crew. Set a course to our next resupply coordinates and get out of the sight of the pirates for the moment.", said Captain Hawke.

Captain Hawke, talking with the marine commanders asked for continuous guards and some spy ships sent out to find the rest of the pirate fleet and report back.

A few days later the supply ship was spotted. At resupply, medical treatment and repairs to the Ajax were undertaken. The supply ship departed with mission statuses from Captain Hawke and some injured crew unable to resume stations.

Admiralty,

We had successfully prosecuted pirates thus far in two battles with the twenty-five-vessel strong pirate fleet. We have destroyed a total of fourteen ships as of this dispatch..

The Ajax sustained some damage and we made repairs at the last resupply. We as well sustained several crew injuries. Those that could not continue were removed to the supply ship to retreat to Portsmouth. While others injured that could continue returned to duty aboard the Ajax after medical treatment.
We are currently on station searching for the rest of the pirate fleet. When we find their location, we will engage them and destroy them.

Captain Hawke, Commander HMS Ajax

"Captain, we have located six large pirate ships harbored at Fajardo harbor on the eastern coast side of the Puerto Rican Island. Shall we enter the harbor and engage them?", asked the Exec.

"No, we will not put the Ajax and crew at risk. The harbor takes away our advantages of maneuverability and our superior guns and keeping out of range of their guns. But we cannot wait for them to leave harbor as well.

I did spot something very interesting in the nine ships we have encountered in our first battle in the intelligence reports..

Ask the marine commander to come to me and to bring his black power expert.

You will attend this meeting as well. I will be in my cabin. I want the best map we have of Fajardo Harbor.", ordered the captain.

A short time later, the marine commander and his black power expert with the Exec and Fajardo Harbor maps in hand knocked on the door to the captain's cabin. At given leave they entered the cabin.

"Commander, as you know we have identified six pirate vessels harbored at Fajardo harbor. We will not put the Ajax and crew at risk and enter the harbor to engage these ships. And we cannot wait for them to set sail then set upon them at sea. This could take some time since they could leave one at time or may be two but they might not leave at all.
However, I noticed something about the pirate ship we have inspected. They locate their power magazine above the waterline and at the starboard side of the vessel. You understand what this means?

They have disregarded any care of ignition and the consequences. Here look at the reports. I have marked them well", asked Captain Hawke.

"I missed this detail.", mentioned the marine commander.

"I want to consider sending several teams with gun power charges, that are big enough and shaped enough to ignite and blow a hole in the side the vessel above and below the water line. If the power magazine is there the explosion will ignite the powder magazine and destroy the ship. If the magazine is not there the hole created will sink the vessel.

Either way the vessel is destroyed.

We have a several challenges to consider yet. How do we create a charge that is water proof, how do we deliver the charges, how do we attach the charge and ignite the charge. And do all of this undetected and getting our men back to the Ajax.

Let us start at the beginning.......

I would like to know if this is possible. If so, can we create six charges big enough to blow a hole in the side of the ship and ignite the powder room of they are located above the water line.

Next can we deliver the teams and charges without being detected and can we get our men back on-board Ajax safely?"

"This a bold plan. We have very skilled fighters that are the best in water, but we have never attempted a mission such as this", said the marine commander.

"We can use fake charges on the Ajax to practice the teams. You, power expert, can we create charges that are big enough to blow that hole in the side, shape the charge to explode into the ship so as to ignite the power magazine if located there or sink the ship?

Would it be small enough to swim the charge to the ship and not be seen?", asked captain Hawke.

"The charge will have to remain dry for it to explode. We will have to shape it like this to assure an into the ship blast. And it cannot be larger than this size else it will hard to swim to the ship and not be seen.", mentioned the power expert working on the problem directly.

"We will have to select the teams and begin practice using the Ajax. As soon as we have a prototype of the charge lets convene to discuss how the practice is progressing, what the charge will look like and how not being detected and returning to the Ajax may be best played.", said the marine commander. We will have to swim a charge out and attach it to one of our small boats with the intent to ignite it and assure the charge works as designed.

"Let this be the plan.", replied captain Hawke.

Two days later, the marine commander notified the captain it would be a good time to continue discussion concerning the topic of charges. The captain concurred and a meeting was set.

"Marine Commander, you have the deck.", said captain Hawke.

"We practiced transporting six teams to the location using two of our surveillance boats at three team per boat. We can transport undetected. We practiced swimming mock charges, of the size and shape expected from the power expert, to the vessel and found the best ways to not be detected. We know have an understanding of the charge to be used and it is smaller than the mock charge we practice with. And we practice swimming back to the surveillance vessel for a return trip to the Ajax. Today we ignited one of the charges timing the team getting away and were successful with igniting the change and the getting away.", reported the commander.

"Shall we talk through the charge to be used on these vessels.", asked captain Hawke.

"Yes. The charge will look like this and be of a dimension as you see here. We created six charges. The power of the explosive, the shaped blast and fusing is such that this will explosion will blow a hole inward in the side of the vessel, if that is a powder magazine on the side of the hull it will ignite and destroy that ship else the size of the hole will let water in and sink the ship.", said the power expert.

"How confident are you in the plan?"

"We feel certain of the plan, of getting the charges to the ships and return of the man to the Ajax.", said the commander.

"How confident are you in the charge and its ignition with time for the men to swim a safe distance and to the surveillance boats?", asked the captain of the power expert.

"Very confident captain.", replied the powder expert.

"Intelligence what is the state of affairs at Fajardo Harbor?", asked Captain Hawke.

"All quiet in the harbor. No preparations to sail. Most ship personnel are on shore. Each ship has a skeleton crew. If you plan to go forward Sir, tonight is the night. Even more so with no moon."
"Exec call general quarters, I will address the crew.", ordered captain Hawke.

Addressing the crew, "As you know we spotted six pirate ships at Fajardo harbor. We looked at our options. We could sail the Ajax into the harbor and risk the ship and crew and decided we will not do this. Another option is to set charges on the hull of each of the pirate ships, and detonate these to sink the ships. We would do this using six marine teams who would swim the charges to the ships without being detected.

As some of you know we have been furiously practicing each aspect of the mission. Today we reviewed the plan, the intelligence reports and the progress and confidence of the teams and decided to move forward with the plan. Two surveillance ships will be used to transport the marine teams to a location out of sight and close enough to swim undetected to the pirate ships and set the charges. The plan is a go.

Let us all pray for our men. Please bow your heads. "Heavenly father, we ask your grace and blessings for our brave men both on the Ajax and our marines about to go into harms way. We depend on your protection. The mission we send them too will take great courage, great strength and great patience. Please Father guide them every step there and back safely. In the name of the Father, Son and Holy Ghost. Amen.

Let us support our marine teams. From the moment they leave and until their return send them your strength.

The Ajax is now on high alert, battle station until our all our teams return. Ships carpenter's crew go through both of the surveillance ships with a fine-tooth comb. Make double sure each boat is in perfect condition.

Marine teams, you will leave tonight at ten on the hour. That will put you there around eleven on the hour. At twelve on the hour the charges will all be set and detonated. By one in the morning, you will be arriving at the Ajax.

That is all, battle stations.", ordered captain Hawke.

"Commander, ask your powder expert to recheck all charges, assure water proofing and review detonation instructions with the marine teams as a final check.", ordered captain Hawke of the marine commander.

"It will be so captain.", replied the marine commander.

At ten on the hour the marine commander said, "Captain, at your order we will leave for the mission.", asked the marine commander.

"Have all my previous orders been completed and the teams concurred?", asked captain Hawke.

"Yes, captain. All is ready.", replied the marine commander.

"Proceed with the mission. Tell them, God's speed and safe return.", ordered captain Hawke.

The two surveillance boats slipped into the darkness of the night as the crew at battle stations all paid close attention sending those on the mission every success and wishing them a safe return.

"Captain Hawke was right to go to battle stations. This activity gives the benefit of assuring the Ajax is ready to fight but more importantly this keeps the crew busy during these tense hours.

"Sir, it is one in the hour this morning.", said the Exec with captain Hawke's head down writing a detailed status report to the admiralty in his cabin, and acknowledging the time and not lifting his head.

"Sir, one surveillance ship have arrived with a report.", said the Exec.

"Send them straight through.", ordered captain Hawke.

"Captain", said the Intelligence officer.

"Report", ordered the captain.

"All pirate vessels have been destroyed. By now they are either on fire or have sunk Sir. All teams returned to the two surveillance boats and are on their way back. The mission was a complete success. Sir. Congratulations.", reported the intelligence officer.

"Exec, inform the crew of the success. Remain at battle stations. The marine teams are on their way back. Write a detailed report of the happening at Fajardo harbor this evening. We will be meeting the resupply vessel in a couple of days and this will be added to the mission details.", ordered the captain.

The Ajax crew breathed a sigh of relief when both surveillance boats arrived with all marines accounted for. Captain Hawke as well greeted them. The crew assured they all had any medical items dealt with and a hot meal waiting them.

"Exec, get us underway directly and have our surveillance ships watching our part of the seas in case we encounter more pirates vessels. Maintain battle stations until further notice. Rotate teams to provide for rest periods.", ordered captain Hawke.

A few days later the Ajax rendezvoused with their resupply ship. Since one of the marines had injuries, non-life-threatening, he would be moved to the resupply vessel to be sent to Portsmouth. When the admiralty received the latest Ajax mission reports. A messenger was sent to Charlton and Admiral James asking him to come to Portsmouth directly. An officer was sent to the Royal Naval Hospital Haslar where the injured Ajax marine was being treated for some cuts and burns, to interview him.

"Vice Admiral Winston, I came directly.", said James.

"Your son, what have you been teaching him. It has been almost three and a half weeks and he has destroyed fourteen of the twenty-five ship pirate fleet. At his last exploit he sent marines into Fajardo Harbor to set charges to six pirate ships sinking all six, keeping the Ajax out of danger and retrieving all marine teams. We have never conceived of these tactics and use of marine forces and reconnaissance ships in this way. The planning and build of explosives are all new to us. The use of intelligence to discover the power rooms were set above the water lines. Battle tactics to disable ships and so much more. .

One of the marines was injured on mission. Non-life threatening but needing better care than the Ajax could provide. He is here at Haslar receiving treatment and is recovering. We interviewed him and found the reports to be very conservative in details to that of a participant in the hostilities.

We have those at marine headquarter asking for details of the mission so they can train the new recruits. We have the Academy asking for details wanting to make this required reading on how to plan and execute dangerous missions at sea. I hardly know where to start in this case. I reminded to all those asking that the Ajax is currently in a live hostile action and they will all have to wait.

Your son reminds me so much of you, we were all in awe at the daring and courage and the brilliance in successfully completing missions and bringing ship and crew home.
The latest note is from the King and the Royal family wanting more information. If he continues and smashes more pirate ships he will have to be knighted, you know it is coming. Oh, by the way our dear captain put a post in the mission bag to his wife and another note with your name on it.

I thought I would give these to you since lady Sofia would appreciate you delivering this letter. As well, you might want a note from your son.", said Vice Admiral Winston.

"Thank you, Vice Admiral. I would like to read the mission reports and perhaps chat with the marine at Haslar?", asked James.

"You may, then give the admiralty your impressions and advice.

In the west indies, the Ajax remains cautious as ever. Sailing just outside of the Caribbean waters so to remain out of sight of the remaining pirate fleet while reconnaissance ships kept a close eye on the remaining pirate fleet movements.

"If we did not get the pirates attention before I am certain we now have.", said the exec.

"We have their attention. I will meet with all officers this evening to go through what to expect please inform them. Be in my cabin at seven this evening.", ordered captain Hawke.

In the captain's cabin, seven in the evening, "Are all the officers in attendance?", asked captain Hawke to his exec.

"Yes, Sir", replied the exec

"Men, we remain just outside the Caribbean waters for several reasons. One, was to give the crew a chance to rest and regain their strength. I believe we have accomplished this.
Two, is to remain invisible to the remaining pirate fleet. As you know eleven ships remain in their fleet. When we enter the Caribbean waters, they would have had spies on every island with a means to communicate our position. They are hunting the Ajax now.

The Pirate leader, Roberto Cofresi knows he will not remain the pirate leader for long if he does not destroy the Ajax and crew.

We have advantages. We will determine the place of the battle to come. We know they will know our position. They believe we are drunk in confidence and will be subject to surprise. They don't understand our strength.

I expect within a week of being visible they will make a play to destroy us. We will practice all gun crews, marine practice sharp shooting, navigation practice directional changes and keeping the Ajax at the advantage in the winds and seas. We should have all surveillance boats out and about so we are not surprised.

As a contingency have gun crews ready at a moment's notice, marines on deck in shift at the ready, and the general crew at stations ready for the order to battle stations.

At the admiralty, "Now that you have reviewed all the battle details Admiral would you give us your thoughts?", asked Vice Admiral Winston with Admirals listening intently.

"You were correct, this strategy is new and very brilliant. The captain's report is conservative compared to the marine eye witness report given. The use, training, practice and support by the crew was very well thought out.

Not putting the Ajax in the harbor and at risk to ship and crew. The adding of intelligence about the pirate ships, their crews, even the moon that night made decision to proceed mission a surprise to the pirates. The status, the double checking of many key pieces assured the plan would have every possible success. All that was left was the decision to execute the plan and the return of the marine teams. Very little was left to chance.

Never before has marine units been used like this in concert with intelligence and the use of surveillance boats to transport forces to the target undetected, the creation, practice and testing of explosive charges and using these skills to destroy targets, then the return of marine teams back safely.

My advice is, assuming a final battle, that destroys the majority of what is left of the pirate fleet that these new tactics and strategies be taught at the academy, added to marine units training and brief all active captains at once.

That marine units are trained in these ways offer an option to captains of His Majesties navy not known before. That we train captains across the fleet in this new way of thinking offers advantages.

Finally, at success, prepare to give the captain and crew of the HMS Ajax decorations for actions well above the call of duty.", said James.

I have captains across the fleet who have gotten wind of what the Ajax and crew are up to in the west indies and are asking for briefings when in port and rested.

The Ajax entered Caribbean waters knowing they would be spotted. The Ajax maintained a quadrant that gave them the full knowledge of the winds and sea currents as an advantage knowing the pirate my dictate the day and the hour of the fight but the Ajax would dictate the battlefield. "Here we own the winds and the sea.", said captain Hawke.

Intelligence noted pirate ships assembling at San Juan. Still not the full complement of eleven. During this time the Ajax gun crews, marines, navigation and other practice over and over so that their roles were second nature. The men were fit and able, ready and determined to finish the job.

Three weeks from entering Caribbean waters intelligence noted the full complement of pirate ships had assembled at San Juan. They expected the Ajax to come for them but after another week they realized they would have to come for the Ajax.

It became clear that Roberto Cofresi himself commanded the fleet of ships.

"Assemble the crew.", ordered captain Hawke of his exec.

"Men, the pirates have assembled at San Juan. All eleven ships are just outside the harbor. Intelligence tells us they are just days away from coming for us. We will engage them here where we have the advantage of the knowing the winds and seas.

All of you have trained hard these last weeks. We are ready. Navigation can spin this ship around keeping us in the wind, the marine sharp shooter are deadly accurate, the gun crews have readied the guns and trained to aim and shoot with accuracy, at command.

I have placed extra guns at the bow and stern. These are very powerful, and will blow holes in the pirate vessels that cross by that way. We have learned from the pirates a trick or two.

The Ajax is ready. We will be patient, stay just out of their gun range, disable their ships, then come about and destroy them. Navigation will keep us maneuvering before they can react and use our longer range and more powerful guns to end the threat. The marines will disable their ships commander.

We are now at battle stations, with rotating teams taking breaks so we are not over tired for the battle. Please check and recheck your equipment to assure we have all hands for the battle to come.", said captain Hawke.

"Battle station! Battle stations! All stations on high alert!", barked the exec.

At Charlton, "Sofia, how is our Richard.", asked Victoria with Anne and James in the drawing room listening intently.

"He is well and such a strange being. I mean, he worries about me and the twins about the two of you and the horses, all the while fighting pirates bent on destroying the Ajax, her crew and him. I know him so well but can't understand the courage that drives him.", replied Sofia with watery eyes.

"It is not the lack of fear so much as one walks through it and completes the mission. Richard feels it, the weight of protecting the crew and the ship and completing the mission successfully.

When Anne would write, to me, about her daily life events, I so much looked forward to this because it became a rest bit. Indeed, courage is hard to understand and until one is in the heat of battle do they know if this is part of their character.

Richard is very courageous. I hope I taught him an equal amount of patient and not to rush into battle. I did receive a note from Richard.

I kept it to myself since most of it is between a father and son. He mentioned all of us in it and asked I send all his love. He and the Ajax are all well at the time of writing.", said James knowing the threat he is now facing.

Late afternoon, there was a ring at the door. "Sir, there is a commotion in the front part of the house. I am not sure what to make of it but they are asking for the Admiral Sir James Hawke.", said the servant flustered at the unexpected crowd.

At the door James surveyed the crowd. "Clearly Navy folk. Can I help you?", asked James.

"We were here first Sir. We would like to speak with the Admiral Sir James Hawke.", said one of three young captains standing with their marine and intelligence officers.

"You have the pleasure of speaking to the Admiral Sir James.", replied James with Anne and Victoria astonished with the scene.

"Are these cadets with you?", ask James.

"No, Sir. I believe instructor Grimms is just there and leading the cadets Sir.", said one of the captains.

"Instructor Grimms, I was not aware I was hosting an academy class today.", said James with a wicked smiles knowing Grimms for a very long time.

"Well, Sir we could not wait any longer and had to see you. Our hope is to ask for your instruction on the sea battles currently occurring in the west indies. These are graduating seniors. Would you consider some time with the senior cadet class Admiral?", asked Grimms.

"Indeed, let us get organized first. We have two houses on the property. Captain's, I take it you're in the same boat?", asked James.

"Yes, Sir.", replied the captains.

I have two houses on the property. Captains you will be settled in the White house and the cadets and Grimms will need the Hill house.", said James calling the servants to assist both groups to the settle.

Talking to Grimms and the captains it was decided the visitors will relax this evening and then after an early breakfast the groups will gather at the big house to talk through the navy mission to dispatch the pirates in the west indies.

On the Ajax, the intelligence officer reported the pirate ships moved out of the San Juan area into the open seas. Captain Hawke informed the crew they can show up at any time. The surveillance boats were kept in a parameter around the Ajax so there are no surprise visitors. As well, after dusk the Ajax maneuvered in a different direction so the enemy could not anticipate its location. Navigation kept the ship hard to find all night so not to be easily spotted.

On the fourth morning just after dawn, the pirates made themselves known sitting on the eastern horizon. Probably wondering how one ship could cause so much trouble and the loss of so many ships to their fleet.

The men on the Ajax, now experienced with fighting pirates, they focused on the job, on the task. Every aspect of the ship was completely primed. The crew checked, double checked and triple checked every gun, weapon. Navigation was keenly tracking the wind, the see currents so they could take full advantage and keep the Ajax just ahead of every pirate reaction.

Captain Hawke watched the pirates real-time and their actions. He assessed the condition of the ships, their ability to navigate, the crew's ability to manage the sails, who was barking orders.

What his crew knew was the most likely location of the power magazines and that his gun crews practiced hitting that part of the ship accurately.

As the pirate ships approached, they split into to offset lines of five ships and six ships. Marine sharp shooters where ready to do their part. While the gun crews readied the batteries.

"I do not think the pirates have notice our guns at the bow and stern. If the coming battle calls for it, they will find out. Are all stations ready.", ask captain Hawke of his exec.

"Yes, awaiting you orders captain.", replied the exec.

"Patience and be ready.", whispered Richard.

"Master, take us into the wind. We will sail to the starboard side of the two lines of ships and just out of range of their guns. Gun crew remember the location of their power magazines focus power there and blow them up. Sharp shooter take away their command.", ordered captain Hawke.

As the Ajax made a first pass the guns crews managed to ignite the power magazines of six ships immediately disabling them and rendering them unable to maneuver with heavy damage, and sinking.

The Ajax swung around taking advantage of their knowledge of the winds and sea currents and using it to catch another two ships before they could react pounding them with heavy shot to the point, they had no masts with sail leaving them listless and nothing to do.

Into the wind the Ajax used the bow guns catching the pirate crew by surprise hinting their navigation and finally igniting the power magazine ending many a ships life as they slowed burning in place.
Two ships moved away with full sail lighter and fast moving so not to be caught. One of the ships was captained by Roberto Cofresi. They got away in the dusk, not to be found this evening.

Captain Hawke left the nine burning pirate ship to their fate staying at a safe distance observing the scene to assure all ship eventually sank.

A couple of weeks later the Ajax moved out of the Caribbean waters to reduce risk of surprise attack and give the crew a much-needed break. At the resupply rendezvous point they met the supply ship, made repairs to the ship, offered medical treatment for some of the crew and took on new stores.

It was two weeks later then a Royal Navy warship, the HMS Pegasus took up position to the starboard side of the Ajax. New orders were transferred to the Ajax.

"We are recalled to Portsmouth. With congratulations on a successful mission. The HMS Pegasus will take up station here.", announced captain Hawke.

The captain of the Pegasus came aboard the Ajax to be briefed on the current state of the Pirate fleet. "Captain Hawke what you have done here is astonishing. The pirate fleet is crushed with only two ships left. I have to say, when the admiralty elevated you from acting captain to permanent, I had my doubts Sir. I can tell you the entire captain's ranks are so very proud of you and want to know you.

I was wrong to have had that opinion, you are a captain equal and better then most. I am glad to know you Sir and would be honored to fight at your side if ever you need me.", said the captain Smart, of the HMS Pegasus.

The crew of the Pegasus saluted the crew of the Ajax with a hip hip ha ra! Hip hip ha ra! Well done, Ajax! Safe sail back to Portsmouth and a well-deserved rest.

Arriving at Portsmouth, some weeks later very early morning the ship moored at the appointed dock and with the last rope-tired captain Hawke found all stations secured and dismissed his crew.

Hawke made sure he was the last one on board beside the marine guard, at station, to protect the Ajax.

Packing his bags, Richard was interrupted by representatives of the Admiralty, there to escort him to his debrief. James, Anne and Sofia where there at the dock as well eager to see their Richard. "Richard, Richard. We are so glad you are returned to us. How are you?", asked Sofia.

"Dear Sofia, I want to see you but I am on mission and obliged to debrief the admiralty first before I am dismissed. I am so glad to see all of you but have to go. Father, will you come to the debrief. Then, I shall see you at the house. How are our twins?", asked Richard as he began to walk away.

"They are very good. Victoria stood back at Charlton to be with them. We will be at the house waiting for you darling.", replied Sofia to her exhausted looking husband.

"Ladies, I will lead you to the carriage that will take you to the house since I will sit in Richard's debrief of the mission. He and the crew seem to have done the extraordinary in many respects. He unknowingly has rewritten the navy books on tactics and strategy.", said James in the navy way, as the carriage drove away with the women he headed to the admiralty so not to miss the debrief.

Welcome captain Hawke, let us begin the debrief. Typically, we have just those that document your verbal report but today we will as well have the entire admiralty staff here in attendance. Please begin sir, take us through the mission and prepare for questions.

After the debrief Richard was congratulated by the admiralty on a successful mission and was dismissed for four months leave. Repairs to the Ajax would need about this amount of time and the captain and crew, they could see, were exhausted.

After taking his leave Richard walked out with his father, "Richard, what you did on this mission is extraordinary. The tactics and strategies will be required reading at the academy. We had three captains and the entire senior class from the academy come to Charlton, unexpectedly, wanting a full brief. I did my best. If you were there you would have better explained the reasoning and execution.

Expect more visitors as many in command want to know and master these new ways.", said James very proud of his son.

"Indeed, father.", replied a tired captain.

"Let me get you to the house, get some home cooked food into you, and to your women and a bed to rest. Well done son, I am so proud of you. Extraordinary, just extraordinary", said James.

Walking through the academy ground on the way to their waiting carriage entire cadet classes recognizing the captain of the Ajax stopped to salute a now role model and hoping he might recognize them. Richard understood and made sure to return the recognition by saluting and bowing.

"I may have to spend a few days here talking through the mission with the cadets before next mission.", said Richard as he and James now aboard their carriage headed to the house and a much-needed rest.

"Richard, it is so good to have you back. We will rest today not asking questions and knowing how tired you must me, in the next day or so discuss when to leave for Charlton.", said Anne.

"Darling, how about a meal and up to bed. I can see you are exhausted. I can be patient a little longer. We will have many days to catch up.", said Sofia.

"Thank you, dear I am indeed drained.", replied Richard in a tired voice.

"Late in the evening James, Anne and Sofia sat by the drawing room fire.

"James, what is a debriefing?", inquired Sofia.

"This a meeting where a captain talks through the mission they just completed. The captain talks about all the decisions made, mistakes, the successes. Many debrief's go well with successful missions completed. While other debriefs are tough describing failed missions.

These debriefs are necessary to help the admiralty better understand what captains face on the seas. The admiralty usually never attend but read the reports later. This debrief, all members of the admiralty attended personally.

Richard, debrief went very well. He has advanced many strategies and tactics thought to be settled. Much of what he and the crew of the Ajax did will be required reading at the academy. I expect many visitors to Charlton asking to be briefed. I expect Richard will be invited at the academy to speak. Today when we walk across the academy campus many a cadet class stopped and saluted Richard out of respect and admiration.

The mission he was on was quite dangerous. He was one warship to twenty-five pirate ships. They knew the waters and he and crew had to learn quickly. His first battle saw eight pirate ships fall to the one Ajax. His tactics and strategies were so brilliant he caught them unawares. The Ajax destroyed all eight.", James.

"Well seven, father. The eight ship almost disabled was used to collect all the surviving pirates and aimed to shore at the island of Puerto Rico. After all we are not savages the Royal Navy.", said Richard walking into the drawing room.

Richard, what are you doing up. I thought you would sleep all night.", asked Sofia surprised.

Well, as father knows, I am in the pattern of sleeping a couple hours at time. It's a captain's lot worrying about the ship and crew.

I am sure when you are at my side tonight, I will sleep the whole night.", said Richard

I could use a proper cup of tea and biscuit. It is the little things one misses when in the middle of the ocean.", said Richard sitting beside Sofia with her arm around his waist.

James had the servants bring a piping hot pot of tea and an assortment of biscuits. As they all sat together listening as Richard described the west indies mission.

The next morning, before breakfast Richard and Sofia sat together. One could see the conversation back and forth, laughing and some seriousness at other times. They held hands and other times expressed ideas using their hands.
"Let us not interrupt them, Anne. I am glad he is here and with us.", whispered James.

"It is good to see him and Sofia so engaged.", replied Anne having experienced a career of separation from her James when he was away at sea and knowing not to interrupt a reunion.

A couple months later, at Charlton, the weather warm and glorious with green springing out everywhere. Anne and Victoria agreed to take the twins so that Sofia could go for a ride with Richard.

"I am glad we both love the twins.", said Anne to Victoria.

"Especially now, they do not need every moment care.", smiled Victoria.

Meanwhile, Sofia and Richard rode along a familiar country path lined with trees and a tall green hedge with wild flowers, blue bells, and lingering snow drops this time year.

"Darling, I worry when you're out to sea. What I read in the paper gave me pause.", said Sofia.

"The papers exaggerate just a bit. Adding this or that but having not been there to see, they know more than those that actually where in the events.

Dear, I always protect the ship and crew, and not taking unnecessary risks. I do exactly what father taught me, that is to think first don't rush in and don't react make the enemy react.

I know this will not stop worries but know I have you, the twins and the family in mind, my crew and ship, and will not risk foolishly but be deliberate.", replied Sofia.

"I have some good news for you.", said Sofia.
"What is it?", replied Richard.

"I am with child. Mind you it is still early but all the signs are there. A woman that has had a child knows the signs. I see the physician in a couple of days to confirm.", said Sofia.

"Sofia, this is so exciting! I hardly know what to say! Are you healthy?" Do you feel well?", reacted Richard holding Sofia.

"Yes, and Yes", replied Sofia.

"Yes, I am healthy and Yes, I feel good.", said Sofia smiling.

"I think this will be a February or March baby.", said Sofia.

"I am so excited Sofia.

I wish I could be here at Charlton but I have a few months over two years yet to complete of navy obligation.", said Richard a bit sad.

"I am so grateful for James, Anne and Victoria. They are such a help and a strength for me. When you are gone to the sea, they are such a support to me and the twins. It is hard not having you just here but they make it bearable.", replied Sofia.

"Sofia, one item I have not talked about, since this navy mission is, we have become independently wealthy. I have to chat with father about the best way to invest for our and the children's future.", said Richard.

"This is very wonderful to hear that we can provision for the children and more, dear.", said Sofia.

"The family should know about your condition.", said Richard.

"I will tell them tonight at supper. I wanted to be sure you knew first, you are my husband after all.", relied Sofia.

At supper James, Anne, Victoria, Sofia and Richard sat in the usual spots. Sofia, tapped her glass, with her knife, to get everyone's attention.

"I have an announcement to make,

I believe I am with child.", said Sofia, to the group gathered around the table.

There was silence and a wonder, then, "I, for one, am so glad the house is full of the laughter and challenges of our grandchildren.", said James smiling and breaking the silence.

"Many congratulations Sofia!", said Anne.

"This is indeed wonderful news.", said Victoria.

"The physician will be here in a couple of days to confirm I am with child. However, as a mother I can see all the signs.", said Sofia.

We will go to the Royal Court next week. Will you be strong enough to go Sofia?", asked James.

"Yes, I will be fine. This condition is very early. As long as I do not overdo it, I will be able to be at my Richard's side. I am planning to go. Perhaps, one dance while there husband?", asked Sofia.

"A dance, of course. As many as you want.", replied Richard.

"We will meet the Royal family. They want to congratulate you over the success of the west indies mission.
Many others will want to know the Crown's servant.

It would be best that you wear your naval dress uniform and look the part. You are in fact the captain of the HMS Ajax one of the most powerful warships in the Royal Navy.", said James.

"I will do as you have advised father.", replied Richard.

"The special evening of the visit to the Royal Court is here and so suddenly. I hope our time there goes much slower so we can just enjoy it all.", said Anne to James concurring.

"Sofia, you look magnificent. I will stay close to you since many men will look at you.", said Richard moving close to Sofia.

"Have no worries, husband. I only have eyes for you, our child and family. I have no need of more men.", smiled Sofia , taking Richards's arm firmly.

"You, radiate courage and strength in your dress uniform. I fear the ladies will gravitate to you.", said Sofia.

"Ha, ha! No, I am always polite but you I come with, dance with and go home with!", replied Richard kissing Sofia.

With everyone ready, the group set off for the palace and the evenings events. They were announced at entry. The Admiral Sir James Hawke retired and the Lady Anne. The Captain Richard Hawke, Baronet and the Lady Sofia Baroness as many stopped to view the captain of the HMS Ajax and hero of the west indies mission.

Walking along the ballrooms many a gentlemen and lady paused to give their congratulations to the captain of the HMS Ajax. With the dance floor open and at Sofia's prompting Richard led her to the dance floor for a dance. Many dancers gave way to Richard and Sofia paying respects to the brave captain and his radiant wife. James and Anne watched from the side.

"He is so much like you James at your time. Even the giving way on the dance floor is something we experienced.", said Anne to James's concurrence.

Later in the evening and quite unexpected the entire crowd split in half to give way to the King and Queen and several of the Royal family. Several Admiralty moved to Captain Hawke's and lady Sofia's side. James carefully moved Sofia and Anne to his side to be seen but not to interfere.

"You Majesties.", said captain Hawke, bowing.

"Captain Hawke, I wanted to congratulate you. Thank you for upholding the Crown in the West Indies. We realized the HMS Ajax would be the only vessel against a fleet of twenty-five pirate ships. The admiralty was doing everything to free more warship to give you support but were unable with actions in the east indies raging.

However, the Ajax applied new thinking, new methods with the result to destroying all but two pirate ships and at lightning speed. I had the opportunity to be briefed in detail of the battles, your methods and approaches. I am very impressed with how you protected the Ajax and her crew, yet dispatched the pirate fleet.

You set a new standard for what a single Royal Navy warship is capable of doing. What you accomplished has never been done before.

Captain Hawke, after consultation with the Admiralty, I am ordering you be knighted by my order as King. My secretary will contact you with details after scheduling with the Admiralty.", said the King with many on lookers and admirers witnessing history.

"Lady Sofia, I understand you have two young twins? And are with child.", asked the Queen.

Bowing first, "Yes, your Majesty. They are home at Charlton being cared for by my mother, the lady Victoria.", replied Sofia.

"I am aware of the sacrifice you make with not having your husband home at times, especially when he is at sea on Crown business. Are you able to manage?", asked the Queen sincerely.

"Yes, this is a sacrifice and Yes, I am able to manage with having my father Sir James, Mothers Lady Anne and Lady Victoria to surround me when Richard is gone to sea,", said Sofia.

"I am glad to hear this. Thank you for the sacrifices you make for the Crown. This does not go unnoticed.

"Sir James, Lady Anne it has been a while since we have had the pleasure of seeing you at court.", mentioned the Queen.
"The twins take up a lot of time these days.", smiled James.

"One can imagine. Do have a wonderful evening. If there is anything I can do to make your evening do not hesitate to mention it and if it is within my powers, I will grant it.", said the Queen.

"The evening ended on a high note.", recalled Anne as their carriage sped down the lane from town to Somerset and Charlton.

"Son, if I recall I was knighted around the same age in my career. Save you are captain of a more powerful warship then me. Ha ha.", said James.
"I noticed. It is hard to imagine such goals. I give you all the credit father, all the many naval lessons you guided me through, the encouragement, the experience you imparted.

Continued, in Sofia and Richard, book 2.

# # # # #

www.ingramcontent.com/pod-product-compliance
Lightning Source LLC
Chambersburg PA
CBHW030744310726
48969CB00005B/1317